BLAME IT ON THE TEQUILA

Blame it on the Alcohol Series

FIONA COLE

Copyright © 2021 by Fiona Cole

All rights reserved.

Cover Designer: Najla Qamber, Qamber Designs

Photographer: Regina Wamba

Cover Models: Jared Sternaman, Hannah Peltier

Interior Design: Indie Girl Promotions

Editing: Kelly Allenby, Readers Together

Proofreading: Janice Owen, JO's Book Addiction Proofreading

No part of this book may be reproduced or transmitted in any form or by any means, electronic or mechanical, including photocopying, recording, or by any information storage and retrieval system without written permission of the author, except for the use of brief quotations in a book review.

This is a work of fiction. Names, characters, businesses, places, events and incidents are either the products of the author's imagination or used in a fictitious manner. Any resemblance to actual persons, living or dead, actual events, or locales is entirely coincidental.

Playlist

THERE'S A LOT

Open Hands - Ingrid Michaelson (feat. Trent Dabbs)
Is That Alright? - Lady Gaga
Grace - Rag'n'Bone Man
Your Name Hurts - Hailee Steinfeld
Glitter In the Air - P!nk
Right Now - One Direction
Take Me Home - Chord Overstreet
Hello - Adele
Falling like the Stars - James Arthur
Happy - Leona Lewis
Sorry - Mali-Koa
coney island - Taylor Swift (feat The National)
If Our Love is Wrong - Callum Scott
New Year's Day - Taylor Swift
Take on the World - You Me At Six
Rise Up - Imagine Dragons
Love in the Dark - Adele
evermore - Taylor Swift (feat. Bon Iver)
Hurricane Drunk - Florence + the Machine
Won't Let You Down - Callum Scott
Always Remember Us This Way - Lady Gaga

Looking Out - Brandi Carlile
Is There Somewhere - Halsey
Even If It Breaks Your Heart - Eli Young Band
Bill Murray - Matt Nathanson
Where's My Love - SYML
Tempo - Lizzo (feat. Missy Elliot)
Cuz I Love You - Lizzo
Feel Something - Landon Austin
Always Be Loving You - My Brothers And I
Breakups - Seaforth
Shut Up and Dance - Walk the Moon
Leaving My Love Behind - Lewis Capaldi
Always - Isak Danielson
First In Line - Matthew Mayfield
when the party's over - Billie Eilish
Take Me to Church - Hozier
Therefore I Am - Billie Eilish
Lo/Hi - The Black Keys
Jump Around - House of Pain
Wish That You Were Here - Florence + the Machine
Secret Love Song - Little Mix (feat. Jason Derulo)
You Are the Reason - Callum Scott
Say Something - A Great Big World & Christina Aguilera
Way Away - Yellowcard
I Forgive You - Kelly Clarkson
Heat Above - Greta Van Fleet
Pain - Nessa Barrett
Two of Us - Louis Tomlinson
Falling - Harry Styles

To Mama Lucia.

Prologue

NOVA

PAST

"I'm so sorry, Nova."

I watched Parker's head drop to the white sheets of my hospital bed, his dirty-blond waves looking almost white in some spots from the harsh fluorescent lighting.

Lifting my hand slowly, I dragged my fingers through his hair, enjoying the thick texture, remembering just days ago that I thought I'd never feel it again.

"It's okay."

He shook his head hard and lifted upright, but not pulling away. As if struggling to do so, he hesitated before meeting my eyes. His usual ocean blue eyes dulled against the dark circles and bloodshot exhaustion, but they flared with his flexing jaw.

"It's not okay. It's not okay, Nova. Jesus. It's—"

The deep lyrical voice I loved to listen to cracked, and he looked away, dropping his chin to his chest.

He was right. It wasn't okay. None of this was okay. The part he played wasn't okay.

But right then, I needed him by my side more than I needed to blame him for what happened.

So, I slid my hand up his forearm until I could link my fingers with his, careful to not bump the IV rehydrating my body.

He held on tight and kissed one knuckle at a time with reverence and so much more.

"Just talk to me," I requested on an exhale. I'd barely woken up from my last nap, and already I could sleep again.

"What do you want to talk about?" he asked.

I started to say anything when a floppy-haired blond popped his head around the corner, his goofy smile flashing behind a handful of wildflowers.

"Did you tell her?" Oren asked, maybe a little too excitedly for the situation.

I darted my eyes to Parker because I had no idea what the hell he needed to tell me and found him with a shut the fuck up look on his face.

I flashed back to Oren just in time to watch the smile drop. "Ohhhhh. Well, my bad." He sat the daisies down on a chair next to him and started backing away with an awkward laugh, only to bump into the other two members of the band, Ash and Brogan.

"What the fuck, dude? We want to see her," Ash grumbled.

"He hasn't told her yet, and the look he gave said to get the fuck out," Oren tried to whisper, but he sucked at it, so we all heard.

Parker groaned and dropped his head.

"We'll be back," Brogan called as Oren ushered them out.

As soon as they left, I focused on Parker, who chewed on his bottom lip *and* rubbed a hand over his face. Never a good sign for him to do both. One meant stress, and both meant I needed to brace myself. In the few years since Parker Callahan came crashing into my life, I'd only seen the combination a handful of times.

"Tell me what?" I asked. I was too tired to brace myself or dig it out of him.

"It's nothing right now."

Heaving a sigh, I dropped my head back on the pillow. "Distract me, Parker. Tell me."

"Are you hurting?"

"No, I'm fine. I just want to not think about lying here right now. So, just tell me."

One more hand swipe across his face, over his head, and around the back of his neck. "The music executive at the show offered us to go on tour with Rufio."

"Holy shit, Parker." My whole face broke into a grin, so excited for him—for the band to get an amazing chance. This was what we'd all been working for, and it was happening. "Freaking Rufio. How insane is that?"

I barely had any energy left, but I used it all to feel joy for my best friend—my stepbrother who became so much more despite our best efforts. But as my energy faded, reality crept in. I took in his hesitant smile and realized I hadn't heard the whole story.

"When do you leave? Where are you going?" I peppered him with questions, hoping to ask the right one—hoping it wasn't the omen lingering in the background of the conversation.

"They start touring next week, and they want us there for all of it."

"Oh, wow. That's…a lot."

"Yeah." A lip bite was my only warning. "Do you think you're up for it?"

"For what?" Surely, he couldn't mean me going with them. The very idea of it had tension and fear crawling up my throat, but I swallowed it down, waiting for his answer.

"To tour. You're part of the band."

I was shaking my head before he even finished. "No. No, Parker." The trembling started deep inside and vibrated through every inch of me, and yet, nothing actually shook. "I can't."

"If you're not ready yet, I can ask if you can join us later?" he offered, trying to look hopeful, but I saw the truth lingering in his gaze. He knew.

"*I won't,*" I clarified.

His shoulders dropped, and just before he looked away, I saw his lip get trapped under his teeth again.

The boy I loved sat before me, indecision and guilt weighing on him, holding him down in an awkward position that looked ill-fitting. The boy I loved, whose dream he worked so hard for, sat there unable to be happy, and I loved him enough to absolve him and push him to take that dream.

I squeezed his palm in mine as hard as I could. "Parker," I said and waited for him to face me. "The band was never mine—it was never my dream. You just let me be a part of it. It was fun," I managed to say despite my throat closing around the words. "But I can't do this. I can't ever imagine putting myself out there. I can't—"

His face crumpled, and despite all I'd been through, I hated watching him hurt. He leaned forward and rested his forehead to mine, our breaths mixing in the space between. "I'm so sorry, Nova," he said again.

"I know, and I'm telling you it's okay."

He dropped his head to my shoulder, and like so many nights before, he crawled into bed against my side. We laid there silently, my hand in his and the other brushing through his hair.

I was young, and my future loomed with so much uncertainty. I had no idea how I'd take the next step or where it would lead, but I did know one thing: I loved Parker Callahan, and no matter what he'd done, I couldn't let him give up his dream for me.

"Go."

He shifted to his elbow, looking down with his brow furrowed. "What?"

"Go on tour. Go get your dream. Prove to them that you can."

He shook his head. "Nova, I—"

"You can. And you will."

I scrounged up ferocity I was far from feeling and dared him to challenge me. He studied my face, looking for holes and lies in what I said. When he didn't find any, his face softened, and he stroked his thumb along my cheek.

"Fucking, Supernova. Bright and powerful."

I leaned into his touch and heaved a sigh of relief when he retook his spot against my side, and I could relax from holding strong when all I wanted to do was cry.

I needed him more than ever before. The future loomed a little darker, but I refused to let anything of mine hold him back. Imagining him gone next week had fire burning up my throat.

"You'll call?" I asked.

"All the time. And I'll come back for homecoming and the holidays. I can't miss your senior homecoming."

"Especially since you missed yours," I joked, remembering the guys going to a concert instead of the dance last year.

"If I couldn't have the date I wanted, then I didn't want to go. But I have you now and I'll be there."

"You promise?"

"I promise," he said meeting my eyes with sincerity.

"Promise me on your vintage Fender," I demanded. I needed him to know how serious I was and that Fender was his favorite.

He slipped his pinky through mine and squeezed tight, not looking away, "I swear on my Fender. I'll call and I'll be back for you."

"You better," I whispered.

"I promise."

But all too soon, the calls tapered off or went missed and unreturned. Parker didn't make it to homecoming. I'd sat at home, all done up in my blue dress because it was his favorite color, and never even got a phone call.

He didn't make it to Thanksgiving either. While his world just started taking off, mine fell apart at the seams, and I was too weak to fix it alone.

With each broken promise, I frayed a little more, leaving gaps for the resentment and anger to slip in.

I couldn't believe he went back on his word. I couldn't believe he kept blowing me off. I couldn't believe he wasn't there. I couldn't believe he left me alone.

So, the next time he called, I hit ignore.

When he said he'd be home for Christmas, my trust was already gone. This time, I didn't wait around for him to let me down. I left before he could pull at my strings anymore.

I left with a promise of my own.

I would never let Parker Callahan put me second to his dreams again. No matter how much I loved him.

ONE

Nova

FIVE YEARS LATER

"Yasss! Naughty Nova is here tonight!"

I shimmied toward Raelynn, my best friend and co-bridesmaid. The silky material of my bridesmaid dress barely moving.

"And a shimmy?" She bit her knuckle like she could barely hold back taking a bite out of me. "I think this calls for another round."

"Hell yeah," I cheered.

Austin, Rae's best guy friend, groaned from where he leaned against the cloth-covered table.

"Don't act like you're not wanting another one, too," Rae reprimanded him with narrowed eyes. "Come on, we have rooms here tonight, and if you're lucky, I'll let you take advantage of me later."

"You mean keep your feet warm and watch Netflix?" he deadpanned.

"Don't act like you didn't love binge-watching *Bridgerton* with me."

"Awe," I cooed. "You guys are such a cute couple."

Rae playfully rolled her eyes, somehow missing Austin

avoiding the topic. Hell, I was four shots of tequila and three glasses of champagne in, and I saw it.

Not that I had time to dwell on it because Rae linked her arm with Austin's and mine and dragged us to the open bar in the corner of the wedding reception room.

"*Tres Patron, por favor.*"

The bartender finished drying a glass before grabbing the squat bottle of clear liquid.

We gripped our glasses and limes, holding them up to tap them together.

"To Vera finally getting over her stubborn ass and hopefully riding Nico all night long."

I snorted. Only Rae.

I nodded my agreement and licked the salt from the rim before tossing the shot back and sucking on the lime, wincing at the burn and tang.

We set our glasses down only to ask for another.

Just then, my phone lit up, and I pushed my glass toward Rae. The hangover that would hit me hard tomorrow was already knocking on my head. Pulling up the email, I squeezed my eyes open and shut, trying to focus on the blurry words.

Nova,

One of your paintings from your Instagram post last week sold. I'll take care of shipping and payment this week.

Also, I've got another interested sponsor in your Instagram account, but they're hesitant because of the lack of personal connection. I know how we discussed your priority to keep your face out of the photos, but this is the fifth interested business this week that has expressed similar concerns. You hired me to help you manage your various business ventures. If you want to expand on the Instagram front, then I think you need to revisit your decision to continue not showing your face. I have ideas of ways to expand into new areas that match your other businesses. Think on it, and we can talk next week.

Aiken

"Ugh," I groaned, dropping the offending device to the bar and pushing it away.

"Hey, now. We don't make those sad noises when we look this pretty," Rae scolded. "Tell Mama Rae what's up."

"It's Aiken."

"The advisor you hired to streamline your erratic and eclectic ventures into something resembling a business that can function on its own?"

"Yup. That guy. He's back to pushing me to change my Instagram."

If I was looking for sympathy, I sure as hell wouldn't get it from Rae. "Listen, the fact that you're even kind of able to make money from Instagram is blowing my mind. I've never seen anyone stumble upon becoming an influencer without trying."

"I'm not an influencer." I scrunched up my face at the word.

"Yes, you are," she said without missing a beat. Before I could pick up the same argument we'd had since our junior year of college, that I wasn't one of those girls who took perfect pictures and had obviously placed ad-like posts, she held up her hand. "Don't start. Now, you hired Aiken for a reason. What's that reason?" she asked like a mother asking a child to recall the rules.

"To have a van of my own, so I won't have to get a rental every few weeks when I travel," I answered in rote.

"And how do we do that?"

"By combining my art, travel, and writing into a single entity," I continued the routine answer.

She beamed. "Exactly. So, suck it up, and don't worry

about it tonight. Because tonight, Naughty Nova is coming out to play. Although, I'm sure your followers would *love* to meet her. You'd probably get sponsored by Patron."

She was right; I didn't need to worry about it tonight. Pushing the phone aside, I snatched the shot glass and tossed it back, trying to block out the impending doom of tomorrow morning's headache. Just as I set the glass down, Lizzo's *Tempo* came on.

"Oh, my god. I love this song."

"Hell yes, you do." Rae smirked, snatching my purse, knowing damn well what was coming next. "Get it, girl."

I swayed my way to the dance floor, the lights flashed, spotlighting my every move.

Looking around the large gilded room, I realized we were the only ones still lingering. Staff at the hotel moved from table to table collecting dishes, and yet here we were, enjoying the still dim lights and open bar.

And I planned on enjoying every second of this song.

I pushed my lips out and channeled my inner diva, shaking my ass.

After a spin, I looked up to find Rae holding my phone. The alcohol swam through my veins, the lights swirling, and my hair sticking to the damp nape of my neck.

"Don't you dare record me, Raelynn," I said, but it came out breathless and was only enforced with a half-ass arm lifted to block my face. It dropped quickly when I moved my hand to my rolling hips.

"I would never," she joked, her voice heavy with the lie she didn't bother to make me believe.

Fuck it. I weighed my options and figured the recording would be blurry at best with how much she moved around with me. I'd delete it later. There was no need to stop enjoying the music.

My limbs tingled, and I laughed as the weightless joy carried me around the floor. I stumbled but recovered quickly, placing both hands on the floor and shaking my ass like a stripper.

Rae catcalled, and I went with it, letting the thud of the bass fuel my movements. I loved music. It was built into my DNA. But having music as part of my life didn't make me the best dancer. It did give me enough musicality to hit the beats and make it work. With the tequila infusing my confidence, it made up for anything I lacked.

I didn't drink often, but when I did, I went for the gold. That was when Naughty Nova came out, as Rae called me. I'd earned that title when we'd met in college. After a couple months of always being the designated driver for her and Vera, I cut loose and agreed to an Uber. We did shots of tequila, and I ended up dancing on a table.

And Naughty Nova was born. Or at least named. She'd always been there before, eager to break the chains I kept her in.

Lizzo ended, and Muse's *Pressure* blasted from the speakers. I turned to face a smiling Rae next to a wide-eyed Austin. His eyes flicked to my phone screen and back to me, looking like a deer in headlights bracing for impact. Probably just holding his breath, waiting for Rae to drop the phone and start dancing around him. I focused my attention on her, planning to take the phone and shove it aside so she could dance with me.

I rolled my shoulders and gave the camera my most seductive look. Why not? It was getting deleted tomorrow, anyway.

"Oh, yeah. Give it to me, baby," Rae cheered.

Another shimmy and ass shake.

Then Rae turned the phone to show me the screen, and although the music still played, a record scratched to a halt in my mind as I met the bluest eyes I never thought I'd see looking back at me ever again.

"Damn," the man on the screen said.

And he was a man. His scruff covering his cheeks, hiding

the lines I knew were there when he was clean-shaven. His arm flexed, showing off more tattoos than I remembered, when he pushed back the wavy dirty-blond locks that I knew lightened over the summer when he spent too much time at the pool.

"I'm sorry. I couldn't help myself. He was doing an Instagram live and picking fans to go live with him. I at least had to *try*, and he picked me," Rae explained, laughing. She moved to stand beside me and put us both on the screen. Her smiling face next to my shell-shocked one. "She's like your biggest fan, and when I saw you go live, I figured, why not." She bumped my shoulder. "Can you believe it?"

I couldn't tell what caused the lights to spin and twist this time, the tequila or the shock. Rae said some more words, but it barely breached the rush of blood blocking out everything—pulsing like I floated in the ocean. His lips moved, but I was too focused on his tongue chasing the words, remembering all the times I'd watched it when he sang.

Another bump to the shoulder and all my sense crashed back at once.

"Nova!" Rae squealed. "It's Parker freaking Callahan. Say something."

Too loud, too bright, too much.

I snatched the phone and exited the app.

"Uhhh." Rae's jaw hung open, and I struggled to come up with a valid reason for ripping the phone from her hands.

"Umm…" I forced a laugh which was more of an expulsion of air with a squeak. "That was awkward."

The phone vibrated in my hand, and I glanced down to see an Instagram notification.

Fuck. Shit fuck. Fuck shit fuck.

"Dude," Rae said, unimpressed with my response.

"More shots," I shouted. Me drinking always distracted Rae.

She shook her head and smiled. "Missed opportunity, homegirl."

My phone vibrated again, and I shrugged. "Let me run to the restroom, and I'll meet you there. Grab me two." I was going to need it.

She snagged Austin and tugged him behind her. With a shaking hand, I swiped open the notification.

Parker Callahan: Give me your number.
Parker Callahan: If you don't, I'll figure out who your friend is and ask her. She seems eager to connect us.

Oh, shit snacks.

I imagined him figuring out who Rae was. It wouldn't be hard. My profile was public even if I used an off name and never showed my face. She splashed her face all over her feed, and it wouldn't take much to connect the pieces through our friendship. I imagined the conversation and cringed when Rae would eventually find out that I wasn't just a fan of Parker Callahan from The Hidden Obsession but had been in love with him once upon a time when he'd not only been my biggest crush but my stepbrother, too.

Psithursm: I don't want to talk.
Parker Callahan: Is she Raelynn Vos?
Parker Callahan: I only saw her in the dark, but I'm willing to guess.
Psithurism: Fine.

I sent him my number and held my breath.

Within seconds my phone vibrated with an unfamiliar number and a New York area code. Part of me half expected his name to pop up like it had all those years ago, like maybe he kept the same number.

Taking one last deep breath, I accepted the call and lifted

the phone to my ear, pinching my eyes shut, bracing for impact.

But nothing could prepare me to hear him say my name again.

"Nova."

Damn.

Just my name and all the emotions I'd fought to block out years ago flooded back, rendering it impossible to do anything but wince at the pain and smile at the memories.

Because Parker Callahan always came with both.

PARKER

"Parker."

I never thought I'd hear that voice again. I'd let go of that dream a long time ago. But just my name, and it stirred all the old emotions that came with it.

The swell of heat. The rush of need.

The resentment.

The anger.

The hurt.

"Hey," I finally responded, at a loss for words for the first time in my life.

"Hey."

We both laughed at the one-word greetings.

"Were we always this awkward?" I asked.

"I was," she admitted. "But you? Never."

"I was with you."

"Bullshit," she crowed.

"Please. You came in all cool and collected, and I just jumped at the chance to pull you out of your shell so I could talk to you."

"I think we remember things a wee bit differently, Parker Callahan."

"Nah, I'm always right," I said, flopping back on the couch in yet another hotel.

"Yeah, right."

I could still hear the music in the background through her phone, but it faded as if she left the room she'd been dancing in before.

Of all the ways I imagined seeing Nova Hearst again, watching her twerk on an empty dance floor in some kind of champagne silk that clung to her soft curves on an Instagram live would have been my very last guess. It wouldn't have even made the list.

Accidentally running into her at a library, coffee shop, or art show sat at the top of my list of places to possibly find the girl who vanished into thin air. I didn't even like art shows, but I'd gone to more than I'd care to admit on the off chance she'd be there.

A tired, heavy sigh reached through the phone, and I didn't know what time zone she was in, but my clock read eleven-fifty-two. The Nova I remembered never could stay up too late. Always an early riser looking for the best morning light for her art.

"How are you, Nova?"

"I'm…good." I liked that I could hear the smile in her answer. I liked finding out she was happy because she deserved it after what she'd gone through. After what I'd failed to protect her from. "I'd ask you how you've been, but it seems redundant when it's all over the internet."

"That's the internet. You should know it's not always right."

"True. So, I guess I'll go ahead and ask. How are you, Parker?"

After a long pause, leaving her hanging, I answered. "Good."

A giggle came through the phone and squeezed my chest, forcing my heart to pump harder. Damn. She still had the same effect even after all these years, even over the phone. I couldn't help but laugh with her.

"You're on tour, right?"

"We sure are."

"Where are you now? Dallas?"

"Ahhhhh. I see how it is." My smile grew at her slipup.

"See how what is?"

"You keeping up with us, Nova?"

She scoffed—twice—before deciding she'd been caught. "Maybe. I may have seen a show or two."

"Shut the fuck up." The words escaped on a gust of air like I'd been sucker-punched in the gut. I'd done a double-take on every willowy redhead in the last five years, and she'd been right there. A bobbing head and screaming fan in a sea of darkness impossible to see past the blinding lights.

So fucking close.

She giggled again. "Nope. Jammed out with all your fangirls."

"I just…" My mind struggled to process it. "I didn't realize how close you were."

The shock faded enough to let another emotion take over—hurt.

Her lighthearted giggle stopped, unable to miss the way the emotion hung from my words. "Yeah."

Another strained silence, and I imagined her teeth digging into her plump bottom lip. The memory of watching her do it across the dining room table one of the first times we met hit me, and I missed her all over again just as hard as the first day I realized she left.

Jesus, I hadn't even known I was capable of such a strong emotion after all these years. It knocked me sideways enough to slip honesty past the superficially light conversation.

"I looked for you, Nova."

"Oh," she whispered.

"I looked for you," I repeated, willing her to hear all the days, weeks, and months I'd held my breath in hopes of her coming back to me.

A thud came through the line, and it was like I was there, watching her lean against a wall, the phone to her ear, her pink lips even rosier from the assault, tipping her head back to hit it against the wall. *Just to jar the thoughts free*, she'd explained the first time I caught her doing it.

"Listen, Parker," she finally said. "I'm pretty drunk right now. My friend just got married, and I've done more than my fair share of shots."

"Supernova," I said softly, wanting to stop the exit she tried to make while simultaneously reminding her of the nickname we gave her when she let loose.

"It was good catching up," she said more firmly. Now I could see her stand up and pull her shoulders back, full of false bravado. I could imagine every move—saw it so clearly in my mind. "But I'm about to collapse where I stand."

I sat up and pulled my shoulders back too, enforcing real bravado against her fake one. I refused to let her end this as soon as it started. "I'm calling you again."

"I-I don't know—"

"I do."

"Parker."

"Go sober up, Supernova. But I'm calling again. Soon. Make sure you pick up." She let loose a heavy sigh. "Don't get all huffy on me. I'll contact your friend," I threatened playfully to lighten the mood. Maybe if we ended on a lighter note, she'd be more willing to pick up.

"God, no. Anything but that."

"Is she that annoying?"

"No, not at all. But she'd chew you up and spit you out once she got everything she needed from you."

"Challenge accepted."

She groaned but laughed.

"Pick up, Nova."

"We'll see."

"You fucking better."

"Night, Rock Star."

"Night, Supernova."

The line went dead, and I fell back on the couch, an ache in my chest and a smile on my lips.

She'd called me Rock Star.

Just like she had the first night we'd kissed.

TWO

Nova

PAST

Most kids got a car for their sweet sixteen. I got a new life.

Okay, maybe a little dramatic.

My mom married her long-distance boyfriend, and we moved into a stupidly big apartment in the city like some kind of mini-Brady Bunch. The apartment also came with my new stepdad and stepbrother—Parker Callahan.

I hadn't met him too many times other than short trips where I kept mostly to myself. The few visits Brad made to visit my mom, Parker stayed with his mom in Chicago, not leaving us much time to get to know each other. Living together hadn't changed that much either since he was always out.

"Nova," my mom called. "Time for dinner."

Except for tonight, when my mom was forcing a family dinner, where we would all sit around a table like a happy family.

Dropping my charcoals on the desk, I rolled my neck and arched back, spreading my cramped fingers like if I reached hard enough, I'd be able to touch the ductwork in the ceiling of my room. My fingers matched the darkness beyond the lamp illuminating my desk, and I dabbed them on the cloth I kept. Not that it worked since I'd overused it, and it only served to smear the dark color more.

Making a better attempt to scrub them clean in the bathroom, I looked myself over in the mirror. My hair piled messily on top of my head, my shirt had smudges, and my cut-off shorts had fraying strings. I considered changing but shrugged off the idea as soon as it came. If my mom wanted a family dinner, then we'd stick to the norm and keep it casual.

I walked out just in time to watch Parker fall back into one of the chairs around the table. He pulled out his phone and scrolled, giving me time to take him in—something I liked to do whenever I got the chance.

Parker Callahan was hot—really hot.

He was only a year older than me but carried himself like he'd lived an entire life to find the confidence he exuded. His arms flexed against his black T-shirt and his legs strained against the jeans. Not like the football players at our school, but like a swimmer.

Every time I saw him, I cataloged something new. How he stood so much taller than my five-foot-eight frame—definitely over six-foot. The ropey muscles stretching down his arms to his agile fingers. The way his lips curled up a little higher on one side when he smiled.

One beautiful moment stood out the most. I'd caught him coming up from the pool downstairs in shorts and a towel, displaying a light dusting of hair that perfectly matched the dirty blond waves on his head. I almost drooled when he deflected a punch from his friend, and he flexed, showcasing perfectly lined abs. God, even his strong legs leading to his feet had been drool-worthy.

This time I noticed a small black mark—a tattoo—on the inside of his right middle finger and made a note to try and figure out what it was.

"Nice shirt," he said, jarring me out of my perusal.

Blinking, I looked down at my oversized white tank with The Black Keys emblem. "You know them?"

He pinched one corner of his shirt to show off the same band name over the left side of his chest. As if connected to the material, one side of his mouth quirked up too, rendering me speechless.

"Cool," I muttered.

It was his turn for his gaze to take me in, and it dropped to my bare legs exposed beneath the edge of my tank, grazing my thighs.

"I have shorts on," I blurted, real smooth-like. To add insult to injury, I lifted the hem of my shirt to show the cut-off jean shorts.

Heat bloomed across my cheeks as the other side of his mouth kicked up in a delicious smile. He lifted his hands and laughed. "It's your house. You can wear whatever you want."

"Well, not really my house."

"Not really mine either."

My green eyes clashed with his blue ones, and a moment of understanding passed between us, followed by a laugh.

"It's weird," I said.

"That it is," he agreed. "At least you have your normal school."

"Yeah." I dug deep for normalcy to fill the small talk while we waited for our parents to join us at the table. "Are you bummed to leave your old school your senior year?"

He shrugged. "A little. But it's a cool adventure. New York is bigger than Chicago, and I'm always up for exploring."

"I have no doubt you'll fit in perfectly."

"I hope you don't mind breakfast for dinner," my mom said, walking in with a platter of pancakes for an army. Brad followed behind, his hands equally as full as my mom's.

"Breakfast is good at any time of day," Parker answered.

"Nova loves breakfast, too."

Parker nodded with approval, and my heart jumped for

joy like I'd been admitted into a club. Although, when Parker squirted grape jelly over his scrambled eggs, I wasn't sure I wanted to be in the club anymore.

He looked up and laughed. "Don't judge me, it's good. Have you ever had it?"

I tried to pull the look of disgust off my face and failed. "No. Because it's grape jelly and eggs. I don't need to try it to know those don't go together."

"You're missing out," he explained around the huge bite he took.

"So, Parker," my mom started. "I see you're fitting into New York well. You've definitely been busy."

That was putting it lightly. In less than a month of moving to New York, Parker came and went like he had the social calendar of the queen.

"Yeah, I met Ash almost as soon as we moved in."

"Ash?" I asked.

"The guy who lives three floors down. He said he goes to school with you."

"Oh, yeah." I played it off like I knew who it was the whole time when in reality, I only recalled dark hair and a tall body. I kind of kept my head down for the most part at school, preferring to sit back and observe and lose myself in art.

"Ash plays bass, right?" Brad asked.

"Yeah, he's going to introduce me to his buddy, Oren, who plays drums. With me on guitar, we were thinking of seeing if we could get a band together."

My mom stiffened, her fork freezing over her egg whites. She'd been married once before, to my dad, who'd been an aspiring musician. One who'd been blindly ambitious to anything but his own dreams, leaving us behind in the process —but not before he tried to use us to get ahead. I watched my mom carefully school her reaction with a smile.

"That's right, you were part of a band in Chicago." I had

to give her props for at least sounding interested and not letting her existing experience shut him down.

"Yeah, kind of. We really just jammed. I was the only one serious enough to want more."

"You'll get there," Brad encouraged.

"I know," Parker answered, not a drop of doubt lingering behind his words.

"You know, Nova's pretty artistic," Brad said, turning the spotlight to me. "You should check out some of her art."

"Oh, no." I waved the suggestion away. "I'm sure he's busy." I imagined watching Parker take in my work and cringed internally. I loved my artwork—wanted to share it with the world. I just didn't want to stand there and watch them study it…in my room. Which was where I kept everything.

It felt too…personal, and all I could imagine was him forcing interest in something he thought was lame.

"Nah, I'd love to see it." He pushed past my objections, and I forced a smile, desperately trying to hide my discomfort. I'd probably need to practice that face when he laughed at some of my drawings.

"You two should hang out more," my mom said. "Nova always wanted a brother."

And just like that, my cringe was back. I dropped my gaze to my plate, not wanting anyone else to see my reaction to calling Parker my brother. The last thing I thought of when looking at him was brotherly. When I braved a look up at him, he watched me in a way that didn't remind me of a brother either. But as soon as I met his blue eyes, he looked away, making me wonder if I made it up.

By the end of dinner, I hoped he'd forgotten about the suggestion, but no such luck. We dropped our dishes off at the sink, and before I could make a break for it, he stopped me.

"Ready to show me your art?"

"Oh. Umm…"

My eyes shot wide, bringing a full laugh from his parted lips. I could imagine then that he sang as well as played the guitar I heard through the walls occasionally. There was no way a guy could have a laugh that melodic and not sing. The deep timber filled the room and sank into my chest, making me feel more at home than I had since we moved here.

"Don't worry. You don't have to show me."

"I just don't usually show anyone, and you were kind of cornered into it, so no pressure to turn back. I know you've got plans."

"I've got time. Besides, I'm interested. And we're family now, right?" he joked.

That was *not* the reminder I needed right then as I wondered what his laugh would sound like with my ear pressed to his chest.

I hesitated, a million possibilities playing out in my mind. What if he laughed and hated it? What if he made fun of me? What if he tried to placate me and pretend he liked it when he thought it sucked, and then he made fun of me behind my back?

But then he smiled and closed the gap, his height more intense with each step closer. The doubts passed, and I clung to the warmth of home he ignited. Before I could question it anymore, I murmured a quick, "Sure."

"Sweet."

I laughed, shaking my head at his excitement.

Trying to brush off the nerves and act as cool as him, I turned toward my room. By the time we walked through the bedroom door, my legs shook like jello, and my lungs worked overtime.

Be cool. Be cool.

"Man, I think you got the better deal on the room," he said, looking around.

I remembered the first time I saw the apartment and requested this room. My mom hadn't understood when it was more of an oversized office with no closet. But she never did. She never saw the natural light streaming in the windows from all sides. She didn't see the space to have my bed *and* a large enough area to keep my oversized workbench.

But Parker did.

"I bet you have a hard time leaving in the morning."

"Why's that?"

"The morning light through these windows has to be inspiring."

A slow smile stretched my lips. That sensation of home grew almost too big. "Yeah, it is," I agreed softly. "I get my best work done then."

He turned away from the art tacked to the wall and smiled. In that moment, I realized maybe Parker and I weren't so different after all. He may be outgoing while I hung back, but I think we both searched for a little understanding. Not many people understood the unique traits of an artist.

"What are those?" he asked, nodding behind me.

I whipped around, fully prepared to find a stack of my bras or something.

Worse.

My stack of journals piled as high as my nightstand. If I thought my drawings hinted too much to my inner soul, it was nothing compared to the nakedness that overwhelmed me at the thought of him reading my scribbled notes and poetry.

"Oh, um, just some writing stuff." I waved my hand, trying to play it off.

"Cool," he said, walking past me to the pile.

It took all I had not to slap my hand over the pile when he brushed his finger over the top one.

"Can I?"

No. Hell no.

"Um, sure."

Wait. What?

All air ceased in my lungs, and blood rushed to my ears as

he flipped through the pages. Maybe if I stood super still, I'd disappear, and I wouldn't have to face the outcome of him looking over my words.

"You look at me, but you don't see. You hear me, but you're not listening. Why exist at all when the real me is a ghost haunting the person you really wanted?"

Hearing my words in his masculine voice turned my body into one live, vibrating pulse. This was it. This was the moment I'd pass out and make it a million times worse.

He flipped a few more pages, and I stood frozen like a statue.

"You should write music," he finally said.

"What?" I squeaked out.

"Yeah. Your words are amazing. I could totally put this to a beat. I can already hear some of it in my head." He bobbed his head to a tune only he could hear.

"Oh. I've never thought of that. They're just random things. Nothing, really."

"No." He shook his head and looked up from the pages, meeting my eyes, and unlike the poem accused, he definitely saw me. "These are great."

Fluttering fire burned its way up my chest and into my throat. My cheek twitched, but I stood in too much shock and awe of his compliment to even form a smile.

He obviously didn't have the same struggle I did. He smiled enough for both of us, and it washed over me until finally, I found enough strength to smile back.

"Thank you."

He opened his mouth, but the shrill ring of his phone shattered the moment. He closed the book and carefully placed it back as he tugged his phone out of his pocket. "It's Ash. I was waiting for him to call."

"Of course."

"I'll see you around."

"Yeah."

With a head nod from him and an awkward finger wave from me, he left.

I didn't know how long I stood there trying to see my small corner of the world from his point of view, but when I finally fell back on my bed, I saw it with more confidence than ever before.

Parker Callahan had been in my life for a few months, and already he was changing it.

THREE

Parker

"You waiting on a booty call?" Brogan asked. "That's the five-hundredth time you've check your phone this week."

I expertly dodged the bass pick he flicked my way from where he sat perched on the edge of the stage. However, I missed the guitar pick Ash hit me in the side of the head with. Brogan high-fived Ash when he plopped down next to him, both their feet dangling like kids.

"I've barely looked at my phone." The guys snorted and gave me matching looks that called bullshit. Rubbing a hand over my face, I glanced down at my phone again, like maybe a return message from Nova would randomly appear.

Still not there. But my seventeen messages stared back at me.

"You'll never guess who I stumbled across."

"Angelina Jolie?" Oren guessed, coming up behind the rest of the guys. "Please say Angelina Jolie. And that she's coming to our show tonight and then back to the hotel to see me because she was just using you to get to me."

"Wow, that's detailed, bro," Brogan said.

Oren shrugged. "We're on tour," he said like it explained it all. And it kind of did. The days blurred, and the mind struggled to keep up, even only a few days in. So, random ass thoughts and fantasies made sense.

"Who?" Ash asked, bringing us back to the point of the conversation.

For a second, I considered lying and avoiding telling them like I had all week, but frankly, I needed to get it off my chest, and no one knew what I'd gone through with Nova better than them.

"Nova."

I wished I had a camera out and ready to snap the various stages of shock marring their faces. It ranged somewhere between the same wonder I felt and a minor flicker of hurt that they carried around with them, too.

"Shut. The. Fuck. Up," Brogan said first.

"How?"

"When?"

"Dude, how?"

They pestered me like a crowd of rabid fans rather than my three bandmates.

"Calm the fuck down," I shouted.

"How am I supposed to calm the fuck down when you drop that bombshell," Oren asked. "It's fucking Nova."

I shook my head, still unable to believe my luck last week. "I was doing my usual Instagram live with some fans, and I randomly picked a person. At first, it was someone else—her friend—and then she flipped the screen, and there she was."

"Oh, shit," Brogan said.

"Dancing in some bridesmaid dress."

"What?" Oren screeched.

"Remember that one house party we went to, and she danced," I reminded them.

"Oh, fuck yeah, I do," Ash said with his devious trademark smirk.

"She was dancing like that."

"Fuck," Ash shouted. "You should have come and got us or screen recorded it or something."

"How is she?" Brogan asked.

"*Where* is she?"

"Do you have her number?"

"Did you actually talk to her or just watch like a perv?"

"Are you talking to her again?"

"Does she miss us?"

"Did you ask her why she left us?"

"Jesus, you guys," I said, holding my hands up to slow the barrage of questions. "One at a time."

"Well, stop pussy-footing and speak," Ash ordered.

"She's…good. And yes, I actually spoke to her. I may have had to threaten to contact her friend for her number if she didn't give it to me."

"Is her friend hot?" Brogan asked.

"Is she single?" Oren added.

I pinched my lips and gave them a hard stare. They held their hands up in surrender before motioning to continue.

"So, I call her, and we talk. It was short, so I didn't get to ask where she was or anything."

"But you have her number?"

"Yeah."

All three of them moved at once and swarmed me. Next thing I knew, Oren held my phone up in victory and entered my password, quickly scrolling for Nova. Before he could hit her name, I snatched it back.

"I talked to her last week, and she hasn't picked up when I've called or responded to any messages since."

Some of the excitement dimmed, and reality crashed back in. The guys sunk back to lean against the stage, searching the ground like it held the answers about the right way to feel. In reality, we all hurt and didn't want to see it mirrored back at us when we looked at each other.

We'd been a family—an immature one that made

mistakes. Mistakes I knew clung to each of us in different ways. However, even when you made a mistake, it didn't make the consequence any less difficult to deal with.

Like losing part of your family. Or for me, losing everything.

"I don't really blame her," Brogan muttered, digging his toe against the ground.

"It still would have been nice to see her," Oren added.

"How did she look?" Ash asked.

I smiled softly, remembering those green eyes lowered seductively as she danced toward the camera. "Amazing." I recalled how many times she'd looked up at me with those same heavy eyes, only this time, they held a wealth of understanding that they hadn't when we were teens. "But I didn't get to see much of her. As soon as she realized what her friend had done, she'd looked like a deer in headlights and left the live video."

"Oh, man," Oren laughed, slapping his thigh. "I bet it was epic."

"It was pretty funny."

"Remind me why you haven't talked to her again," Brogan asked.

"She hasn't picked up. According to her Instagram, she's on a trip. But I also think she's avoiding me."

"She has Instagram?" Ash asked, pulling out his phone. "What's her name?"

"Psithurism." His brows shot up, and I spelled it out. "Apparently, it means the sounds of the wind in the trees."

The guys crowded around Ash, and I already knew what they'd find since I'd scrolled through each picture a million times.

"Dude, she's got a million followers," Brogan said.

"Are you sure this is her?" Ash asked. "She doesn't show her face at all."

"Yeah, it's her." I had no doubt. I'd know that red hair

anywhere. I'd dreamt of those long limbs almost every night. Then there was one of the photos that showed part of her profile, and I noticed the beauty mark just behind her ear that always sent chills down her back when I kissed her there.

"Daaaaaamn," Oren crowed. He didn't have to explain. I knew they stumbled on one of the many that she posted of her naked back as she lounged in a lake or on the edge of a cliff.

"All right, ladies," Aspen, our manager, called from the stage. "Equipment is setup, so let's get going."

She stood taller than her five-foot-four frame, her attitude and confidence adding a few more inches—the black stilettos helped too.

Ash shoved his phone back into his pocket. "If you hear from her, let us know."

"Sure."

Once upon a time, I'd worried Ash also had a thing for Nova, but in one drunken confession, he admitted he would flirt with her to push my buttons because it'd been the only way to make me take what I so obviously wanted. It'd just been hard to take when that someone was your stepsister.

"Parker," Aspen called. "Can I talk to you for a minute?"

I headed her way while the guys strapped up. "What's up?"

"I know you're struggling with lyrics," she started, and I rolled my eyes before she finished. "Don't give me that. This is your job, and it's my job to make sure you do your job. If you can't do your job, then it's my job to do what I can to make it happen."

"I'm working on it."

"I know. And usually, that would be enough, but we're doing a big push this year. You're on the cusp of being a great. A Rolling Stones, Foo Fighters, Led Zeppelin. Parker, this is the push to be legendary forever and not just a forgotten band who almost made it."

"I know that," I growled.

"Good, because I wanted to talk to you about bringing on a songwriter."

"No. We write our own music."

"And if you were actually writing anything, I'd believe you." She matched my glare with a dark one of her own. Aspen was the record label owner's daughter. She had a lot to prove, and because of that, her determination to see us succeed broke through any barrier in her way. "Listen, I get writer's block," she said softer. "I'm not saying we just buy some lyrics. I'm saying we find a way to get someone to work with you. Even if that person just comes in and says something absurd that sparks a song for you, then that's good enough. Even if you don't use a thing they create, I just need *you* to create."

Pacing away, I dug my hand into my hair and tugged before walking back. "And what about the tour? How are we doing all this? We're already planning on recording on the road where we can."

"Leave that up to me. I just need to know you won't fight me on this if I set it up."

I wanted to. I wanted to tell her and whoever she hired to fuck off because I didn't need them. The guys' laughter nabbed my attention, and I looked over at the three guys who I'd do anything for.

I hated this rut that shrouded my thoughts in nothing. Lyrics usually came to me like oxygen to my lungs, but lately, I'd been deprived. Probably because on this path to becoming legendary, there was limited rest. I loved every part of this job —it'd been my dream since I was a kid, and every person that doubted me, only drove me harder—one person in particular.

When that one person was your own mom, you didn't take breaks, and you didn't pull back from the hard stuff to succeed. I just wish succeeding could feel a little easier for once. Kind of like it did when I'd had Nova at my side. She'd slipped her hand in mine, and the future flowed together like pieces of a puzzle snapping in place. I'd almost hoped talking to her might have caused another surge of inspiration—she'd always been my muse.

But it was hard to use your muse when they didn't pick up the phone. Which left me still stuck in my rut.

"I won't fight you," I gave in.

"Good," she said, her red lips stretching into a smile.

I walked up on stage and grabbed my guitar. Aspen rambled on about our schedule while we got ready to run through our set.

"Also, Parker, you have a date with Sonia tomorrow night."

Sonia was a model-turned-actress I'd been photographed with at an awards afterparty last year. When the media had a field day with the photos, Aspen concocted a plan to formulate a fake relationship between us since the fans went crazy imagining all the songs we wrote were about Sonia and me. Our sales skyrocketed, and Sonia hadn't hesitated to use me as much as I used her.

I didn't hate it because every once in a while, Sonia and I fucked after our dates and the release without any pressure of what came next was nice. It didn't hurt that her hair looked a lot like Nova's.

Not many women had that deep red hair, but I did my best to find them all and fuck the desire for redheads out of my system. Spoiler alert: it didn't work. I just got labeled as having a type. Which I guess I did.

Anyone who reminded me of Nova.

Aspen being the businesswoman she was, turned it into a contract that strangled me more than helped.

"It's dinner at a restaurant opening, so maybe get the scowl off your face," Aspen reprimanded. "It should be nice."

"Yeah, nice," Ash scoffed, imitating a blow job.

Brogan made humping motions, and Oren wrapped both

arms around himself like he was mid-make-out session, adding breathy moans for effect.

"You guys are gross," Aspen sneered. "I'll see you in the morning. Don't be late."

Before I could object, she turned away. Usually, I didn't mind the arranged dates, but ever since seeing Nova—even for that quick flash—a date with Sonia was the last thing I wanted to do.

"THANKS FOR DOING THIS," Sonia said as I helped her into her jacket.

"Of course. I was just happy it wasn't a shopping trip again."

She turned, pulling her sleek hair out from under the collar, her full lips stretched into a perfect smile. She was on. Probably because we stood in front of the restaurant we just ate at with a glass wall between the lingering paparazzi and us.

"I'm at your mercy whenever you need me." She stared up at me from under her lashes as best as she could when she was only three inches shorter in her heels and closed the gap between us. She gripped the lapels of my coat and adjusted them before resting her palms on my chest.

The moves came naturally as we'd done them time and time again. I even knew when to angle a few degrees away from the window, making sure she stood in the perfect spot lined up for a photo that got her good side.

"Unless you're not ready for the night to end," she murmured. "You know I'm always up for a quickie."

I remembered the last quickie when she'd sucked me off on the drive back to her apartment. She'd paid the driver two-hundred dollars to not tell anyone but secretly hoped he would to beef up our lie.

But even that memory couldn't block out another redhead, and when Sonia leaned in to close the gap, I gripped her biceps, holding her back, making it look more like an embrace rather than a rejection. Even with only a moment from Nova and that was all it took to remind me of what we had. With those memories came the ones of how I hadn't needed to work so hard—hadn't needed to go on arranged dates I didn't want to go on.

"Not tonight."

Her eyes narrowed only a fraction before the coy smile slipped in place. "Oh, Parker," she said on an exhale. "Are you seeing someone?"

I laughed. "No."

But I was thinking of someone I desperately wanted to see, and the thought of putting my lips on Sonia's when all I could do was remember the few sparing times I'd put my lips on Nova's, rubbed me the wrong way. Everything in me screamed no.

"I'm just not wanting to put on that much of a show."

"But we always kiss at the end of the night."

"Just…not tonight."

She studied me a little longer before relaxing and sliding her hands down my chest, pulling away to turn to the door. "Okay. I can respect that."

She reached her hand for mine, and I dutifully grabbed on, pulling back on the affection I usually delivered with every smile. We stepped through the doors, and cameras went off. Normally, I blocked them out, not really caring what I looked like. But tonight, my hair stood on end, every muscle on high alert of how I positioned myself around Sonia, wondering what the pictures looked like to an outsider—to Nova.

Sonia's car pulled up, and I opened the door for her, waiting for my own right behind hers. Before getting in, she turned to me one more time, stepping close and brushing her fingers along the scruff on my cheek. It was the only warning

I got before she closed the few inches between us and pressed her lips to where she's just touched, dangerously close to my lips.

My hands tightened on her hips, barely fighting the urge to shove her away. Before she pulled back, she whispered, "A deal is a deal, Parker. Be happy I didn't go for a full kiss you couldn't pull away from."

I ground my teeth, not liking the walls closing in around my natural reactions, trapping me into a role I didn't want to play tonight. She pulled back, stroking her thumb along the red lipstick I knew marred my cheek.

"Hopefully, next time, you'll be more willing to play. It was the best bonus of our deal."

And with that, she smiled at the camera one last time and got in. I waited until her car drove away before I moved to mine, collapsing into the back seat, grateful for the blacked-out windows.

FOUR

Nova

For the seventh time, I dropped my book on the mattress beside me, unable to sleep. Abandoning trying again, I readjusted to my back, bringing my head to the edge of the mattress to peek out at the stars beyond.

I wouldn't be able to keep the back doors of the van open much longer. As the days crept deeper into fall, the nights got colder, even in Georgia. Peeking out of the corner of my eye, I stared at my phone, the urge to pick it up hitting me like a ghost haunting my body.

It always did.

But I never gave in.

It'd been a little over a month since my digital run-in with Parker. A month filled with indecisions, doubt, memories—happy and...not so happy—curiosity, more doubt, and another dash of doubt for good measure. Add in the wave after wave of remembered feelings, and I barely came up for air. I'd traveled more, trying to find a comfort his phone call disrupted. I'd put off Aiken's emails and not so gentle nudges to make decisions about where I wanted to go with my conglomerate of businesses.

Instead of thinking about how I wanted to plan my future, I lingered over the past.

That first week, he'd called, messaged, and stalked me on Instagram. Then they slowed down a little more each week. I held my breath for the moment he followed through, and Rae came to me to let me know Parker Callahan reached out to her. I called his bluff, and part of me wished he hadn't been lying.

However, he still called me. Just not as often. Just enough to never let me sink back into the normalcy I'd found over the last few years. It was like as soon as I shut the door, he'd stick his foot in it just in time to make me keep it open.

Usually, I resisted.

When I came close to giving in, I shoved past the good memories and remembered all the reasons why we were apart. I remembered every ounce of loneliness that consumed me. I remembered the fear and pain. I told myself he was just like my father and would always pick his dream over me. I told myself I deserved more than these doubts, and that helped to shove the phone away when his name popped up.

But tonight? Tonight, I wanted to call him. Something about the stars and the air and the aching hole in my chest he'd left behind. Maybe he'd ripped the flimsy band-aid off, and without it, it grew a little more each day, and tonight it finally grew big enough to not ignore.

Whatever the reason was, this time, when my fingers twitched with the need to call him, I did. I held my breath with every ring, hoping it went to voicemail and dreading that it did. My heart thundered so hard the beating pulse almost blocked out all other noise. It worked too hard, and my lungs struggled to keep up.

Just when I planned to pull back and end the mistake before it began, the ringing stopped.

"Supernova," he answered.

The organ in my chest came to a screeching halt, and I sucked in a breath. "Hey, Rock Star," I exhaled.

Some of the tension eased when I heard a huff of laughter on the other end of the line at the nickname I gave him. It was better than the *fuck you*, I expected.

"I'm pretty sure we said the next day, not the next month."

"Yeeeeaaaah, about that...Life got a little crazy." The excuse sounded lame even to me, and he didn't hesitate to call me out on it.

"For a month? For even a text response? I live one of the most hectic lives, and I was able to find time to call you."

"It wasn't always that way." The sharp words slipped past my lips before I could think better of them. That was the thing about the past; sometimes, those hurts lingered in the shadows unnoticed, popping out when you least expected it. Sometimes you forgot they were even there.

"Yeah, it wasn't," he admitted sullenly.

I winced. We'd been on the phone all of two seconds, and I'd already brought up the bitterness of our past and how *he'd* been the one to not respond or call. Maybe I'd been subconsciously punishing him with my lack of response.

But *I'd* called *him*. And not to fight about what was already done. In fact, I didn't even want to think about it, let alone talk about it. "Sorry. I didn't mean that." We both knew I did, but before he could call me on it, I pushed on. "I *did* get busy and lose service on that first trip, but when I got back, I got lost in my head, and...I don't know."

"What don't you know?"

"I don't know," I laughed, looking up at the stars for answers. "I guess, maybe I wondered if talking would be good or bad. I wondered if it would be better or worse or if maybe we'd changed so much, we didn't have anything to talk about. Or our lives were too different, and we didn't have room for anything else."

Or if we had someone else in our life that may not like us talking to each other. I recalled the image of him with Sonia at a dinner and the way her glossy hair shined as her red-painted lips smiled adoringly at him. Remembering the photo that had been splashed all over Instagram had jealousy punching me in the gut, almost forcing the words up and out, but I bit them back. I'd already let enough bitter comments slip free.

"Talking to you is always good, Supernova. Even when it's bad."

"Thank you?"

His laugh rumbled low like the deep ocean waves, and I closed my eyes to let it wash over me.

"It's a compliment. Even when you were a feisty pain in my ass, I enjoyed your company."

"I'll be sure to list it on my resume."

A silence fell between us, and I wondered where he was. I'd made a point to take off the Google notifications I had set up. The less I knew, the better.

"How about this," he started. "We just talk—like old friends, and we skip the past."

Another chord of tension around my chest broke free. "I like the sound of that." I made it a point to always skip talking about the past. Even Rae and Vera didn't know my history.

"And Nova?"

"Yeah?"

"There's always room in my life for you."

Unbidden, the past crept out of the shadows, but I saw it coming and shut my mouth before it could escape.

You hadn't always. Once upon a time, you'd forgotten me as quickly as you'd known me.

But we weren't talking about the past.

"So, what are you up to?" I asked instead.

"Lounging in my hotel room."

"So, fancy."

"Beats the bus. Don't get me wrong, I love it—but four

guys in one small space starts to smell bad. It's good to air it out."

"Gross," I laughed.

"What about you? What are you doing?"

"On another trip in a van."

"Damn. Again?"

"Yup."

"You must love it."

"I truly do." The freedom. The solitude. The fresh air and exertion. Only me and wherever I landed to take pictures or set up an easel and work on a new painting or sketch to sell. I never worried about being closed into a cubicle at a big publishing company like my mom hoped. I was free.

"How does one come to love the van life?" he asked.

I heard the rustle of fabric and closed my eyes, imagining him leaned back against the pillows, his arm behind his head, a few more tattoos than last time peeking out from his short sleeve shirt. I saw the ink on his arm grow in pictures, but I never let myself study it enough to see what the new tattoos were.

"Well, I randomly rented one with my birthday money one summer between my sophomore and junior year, and it was the best experience of my life. I knew I had to go back. I did it again after my junior year, and I began saving so I could do it for longer after my senior year."

"I bet your mom loved that," he muttered.

"She definitely did not. At first, she hoped it was a phase, thinking I would get it out of my system. She never outright vetoed the trips until I turned down an internship after college. Then she gave me all of six months post-college to get a reputable job she approved of, or she would pull any support."

"Shit. When is that?"

"Last week."

"So, does that mean you're in a van because you're homeless?"

"Nah, I worked odd jobs over the summers in college and saved as much as I could. And now, it's those odd jobs that are helping me establish contacts I'm using now to build something for myself."

Just not building fast enough. Which was what I needed Aiken for. Sponsorships on Instagram and my sporadic art, articles, and music sales didn't quite cover the tiny loft in New York. Let alone, van rentals and trips. I didn't *have* to live in the city, but my family was there—Vera and Rae. My life was there. And eventually, I'd have to cave to Aiken's ideas—like showing my face—if I wanted to stay there.

"Damn, Nova. I always knew you'd be amazing."

"I definitely try. Wanting to eat and keep a roof over my head definitely acts as motivation."

"That it will. It sounds a lot like our first year on the road. Brogan may have danced a night or two at a local club to get some cash."

"He didn't?" I gasped.

"He sure did."

I tossed my head back into the pillow and let my laugh bellow free into the night, imagining the big blond swiveling his hips at some club. "Did you?"

"Maybe," he muttered.

I curled to my side, laughing so hard.

"What about your friends?" he asked. "Did anyone you know have to strip or sell blood to survive? College can be expensive."

"I went to Wharton," I deadpanned. "Everyone came with a silver spoon."

"Fair enough."

"Really, though. My two friends, Vera and Rae, didn't even need scholarships."

"Rae. Is she the one who I talked to?" he asked.

"Yup."

"I like her."

"Most guys do." I usually didn't mind but having one of those guys be *my* Parker stung a little more than I wanted to admit. At least until he admitted why he liked her.

"Well, I like her for bringing me to you. "

His sincerity popped any bubble of jealousy and left behind a warm goo that eased past my defenses. I rolled to my back and looked up at the night sky, unsure what to say. In the end, I went with a topic I said I'd avoid. "Are you seeing anyone?"

I cringed as soon as the words left my lips. *Stupid, stupid, Nova.*

"As a matter of a fact, I'm not. Did Google not tell you that?"

His easy answer, not at all what I expected it to be, threw me for a loop, and confusion lowered my filter even more. "Google just shows you with a bunch of girls."

"Ohhhh," he said, laughing. "So, you've checked?"

My face would be permanently twisted in a wince of regret if I didn't think before speaking. But the truth was, I checked more than I liked to admit.

Again, I thought of Sonia and how I never failed to glare at her picture like it would make her any less gorgeous. She even had good taste in shoes, which made me equally envious, and also want to ask her where she shopped.

"I mean, it's hard to miss," I said flippantly, trying to backtrack.

"Mmhmm," he responded with disbelief.

I had some disbelief of my own. He didn't even hesitate when I asked him about dating, but he seemed awfully close with Sonia when she pressed her lips to his in the photo. They looked awfully close in every photo they'd been in over the last year. It'd been on and off with others mixed in, but still. Interviewers always implied that his love songs were about her, but he never confirmed or denied it.

Had I read it wrong? Was he really single?

Did it matter?

"So, what about you? Any guys in your life?" he asked, pulling me out of my inner revelry.

Warmth bloomed in my chest at his curious tone. Part of me wanted to lie and say yes, but I resisted the petty urge. "Just me, my van, and my girls."

"Anyone serious before? In college?"

I paused, noting this question held more weight—more than conversational curiosity.

"No. Maybe a boyfriend or two, but no one serious." Just someone I gave my virginity to and another I wasted six months on. My most serious relationship was with my porn collection I'd take to my grave.

"Cool."

A silence lingered, and I connected Orion's belt thinking over what to say next. "Is your dad still in New York?"

"Back in Chicago, but visits New York a lot. What about your mom? Is she still in New York?"

"Yup."

"And you?" he asked softer. "Are you still in New York, or is home somewhere else now?"

"Yeah. I'm still there," I admitted like I expected him to narrow down the addresses in all of New York and pop up at my tiny apartment. "Just a small home base."

"Yeah. I have a home base there, too."

My heart skipped a beat, wondering how far he was from my apartment.

"Upper East Side. Nothing big."

I laughed, imagining his nothing big was a whole lot different than my less stylish, nothing big, in an up-and-coming neighborhood.

"I'm sure it's a shack," I said dubiously.

"Everything is a shack in New York."

"Very true."

"Either way, it's a good enough place to rest my head and write some music in my downtime."

"You still write the songs?" I asked.

"Almost all of them."

That made more sense than I wanted it to. I thought back to all the angry songs from their first album that I convinced myself weren't about me. Seems like maybe they were.

I wrote more than my fair share of angry songs at the same time. The difference was that I sold them to other bands rather than sing them myself. One of my many business ventures Aiken wanted me to combine with my Instagram business to build a *brand*.

The thought of everyone knowing the songs I wrote left me anxious thinking about them hearing the lyrics and getting a peek inside my soul. It left me exposed and naked.

I currently used a private LLC to sell my music through online avenues. I took every precaution to protect my identity. Before I left high school, I deleted all my social media, only starting up the Instagram I had now because I wanted to share my art and travels, and someone told me I could probably start selling art on Instagram. I made sure to never show my face and used another LLC for that too. I didn't want to be in the public eye—especially with any connection to the music world.

I'd done that before, and it had been the worst experience of my life.

The one that had pulled me away from Parker Callahan when I'd needed him most.

The one that had left me yearning for a man who stole my heart and ran away to a life I could never be a part of.

"At least I used to write our music," he grumbled, interrupting my melancholy.

"What do you mean?"

"I've…" His exhale carried so much weight even I could feel the pressure of it through the phone. "I've been in this writer's block."

"Shit. That sucks."

"Tell me about it. We're supposed to be working on an album soon, but I don't have any lyrics to sing. I highly doubt our fans will be thrilled with a purely musical album."

"Probably not," I agreed. "Why are you pushing making an album while touring? That seems awfully crunched, and I'm sure it's not helping the stress."

"Aspen, our manager, has built us up to this point. It's our year to take everything we worked hard on and shape it into something epic. And that means constantly pushing out product."

"Wow. That's a lot of pressure."

"Tell me about it."

"I have no doubt you'll get there." It was on the tip of my tongue to offer to help, but I bit it between my teeth, holding it back, not wanting to tie myself to him anymore. When we'd written music together before, it'd been intense and intimate. Putting myself in that position sounded a lot like asking for more hurt and pain.

"Yeah," he sighed, not sounding convinced. With another deep sigh, he changed the subject. "Where are you tonight?"

"In the Smoky Mountains, skirting the Tennessee border in Georgia. Where are you?"

"What? Not keeping up with our tour schedule?"

"Yeah, right," I scoffed. "I wouldn't know if you were in Seattle or Miami."

"Mmhmm," he said doubtfully. "We're in San Diego right now."

"Good ole California."

"Have you been?"

"Not yet. But I want to. I'd love to hike the Sierra Nevada."

"You'd love it," he agreed.

"You've done it?" I asked, jealous but excited to hear his story.

"We did a small hike one day to an alpine lake. Oren and Brogan apparently wanted to skinny dip in liquid ice."

"Oh, man." I laughed, imagining it. "Did you do it?"

"Hell, yeah, I did. It was a long-ass hike."

"I'm so jealous."

"I'll take you there someday," he promised softly, like maybe if he said it too loud, I'd run. And honestly, I kind of wanted to.

His promise sat like an anvil on my chest, choking the air in my lungs. We could avoid talking about anything from the past, but it didn't mean it wasn't there, making itself known with the simplest of words. His statement was easy—something anyone would say but came with a wrecking ball of meaning, knocking down the veneer of lies I tried to hide behind.

"It's a beautiful night tonight," I whispered, changing the subject.

"Now *I'm* jealous," he joked. "I'm stuck in a hotel, and it's raining here."

"Ew."

"Tell me what you see. Tell me about where you are," he requested. "I'm gonna lie back on the bed, close my eyes, and imagine I'm in the van with you."

Another anvil. This one lighting a fire up the back of my throat.

Like I had a million times before, I closed my eyes too and imagined his weight dipping the mattress beside me. How many nights had I looked up at the sky and wished he'd been right beside me? How many moments had I closed my eyes to imagine him there, sharing the life we painted when we were kids?

Too many to count.

More than I wanted to admit.

And to have his voice in my ear, it was the closest my dreams came to reality. I just didn't know what that reality came with. Being faced with it now, I worried it came with more hurt than anything else I'd imagined.

With a deep breath, I swallowed back the fire and opened my eyes to look up at the stars.

"You can see everything. Without the light pollution, you can see everything."

"Tell me," he pleaded, almost desperate. "I want to be right there."

I wanted him to be right here too, I admitted to myself, and that terrified me. It scared the hell out of me how quick these feelings came roaring back and how quickly I wanted to pretend they were all that existed. I knew better. I knew life was more than the fantasy we wanted to believe—more than what lay on the surface. Yet, there I was, only wanting to see this moment and nothing else.

Two minimal conversations over nothing, and Parker managed to shine a light on the gaping space I'd tried to cover. He found a crack in the flimsy wall and pulled loose a brick covering the place in my heart he'd made for just him years ago.

Fire tried to climb its way free, but I refused. I *refused*.

I swallowed it down, and I forced my eyes open—forced myself to keep pretending the hole wasn't there. "You think you know how many stars there are, but until you're here and the sky is almost completely covered with them, you have no idea. And the Milky Way? We learn about it all through school. We know it's out there, but until you see it, it's kind of like Neptune. Just an idea. A picture we've been shown. But Parker, I see it every night, and it's beautiful."

"Yeah?" he whispered, matching my quiet tone.

I wondered if he heard the double meaning. That so many nights I'd looked up, and I saw him—I saw us. Something that had been surrounded by so much youth and lights that we hadn't been able to see it for what it was. I hadn't been able to see or understand how much I'd loved him until he was gone and took something vital with him.

"A glowing cluster like a fading cloud with a dark vein running through it," I continued. "One of the most beautiful things I've ever seen. I had no idea. Living in the city teaches you a lot, but it doesn't teach you this. The city is full of art, but this…I'd never be able to match this."

"You already do," he said almost too quietly for me to hear.

"Parker…" I whispered, almost pleading. Pleading for him to not do this. Pleading for him to stop.

"We should see each other," he stated. "Meet up so you can't ignore my phone calls again."

Yes.

My mind worked overtime imagining seeing him. How many times had I imagined running into him, smiling, and running into his arms to feel the hug I'd missed so long? But just as quick as that yearning came, the reminder of why we parted—how he put his career first and left me alone smashed it apart.

The mix of emotions swirled even more violently with him so close, with his voice in my ear. Each thought bombarded me until I feared losing myself altogether.

I want to see him.
I can't see him.
I miss him.
He left me.
I love him.
I hate him.

One freaking phone call and look at me—a mess.

What would I look like if I actually stood before him? What would I be willing to sacrifice just to have a piece of him? I wasn't willing to find out.

"I can't."

"Why not?"

"I-I...I just can't, Parker. I'm sorry."

Silence. So much silence until I feared he'd left me, but I knew he was still there when I heard the occasional huff of air. I chewed my lip, struggling to let him process but knowing I had no other words to give him. I didn't want to explain how seeing him would be too real. I didn't want to explain that if I saw him, I wasn't sure I would want to leave. I didn't want to explain because I wasn't even sure I could explain it to myself.

We hadn't talked for five years, and yet here I was on the verge of crying because...because...

I bit back my groan of frustration, irritated with my inability to put it into words.

But that was Parker. Always stirring emotions deep within me like no one else ever had.

"Can we talk again tomorrow—actually tomorrow?" he finally asked.

I breathed a sigh of relief that he dropped it and answered vaguely. "I don't know if I'll have service, but I'm heading home soon for an interview."

"Yeah? Where at? Are you going to settle down to that office job?" His laugh was fake, but we both ignored it, latching on to the reprieve.

"Yeah, right. It's just a freelance job. Writing an article for an online travel magazine."

"You'll nail it."

"How do you know?"

"Because you're the most talented person I know. How could they not want you?"

"You do good things for my ego," I laughed.

"I do what I can."

"Well, thank you."

"Keep me updated. And send me a picture of you on a mountain somewhere."

"I have them on my Instagram."

"No. I want one with your face. I want to see you." When I didn't answer right away, he added, "Please."

"Okay," I found myself agreeing.

Because why not? Parker Callahan could always get me to do anything.

FIVE

Nova

PAST

"Oh, my gosh," a girl, whose name I think was Amber, practically squealed when she leaned beside my open locker. I froze, wide-eyed, alarmed, and wondering if she thought I was someone else. We'd definitely never talked before. "I had no idea Parker Callahan was your brother."

"Stepbrother," I corrected on rote, cringing even over admitting that.

"Yeah, when Dr. Brooks mentioned he had your brother in his morning class, I couldn't believe it. How cool to have the same classes as your brother. You could totally study together at home," she continued like I hadn't spoken.

"Yeah. Cool." My interest in the conversation went from minimal to non-existent. It'd only been a couple of months, but she wasn't the first girl to randomly approach me to ask about Parker. I could already play out the rest of the conversation, it happened so frequently.

"I mean, he's so hot. Not that you would notice since he's your brother. Which is totally unfortunate because that would be like incest."

"Stepbrother," I grumbled, knowing she probably didn't even hear me, cringing over the incest comment.

Maybe if I said it enough, *I'd* start listening because when I looked at him, he inspired anything but brotherly feelings.

The flicker in my chest started over the summer before I was faced with public thoughts and queries like this one. It'd been easy to feed into the feeling growing in my chest because the situation made us more like roommates than family. Or friends that just happened to live together, and there was no harm in drooling over your ridiculously sexy friend. There was no harm in wanting to abandon your naivety and explore the heat he created in the pit of your stomach. There was nothing wrong with the thoughts I had about my friend.

Until school, where people like Amber and Dr. Brooks reminded me at every turn that he was my stepbrother.

"But still. You're so lucky. He seems so cool. Caitlin hung out with the band last week and said he's like the best kisser ever. I mean, those lips. I asked her if they went further, but she wouldn't tell. I totally bet they did. I hear he's slept with quite a few lucky ladies."

God, if you're listening, kill me now, and please stop this fire blazing inside my chest.

"Oh, my god, Nora, we should totally do a study group."

"Nova," I corrected.

"What?"

"My name. It's Nova."

She blinked, almost like she was seeing me for the first time. "Right. Nova. Silly me. So, how about it?"

"You know, I'm pretty busy." *Liar.* "And Parker is gone a lot anyway. So, we rarely study together." *Unfortunately, true.*

"Yeah, probably with the band," she said slowly, like it was just hitting her. "I should probably ask Caitlin what she did to hang out with them."

"Probably just talking to them would work," I offered, my voice doing nothing to hide my desperation for it to be over. Not that she noticed.

"Yeah, right. I need him to, like, notice me."

"Well, good luck with that."

"K, thanks, Nora."

"Nova."

But she was already gone. A bummer for her because less than a minute later, Parker walked up.

"Ready to head home?" He replaced the spot she leaned against moments ago, and already my mood improved.

With a smile, I closed my locker and followed him to the subway.

Watching his broad shoulders part the crowd on the sidewalk, I thought over Amber's comments and the others like it. All the daily reminders served to do was make this growing attraction feel more uncomfortable than it already did. As if the fear of my crush being outed wasn't hard enough.

But sometimes, I wondered…was my crush one-sided? Sometimes I noticed him watching me like I watched him. Sometimes, I noticed he could move away from touching me but didn't. Kind of like he did then when he sat next to me on the ride home, and his thigh pressed to mine. He could put a seat between us or scoot over, but he didn't.

I knew we'd formed a friendship—but I wondered if maybe something more lingered under the surface. I wondered what the hell to do with it.

Nothing. Because I didn't know the first thing about being with someone like Parker. Hell, the whole friendship thing was new to me. I'd been pretty inexperienced, unlike him, who'd apparently hooked up with everyone like Amber claimed. I had no idea what having someone as intense as him focusing his attention on me would feel like. But I sure as hell wanted to know. He made me want to explore.

When we got home, the apartment was empty, and without any words, we fell into our usual pattern. It'd been a couple of months, and this was our norm. Him working on his art while I used him as a muse for mine. Sometimes, he'd even prop up a canvas and join me as we listened to music, seeing who could guess the song before the other. Or we'd debate the merits and pitfalls of each song. Or we'd just sit in silence and enjoy the company of someone who got us.

It was easy.

So easy that hours passed before I knew it.

The scrape of my paintbrush against the canvas matched the strum of Parker's guitar. And when he started humming, I closed my eyes and absorbed the music we made together in my quiet room.

The strumming turned to quick plucks, and pitch changes. Unable to help myself, I put lyrics to the tune. Not that he needed to know. I kept that portion of the song in my head. I just couldn't help but let the upbeat staccato tune that bled into long mourning chords pull the words from my head. Like he'd plucked them himself the same as he plucked the strings.

When he stopped, I opened my eyes to take in the canvas and what our music created—the way the bold blue in the corner bled into the pale, neutral pink. Kind of just like how Parker bled into my life a little more each day. I turned to watch him jot notes down on the notebook beside him on my bed. He propped himself upright against the pillows, one leg bent, and the other stretched out, his bare feet their own work of art.

Dragging his hand through his wavy hair, I watched the music note tattoo on the inside of his bicep dance with each flex. He had a small handful of tattoos apparently his mom signed off on. They were small, hidden like a treasure hunt I loved to play.

"Let me see," he said, interrupting my perusal.

I blinked and met his smirking face. Even when he didn't smile, his face looked like he was smiling. The happiness shining from his blue eyes like he had the world at his fingertips, and he knew it.

"Oh, I don't think it's done," I said, turning back to the canvas, assessing it.

I tipped my head back and forth, squinting my eyes to try and see it from another angle. His bare feet padded across the floor, closing in, and I held my breath. This was my favorite part of our time together.

His hand rested on my shoulder, sending a blazing path down my chest like I'd never experienced before, and his warmth surrounded me when he leaned over, resting his other hand on my table. With his face next to mine, the painting faded away. All I saw was Parker's profile staring at my art, only a small distance from mine.

He tipped his head too, and the seconds ticked by. Part of me never wanted him to move, while another part needed him to before I passed out from holding my breath.

Finally, slowly, his cheek ticked up, and he stood. "Damn, Nova. This is good."

The air whooshed from my lungs, and I swear I almost collapsed off my stool.

"One more thing though," he added.

As if in slow motion, his hand reached across my body for the paintbrush I still clutched in my grip. Without removing it from my hand, but instead wrapping his fingers around mine, he dabbed the brush in white and placed the tiniest dot inside one of the blue circles. Usually, if anyone tried to touch my art, I'd cut their arm off. But just like relaxing in the room together, this was also our norm. He'd asked the first few times he'd added his special touch, and I'd been useless to say no. But now, he did it at his leisure, and I let him.

When he let go of my hand, I wanted to chase his and beg him to never stop touching me, but he stood, and I managed to control myself.

"There," he said, standing tall, nodding at the painting with crossed arms. "Now, it's our art."

And that was why I let him do it. Because when we were in my room, it was *our art*. Even if he only added a speck of paint that anyone could barely see, the reality was, he filled every stroke, line, and dot I created with his music as my backdrop.

"Yeah," I breathed. "Perfect."

He turned, and like always, his smile brought mine out to play. As if in slow motion, the shift from friends to something else started. His smile faded, and his eyes dropped to my mouth. Unbidden by me, my tongue peeked out to slide across my parched lips.

Maybe it was good that Parker wasn't home as often because this band around my chest squeezed tighter and tighter with each passing second, and I was scared of what would break free when it snapped.

I'd had crushes—this wasn't new. I'd kissed boys and even let them put their hands on me, but I'd never had this. I'd never had the all-consuming urge to go, go, go until we were one. I'd never had the urge to crawl inside someone and never come out.

Until him. It kind of scared the shit out of me at the same time as exciting me. It made me want to give in and pull back. Especially when I had the daily reminder of him being my stepbrother from everyone in the world weighing on me. It was one thing to crave a boy—it was another when that boy stood across a forbidden line with a million consequences on the other side.

I broke the stare and cleared the need crawling up my throat. "What time are you meeting Ash?"

He tugged his phone from his back pocket and checked the time. "I should probably head down there now."

"Cool. I'm probably going to hop in the shower to get all this paint off."

"Yeah, you might want to start with your face," he said, poking my cheek.

I tried to dodge his finger and rolled my eyes. "Damnit. I thought I did good not touching my face."

"Maybe one day you'll get through a project without being

covered in it." I raised a doubtful brow, and his smile broke out. "Yeah, probably not. You should just go ahead and own it. Maybe get shirts made. *I'm an artist. Ignore the paint in my hair and the charcoal on my...everything.*"

"You're sooo funny."

"I know I am." He backed away with a bow and collected his stuff from the bed. "I'll see you later?"

"I'm always here."

"You know you could come, right?" he offered.

"Yeah, but I'm good hanging out here."

I did, but I never took him up on it.

He'd won me over at school, slowly pulling me over to sit with him at lunch, but my introvertedness kicked in each time he invited me to go with him to see the guys. They were great, but maybe subconsciously, I was trying to keep some distance between us. Maybe subconsciously, I was trying to protect myself from others noticing what Parker did to me. I could only imagine what everyone would say—all the rumors.

Incest. Illegal. What do your parents say?

Nothing because despite everyone calling him my brother, Parker Callahan wasn't my brother.

He also wasn't mine, and it was good to remember that to help control my growing fantasies. Fantasies that came to a screeching halt when girls tagged along with the guys. As much as I wanted to control this desire, I didn't need to stab it with a knife, creating painful jabs from watching some girl hang all over him. Last week, I saw him kiss a girl in school and immediately wanted to bleach my eyes and scrape the memory from my brain and heart.

Yeah, I was good with not hanging out with them.

"Thanks for the offer, though."

With a nod, he left, and I gathered my things to shower just as the front door closed, marking Parker's exit.

Silence. The apartment didn't make a noise beyond the

quiet hum of the heater kicking on. I didn't mind because, like a total cliché, I loved to sing in the shower.

Rubbing the loofa across my chest, I was about a minute and a half into belting out the best part of my favorite Adele song when the door banged against the cabinet drawers I always kept open for just this purpose of alerting me if a serial killer was breaking in to kill me. My vocal cords seized up, choking off all sound.

My heart thudded faster and faster. Adrenaline flooded every ounce of my body. In those point two seconds, my mind whirled with possibilities, and I slapped a hand to my chest as if to hold my heart inside and scanned the shower for a weapon. Why didn't I put a weapon in the shower?

"You can fucking sing," Parker crowed from beyond the curtain.

Just Parker. Not a serial killer. Not someone I would have to throw shampoo bottles at and try to shave to death as I stood there naked and wet.

My legs almost gave out when the adrenaline ebbed.

Only to come roaring back because *Parker fucking Callahan was just on the other side of the shower as I stood there naked.*

"What the *fuck*, Parker," I screeched.

"You can fucking sing," he repeated, this time the words slowly processing.

Except, it didn't change my response because Parker was still there while I was still naked. "What the fuck are you doing in here, Parker?"

"I came back in and heard you singing and kind of just acted."

"What if I had been naked and not in the shower?"

"I have my eyes closed," he explained like that made everything all right.

"Jesus Christ," I screeched again. It was about the only pitch I could make with that kind of shock zinging through my body. "How would you feel if I barged in on you in the shower?"

"Uhhh…" he dragged out. "Not sad."

Wait. What?

"What?"

For an answer, I got a cleared throat and change of subject. "Nova, your voice is amazing. I had no fucking clue, and it's so fucking good."

"Parker!" I shouted.

I stood there with my arm across my chest and the other blocking the apex of my thighs just in case the shower curtain collapsed or something, and he wanted to talk about my voice. I couldn't even fathom dwelling on the comment he made about not being sad if I barged in on him.

"Fine, fine," he said, exasperated. "But we're not done with this. I'll be outside, and we can talk then."

"What about Ash?"

"He's on his way up. I was halfway down the stairs when he said his parents were home, and we decided to meet here."

Keeping my arm across my chest, I abandoned my groin and held the curtain back just enough to peer out and narrow my eyes at him. Hearing the rustle of the rings against metal, he cracked one eye open, and I gave him my most deadly glare. "We will *not* talk about this with him around."

As if I yanked the curtain back to bare my whole body, he stared, taking in every minuscule inch bared of my shoulder and face. Heat burned where his eyes touched, but I couldn't tell if it was from his look or embarrassment.

"Parker," I snapped.

His eyes shot to mine before slamming closed again. With his hands up, he backed away. "Fine. But we *will* talk about it." Before the door closed behind him, with his lids still squeezed shut, he brought two fingers to his eyes and then pointed at me. He looked so ridiculous that even though images from my possible death by serial killer in the shower still played, I laughed.

Not making another peep, I quickly finished up my shower and took the time to blow-dry my hair and put on makeup. My plan was to take so much time in the bathroom that they forgot about me, and then I'd dash to my room and lock the door.

I held my breath and turned the knob, pulling it open just enough to slip past and tiptoe down the hall. I was halfway there when they beckoned.

"Nova," Parker called. "Come hang out."

"Yeah, Nova."

"Come on, Nova."

Accepting defeat, I pivoted on my heel and tried to hide the fear that Parker would blurt out that I could sing and then I'd get harassed forever and ever. As soon as I rounded the corner, I met his smile with a glare.

"Damn, Nova. Looking good," Ash complimented, looking me up and down. His dark perusal wasn't completely hated.

I'd grown comfortable with the guys—at least a little bit as I stuck to the periphery of their group, but they did their best to pull me in. Oren did it with playful jabs and jokes. He acted the most brotherly to me. Ash won me over with flirtatious comments I put down to his own version of joking. Because even considering Ash wanted to seriously flirt with me was a joke.

I stepped into the semi-circle of chairs and couches, and Ash patted the minuscule amount of cushion next to him. "Come sit with me."

"I'm small, but not that small," I laughed.

"Then my lap it is," he said, now patting his thigh.

Oren snorted, and I think Parker may have growled. Before I could dwell more than a second on why he'd growl, his hand slid around mine, tugging me to the space beside him and nowhere near Ash. Not that Ash seemed to care. He met Parker's glare with a devious smirk.

"All right, ladies," Oren interrupted. "Are we going to work or just stare longingly into each other's eyes? I mean, I get it, Parker has those baby blues you could get lost in, and Ash yours are dark like the pits of hell, so anyone could take a wrong turn there, but I thought we were in a band, writing songs and not a circle jerk."

"Tell them how you really feel, Oren," I laughed.

"What?" He shrugged. "They have pretty eyes, but we also need to stay focused. We got that gig coming up."

"You mean the basement party?" Ash deadpanned.

"Hey, dude. A gig is a gig. We'll get more."

"Okay, okay," Parker said, grabbing his guitar. "I was working on this earlier."

He strummed the tune, and Ash picked up his bass to find a rhythm with him as Oren tapped out a beat. I leaned back into the corner of the couch, observing them work—enraptured by how they fed off each other. They joked and ribbed, but all in good fun. It was like I didn't exist in their realm, and I was completely okay with that. I just wanted to be close enough to watch the magic.

They got through the second verse and struggled over the ascending climax. I closed my eyes, listening to the beat, bobbing my head, quietly humming along.

"Uggh," Parker growled. "It's not right."

"What if..." I spoke up before I could think better of it. I wanted to choke the words back as soon as they escaped, and I could only hope they hadn't heard my quiet voice. No such luck, because a second later, all eyes were on me. I swallowed my nerves and forced myself to step out of the shadows. "What if you played something like this, Parker?" I hummed a quick tune with a slower beat. "And then you did a little lower like this, Ash?" This time, I hummed a quick pace similar to Flea from Red Hot Chili Peppers. "And,

Oren, your beat could match the bass. Maybe heavy cymbals?"

I stopped talking, but no one followed up. They all stared, blinking, and I worried that I had a booger hanging out of my nose. Or maybe a giant penis randomly sprouted on my forehead. That's the only thing that made sense for why they kept staring in silence.

"Damn, Nova," Oren said first. "That's some shit. I didn't even think of it. Let's give it a try, ladies."

Parker looked away last, his eyes hinting at a smile I knew laid just below the surface. They played what I suggested, messed up, and tried it again. By the third time, they nailed it, giving each other high fives with cheers of delight.

Oren wrapped his arm around my shoulder and jerked me into his chest. "Magic, guys. She's fucking magic."

Tucking my chin to my chest, I basked in their cheers, my face almost splitting in two from smiling so hard.

"What else do you have tucked up your magic sleeves?" Ash asked.

"Well," Parker started, and I jerked a wide-eyed glare to him. With a shrug that was anything but apologetic, he announced, "She can sing. Like really, *really* fucking sing."

"What?" Ash screeched.

"Hell, yes!" Oren said, clapping.

"Fuck you, Parker," I grumbled under my breath.

"What? Don't hate me. It's awesome."

"Sing for us," Oren demanded.

"Um, I don't think so."

"Oh, come on," Parker cajoled, shoving his shoulder against mine. "Don't think I don't know you have at least *some* lyrics for this song. I saw your lips moving when I was playing earlier."

My jaw dropped. *Holy shit.* How had he seen that? I hadn't even known he'd been watching. I'd been sure he was too engrossed in his music to notice I was even there. Had he noticed me watching him? Heat bloomed in my cheeks, and I considered the chances of making it to my bedroom before they stopped me.

Probably not good.

"I don't sing in front of people."

"But we're not people," Ash cajoled, giving me the most devious puppy dog eyes, his full bottom lip sticking out. I bet he got a lot of girls with that look, especially with that dark hair that matched his dark eyes. I knew for sure in school they tripped over themselves for a taste of him. He looked like sin, and I wasn't even sure I could fathom what sin tasted like at sixteen, but he made all the girls want to find out.

"Yeah, we're like family," Oren added.

"Well, Parker actually *is* family," Ash said, laughing. He laughed even harder when Parker screwed up his face in disgust.

"Come on, Nova. It's just us," Oren begged. "Pleeeease. Pretty, pretty please."

The guys started chanting my name, and I buried my head in my hands, groaning and laughing. I tried to picture singing and what it would feel like to do it in front of them, and just the thought had my hands trembling.

But the cheers …

"Ugh. Fine," I finally caved. I knew it'd been inevitable as soon as I'd opened my mouth about the song. I snatched the paper from the table and jotted down the lyrics that had floated through my head earlier.

With a shit-eating grin on his face, Parker opened the song, and the guys joined.

And like I was supposed to be there all along, I hopped in with the lyrics, joining the band.

SIX

Parker

PAST

SIX MONTHS LATER

"Come on, Nova," I pleaded.

"Why?" she asked from where she lounged on her bed, messy bun in place. "It's not like you're playing or anything? It's just a party."

"Because it's a Saturday night, and I want you to come hang out."

She looked up over the edge of her book and cocked a brow. "What? To be your wingman?" She rolled her eyes and went back to the pages I knew damn well she wasn't reading. "I really don't feel like being left behind while you screw off with Kelly."

Kelly. Yeah, I guessed she'd be there too and probably join in, but she wasn't one of us. She was more of a…distraction.

A distraction from this growing attraction to Nova. And not the normal one that most teenage guys had. I had that too since I first saw her. No, this attraction crept into my very being, planting itself in my bones until it became part of me —until I feared I wouldn't be able to live without it. Which was why I had to try and stop it before I couldn't.

Nova was my stepsister, and I struggled to sit across from her at dinner like some kind of happy little family when all I could think about was what her lips would taste like. If her skin was as soft as it looked. What her moans would feel like against my tongue. I knew what her annoyance, happiness, frustration all sounded like, but I constantly wondered what her pleasure sounded like. Would it be just as unique as her?

How would she fit in my arms if I snuck into her room at night and pulled her close? Probably better than Kelly did, who wrapped around me like an anaconda. But it was fine because I didn't plan to be with Kelly forever. Like I said—a distraction.

A distraction that worked as a double-edged sword and sparked Nova's jealousy.

That was the thing—my attraction was only half of it. The way Nova looked at me more than filled in the other half. One of us had to try and put up walls. Nova had her shy, passive personality that would prevent her from making a move, so I used Kelly because I didn't have a shy or passive bone in my body. I needed physical objects that would at least try to slow down my get, get, get attitude.

"I wouldn't leave you behind. Come on, the guys will be there, and *I* want you there." That got her attention. "Please, please, please, please, please."

Her eyes met mine over the edge of the book, and I held my breath, unsure of how I wanted her to answer. Despite needing to keep her from becoming too much a part of me, she'd already planted roots, and I also hated having her away—like I left my arm at home or something.

I wanted to rip out my hair. I hated not being able to make a solid decision about Nova and just stick with it. I guessed this was part of being a teen—all the angst and being unable to follow through on what you needed because of what you wanted.

She sighed and tossed her book aside. "Fine."

"Yes," I shouted, arms tossed in the air. I did a victory lap around her art table and back to her bed like Rocky Balboa. She shifted to the edge, laughing at my antics. I gripped her shoulders and hoisted her up, turning her toward the bathroom.

"Listen, you don't have to get changed, but maybe wear something other than slippers. Also, brush your teeth, so you don't clear out the house the first time you speak."

"Oh, fuck you, Parker."

"Oohhh, shit. Nova just swore. It's gonna be a good night," I cheered.

She rolled her eyes just before slamming the bathroom door in my face. Turning, I leaned my back against the wall and smiled, inhaling as deep as I could to stretch my lungs. It *would* be a good night. As long as I could keep my hands off my stepsister, we'd be fine.

By the time Nova emerged, Ash was waiting and whistled, looking her up and down.

"Damn, Nova. Those boots were made for walking, and they can walk all over me," he declared.

She did a twirl, her long hair fanning out like a spreading wildfire, lifting one of her grass-green, crushed velvet boots. Nova had a thing for shoes, and I remembered when she came home with those. She wore them around the apartment for days, even in her pajamas, because apparently, she needed to break them in before taking them out on the town.

"Come on," I grumbled, playfully shoving Ash toward the door—kind of.

By the time we walked into the industrial loft, the party was in full swing. As soon as we cleared the doors, Kelly threw herself at me, making me bump into Nova.

"Parker! You made it."

The beer on her breath almost took me down faster than her surprise attack. "Already drinking?"

"Just a little." She held her thumb and pointer finger

barely apart. "Hey, guys." She waved at Nova and Ash, not bothering to untangle her arms from my neck.

Kelly smacked a kiss against my cheek and caught me up on what had already taken place. She was a cool girl. Laid-back and easy to be with. We both knew she liked me more than I did her, but it never stopped her from wanting to be with me.

She was the perfect distraction—her black hair and tan skin making it impossible for me to imagine Nova whenever Kelly and I fooled around. I already struggled to keep thoughts of Nova from my imagination. I definitely didn't need a picture of a redhead bobbing over my lap to go along with those fantasies.

"You want a drink?" Kelly asked.

"Sure."

Before I could say anything, she tugged me to the kitchen, Ash and Nova following behind. Kelly poured two drinks and danced around me, doing her best to get my attention, but I couldn't stop staring at Nova as she accepted the shot of tequila. I stood right next to her but somehow barely hung on the fringes of the attention she gave to Ash. I watched her take the shot, her delicate throat swallowing it down. She cringed and coughed before tossing her head back, laughing. The lights from the living area flashed, and I couldn't take my eyes off her.

Pinks, blues, greens splashed across her smiling face, and I thought about our recent science lesson. "Supernova," I whispered, not even realizing I'd said it until all attention was focused on me.

Her big green eyes looked at me, and I couldn't look away. It wasn't until her nose scrunched up that I realized I spoke loud enough to hear.

"Supernova?" she asked.

I knew I should be aware of Kelly still clinging to me, but I couldn't make myself care. "Yeah. You're like an exploding star—all bright lights and energy."

The confusion dropped from her eyes like a gate being let down, and a flash of honesty flared like a flame hitting me square in the chest.

"It's totally the red hair," Kelly announced, bringing the gate back down over Nova's gaze.

"And those green shoes," Ash added, thoroughly breaking the moment.

"Thank you?" Nova responded, laughing, but still looked at me curiously.

"What is up, my buddies?" Oren greeted, saving me from explaining more. He walked up behind us with his arms spread wide. The giant linebacker behind him looked a little out of place in our crew but had managed to find a spot.

While we wore band tees and relaxed jeans, Brogan Carmichael wore a polo and perfectly pressed jeans—his blond hair styled to a T. He was the star linebacker for our football team and also the new rhythm guitarist for our band. Like me, he'd just moved here, and through an unlikely run-in, we made fast friends.

"Shots, man. Join me," Ash said, flipping over more solo cups.

A giggly Nova turned to Oren, the tequila already seeping into her veins. "I'm a supernova."

"Damn right you are," Brogan agreed, holding his fist out.

She bumped hers to his and edged back to make room in the circle for everyone, holding out her cup for more tequila.

We all tapped cups and tossed the shots back. Nova brought the lime to her lips, and I almost choked on my tongue when her usual bright eyes met mine, growing darker, filling with something I'd never seen from her before. *Desire.* Unlike the curious glances she gave me before, this one screamed want and need. She dragged her tongue along her bottom lip. I could have basked under her stare all night, but it vanished when Kelly ducked under my arm.

"Pour me a shot," she told Ash.

"Pour me two," Nova shouted like it was some kind of competition.

Oren cheered. "Me too. Let's do it, Supernova."

She lifted her cup and started singing *Shots* by **LMFAO**. Oren danced, and Nova joined in, stumbling.

"Hey, why don't we slow down," I said softly.

She stopped dancing and looked from me to Kelly and back to me. "Nah, I want to enjoy the party. That's why you wanted me to come out, right? Have fun on a Saturday night?"

"Yeah," the guys cheered in chorus.

I wanted her to come out and have fun, but I didn't want her to end up miserable and blacked out drunk.

Thankfully, *Uptown Funk* came on, and Nova abandoned her plan for two more shots, brushed past the guys with her arms already up as she danced her way to an open spot. Oren took her shot for her and followed behind. Brogan and Ash joining them.

"Let's dance. I love this song." Kelly grabbed my hand and pulled me to the group. She shook her ass and rolled her hips, holding my attention—for the most part. Nova danced beside us, tempting me to watch her.

Determined to focus on Kelly, I gripped her hips and moved with her. Two songs later, she asked if I wanted another beer, and I jumped at the chance to put distance between Nova and me. But it backfired when we stood on the edge of the dance floor with our beers, and I had a perfectly direct view of Nova dancing.

Kelly stood in my arms, her back to my front, ass firmly swaying against my dick. It should have been all I could think about, but I couldn't help but focus on Nova dancing with the guys.

Songs blended together, and she twirled away from Ash's arms and into Oren's and then Brogan's. She rotated between them until they began pairing off with other girls. Then random guys moved in, trying to capture the supernova shining on the floor, and I reached my breaking point.

"I'm gonna keep the other guys away from Nova," I said against Kelly's ear.

She turned back, her face twisted in confusion. "You're going to dance with your sister?"

"She's not my sister," I growled. "And I promised our parents I'd keep an eye on her," I lied.

Kelly's face softened, and she kissed my cheek. "You're a good guy, Parker."

I snorted. Yeah, a good guy. Totally noble.

NOVA

My head swam from the quick succession of tequila I'd consumed upon entering the party. I knew I'd regret it later, but right now, with the music blaring, the lightheaded happiness that kept me from dwelling on anything other than moving my body to the beat, I didn't care.

Every time I looked over to find Kelly grinding on Parker, all I had to do was turn into whoever's arms I was dancing with, and all was forgotten. All I had to do was close my eyes and pretend it was Parker's arms wrapped around me and it was like Kelly never existed.

But she did.

And it had guilt bubbling up because Kelly was cool—other than her being with Parker.

I wasn't even sure if they were dating, but fantasizing about a guy who even kind-of-slightly-might belong to someone else wasn't me.

At least it hadn't been me.

I didn't want it to be me.

"Move," a deep voice ordered, interrupting my beat.

I stumbled and turned, watching my dance partner hold his hands up to a scowling Parker and back away.

"What the hell, Parker?"

"You just going to rub your ass on anyone tonight?" he asked with none of his usual relaxed humor.

"I'm just dancing," I said, rolling my eyes. "It's not like I'm letting my girlfriend dry hump me in front of everyone."

His brows shot up, and I looked away, hating that I admitted my irritation.

"She's not my girlfriend."

"Well, whatever. I'm just dancing."

"With strange guys."

"Half of them go to our school."

"Well, now you can dance with me."

"I-I—" I sputtered, trying to process the thought of Parker actually wrapping his arms around me, his clean, spicy scent engulfing me. "What? Won't Kelly care?"

"No. Like I said, she's not my girlfriend." The song changed, and his smile came out to play, luring me in. "Now, shut up and dance with me."

I laughed, hearing the opening to the song, giving in to the music. I bounced on the balls of my feet and swayed side to side, singing the words to him. When the chorus came on, I acted out the lyrics, holding up my hand and demanding he dance with me.

His perfect smile grew, and we danced around each other, singing back and forth. When the lyrics weren't there, I played drums while he played air guitar, just to go right back to dancing—never getting too close. The only time we touched was when he held my hand and turned me in circles.

At least until a slow beat came through the speakers, and my inner ho came out. The gritty bass opened the song, and I moved my hands up my sides, into my hair, dipping down to rock back and forth. I rolled my hips and neck, turning around to meet his ocean blue eyes darkening under his heavy lids. He stood there motionless other than his hands flexing along with his jaw, watching me.

The rest of the room faded, and I basked in his heated gaze, putting on a show. Stepping close, I moved his hands to my hips before turning and continuing my dance. His hands gripped tight when my ass brushed against his groin the first time. I half expected him to step back, but a moment later, his heat came into full contact with my back and enveloped me. He wrapped around me, moving his hips, leaning his head next to mine, breathing deep. I tipped my head back, giving him every temptation to bury his mouth against my neck. The desperation to feel him overwhelmed me. Sweat dripped down my spine. My thighs burned from dipping low and pushing back against him.

His long fingers dipped beneath my hip bones, and I lost myself for a moment, placing my hand over his, lacing our fingers, holding him in place while I pushed back and moved side to side. I felt his rumble against my back more than heard it, my heart jumping in its confines when my ass encountered a hard ridge.

The high of making Parker Callahan hard hit me, and I never wanted it to fade.

The dry humping I accused Kelly of performing on Parker earlier looked like the hokey-pokey compared to what Parker and I were doing.

Before now, I rarely thought beyond my own desires. I never allowed myself to wonder if Parker might feel the same way because it'd been so easy to scoff at. Parker would never go for someone like me—someone as complicated as his stepsister. But the way he held me tight and inhaled against my neck like he wanted to make my essence part of him, I couldn't brush it off and wondered if maybe he looked at me as something more, too.

The song faded, and I turned back around, our foreheads almost touching, His eyes were glued to my mouth, and his hands still held me close. On impulse, I slicked my tongue across my lips before digging into the tingling flesh. One of his hands abandoned my hips to tug my lip free and slowly drag his thumb along the abused flesh.

It would be so easy to suck his thumb into my mouth—to cross the line—to drop a bomb on the line and forget why it even existed.

I almost did when a catcall preceded Oren bumping past people and emerging in our little bubble, Brogan and Ash close behind.

"Damn, Supernova. That was H-O-double-T—hot. I think I got a half-boner just watching."

Parker pulled back to a respectable distance, breaking the connection like it never existed in the first place.

"Ew, Oren." I tried to say the words like I normally would, but they came out breathless. Still a little lost in the moment.

"Yeah, ew," Brogan agreed, slapping the back of Oren's head.

The guys danced around and joked. I tried to get into it, but the weight of my desire made it hard to lose myself like I had before.

Halfway through the song, Kelly made a reappearance and tugged Parker down to whisper in his ear. His eyes flicked to mine before he nodded and followed her off the dance floor.

Questions bombarded me as I watched them move out of sight. I tried to ignore them and failed.

Where did she take him?
What are they doing?
Maybe he'll be right back.
Maybe it's nothing.

Maybe everything was nothing.
Maybe I'm imagining it.
What if it meant nothing, and he was hard because he was thinking of Kelly?

Shaking my head, I finally gave up on dancing by the third song. The pendulum of emotions from high to low wiped out any lingering energy, and every bone in my body called for a bed.

But first, my bladder called for a bathroom.

I let Ash know and made my way down the single hallway, almost pouting like a child when I took in the four doors on each side. With a deep breath, I sent up a quick prayer I didn't walk in on anyone fucking.

First door, empty bedroom.

Second door, group of pot smokers. After politely declining, I resumed my search.

Third door, locked. God, I hoped that wasn't the bathroom.

Fourth door—I didn't bother because I could hear the couple banging against it on the other side.

Only four more to go, I promised my bladder.

Fifth door, a guy getting a BJ on the edge of the bed.

Fifth door, I cringed, about to shut it when my heart dropped. My bladder was forgotten, and every ounce of tequila threatened to come up with each rioting roll of my stomach.

Fifth door, I shattered, not knowing how much I cared until watching the possibilities be snatched away.

Fifth door, Parker leaned on the bed, his lips parted, head tipped back, and eyes closed as a girl kneeled between his parted legs, her dark head very clearly bobbing up and down.

He groaned, and his eyes slid open, locking on mine, widening.

"Shit."

Blame it on the Tequila

I jerked back into action, shoving all hurt aside and locking it away. "Fuck this. I'm leaving."

He promised to not leave me for Kelly, and yet here he was, getting his dick sucked, leaving me stranded with the guys. Maybe he really did need me as a wingman, and he was dancing with me to get Kelly going. Maybe this was all just a fucking waste.

"Nova," he called just before I slammed the door.

Keeping my head down, I barreled through the crowd, blocking out anyone calling my name. I made it to the elevator, the doors just opening when the music blared into the hallway with the opened door.

"Dammit, Nova. Stop."

I willed the doors to close faster but didn't get that lucky. He stopped the door and climbed in with me.

"What are you doing here?" I sneered.

"Making sure you don't run off half wasted and get hurt."

"Like you care."

I kept my eyes glued to the panel of numbers, begging the elevator to move faster. From my periphery, I watched his hands dig into his hair. He let out a frustrated growl before facing me.

"What do you want, Nova?"

"Nothing I can have," I grumbled, letting some honesty slip free.

He shook his head and huffed a laugh. "You're drunk."

"And you're a whore."

"No. I'm a seventeen-year-old guy."

"Exactly," I snapped. "A fucking whore."

"Jesus Christ," he laughed without humor.

For as much as I stayed still and kept my eyes forward, he moved. His arms flew out in exasperation. He paced the small cube, rubbed his mouth, and shoved his hands back into his hair.

"You know what? Fuck it," he said, stepping closer. "I

went with her because if I stayed with you, I'd have taken *you* to that back room, and that can't happen."

That got my attention. I jerked my head up, meeting his angry, heated eyes.

"Yeah. Exactly," he said, like my shock confirmed he made the right choice. "I would have taken you back there and made you dance for me again, this time taking your clothes off until I had access to every inch of you and could do what I really fucking wanted. And the only reason I'm telling you this is because you're too drunk to remember in the morning."

I couldn't ever imagine *not* remembering this. This moment when his words set me on fire. When my cheeks flamed with the thought of being naked in front of Parker. Embarrassed that I liked the image he painted. Terrified of wanting it too.

"Why didn't you?" I challenged.

"Because it's not right, Nova. It's too complicated."

The obvious answer fell from his lips like he hated saying them as much as I hated hearing them.

"Parker…" I said his name because I think I just needed to hear it, but I didn't know what to follow it up with. In the end, he was right. The can of worms giving in would open wasn't worth it. At least, it wasn't on paper. The tequila made everything swirl in a not-so-fun way, and I just wanted to go home.

"Yeah?" he asked when I didn't say anything else.

"I'm tired."

He heaved a relieved breath like I'd pardoned him from death, and I understood it at the same time as hating it. The door slid open, and he held his hand out. "Let's go home."

I latched on gratefully and let him lead me home. Usually, we took the subway, but after such a long night, we opted for a cab.

By the time we made it home, my exhaustion had turned a

little crazy, and every time I stumbled, I giggled like an idiot. Parker did his best to keep me upright, laughing with me.

"It's not fair that you're not drunk with me," I said, almost falling into my bedroom.

He shrugged. "Life's not fair, Supernova."

"Truth." I blew out hard and fell back on the mattress.

I managed to get my shoes off and shimmy out of my jeans, not really caring that Parker still stood there, a bottle of pills in one hand and a bottle of water in the other.

"Uhhh …Nova."

"Relax, I'm just too tired to care. Toss me my shorts."

He did and finally relaxed once I had them over my hips. I climbed under the covers and gladly took the water and meds. When he tried to walk away, I snatched his hand.

"You need something else?" he asked, looking at my hand clutching his.

"I just don't want to be alone. I'm not ready for you to leave."

When he didn't move, I tugged him softly, nodding toward the empty spot in my bed. After a moment, he finally caved, kicking off his shoes and climbing in, turning off the lights before lying next to me. We both laid on our backs and stared up at the ductwork decorating the ceiling.

"What's not fair to you?" I asked softly, not wanting to disturb the moment.

He blew out a breath, and I wondered if he'd answer. Parker was light and smiley, but I knew things plagued him. I heard it in his music, in the moments he thought no one was listening.

"My mom left us." He stated the fact so easily I could have believed it meant nothing to him, except for the shuddering breath afterward. "Just started a new family like ours wasn't enough. Like *I* wasn't enough."

I reached over and snagged his hand, linking our fingers.

"And when I wanted to rant and rage over it, I was told to just smile—to push it aside, and it would fade with time."

"Did it?"

"Maybe a little. What didn't help was her constantly pushing me to be someone else. She thinks my music is a waste and that I don't have what it takes to get there. So, the only time she tells her new circle of friends about her son is when it involves school."

"I'm sorry, Parker. She has no idea what you're capable of. She must have never seen you play because otherwise, she'd never doubt your talent."

"Even if my talent isn't perfect. I'm going to make it, Nova. Come hell-or-high water, I'll make it. If only to make her see me."

"I see you, Parker. I want *you*—the real you."

His hand squeezed mine, and I held on tight.

"I forgive you," I said after a stretch of silence.

"For what?" he asked incredulously.

"For abandoning me to get your dick sucked."

"Uhhh…"

"Especially since you didn't come."

"What?" he asked, laughing.

"I mean, you still looked hard when I walked in, and unless you came in point-two seconds—which would be sad if we're being honest—you didn't finish before you followed me."

"I assure you, I'm not a minute-man."

"Okay," I said, full of sarcasm.

"I'm fucking not."

"Okay, okay. I believe you. No need to get your panties in a twist." I barely held in my peals of laughter at his indignation. "Minute-man," I added, unable to help myself.

"Fucking Christ, Nova," he groaned but also laughed. "Please don't call me that in front of the guys."

I laughed harder, and he joined me.

"You'd never live it down."

"I sure wouldn't."

When we both settled, my eyes weighed heavy, and I was finally ready to succumb to sleep.

My fingers still linked with his, and I stroked my thumb along the soft skin between his thumb and forefinger.

"Thanks for following me, Parker." I didn't want to think how this night would have ended if he hadn't.

"Always," he promised.

SEVEN

Nova

"Who's Rock Star?" Rae asked just before sipping from her champagne glass.

I almost missed my chair from the jolt of shock as I sat back down. Readjusting myself, I struggled to school my features into something other than the wide-eyed panic I could feel it stretched into.

She waited patiently, a docile smile on her pouty lips, looking exactly like the polite, politician's daughter I knew her to one-hundred-percent not be. Meanwhile, Vera's eyes flicked between the menu, to me, to Rae, and then back to the menu, trying to appear like an innocent bystander.

"What?" I choked out on what little air still lingered in my lungs. I come back from the restroom, and all of a sudden, the easy conversation about how Rae's trying out a boyfriend for the first time ever vanished, and all lights were now shining on me.

Raelynn's eyes narrowed the slightest bit, the only hint to the devious lioness lingering underneath her perfectly made-up face. I needed to get myself under control, or she would eat me for breakfast, lunch, *and* dinner.

"Your phone kept going off while you were in the restroom," she answered easily.

"I tried to stop her," Vera finally joined in.

Rae scoffed and rolled her eyes over to Vera. "Liar. It was your idea."

"It was not," Vera denied, looking beyond offended.

"What if we looked?" Rae said in a softer voice, repeating Vera's supposed idea. She added an over-the-top giggle Vera would never do and continued. "I mean, not that we would. But who could be messaging so much? It could, like, maybe be an emergency."

"I do not sound like that," Vera argued.

While they bickered, I quickly dug through my purse with trembling hands. This is what you got for not immediately spilling to your best friends from college that your ex-step-brother, who just so happened to be a rock star, started talking to you again. Oh, and that you used to be in love with him and maybe kind of still had some of those feelings lingering about.

Just as I pulled out my phone, it lit up with another message from Rock Star, still unopened by Rae, the messages hidden until it recognized my face.

I heaved a sigh of relief until Rae reminded me I wasn't out of the woods yet.

"Anyway, I peeked, and it said Rock Star. Soooo…"

Stuffing my phone back in my purse, I swallowed, trying to take discreet deep breaths.

"Gosh, Nova," Vera said. "You're like a deer in headlights. I'm a little scared."

Pull it together, Nova.

One more deep breath, and I managed a somewhat normal laugh, resting a hand against my thudding heart. "You just caught me off guard," I answered. Digging deep, I shook my head and rolled my eyes at myself, going for my usual self-deprecating sense of humor. "I'm…I—"

I what?

I looked from Rae's face to Vera's, both waiting expectantly, and I gave up pretending I was anything other than the mess I'd been since Vera's wedding.

My shoulders dropped, and all pretense of holding it together dropped with them. "It's Parker."

Vera's face scrunched in confusion while Rae's dark brows slowly ascended toward her hairline. "Parker? As in Parker fucking Callahan? The one you danced for on Vera's wedding night."

"I didn't actually dance for him," I corrected. "Someone caught me off guard."

"Holy shit," Vera muttered, her jaw dropping more than Rae's.

Rae recovered first, her shock slowly morphing into a smile that had me bracing myself. Rae gave bold honesty a new meaning, and I never knew what would come out of her mouth. To stem whatever swirled in her head, I rushed to splash water on her flaming imagination. Except, hearing the truth of my situation out loud for the first time made me realize Rae's imagination might have been better.

"The thing is that Parker's dad married my mom when I was sixteen, and we lived together for a while, and I kind of fell in love with him completely until he left me to follow his dreams of becoming a rock star."

"Holy. Shit," Vera muttered again, slower this time.

"Parker Callahan is your brother?" Rae almost shouted. Then to add insult to injury. "You loved your brother?"

"I swear to all things holy, Rae, I will stab you if you don't keep your voice down," I practically growled. "And he's not my brother."

If I expected any of this to dim her smile, I was wrong. If anything, it just grew more and more.

"Holy, freaking, shit," Vera kept saying.

"So, yeah," I sighed. "And I changed my mind, I want that

glass of champagne." Without one in front of me, I snagged Vera's and drained it.

"Okay, okay," Rae took a calming breath with hand movements and all. "So, *Rock Star,*" she enunciated his nickname, "was your *step*brother, but then your parents got divorced. And you guys just…stopped talking?"

"But you were in love with him?" Vera added.

"Did he love you?"

I winced hearing it played back, pulling a Parker-like movement and running my hand through my hair. "I…I thought he did."

"So, what happened?" Rae asked.

I closed my eyes, running over the moments of the past, feeling the familiar ache.

The excitement.

The fall off the cliff.

The fear.

The crash.

The pain.

The anger.

The sadness.

I swallowed, struggling to formulate the words. "He left me when I needed him." *More than once.* "And I was young and angry, and I ran away from it."

"But he left first?" Vera confirmed.

"In short, yeah. Our parents got divorced, and he never came back."

"I'm guessing it wasn't a good departure," Rae surmised.

Memories flashed leading up to him leaving, filling in the gaps, poking at all the sore spots I thought had healed. Time had softened them, but they had left their mark and would always be with me. It was all too much to bring up over dinner, so I kept it simple. "Yeah. Not good."

"So, the Instagram was the first time you saw him?" Rae asked.

"Pretty much."

"Damn. Your reaction makes a lot more sense now." She winced. "Sorry 'bout that."

"Yeah," I deadpanned. "Thanks."

"Well, how's it been going? He's obviously texting."

"Yeah. Kind of. I don't think I know what to do. I avoided him for a while, realizing how angry I've been over it all."

"Rightfully so," Vera interjected.

"But Parker is…Parker. He's…"

"You still love him?" Vera guessed.

I huffed a laugh and swallowed down the lump of emotion that randomly rose up. Maybe this was why I hadn't told them. I knew they'd ask questions that made me face the truth inside me. "Yeah," I admitted. "I guess I do a little. Or I loved who he was and who we were. I don't know him anymore."

"Then get to know him," Rae stated. "Play twenty questions and forge a path. He obviously wants to talk to you."

Another laugh bubbled up. She made it sound so easy. "What if we don't fit anymore? Or what if we do, and I get hurt again? And who says he gets another chance to know me after he left me?" I asked, some of my anger slipping free.

"Well then, just fuck him at least," she said with a shrug.

A real laugh burst free, and I looked from one to the other, grateful for these women. "Someone recently told me that I shouldn't make decisions from anger," Vera said, gently reminding me of when she called me for advice about her husband.

"That someone was obviously full of shit," I joked.

"Well, it worked out pretty well in the end. I think it was great advice."

"Look," Rae stated, all smirks gone. "You are a grown woman, not a naïve teenager. You're Naughty Nova. Be brave. Be brash. Don't let this go by without at least trying. You can try cautiously, but damn girl, you at least have to try. You don't have to marry him, but you could at least go see him. Maybe even fool around and give me all the details," she finished, her smirk back in place.

"Don't you have a boyfriend now?" I asked.

"Meh," she shrugged. "But this isn't about me. What are you going to do?"

I looked to Vera. "Don't make decisions from anger," she repeated.

I closed my eyes and imagined seeing Parker—really seeing him. I imagined calling him and letting him know I wanted to meet after all his pestering to do so. With a deep sigh, I opened my eyes. "Okay."

"Good. Now that that is solved, how are things going with Aiken?" Vera asked, like we were checking off bullets at a meeting.

With a groan, I grabbed the almost empty glass in front of Rae and finished it off.

"Sounds great," Rae teased. "Especially if it's making you ballsy enough to take my alcohol."

"I think I'd almost rather talk about Parker," I grumbled.

"C'mon," Vera cajoled. "You can always bounce ideas off me. I'm not an influencer, but a business is a business."

"I'm n—"

"An influencer," Rae cut in. "We know. But you are an artist with work to sell and a platform to sell it on."

"Exactly," Vera added. "I know you don't like putting yourself out there, but with Aiken's help, you can control how much as you blend your worlds together."

"This was so much easier to do when I randomly started them in college."

"Oh, college, the good ole days," Rae sighed.

"So, what has he recommended?"

"He wants me to post more pictures of me at least creating my art. That should be easy to add since I already post some of those when I paint on the road. It's the music aspect that I'm not a fan of. I rarely interact with any of the musicians."

"Yeah, your avoidance of rock stars is making a lot more sense. I thought it was just your dad."

"Nope. I have 'leave me behind' written all over me in a language only musicians can read."

"Lucky. I'd love to bang a rock star and have him leave me behind. No romance afterward?" Rae blew a chef's kiss. "Perfection."

"Anyways," I said, laughing. "He wants me to start meeting with the bands and working hands-on and possibly take pictures with them."

"Ew. Gross," Vera said.

"Right?" I exclaimed, picking up on her sarcasm too late. "Whatever. It's not…my thing."

"Well, I hate to say it, but if you want that van you've got your eye on, making it your thing may be your best bet."

I scrunched my nose and pouted like a child, which earned me eye rolls from both of them. "I do want that van. And to stay in my apartment."

"Both are very valid reasons to listen to Aiken," Vera assured. "You may need time to save up for your van—unless you maybe le—"

I cut her off. "Don't even say it."

She said it anyway. "You know we could loan you the money interest-free."

"I know. And I don't want to borrow money from you. I'll eventually get there," I promised. "Besides, Aiken is looking into the music thing and said he may have an option open to meet with a band. I told him I didn't want my identity shared in case it all went to shit, and I panicked. So, I guess as long as he can work some privacy magic, I may be sitting down with musicians and posting elusive photos. Ugh."

"Whatever. It will be great. *You'll* be great," Vera encouraged.

"Let's toast to it," Rae suggested.

She called the waiter over to refill our glasses, and I ended up turning down one of my own, sticking to water.

"To rock stars and stepbrothers and sharing all the dirty details," she said pointedly to me.

Vera and I snorted out a laugh and clinked our glasses together, diving into more details about Rae's new boyfriend and trying to find out how Austin felt about it.

And I thought I was evasive.

PARKER

Supernova: Hey.

I LOOKED DOWN at the phone and smiled. We'd just got back to our hotel room after the show, and we all bounced around on cloud nine. A message from Nova was icing on the cake.

"Aww, look at him, smiling like a cute, lovesick puppy," Oren baby-talked.

"Ha. Ha," I deadpanned, flipping him off.

"You coming out with us tonight?" Ash asked.

"Nah. I'm staying in."

"To talk to his girlfriend," Brogan said.

"She's not my girlfriend." We never made it that far before things always fell apart.

"C'mon, we need to celebrate. Freaking New Year's Eve in New York. It's huge," Ash tried to convince me.

The news hit me all over again, stealing the air from my lungs just like it had when Aspen told us earlier. "I still can't believe it."

"So, let's celebrate."

"Not tonight, bro. I may try to take this high and write some music."

"Ugh. Fine," he finally accepted. "Lifting tomorrow?"

"Yeah, I'll see you in the AM."

Ash and I both got into lifting weights when we could. It started for vanity, but we quickly became addicted to the activity.

Waving the guys' catcalls off, I shut myself in my room and pulled out my phone. Before I could respond, it rang in my hands—Aspen's name showing up.

"Miss us already?" I answered.

"Hardly. I wanted to let you know that Sonia will be at the New Year's Eve performance. That way, you can kiss her at midnight."

On television for everyone to see? No. I wanted to be remembered for my performance that closed out the year, not who I made out with.

And I sure as hell didn't want Nova to see. We spoke on and off for the last two weeks, and I knew I was winning her over to finally meet me at some point, but if she thought I was seeing someone, I knew she'd pull back hard. Not that she'd admit it, but I knew her well enough to hear the flirting every now and then. Besides, I wasn't sure we would know how to be around each other as anything other than what we were.

"No," I answered simply.

"What?"

"I said, no. I'm not making out with Sonia at midnight after a huge performance."

"Uh, yes, you will. You guys are performing your latest song. It will be perfect. Fast paced and about being in love. The fans will love it."

"Maybe the fans will love the music without a lie shoved in their face after."

"Parker," she argued, her patience running thin. "Don't fight me on this."

"Listen, this started as a convenience, but now I'm starting to feel like a show pony."

"Well, you're a show pony who signed a contract to uphold a number of interactions, and you haven't fulfilled them."

"Aspen, c'mon. I'm a musician. Let me be one."

"You're a musician who's managed by your label, and this is part of it."

"No," I said again.

"Parker, this is happening. Accept it." And with that, she hung up.

I fell back on the bed and ran my hand over my eyes, digging in to relieve some pressure.

My phone vibrated again, and I formulated a snarky response before I lifted it to find another message from Nova instead of Aspen.

Supernova: I know it's late, but I wanted to let you know I saw you on that talk show last night. You guys looked good.

The tension drained out of me, like it had every time we talked. Not that it was often, but the few times were enough that I could breathe—almost enough to maybe try writing again.

Me: I always look good.
Supernova: *eye roll* you're so full of yourself.
Supernova: How was your hike?
Me: Good. Short. Ash came with me.
Supernova: Sometimes, a short one is all you need.
Me: Really? I heard nice and long is what most women prefer.
Supernova: Still the same perverted jokes as before. Some things never change.
Me: I blame the rest of the guys. So immature.
Supernova: I bet.

Supernova: So, do you have any pics of the hike? I'm curious.

I scrolled my phone for the picture of the waterfall descending the jagged rocks and the one of the misty forest and fading greenery. To see if she'd mention it, I added the one Ash took with the waterfall behind me. We didn't always have time for much, but we all enjoyed hiking when we got the chance, exploring all the different locations on tour. I'd been so stressed with the tour and the looming album, I pushed it to the side until Nova recommended a few trails.

Supernova: Beautiful.
Me: I know I am.
Supernova: *eye roll*
Me: You know you love it.
Me: Your turn. Send me a picture.

She sent a few of the forest canopy, the reds bleeding to orange and yellow. She sent me her own waterfall. She sent me one of craggy rocks falling off into the abyss. None of them were what I wanted.

Me: Show me one of you.

A moment later, a photo of her standing on a cliff, her back to the camera, looking out at the mountain peaks popping through the thick covering of clouds. My lids slid closed, and I imagined I was there behind her taking the picture. I'd have taken it and then wrapped my arms around her to stare out at the beauty beyond, her long fiery hair whipping around us.

The image settled deep in my bones, but it wasn't the one I wanted.

Rock Star: Not an Instagram one. I want to see you.

I held my breath, watching the bubbles appear and disappear, only to reappear again. Finally, when I was sure I'd pass out, a picture came through.

Her over-exaggerated smile hit me so hard, I couldn't help but laugh. Her dimples showed up in full force. Her full lips stretched over her perfectly white teeth. Small specks of freckles I knew by heart covered the bridge of her nose. The only thing missing was her grass-green eyes hidden behind her lids squeezed tight. Strands of her hair hung from the messy bun piled on top of her head. My fingers twitched around the phone, wanting to reach out and brush them back behind her ears.

God, she was stunning, and each second of not being able to actually see her only served to make me want her more—to touch her and be with her more than just through a speaker.

I tapped her name and hit the camera.

On the third ring, she finally picked up. The same girl in the photo smiling back through the phone.

"Aww, you took a selfie just for me."

"I don't have a ton of photos of myself on my phone," she explained, a perfect blush staining her cheeks.

"What kind of tea are you drinking?"

"How do you know it's not coffee?"

I gave her a deadpanned stare. "Because you'd never sleep if you drank coffee this late."

"Peppermint," she admitted softly.

"Your favorite."

Silence filled the line, and I hoped she was remembering how much I knew her, remembering how close we'd been. Maybe if she remembered that enough, she'd forget the worst part and give in to seeing me.

"Guess where I'm going to be next month?" I asked, my excitement bringing me to the edge of my seat.

"Where?" she asked equally excited. "London? Paris? Timbuktu?"

I laughed at her suggestions. "No. New York," I exclaimed. "We're playing the last two songs of the year on New Year's Eve."

"Holy shit," she breathed, her hand covering her mouth.

"Yeah, that about sums it up."

"Parker, that's amazing." Her face split into the smile I knew better than my own, her dimples digging deep. The green of her eyes sparked with the same joy that shot its way through me every time I thought about playing at Times Square.

"Right? We're so fucking pumped."

"It's not even me, and I'm pumped for you."

Something shifted in my chest, a piece sliding into place I hadn't known was missing. The band had a lot of success, and we'd always shared it with each other, but I couldn't deny how my mind had always gone to Nova, how I'd already reached for the phone to call her. I missed sharing our wins with someone outside of the band who supported me wholeheartedly. That need immediately got followed by the crashing reminder of how she cut me out of her life.

So, I'd taught myself to block out that need to reach for her. Apparently, blocking it wasn't the same as getting rid of it completely because, like it'd been lying in wait, the joy of sharing with her filled me to bursting.

"I miss you," I whispered, scared that if I said it too loud, it would scare her off.

She dropped her face, hiding like always, but I still said it. I missed her more and more with each day. Hell, I'd been missing her each day and not even realizing it until I saw her again. So fucking much that it grew like a drop of blood in water, changing something in me I hadn't known could be changed.

Every day I still looked for her. Every show, I wondered if

she'd surprise me and be out in the crowd. Every redhead sent a spark of electricity through me, only to be doused out before the fire could begin.

I'd told her before I missed her in passing—as a joke—and she'd shut down. But this time, when she looked up, something else happened.

Maybe something was changing in her too.

"I miss you, too."

Maybe this was my chance to get her to agree to see me. Maybe…

I opened my mouth.

"Don't ask," she said, cutting me off before I could get the words out.

"Nova, I—"

"Sing for me," she demanded.

The words I wanted to say fell on an exhale rather than floating through the lines to convince her.

"Please."

How could I say no?

I couldn't.

I sat up and propped my phone against the lamp on the nightstand, grabbing the acoustic I always had with me.

"Any requests, my lady?"

She pretended to think on it, tapping her pursed lips before shrugging. "Surprise me."

Part of me wanted to pick a song I knew held meaning for us, but instead, I opted for a tune that had been whispering in the back of my mind since I saw her again. Unfortunately, no lyrics came with it. Maybe part of me hoped she would hear it and, just like before, she'd come up with the words I needed.

I strummed the chords, occasionally closing my eyes, searching for the words that lingered just beyond the fog. But as soon as I looked for them, they faded. So, I opened my eyes again and watched her watch me with her cup of tea clutched between her palms. She sat back against her couch, a small kitchen behind her. The green eyes I missed in the photo shining bright with a smile.

When one song ended, she demanded another until I played her her own private mini-concert. I played a rendition of Baby Got Back, which she danced to while still sitting on her couch, laughing at me dancing with her.

The night was perfect.

Just like we'd once been.

But just like before—we never got quite far enough to keep it perfect.

I should have known better.

EIGHT

Nova

"Nervous?" Vera asked.

"Yeah," I answered honestly. Nervous didn't even begin to cover the jittery edge I barely balanced on. I took another sip of champagne, looking over the crowd of people mingling throughout the room.

Rae got us into an elaborate party in the heart of Times Square—a perfect place to enjoy the night minus all the crazy crowds.

Everyone sparkled in their New Year's Eve regalia, laughing and drinking, ready to start a new year with a clean slate. Platters of champagne and hors d'oeuvres made circles around the room as everyone talked about resolutions and future plans.

And I was one of them.

I didn't usually get into the whole fresh start belief. January first was just another day, exactly like the one before. Except, this time, it wasn't. This time, January first would mark the first time I'd see Parker Callahan. Maybe even start the beginning of something more.

No parents trying to force us into the stepbrother-stepsister roles. No one telling us we're wrong. No more stolen nights and forbidden touches. No hiding away or denying what we felt. No holding back.

No, at midnight tonight, I really would feel like a new woman. Hopefully, in the arms of the man, I'd always wanted.

I'd concocted the plan around two in the morning after he serenaded me. Watching him sing, even over the computer, brought forth more feelings than I'd realized were still there. I'd avoided talking to him because I didn't want to be hurt again, but after talking to Rae and Vera, I wanted to at least try. I didn't want to be scared forever. So, staring up at my ceiling, trying to track the fan whirring in circles in the dark, I came up with a plan to surprise him.

I'd messaged Aiken right then and there, asking him if he was able to get me a pass to Times Square on New Year's Eve. I played up the business aspect and how I could take pictures and post them to my Instagram. Maybe even go live at midnight or something. I think I would have promised almost anything in that moment of heart-thumping planning. I'd fully been in the moment of making that wild idea come to fruition and ignoring any doubts.

Aiken might have been more excited about the idea than me. Probably focusing on that percent of profits he had in his contract. It took him a while, but he got the passes.

In that time, Parker and I talked on and off over the last month, busy with holidays and work. Mostly we texted, but there were times we Facetimed, and he always sang for me. Sometimes, I'd even dig out my paints, and if I closed my eyes and thought hard enough, I could imagine it was just like when we were teens.

I considered telling him what I was going to do about a million times, but I'd been riding too high on the thought of his face when I appeared to let it play out any differently than I imagined it. I'd been too high for any of the downfalls of my plan to reach me.

They reached me now.

"Did you tell him you're coming?" Rae asked.

"No, I wanted to surprise him."

Their reactions couldn't have been different, and I wanted to block Vera's raised brows and wide eyes from my mind. Instead, I focused on Rae as she clapped her hands, bouncing on her stiletto heels, her champagne jumpsuit sparkling under the dim, soft lighting. She might as well have heart eyes, and that was the positivity I needed right then.

"Are you sure that was a good idea?" Vera asked, not willing to be ignored. Usually, I was the voice of reason, but reason-be-damned.

"Well, I can't do much about it now," I said, laughing nervously.

"You could message him?" she suggested. "I'm just worried that maybe he might have someone with him—"

"He's single," I cut in. He admitted it himself. He wouldn't have anyone with him.

"But maybe he has plans, and we'll miss him."

"Don't ruin this moment, Vera," Rae reprimanded.

"Then we miss him. I just...I just want to try," I said, almost pleading with her to understand.

"I know, I know. I'm excited for you. I promise. I just have to say it. I know excitement can act like blinders, and I wanted to be a voice of reason. If you're committed to this, then I'm here for you."

"I can be the voice of reason," Rae pouted.

Vera and I both laughed, quickly followed by Rae joining us.

"Maybe he'll kiss you at midnight," Vera said, leaving the land of reason and joining us in the land of excited oblivion. She sparkled just as much as Rae, only in a black sequin top.

"Maybe he'll fuck you," Rae said, looking like a kid in a candy shop. I winced but laughed, kind of liking the idea but not wanting to go into details like I knew Rae would. "I mean, I'm assuming that's why you're wearing the skirt. Easy access."

"Oh, my god. I didn't wear it for easy access."

"Either way, it's totally hot. And with the Doc Martin's and his band T-shirt. So sexy."

I looked down the bronze sequin skirt with a slit up to my mid-thigh exposing my black boots, and confidence had me standing a little taller. I'd thought about wearing a cute top but thought it'd be cheeky to wear one of his band shirts tucked into the high-waisted skirt.

"I'm going to go talk to a friend I see over there," Nico interjected. I blinked, completely forgetting he was standing on the other side of Vera.

"Can't handle a little girl talk?" Rae joked.

"I'll pass." He leaned down to press a lingering kiss to Vera's red lips, uncaring she left some lipstick behind on his. "Behave."

"Always."

"I was talking to Rae," he said.

"Always," Rae copied Vera.

We snorted, and Nico shook his head before leaving us girls to gush.

Vera snagged another trio of glasses from a passing tray, handing one to each of us.

"Can we get three tequilas brought over? With lime and salt, please," Rae requested before the waiter could walk away.

"Oh, no," I said.

"Just a few to loosen you up. This is a night from a movie scene, and you can't go walking around like you have a stick up your ass."

"It *is* like a movie scene," Vera agreed. "He'll finish his last note and pass off his guitar, getting ready to walk off stage. But just then, he looks up, and everything stops."

"Because there is the hottest bitch he's ever seen," Rae cut in. "Red hair flowing like the fiery goddess he always dreamed of. Your eyes lock, and a promise of the filthy night to come floats between you."

"Until you can't take it anymore, and you both run into each other's arms," Vera took over. "Ooo," she cooed, the ideas coming faster. "Maybe he'll see how awesome you are and never let you go. You'll get married and have adorable rock star babies."

"A baby musician band," I added, joining in on the crazy fantasy. *Why the hell not.*

"But first, he'll take you back to his suite and fuck you all night long," Rae inserted.

"Yes," I cheered.

Rae's eyes lit up. "Damn, you are excited. You never cheer when we talk about sex."

I shrugged, liking the sound of all night long.

"But before he whisks you away, he introduces me to that delicious Viking man who will end up fucking *me* all night long."

"Uh…" Vera and I shared confused glances at the turn of events. "Boyfriend," I explained.

Rae sniffed in annoyance and ignored us, getting away with it when the waiter returned with our drinks.

"To a new year," Rae toasted.

I skipped my shot and lifted my still mostly-full champagne glass. I didn't need to add any alcohol with the number of butterflies fluttering through my whole body.

As the clock ticked closer to midnight, I finally got a message from the contact Aiken set up for me. I had a press pass of sorts that would allow me free rein. Before we got to the party, I nabbed a few pictures of bands setting up. One more of the hottest rock band, and I'd call it a successful night for business.

We collected our jackets, and with Nico's broad body guiding the way, we made our way over to the stage The Haunted Obsession was performing on.

Nerves started creeping up my throat, and the high that had carried me this far started being weighed down by doubts. What if he didn't really want to see me? What if he really did? What if we do run into each other's arms, and kiss, and… everything else? What if he leaves me again? What if this was a mistake? What if—

My phone vibrated in my pocket, and I pulled it out to see a message from Parker, smiling before I even read it.

Rock Star: Are you going to watch us play tonight?
Me: Of course. Wouldn't miss it.
Rock Star: Make sure you cheer so loud I can hear you all the way in Times Square.
Me: I'll make sure you hear me.

The tension and what-ifs faded away, replaced by a calm, happy, acceptance. It'd been five years since I'd had Parker's arms around me—since I'd felt like I'd found home. Remembering the warmth and strength of his embrace had all the tension melting away. This was different. We were different now. I would be smarter.

Once we reached the stage, we moved past the crowd. The wind bit at my nose, and I shoved my shaking hands inside my faux fur-lined puffy coat, burrowing into my collar. Partially so I could hide my face in case Parker popped around a corner and saw me. I wanted the meeting to be on my terms.

I glanced at the time. Fifteen minutes.

"You're just in time," the guy who approved my pass said. "They just got on stage, getting ready to play one of their songs and then singing the John Lennon song. You can head up and take the pictures you need. Just stay off to the side."

Rae said she would walk up with me as my 'assistant' while Vera and Nico stayed off to the sides.

"No matter what, I'm proud of you for being brave," Vera said against my ear with one last hug.

I knew she was worried, and I appreciated it. I just hoped she was wrong, and we could laugh about it later.

My heart thundered, and the bright lights swirled until I was sure I'd pass out. This was it. This was it. This was it.

On repeat in my head, it was all I could think about as I ascended the few steps on wobbly legs. People filled the edges of the stage, shoulder to shoulder, preparing for whatever came next.

"Happy New Year, New York," Parker's voice rang all around me, and the crowd answered with a roar of epic proportions. Everything else faded away, and my sole focus shifted to the stage. "How about we get a little chaotic before we close out this year?"

The crowd roared again, and the beginning chords of their latest song began. Rae latched on to my arm and shook me in excitement, and I laughed, bouncing with her to the beat, singing each word I knew by heart.

I'd gone to see them a few times in concert because I loved their music—loved to see how they'd grown into themselves and become better musicians. But standing at the edge of the stage—even if I only caught glimpses between everyone moving around—it was something else. Something I'd never forget.

Happiness, like I'd never experienced, had me shaking my ass and jumping up and down between remembering to snap a few action shots and take video. Rae and I shimmied and bumped hips and swayed to the slow break only to start jumping and banging our heads when the beat picked up.

The song ended but quickly shifted, and the soft chords of John Lennon's *Imagine* floated across the crowd. Parker's rough voice sang the words like they'd been made to be sung with a rock vibe. As each lyric passed, the seconds ticked by, and despite the countdown for the new year beginning, mine had already started.

Finally, the song ended, and seconds later, the final minute countdown started on the screen. People moved to collect the equipment, and with a not-so-subtle shove from Rae, I stumbled past a crowd.

Parker stood talking and laughing with Ash, Brogan, and some other people.

Turn around. Turn around. Feel me.

I chanted the plea, hoping he'd feel my need and comply.

Ten. Nine. Eight.

I didn't want to step any further on the stage. All the lights shined on him as people all around paired off.

Seven. Six. Five.

Two more steps. I needed him to see me. To turn around.

Four. Three.

Fuck it. I charged forward, making each step count before we hit one.

Two.

Red hair flew from the other side of the stage and a body leaped into his arms.

One.

And held on tight as she placed her lips on his.

"Happy New Year."

The crowd erupted and the New Year song played over the speakers, but everything pin-holed into the sight of Sonia's lips on Parker's, and for those first few seconds of a brand-new year I couldn't wait to start, my chest crumbled in on itself.

I was wrong. I thought I knew Parker so well—even after all these years, I never imagined him being an outright liar. But glimpsing the way he caught Sonia, single is the last word I'd use to describe him.

I stood under the bright lights, with thousands of people celebrating around me, oblivious to my complete mistake.

All but one person.

"Supernova!" Oren called. I jerked my head to find him coming out from behind the drum kit, only to jerk back to Parker.

His head whipped around, eyes wide, mouth smeared with red lipstick.

I'd already begun backing away when he pried himself from Sonia's arms.

"Nova."

I watched his mouth form my name, but I couldn't hear anything over the ringing in my ears. Not wasting another second, I turned and ran.

NINE

Parker

SHE STOOD THERE LIKE A VISION—LIKE everything I ever dreamed of.

At the completely wrong time.

For a moment, I stood frozen, unsure if she was real or if I'd wanted her there so much that I conjured her in my mind.

"Nova," I whispered.

I'd seen her over many Facetimes, and not a single one did justice to the woman before me. The screen didn't capture the sharp points of her full lips or the line dimpling the center of her bottom one. It didn't capture just how green her eyes were or that perfect shade of deep red in her hair. I never got to see the full length of her long, lean limbs.

It almost stole my breath, taking her all in at once—this stunning woman she'd grown into.

But as quickly as she appeared, she turned and vanished back into the crowd. As soon as she left my sight, the world crashed back in around me.

The blinding amounts of confetti, the loud crowd cheering and dancing to Frank Sinatra's *New York*. Sonia's arms wrapped around me like a spider monkey.

"Fuck."

Uncaring of anyone watching, I gripped Sonia's arms and pulled them off, pushing her back as I took off to follow Nova. I needed to get to her—to explain. Hell, I wasn't even sure what had happened because Sonia appeared just as quick as Nova had. I'd stumbled and had to focus on not falling from the collision; I'd barely had time to register what the hell was going on.

Although, I should have been ready for anything when she appeared right before I went on stage and wished me luck.

Everyone slapped my shoulder as I tried to move past, wishing me a Happy New Year. I think I nodded in return, but I also shoved people out of the way, knowing it was a waste of time but too desperate to care. I'd barely reached the edge of the barricade, and it'd taken almost five minutes. Hands grabbed at me and screaming burst the bubble of my focus. I blinked, taking in the gaggle of women gripping my arm or reaching out to touch any inch they could reach. Some held up phones, and flashes went off in my face making it harder to think. I just needed to think.

It's over. You ruined it.
She's gone forever.
She'll never pick up. She'll never listen.
I'll never see Nova again.
That one glimpse would be it.

That one hurt, slamming me back to earth more than anything else. I needed to get out of there before they tore the clothes from my body. I wasn't solving anything in the middle of Times Square anyway.

Gently prying their hands off me, grateful for when security finally caught up to my mad dash, I smiled and said thank you blindly to anyone and turned back to the stage. Funny how much easier it was to get back on than it'd been to get off. Not that Nova seemed to have an issue.

"Where the hell did you go?" Aspen greeted me first, sounding pissed. "We have photos we have to take."

Aspen.

Seeing her made it all click in place. "You," I sneered. "You did this."

She crossed her arms and lifted her chin. "Why, yes, Parker. I did do all of this. I busted my ass to get you this slot because it's my job, and we don't scoff at our jobs when it gets hard or maybe not everything we want to do."

"Don't. Don't pull that shit. I bust my ass for this job—for this label. I said no Sonia."

"And I said tough shit."

"You had no right."

"I had every right. You signed a contract making a deal with her, and this is part of it. I wasn't going to argue with you anymore. I told you it would happen, whether you liked it or not, because it's your job."

Knowing I wasn't getting anywhere with her, I walked past and rounded the back of the stage, descending the other steps that led to our gear and the guys.

"Dude, that was fucking Nova," Oren exclaimed, bouncing around like a kid with a sugar high. "I had no idea she was coming."

"Me neither," I muttered.

"Nova was here?" Brogan asked. "Where?"

"She totally ran," Oren answered. "Pew," he said with a hand demonstration of her taking off.

"Why?" Ash asked, cutting in.

I ran a frustrated hand through my hair, remembering our last conversation and how she playfully asked again that I hadn't met anyone new.

"Why didn't you see her?" Ash asked.

"He was playing suck-face with Sonia."

I ground my jaw at the reminder. "I didn't fucking know

she was coming," I muttered, like it would have mattered. "And I sure as fuck didn't know about Sonia."

A flash of red hair off to the side had my heart skipping a beat, but then I took in the too-shiny locks and unnatural red. Not Nova. My body deflated and hated everything.

Five minutes in the New Year, and I sat there in a mess of my own making.

No, not my own making.

I didn't do this.

Clenching my fists, I pulled my shoulders back and stormed through the guys, charging at the second culprit. Sonia and I talked enough for her to know how much I hated being a show pony. She knew I didn't want to do this anymore. I asked her to think of other ways of finishing out our contract and still be beneficial. She fucking knew I was done and should have told Aspen no.

"What the hell did you think you were doing?" I growled.

Sonia whirled my way with wide eyes, but a moment later, being the perfect actress she was, her face morphed into a playful smile.

"Kissing you at midnight. Duh."

"I never agreed to that."

"Oh, come on, Parker. You know I never pass up a promo moment. We're both single. I assumed you were just playing hard to get when you told me you didn't want to do this anymore."

"I don't give a fuck about your assumptions, Sonia."

"Parker." Her smile held firmly in place, but her eyes flicked side-to-side, trying to determine if anyone noticed our disagreement. "You're making a scene."

"No, you made a scene with that damn kiss. And you fucked up my plans. It's not always about you, Sonia. Get the fuck over it."

"Parker," Aspen snapped my name, and I met her hard

gaze. "That's enough. You need to get your shit and take pictures. Do. Your. Job," she reminded me.

Taking a deep breath, I tried to calm the rage, finally backing away from Sonia with another glare, redirecting it back at Aspen.

"Where's my phone?"

"I don't know," Aspen sneered. "You have more important things to worry about."

"Where the fuck is my phone, Aspen?"

Her face went placid while her eyes filled with murder. Running a hand over my face, I tried for another deep breath and backtracked. I was pissed but didn't want to piss off the boss's daughter. "I'm sorry. I'm just…trying to fix something."

She nodded but didn't respond.

"Here's your phone, bro," Ash said, holding it out to me like a lifeline. "I'll get your stuff. Go call her."

With a pat on the back, I dashed off to sit in one of the cars that brought us over. With shaking hands, I found her number and hit send. On the fourth ring, the screen came to life, but it wasn't Nova's face I saw.

No, Raelynn's glittery dark eyes glared back.

"Fuck off, fuck boy."

I didn't have time for her strong-girl act. "Let me talk to her," I growled.

"You think because you're some rock star, you can make demands? You think you're such hot shit that you can lie and cheat without responsibility?"

"Dammit. Let. Me. Talk. to her," I tried again.

She narrowed her eyes to dangerous slits. "No."

I snapped. "I don't know who the hell you think you are—"

Her bark of laughter halted anything I planned on saying, and like a fucking sociopath, the laughter cut off, and she morphed into a woman with a death glare, all humor gone. "Who am I? I'm the fucking boss. I'm the dad with a shotgun.

I'm the crazy-ass mom in a bathrobe with curlers chasing you out of the house with a frying pan. I'm your worst fucking nightmare."

Gritting my teeth tighter and tighter with each explanation, I feared they'd crack. There was no way I would get anywhere with Raelynn. I looked around the bar behind her, trying to take in any features that'd let me know where they were at. I'd fucking chase her down all night if I had to.

"Oh, yeah, you see this bar." Rae pulled the phone back for a moment showing me around too fast to pick up anything just to come back to her crazed face. "If you come close to here, I'll nut punch you."

I wasn't getting anywhere with my frustration, so I went for another tactic. Taking a deep breath, I dug deep for a calm I was far from feeling. "Listen, Rae. Can I please talk—"

"No."

And with that, she hung up.

I almost crushed the phone in my death grip, barely reminding myself it was my only connection to Nova before relaxing my fist.

Knocking on the window jolted my whole body, almost making my heart stop. It was already so overworked with anger, I didn't need fear added on top of that.

Oren smiled and waved through the glass.

"You scared the fuck out of me," I grumbled, getting out.

"I know. You jumped like a solid foot. Very impressive for a tight space."

"What the fuck?" I asked.

"We have some shit to do, then we head off and enjoy our night."

"Yeah," I mumbled.

"Did you find Nova?"

"No."

"Bummer, bro." We walked two more steps. "I'm assuming she has reason to be upset about you kissing Sonia?"

"I didn't kiss Sonia. She fucking bombarded me."

"Yeah, she's a little crazy. It's kind of hot."

"Not really."

"You think if I let her know I'm into it, she'll let me fuck her?"

A laugh broke free because Oren said the most random shit that always caught me off guard. I kind of loved it.

"Maybe, man," I said, patting his back.

"Sweet. Let's do this promo shit and then head out."

By the time we finished, I'd figured out the bar Nova was at. I'd had to dig deep in my memories, but a weird-ass painting of a bearded lady caught my eye, and I knew just where they were. I didn't have faith she'd be there, but I had to try. Taking security with me, I had them go in and look, only to come out with a rueful head shake.

Ten minutes after we left, another message came through.

Unknown: Nice try, fuck boy.

I didn't recognize the number, but I wasn't likely to forget the woman who gave me the nickname. I hit save and kept the name under *Crazy Bitch*, never knowing when I'd need it again.

Knowing I wouldn't get through, I hit Nova's name. It rang four times, and I held my breath for each one like maybe —just maybe—she'd pick up. Each ring had my anger rising. I'd spent the last hour thinking over the situation, and while it played out in the worst way possible, all she had to do was stay.

All she had to do was *fucking stay*.

She never stayed.

Her voicemail came on just in time to get the peak of my anger.

"You know, Nova, I shouldn't be surprised, but here I am. Because it's what you do. You always run. When it's hard, you fucking run like a coward. When are you going to actually face your shit? It's been five years, but have you actually grown at all, or are you just pretending?" As soon as the words left my mouth, the regret wrapped itself around my throat. All of it was true, but I could have called her out more softly. Taking a deep breath, I closed out the message with a promise. "You may run like you always do, but I'm not letting you go this time. I don't care what it takes, I'm finding you."

TEN

Nova

I was a fucking idiot. A stupid fool.

That thought ran on repeat the past few days. What a way to start the new year. I just couldn't help but remember the way I'd gushed with Rae and Vera, all giddy and full of hope, concocting stories that hadn't seemed so far-fetched at the time.

I'd been so dumb.

Days later, and my chest still hurt, and I rubbed at the lingering ache behind my ribs.

"I know you're not thinking about it," Rae cut into my thoughts.

"Huh?" I asked, distracted.

She gave me a look that hit me like a verbal smackdown of a reprimand. "You know what I'm talking about."

"It's hard to not feel like a fool and que—"

"We feel like a fool for no man. Ever. He's the fool for lying. He's the fool for missing out."

"But I shouldn't have just shown up like that. What was I thinking?"

"You were thinking you were a blazing hot catch, and he'd be lucky for you to show up. Especially when he'd been asking to see you. It's not far-fetched. All you did was take away his chance to lie his way out of it."

I smacked my head against the back of the car seat. I was on my way to my interview, and Rae had said she would have her driver take me because 'no one should ride the subway on the way to an important interview.' I'd honestly been sleeping so poorly, I couldn't even argue.

"Now, put on your boss-bitch face and show this secret band that they'd be lucky to have you."

Another groan when I thought over Aiken's phone call about my interview. He'd set it up to be double-blind, so no one knew who the other was, protecting identities. I didn't want to shove my identity out in the world just yet, and apparently, the band didn't want to share the news that they needed help writing music.

"Don't pout. This is huge."

"I know. I know."

"I mean, touring with a band? I'd probably pay to do that. And they're wanting to pay you? Hell yeah."

I couldn't believe my luck or the magic Aiken worked. I'd been ready to turn him down as soon as he called on day two of wallowing, and he'd ticked all my boxes to make it happen. I didn't even have to show my face or which band. I could just take pics and hint to writing music on tour with a big band. It was kind of perfect.

"Yeah." I rolled my head to face Rae, smiling. "Enough for a van. *And* a couple months' rent."

"Fuck yeah," she cheered.

She boosted me up just in time to pull up in front of the tall building. It didn't hint to whoever waited inside, instead just a building with offices to rent for meetings.

"Thanks, boo."

"Anytime. Now, forget Parker stupid-fuck-face Callahan and crush this interview."

With an ass-slap and a catcall, I made my way inside.

I tugged my jacket off as soon as the elevator doors slid closed. I'd needed the extra protection against the blundering New York wind, but now my nerves kicked my body temperature into overdrive, and I'd be lucky if I didn't sweat through my oversized sweater.

I stared at my muddled reflection in the glossy doors and tried to position my jacket and purse in the crook of my arms to look like I wasn't on the edge of a nervous breakdown. Settling on a hip-cocked position, I looked down at my outfit. The beige sweater led down to the black wide-leg pants and ended in my black power-pumps, as Rae called them.

Because no woman can walk around in a pair of red-soled stilettos and not feel like the most powerful bitch in the world.

And when I strolled out of the elevator on the top floor, I had to admit, she wasn't wrong. They clicked on the tile, announcing my entrance to the receptionist. She looked me up and down, probably finding my attire lacking compared to her charcoal suit. Not that I cared. I'd always enjoyed my style and how different it was from everyone else.

"I'm here for Miss Quinn," I stated.

With a nod, she picked up the phone, letting them know before going right back to work. Seeing the dismissal, I turned away and paced the open area, trying to discern who I'd be meeting with, and wondered if they knew who they were meeting with. Anyone who looked into SPRNV Music would find a basic website with references and a contact form that went to Aiken.

Despite requesting anonymity, it bothered me to not know the details, but I guessed the most important details I knew: the job itself and the pay. It was the pay that had me pushing aside my usual MO of working with a band over Facetime or just selling the lyrics outright. That and Aiken's constant reminder to explore new tactics if I wanted to grow—tactics like touring with the band while I helped write music.

A big band, if the pay was any indication.

A touring band—like Parker's.

No. Parker and the guys always wrote epic songs on their own—at least after they left me. Parker mentioned he hit a writing slump, but I couldn't imagine him hiring a songwriter.

Definitely not them. Rubbing my sweaty hands on my pant legs, I studied the generic wall art without taking any of it in. Maybe I should have been bothered by all the secrecy, but in reality, it reassured me that the artist valued privacy as much as I did.

Freakin' crap. I didn't know. Maybe this was all a mistake. Maybe all these reasons I talked myself into doing something I wouldn't normally do were really just excuses.

"You can head back. Third door on your left," Miss Cool-calm-and-collected said, yanking me out of my doubts.

Well, no turning back now.

Lifting my chin high, I focused on my heels clipping their way down the hall. *Be a boss. Let them know you're coming. Be a boss.*

My affirmation died a quick death like a tidal wave to a tealight flame when I rounded the corner to find four familiar faces staring back.

"Supernova!" Oren shouted. He hopped over the back of the couch, almost face-planting in his excitement but managing to catch himself and closed the gap between us. Like not a day had gone by, he wrapped his arms around my waist and lifted me off the ground in the tightest hug I'd had in years. Unable to help it, I laughed, his excitement a tangible thing. I braced myself on his shoulders, taking in the breadth of them. His lanky limbs from high school filled out and flexed under my grip. But when he slid me to the floor, he smiled just like he had before—cornflower blue eyes and the most perfect dimples.

"Hey, Oren."

"Get the fuck out of the way," Brogan grumbled behind Oren, jerking him back. "I want a turn." Brogan replaced

Oren and repeated the process of lifting me off the floor in a burly hug. "Damn, it's good to see you."

He held me off the ground and smiled up, the sun shining in through the glass windows, illuminating the changes in his face. He used to be the preppy, football player, but not anymore. His eyes still held that sweet sparkle, but of all of them, Brogan went through the biggest transformation. He was still as burly as ever, but now he had the beard and long hair making him look like the Viking his fans nicknamed him as. He had it pulled back, showing off the ear piercing and tattoos peeking out from the collar of his shirt.

"Good to see you, too."

When he set me down and moved away, I barely got a chance to breathe before Ash engulfed me. He didn't lift me up. Instead, hunching down and wrapping himself around me, pulling me in. I held on tight, feeling an edge of desperation in his hug. I don't know why it was there, but I responded to it. Maybe because I knew that when he let go, there was only one member left to acknowledge, and I wasn't ready to face him—wasn't sure I'd ever be ready to.

"Hey, Supernova," he finally greeted, pulling back just enough to meet my eyes. He brushed a few strands back that had fallen out of my topknot, giving me the smirk that somehow became even more devious over the years. Maybe because his cheeks had a sharp edge to them that had been hidden under his youthful face.

"Hey, Ash."

"Oh, I get it," Oren exclaimed.

Ash let me go to turn and look at Oren, but I still stuck close to him. Maybe he'd be my buffer, and I wouldn't have to talk to Parker at all. Yeah right.

"Get what?" Brogan asked.

"SPRNV Music." Oren wagged his finger at me. "Sneaky, sneaky girl. Supernova lyrics."

I held up my hands. "You caught me."

"Shit, you're the songwriter?" Brogan asked with wide eyes.

"Why the hell else would she show up here?" Ash asked like it was obvious.

"Uhh, because we're her friends, and Parker asked her to come."

I didn't know what hit harder—that he still considered me a friend after not really talking for five years or him referencing Parker's name. It all stole a little extra air from my lungs I didn't have to spare.

Oren slapped the back of Brogan's head and had a whole conversation with just his eyes before a lightbulb went off in Brogan's head. I could only assume he was remembering New Year's Eve.

I didn't turn to look at Parker, but I could feel him looking at me. His stare weighed on me like a fifty-pound blanket, and oh my god, I was going to die in this sweater. I should have just worn the summer dress hidden in the back of my closet. Anything had to be better than the overheating.

"So, you know each other," a petite woman said.

I was forced to acknowledge her and give in to the silent demand Parker gave since he was standing right next to her. Our eyes locked for a moment, but it was enough to strike me like a blow.

A flash of red hair covering his face.

Him turning with red lipstick smeared on his mouth and his arms full of a perfect model.

His mouth I fantasized about for longer than I could remember mouthing my name just before I ran.

One second and each image hit me harder than the last until I forced myself to focus on the woman next to him. While she may have been short, she stood with confidence bigger than anyone else in the room. I'd be that confident, too, if I looked like her. Her hair was pulled back in a sleek bun—

her hair almost as black as her leather pants. A stark contrast to the white silk blouse.

Her sleek brow lifted high, and I remembered she'd said something.

"Uh, yeah," I stuttered.

"We all went to high school together," Ash explained.

"Yeah, and Parker and Nova are stepsiblings," Oren added.

Miss Quinn's other brow joined the first.

"We're not stepsiblings," Parker grumbled, speaking for the first time, making me realize how much I'd missed his voice over the last week.

"Oh, right," Oren said, snapping his fingers like a lightbulb clicked. "Their parents divorced, so they're not stepsiblings anymore."

"Anywho," Brogan cut Oren off when he opened his mouth again. "Nova used to help us with our music back then. She also sang with us for a while."

"Why don't you sing with them anymore? Were you not part of the contract?"

The room fell silent as, all of a sudden, every second of the last five years and why that time existed between us crammed themselves in the room. Everyone's eyes dropped to the floor, no one willing to voice what happened.

"It's a long story," Parker finally answered.

"Oh, well, is it going to be an issue?" she asked, all business. "Because if so, then we don't need to waste our time with this meeting. We need someone who can work with the guys without problems."

They all shook their heads, muttering that they had no issues—even Parker. Four sets of eyes landed on me, awaiting me to join them, and I stood there like a deer in headlights.

Could I do this? The little information given let me know I'd be going on tour with them. I'd be with them for at least a month to write the album. Any hope I had of avoiding

Parker would be a joke. I'd probably be working with him the closest.

I should have turned on my power heels and stomped out of that room, but the guys looked at me with silent hope, and maybe I missed them more than I ever let myself think about. And then there was the money. I'd be able to finally get that van I had my eye on—a better one.

With a deep breath, I made my decision. "No. It's not an issue."

"Fuck, yes," Oren crowed. "With Nova on our side, we're going to be winning Grammys left and right."

"Good," Miss Quinn answered, a slight tip to her full lips the only hint of her approval. "Let's have a seat."

I rounded the couch, picking a chair on the far side away from Parker.

"I'm Aspen," she finally introduced herself. "I'm the manager of the guys and pretty much keep everything in line."

Kind of like what I used to do before they signed a deal. The thought crept in, leaving the bitter taste of jealousy in my mouth. Shaking it off, I shoved it away, knowing thoughts like that would only make this harder.

She pulled out a stack of papers handing one to me before grabbing a seat and proceeding to go over each page of the contract. We went over the privacy clauses, tour dates, non-disclosures, and every requirement in between. Through it all, I could feel Parker staring, his gaze a powerful force urging me to look up and see him. But I refused, focusing so hard on the words they blurred.

When we got to the last page, my heart skipped a beat as she went over travel arrangements.

"Some trips will be by plane with stretches of time in the tour bus. When we fly, we stay in hotels, and you'll have your own room, but the bus is closer quarters."

"Oh," I muttered eloquently.

"Are you okay with sharing?" Aspen asked.

"She can always sleep in my bunk," Ash joked, waggling his brows.

"Fuck off," Parker grunted.

"Don't be jealous that she'd rather curl up with me than you," Ash defended.

"Yeah, right. Nova will one-hundred-percent want to cuddle up with me," Oren claimed.

"Oh, Jesus," Parker mumbled.

I glanced his way just in time to watch him roll his eyes. Brogan laughed, watching the banter like a tennis match. All he was missing was a bucket of popcorn.

"Boys," Aspen called with all the authority of a drill sergeant. "Focus."

The back and forth bickering stopped, and they fell silent. Ash kicked Parker's foot, and just before Parker could kick back, Aspen narrowed her eyes, almost begging them to challenge her. She wasn't even looking at me, and I sat up taller. When they finally complied, moving their feet away from one another, she turned to face me, an expectant look on her perfectly made-up face.

"No problem," I answered. Honestly, remembering when Parker and I wrote together, sharing a bus didn't come close to the intimacy we'd already be delving into to write songs.

"Good. We have a concert this weekend in New York, and then we'll be taking off. The writing can be organic; however, you want to work that out. The guys usually write their own music, but we're…" She trailed off, glancing at a pouting Parker. His jaw ticked, and he stared off at the city, slouched down in the chair with his arms crossed. "Trying something new," Aspen finished.

I couldn't help but wonder what she was going to say originally but figured it had something to do with the few times Parker alluded to writer's block.

"We don't want to push it, but we do have a deadline

before the recording studio. If at all possible, we will try and record a song or two on the road."

"Okay. I'm sure we'll be able to work something out."

"Hell, yeah," Oren agreed, reaching his hand across Brogan. I obliged and slapped my palm to his.

With that, we signed a few papers as the guys talked, and before I knew it, it was done. I was officially helping The Haunted Obsession write their next album and going on tour with them.

Them, as in three guys who used to be my closest friends and one who used to be the stepbrother I loved even before I knew what it meant to love someone so deeply. All of them the guys who left me behind when I firmly shoved them out, slamming and locking the door behind them.

I quietly said goodbye to Aspen, who made me want to be a stronger woman within a few minutes of talking to her, and slipped out the door.

I stood outside the elevator, willing the doors to open for a speedy escape, when he called for me.

"Nova."

The rasp of my name on his lips slipped down my spine, nicking my heart on the way to my core. I hated the juxtaposition of the feeling.

"Can we talk?" he asked, coming up beside me.

I kept my eyes glued to the ascending numbers, too scared to look at him this closely. "There's nothing to talk about."

"Yes, there is," he growled.

"Well, we'll have plenty of time to talk in a few days."

God bless, the doors opened, and I darted in, finally lifting my gaze to his now that escape stood within reach—only to watch him step in right beside me.

"What are you doing?" I almost screeched.

"Forcing you to listen."

God, he was tall. I forgot how he'd made me feel petite next to him despite my height. Add in the brawn that all the guys seemed to have packed on, and he took up more space than just the breadth of his body. It made me want to reach out and feel the changes along with seeing them.

And it pissed me off.

I jutted my chin up and faced forward. "I don't think your *girlfriend* would appreciate you cornering another girl."

"She's not my girlfriend."

I snorted. "You've already lied once, Parker. Doing it again just lets me know how stupid you think I am."

"I'm serious. Sonia isn't my girlfriend. She's…she's…"

His hands waved around as if hoping to conjure an answer with magic, and I held my breath, hoping for the magic of a rational answer. Maybe it was all a silly mistake, and we could fix this.

"She's a contract. We set up a deal to act as a couple when it benefitted us and our jobs. The fans like thinking the songs are about her, and she likes a date with a famous rock star to keep her in the headlines."

I watched in the blurred reflection of the doors as my face screwed up, mulling over his answer. He said it like it all made sense, but it only served to strike another chord.

"So, not your girlfriend? Just a pretend one?"

"Exactly," he said, relieved.

"And you…what? Wanted me to come to your shows and look like the other woman? Is that why you asked me to come?"

"No. No. I wanted to see you. I don't—I don't want to do the thing with Sonia anymore, and I didn't want to do the kiss at midnight, but Aspen cornered me and ignored my request. She made it happen, quoting the contract and how I had a job to do."

Each word weighed on me a little more until I was sure I stood in quicksand. "And what would you do if someone took a picture of me with you, and Aspen said it was your *job* to let them paint me as the other woman?"

"I-I would—"

He floundered, and it reminded me of the few times I could remember my mom pressing my dad for details and only getting excuses of doing it for the job. It reminded me of the phone call when he stuttered through an excuse of why he couldn't come home for the fourth time when he promised this time he would.

There was always a reason. And that reason was never me.

Thankfully, the door slid open, and I walked out.

"I wouldn't let them paint you in a bad way, Nova," he called to my retreating back.

I stopped and turned, realizing how right I was to not let my guard down and remembering to not do it again while on tour.

"I need someone who wouldn't hesitate to even answer. Not someone who can't even defend the theoretical me, because Parker, for men like you, it always comes down to the job. It always comes down to doing what you need to do to make it one step further. I'm more than a stepping stone."

"I know that, and I intend to prove it."

Finally, his jaw clamped shut, but the look in his eyes screamed determination. Well, he could be as determined as he wanted, I wasn't giving in. With a skeptical smile, I turned. "I'll see you next week, Parker."

As soon as I made it to the subway, I got out my phone.

Me: You will never believe who just hired me to write songs with.
Rae: NO!!
Me: Fucking. Yes.
Vera: What did you say??
Me: Well, you just don't say no to that kind of money. Instead, you shove those feelings down and do your job.
Rae: Sounds super healthy.
Me: 100%. Therapist recommended.

Vera: Cool. Let me know how that goes.
Me: Will do.
Me: Also, will you come help me pack?
Rae: Hell yeah! I'm bringing clothes over. We need you looking extra hot on this trip.
Me: I'm good with my clothes. I'm not trying to seduce him.
Rae: Of course not.
Vera: But you do want to make him regret ever hurting you, and what better way than to shove your luscious self in his face.
Me: *looks down at b cup boobs* Luscious?
Rae: Hell yea. FUCKING LUSCIOUS.
Me: Okay. Okay. Maybe a couple low cut tops.
Me: A. COUPLE.

When all I got back was two thumbs up from each of them, I knew I'd be lucky to get anything other than Fredrick's of Hollywood attire for the entire trip.

To be honest, I didn't hate the idea of making Parker drool over me. Especially since he would never have me.

Ever.

ELEVEN

Parker

PAST

"Surprise!"

Nova stood on the sidewalk, wide-eyed and smiling—even if the smile did look a little forced, trying to hide the nerves.

Her eyes bounced from Ash to Oren to Brogan and finally back to me.

"Happy birthday."

"Parker." Her smile softened to a true Nova smile that lit up the dark, pockmarked sidewalk—that lit up the fire in my blood.

Although, it faded back to wide-eyed nervousness when she took in the glowing sign hanging above the heavy wooden doors beyond the guys.

Cap's Apps and Karaoke.

"It's karaoke night, baby," Oren crowed, following it up with a horrible screech that might have been a music note. There was a reason he played drums.

"You don't have to sing."

"But we hope you do," Ash added.

She shook her head, covering her face with her hands. "Oh, my god, you guys."

"Come on, Supernova. We know the guy at the bar, so we're drinking tonight. I'll be your DD."

"We're taking the subway," she deadpanned, finally dropping her hands.

"Whatever, I'll be your designated get-home-safe-guy." She rolled her eyes but smiled, and I knew she was warming up to the idea. "C'mon. You only turn seventeen once."

"Seventeen is the best," Oren said, slinging his arm around Nova's shoulders. "Let's never turn eighteen like these losers."

"Your birthday is next week, asshole."

"Don't remind me," Oren whined dramatically. He turned Nova, placing both hands on her shoulders and leaning to meet her eyes. "Please, Nova. Help me celebrate the last week of my youth."

"For you, Oren?" She rested her palms on his cheeks and smiled like a loving sister. "Anything."

He threw his arms up. "Yes! Victory. Let's go show everyone how it's done."

"Are you going to sing?" she asked him.

"Oh, yeah. Like nails on a chalkboard."

He threw his arm around her shoulder, walking her toward the door. She looked back at me, excitement and mirth bubbling over. "Wait. Can I change my mind? Anything to not hear Oren sing."

"May God have mercy on our souls," I said, laughing.

"And our ears," Ash added.

"The only solution is to drink so much we forget it ever happened," Brogan suggested.

"To the bar," Oren cheered.

Unsurprisingly, Nova stuck to beer, not wanting to repeat her night with tequila. She still didn't drink, preferring to stay home when the guys and I went to the local parties—probably something to do with how the last party ended. Not that we talked about it. We didn't talk about her walking in on me getting head—or what I said when I chased her out.

We didn't talk about how I continued to sneak into her room most nights, waking up curled around her in the morning.

We pretended nothing had changed during the day, sticking to our routine of hanging out—her doing art, and me playing music. Although, more and more, she helped me write the songs, like she was made for it—like she'd lived a thousand lives before, and the words were bursting at the seams to break free.

But in the moments of the night, I burned for her.

Like tonight.

I burned for her, watching the way she danced and laughed—her head thrown back, mouth open wide, arms in the air, and long red hair flowing down her back.

She flitted from guy to guy, and I barely held back from breaking Ash's hands when he gripped her hips and pulled her in close. She mostly twirled with Brogan and jumped around with Oren, but with Ash, she swayed. She let him lead and didn't pull away when he bent his knees to fit his groin against the lush curve of her ass. She laughed when he playfully bit her shoulder and rolled her eyes and shoved his hands back when they inched too far.

I sat at the table watching them, clenching my fists, both intrigued to take in every move and irritated my best friend was dancing with my stepsister like I wanted to be.

Then something shifted, a slow beat poured from the speakers, and her eyes lifted to mine. Her lips parted, and her chest rose and fell a little faster. I locked her in place, unwilling to break the connection. If Ash was going to grind on her, then I wanted her mind on me.

She slicked her tongue across her lips, and I groaned. I had to readjust when she ran her hands up her body, skating over the sheer black crop top I almost swallowed my tongue seeing her walk out in tonight. Ash curled around her, but she was focused on me—she only saw me.

His hands moved further in on her thighs, and this time she didn't pull him away. He dragged his nose up the side of her neck, but I didn't see him, and she sure didn't feel *him*.

She felt me.

We never talked about what we felt—what I wanted. We never went beyond the nights.

But this was the closest we came to admitting it. This was the closest we came to feeling it.

It wasn't Ash behind her, it was me.

It wasn't Ash's hands on her thighs, his cock against her ass—it was mine.

And when the fantasy became too much to bear, I decided to say fuck it and stood.

Her eyes widened as she watched me prowl across the dance floor like a lion stalking its prey.

"Fuck off, loser," I told Ash when I finally reached them.

He lifted his head up from where he stared down her body and met me with smiling eyes, releasing Nova from his hold. When he walked past, he bumped my shoulder and muttered, "Wondered how much you could take before coming over."

I didn't dwell on what he meant because Nova's chest pressed to mine, her hands moved around my back to hold me close. I didn't wait a second longer. With one hand on her hip, the other slid across the bare skin at her waist until I reached the ridges of her spine, rising under the shirt until I hit the black strap of her bra underneath. With one flex of my arm, I jerked her the non-existent distance to me, pressing her soft breasts to my hard chest.

She gasped, goosebumps prickling under my touch, her bright eyes darkening to a deep emerald. Dipping my knees, I slid my thigh between her legs and swayed side-to-side. She mimicked my moves, losing herself to the music thrumming through us, from me to her and back again. It bound us together. It didn't care about the complications holding us apart. It ripped them away and moved us as one.

Her hands drifted over my chest, up my shoulders, and around my neck, driving her fingers into my hair. The scrape of her nails shot down my spine and straight to my cock. When my length grew harder, I knew she felt it. Her eyes flashed with a fire.

We never talked about what filled the space between us. We never talked about what it was—how it was mostly an excitement and comfort in finding a spirit so similar to our own. It hadn't been hard to just let it be and enjoy what we could. But something shifted with her eyes on mine, her heat sliding across my leg, my dick pressing against her—something that felt too important to ignore. This wasn't just a friendship growing into something neither of us understood. No, this was desire, and it burned like a raging inferno, decimating any lines we tried to draw.

I dropped my forehead to hers, closing my eyes, unable to keep looking at her and not devour her right there. "Nova," I pleaded. I didn't know how to stop, and I just hoped she did.

Her head tipped, and I held my breath, waiting for her lips to press to mine, but as promised, like nails on a chalkboard, everything came to a screeching halt.

We both winced and looked to the stage, watching Oren sing *Living on a Prayer* with the passion and confidence of someone much better than him.

Another high pitch scraped along my nerves, and Nova's shaking body snapped me out of the daze I'd been locked in. I looked back to her, watching her cover her mouth and try to hold back her laughter.

The fire ebbed but didn't fade. Enough to at least let me laugh with her, part in relief, part in sheer horror over Oren's singing.

"How is he so musically inclined and yet so tone-deaf?" Nova asked around her giggles.

"Not a clue. I guess that's why he plays drums. He hears it all in beats rather than tunes."

Ash appeared next to me, punching my shoulder, officially making me let go of Nova so I could punch him back.

"Fuck, he's bad," Ash said with wonder.

"But he looks so good doing it," Brogan said, moving to stand beside Nova.

She laughed again and looked to me, her smile softening, letting one last bit of the flame burn between us. It had vanished so quickly, I almost didn't think it existed at all. Wanting to remember a moment longer, I gently reached out and grazed my fingers against hers. She twisted her hand and hesitantly linked her fingers in mine.

With a deep breath, I squeezed her hand, needing to feel her.

I watched her from the corner of my eye, taking in her smile she tried to hide by digging her teeth into the plump flesh. When the lights from the stage flashed over her, I saw the red tinging her cheeks.

Yeah, we may not talk about what grew between us, but that didn't mean we both didn't know it was there.

And it was just a matter of time before we finally did something about it.

NOVA

WE DIDN'T HOLD hands for long, but it ingrained itself in my mind, etched itself into each neuron until I knew I'd never forget the feel of Parker Callahan reaching for my hand.

Marked right next to the feel of his hard length pressed against my stomach.

Holy shit-snacks.

My face heated all over again, joining the fluttery warmth

growing in my belly. Each time I thought of it, my stomach would dip and turn like speeding over a hill too fast.

I couldn't help but hope we got another chance to dance tonight, but as the minutes ticked by, the chances grew less likely. More people from school showed up after Oren posted to Facebook. Some of the girls flocked around the guys like they always did. I cringed when I saw Kelly talking to Parker at the bar, hating that I hated watching her flirt with him.

Parker wasn't mine. He was my stepbrother. A stepbrother I let sneak into my bed most nights. A stepbrother that created a heat burning across my skin. A stepbrother that made me want things I'd never wanted before.

I knew about sex, of course. But beyond some groping and kissing, I hadn't done anything else. No one had made me want to, but Parker had me imagining stripping myself bare to him and begging him to do everything. Anything to make me feel closer to him—anything to help me crawl inside him and live forever like I wanted to.

"Guys," Ash called from a table at the edge of the dance floor. "Get the fuck over here."

I walked over to meet the guys and found ten shot glasses decorating the table with a salt shaker and a bowl of lime wedges.

"Hell yes. This is what I'm talking about," Oren cheered.

"I don't know why I bother," Parker muttered. "I thought I said beers only."

"Beer is for pussies," Oren jeered.

"I'm trying to keep her from getting so drunk she forgets her birthday."

"Meh, Supernova has a liver of a champion. One shot won't take her down." He nudged me, smirking and winking, trying to win me over to his side with his dimples.

"I'll be fine, Dad. Promise," I joked.

"Not Dad. Stepbrother," Oren reminded, missing the way

Parker and I stopped smiling at that reminder we never wanted or needed.

"Calm down, mother hen," Ash added. "We're fucking celebrating."

"What?" I asked.

Brogan slung his shoulder around Ash, his smile so big, I thought it would stay that way forever. "This asshole just got a phone call from George Marcetti," he explained, shaking Ash in excitement.

I had no idea who they were talking about, but the guys must have known because their jaws dropped, and it was like they sucked all the oxygen from our small space and replaced it with a knife's edge of tension.

"He invited us to play at Bordeaux next month," Ash explained.

"Holy fuck."

"Fuck yes."

"Holy shit. This is huge. So big."

"As in the top indie alternative concert bar?" I asked in awe.

"Yes," Parker answered, looking ready to float off the ground. "As in the bar that gave some of the biggest bands their break."

"You guys," I squealed, clapping my hands. "That's awesome."

Ash scooted the shots toward everyone—two each.

"It's a two-shot kind of celebration."

We each grabbed a glass and stood around the round table, lifting the shots to the middle. "To fucking crushing it," Oren said.

"To fucking making it," Parker added.

"To it all being worth it," Ash said.

"To proving we fucking can," Brogan included.

Their eyes turned to me, and I looked back at the four guys who I somehow got lucky to be a part of. "To you guys."

"To all of us," Parker added, his smile soft.

We tossed them back and quickly did the second.

"I declare that to help us celebrate, Nova must sing," Oren announced.

"Uhhh, no thanks."

"Oh, come on, Supernova," Ash cajoled.

"I mean, you can't be worse than Oren," Brogan joked.

Oren nodded. "Truth, brother. Come on. Nova. Nova. Nova."

He started a chant that quickly picked up until there were a few people from tables close by that joined in. I cringed, deciding I'd rather sing than have the entire bar chant my name.

"Fine. Stop. I'll sing. But Parker has to go on stage with me."

"Done," he agreed without hesitating.

I followed him to the stage and stayed back while he put in his request with the DJ.

Bouncing on the balls of my feet, I eyed the stage like it would grow teeth and eat me alive. My stomach turned, and my heart thundered like a stampede of wild horses. I'd never sung in front of a crowd. Hell, the only people I'd ever sang in front of was the guys.

I shook out my hands and took deep breaths, trying to stretch my lungs and release the bands of nerves squeezing them tight.

"You ready?" Parker asked.

"No. Does that mean I don't have to do it?"

He laughed. "Oh, we're doing this. You're amazing. I wouldn't let you up on that stage if I didn't think otherwise."

"You let Oren up there."

"God himself couldn't have stopped Oren from owning that stage."

"This is true." My laughter died, and I went back to

bouncing to expend my energy. "This is the worst. Shit. Shit. What song did you pick?"

"*It's All Coming Back to Me*, I know how much you like that song."

"Damn. I do love me some Meatloaf."

"I knew you wouldn't be able to turn him down. And we sang it together that one night, so it's easy." He gripped my shoulders and bent his knees, so I was forced to meet his eyes, and everything around us faded. "It's just you and me. I'm right here with you."

And just like that, one of the bands snapped loose, making it easier to breathe. It didn't vanish completely, but staring into his blue eyes, watching the thick wave of his hair fall down from where he kept pushing it back, it lightened.

"Okay?" he asked.

"Okay."

We climbed the five steps to the stage, and I kept my eyes glued to the worn and scuffed wood instead of the crowd. A ringing vibrated in my ears. Sweat beaded in my hairline under the two spotlights. No wonder the guys always came off stage sweating, it was hot as hell, and we only had two lights focused on us. Parker passed me a microphone, and I thought it would slip from my sweaty palm.

I didn't think I could do it. I wouldn't even be able to hear the music over my blood rushing through my veins. But then I heard a screech I'd never forget in this lifetime.

"Supernova," Oren screamed-slash-sang. "I love you. Have my babies."

More cheers calling my name broke through the last bit of nerves, and I finally peered up to find the guys right in front of me, their arms up like the best fanboys a girl could ask for.

The music started, and I shifted my focus to Parker. There was no stopping my eyes from going to him. Each note closer to my verse had a lump growing in my throat, but then Parker smiled, and everything eased—at least a little.

Closing my eyes, I imagined I was in my room, doing my art, or in our living room helping the guys create a song—completely normal.

And just like that, the words came. My chest vibrated with the lyrics. I stood taller and sang from somewhere deeper than my lungs. I poured the song out to Parker like I was pouring my soul out to him. His face lit up, and he never looked away—staying with me every second.

Before long, I lost myself to the moment. I even looked out to the crowd, performing just like I'd seen the guys do time and time again. I belted out each note, the euphoria of performing flooding my veins with a bolt of electricity I never saw coming. Every time I considered singing in front of anyone, I shut down. I never thought it would be like this.

This thrilling.

This exciting.

This…everything.

Parker and I harmonized, closing out the song with the last chorus, standing almost chest to chest as we sang together.

I didn't know what perfection was, but this had to be close.

My body vibrated so hard I was sure I'd explode. The excitement filled to overflowing, and I just wanted to scream.

We descended the steps, and I almost tackled him to the ground with the force of my hug. He caught me and stumbled back. His long arms flexed and held me close. I looked up to find him laughing at my exuberance and froze. Maybe it was the shot of tequila. Maybe it was the joy of discovering such a high. Maybe it was the dancing from earlier. Maybe it was every single moment that led to this one right here.

I lifted to my toes and crushed my mouth to his. The kiss was hard and lacking any finesse, but none of that mattered because my lips were pressed to Parker Callahan's.

His body stiffened against mine for only a moment but long enough to pour a bucket of water over my burning excitement.

I was kissing Parker Callahan—my stepbrother—in public where anyone could see.

Every obstacle that held me back before now crashed through my haze, and I jerked back.

"Shit. Parker. I-I'm so sorry," I stuttered.

He blinked, looking down at me like he'd never seen me before.

"I'm so sorry," I whispered again.

He blinked again, and the shock vanished. The next thing I knew, his arms tightened, his hands pressing into my back as he turned us deeper into the darkened corner. The lights and crowd vanished behind him, and all I saw was him.

All I wanted to see was him.

"Parker," I whispered, pleading with him to tell me what to do next.

I could barely see his eyes in the dark, but I could see enough to watch his pupils dilate just before his lips came crashing to mine this time. I gasped, and he took the opening to deepen the kiss, pushing his tongue against mine.

He tasted like the tangy lime and tequila, and I became just as drunk on him as I could ever be on tequila. His spicy scent that lingered in the bathroom every morning encompassed me, seeping into every sense. I clung to his biceps, digging my nails into the flexing muscles, wanting to leave my mark on him.

I didn't even know what that meant, but as he walked us backward until my back hit a wall, I didn't care. I became primal, giving in to my instincts—into the embers that flamed to an inferno. Sliding my hands up, I dug them into his hair, holding him to me, unwilling to let him realize this was wrong and stop. I needed more. I needed to dig deep into this urge he created. I wanted to learn more, and I wanted him to teach me.

I pressed my breasts to his chest, my hips to his, closing every inch of space keeping us apart. He groaned when his hard length grazed my stomach, the sound vibrating against my sensitive nipples.

I ached and whimpered when he pulled away just long enough for us both to suck in air, only to come crashing back.

His scruff abraded my cheek when he dragged his seeking lips down to my neck. The hand pressed to my back slid to my front, gliding up to cup my breast. Needing to see it, I tipped my head, giving him more access to me and watching his long fingers cover my breast, moaning when his thumb grazed across my nipple.

I angled my hips, rubbing back and forth against his dick, needing the friction—needing something.

"More," I begged.

"Fuck," he muttered into my skin. His lips traveled back up over my chin, pinching my nipple through my bra, making me gasp just in time for his tongue to dominate my mouth, to taste me like I wanted to taste him.

We devoured each other in that dark corner, lost in a haze of denied pleasure, ignoring anything that could make us stop.

Anything except the guys calling my name.

Their shouts pierced our bubble and had us jerking back on instinct.

"Fuck," he muttered again, watching me with eyes that looked as lost as I felt. "Nova."

I touched my lips, holding the memory of his on mine close.

"I don't—"

I don't want to stop, I wanted to say, but admitting it felt too much like begging, and I cut it off.

Not that it mattered because he apparently thought the same thing.

"You want to go home?" he asked, but something in the way he asked let me know going home held so much more than our typical routine.

And I couldn't wait to find out.

"Yes. Take me home."

It sounded like begging, but imagining what could happen, I didn't even care. I'd beg him on my knees if it meant we didn't have to stop.

Now that we started, I never wanted to stop.

TWELVE

Nova

———

PAST

The first thing I noticed when walking through the door was the picture-perfect family photo my mom claimed we absolutely needed now that we were all together. Right next to that one was the one Mom made Parker and me take together like siblings.

Not the reminder I needed when my lips still stung from where he kissed me. Not when I wanted to bombard him as soon as the door clicked behind us so we could do it again.

Only the dim light we left on in the kitchen shined around the corner, illuminating us in shadows. But when I turned to face him, I noticed him looking at the same photo, and dread crept its way up my back.

It'd been thirty minutes since I'd first kissed Parker Callahan—thirty minutes too long. We'd rushed our goodbyes and sat silently in the back of a cab on the way home, both lost in our thoughts—me lost in anticipation. I thought maybe Parker had been too, but watching his brows pinch together as he stared at the picture, I worried maybe I'd been the only one.

"Nova—"

"Don't." I cut him off before he could even start his

speech about why we shouldn't. He could have listed off any reason, and none of it would have mattered. I didn't care. Our parents were gone for the weekend and nothing stood in our way. "Just for tonight," I pleaded. "Just for my birthday. Then we can go back to not talking about it."

Just like we had for the last few months. We'd let it linger and fill the wasted space between us and never utter even a hint about its existence.

He finally looked away from the photo, lifting shadowed eyes to mine, and I held my breath, waiting and waiting.

Why wasn't he repeating what he'd done earlier? Why wasn't he dragging me away to his room? Why didn't he look as desperate as me?

"Unless there's nothing to talk about, and I'm making a fool of myself with announcing my one-sided feelings."

At this, he finally reacted. He tipped his head back and barked a single laugh. "Ha! Fuck no. You are one-hundred-percent, not alone in this. Jesus, Nova," he said, sighing, rubbing his hand over his hair and massaging his neck. "There's a whole set of encyclopedias filled with what we don't say. So, trust me, you're not the only one."

"You think about it, too?" I asked hesitantly.

He shook his head like he couldn't understand my question. "All the time," he whispered, slowly closing the gap between us. "Why do you think I come to you almost every night?"

Each step he took, my heart worked harder, pumping the adrenaline like fire through my veins. Each step, I panted for him, desperate and out of breath for wanting him. "My bed is better?" I offered.

His lips quirked up, and his eyes grew heavy. "Why do you think I stay away from other girls?"

"You do?" He nodded, and I swallowed, forming another breathless quip. "Maybe you're holding out for Oren."

Finally, he stood inches away—so close I had to tip my

head back to keep a hold of his heated gaze. He locked me in place, and I was his willing victim. *Take me,* I pleaded back to his burning promise.

"No, Nova," he explained, brushing a loose wave behind my ears, his rough fingers softly grazing my cheek. The caress was nothing, but it might as well have been a direct stroke against an erogenous zone the way it sent goosebumps down my spine. "It's because I can't stop thinking about you. I can't stop watching you—*wanting* you."

I was lost in him, reaching out to grip his waist to hold myself steady. All the blood rushed to my lower body, leaving me lightheaded. I'd seen Parker almost every way you could see someone, but I'd never seen him like this.

I'd never seen him with all his attention focused on me like I was an oasis in a desert. Like I was a 1968 Stratocaster played by Jimmi Hendrix. Like I was the one thing he ever wanted, and now that he had me, he was going to do whatever he wanted.

"I haven't jerked off this much in years. I fucking ache for you."

Heat bloomed across my cheeks. I knew a lot about sex… from reading about it. Experience-wise? I was a novice at best, and I definitely didn't talk about it openly. His blatant announcement conjured an image of his arm flexing, his lips parted, his eyes closed in pleasure. An image I wanted to actually see—needed to see.

"Do you ache for me, Nova?" he asked, backing me up against the wall like we were at the bar.

I was downright panting now and licked my lips to bring moisture back to my mouth. He tracked the movement with first his eyes and then his thumb.

"I think I do," I answered honestly. I didn't know what this tightly coiled tension pulling all my focus into the center of my body was, but I knew I'd never felt it before. I thought about Parker all the time. I imagined kissing him and touching him, but nothing compared to the inferno that consumed me in this moment.

He cocked his head to the side, considering my answer. "Think? Do you touch yourself and think of me?"

"I-uh…umm…" Fuck, words were hard. My brain short-circuited over the question, fighting my instinct to pull away from the topic and also shoving on because I wanted to be all-knowing with him. I wanted to be on his level and show him I could handle him.

"You *do* touch yourself, right?"

"Sometimes," I choked out. "I just…I…I don't know."

His finger abandoned where it rested on my neck and trailed down my chest until he brushed my nipple.

"Here?"

I whimpered when he circled the hard tip, nodding my head.

"What about here?" he asked, dragging his fingertips down my stomach and gently grazing between my thighs like a whisper, there and gone before I could register it.

Again, I nodded, unable to form any coherent words.

"Have you made yourself come?"

Doing my best to hold his gaze, I bit my lip and jutted my chin, trying to show a confidence I was nowhere near having—and shook my head.

"Oh, Nova," he chided. "Then you must ache for me. It's been building this whole time with no release."

His hand rested in the curve of my waist, and he leaned in, running his nose along mine. I clung to his shirt like a lifeline. If he wanted to pull away now, he was going to have a fight on his hands. So, to show him how much I wanted this, even if I didn't fully know what *this* was, I demanded it.

"Show me."

His eyes slid closed, and he sucked in a deep breath through his nose just before he released a growl like a caged animal and attacked. With more experience than I actually had, I met him kiss for kiss. His hands gripped my hips and pulled me right where he wanted me, and I clung to him, letting my hands search the hard planes of his biceps, shoulders, and back. His tongue pushed into my mouth, demanding I taste him, and I pushed back, needing him to do the same, hoping I could leave a part of myself behind and make him crave more.

His lips, teeth, and tongue scraped over my chin to my neck, and I yelped when his roaming hands gripped my ass and lifted me. On reflex, like my body knew what to do more than my mind did, I wrapped my legs around his waist, groaning when my core brushed his abdomen.

"More," I pleaded. I needed more of that feeling.

He continued his assault as he walked us into the living room. I wanted to beg him to take me to his room, to strip me bare and make the ache go away, but I didn't care about a bed anymore when he fell back on the couch with me straddling his lap.

On instinct, I rocked my hips, needing more friction between my legs. He thrust up with a grunt, and I hesitated, worried I hurt him or did it wrong. Not knowing what to do but needing to do something, I pulled back just enough to whisper my plea. "Help me, Parker. I-I don't know."

I struggled to confess the truth when I'd been trying so hard to prove I could handle him, but I wanted this to be perfect, and I didn't know what to do.

He pulled back; the blue of his eyes almost lost to his pupils. They flicked over my face, and I feared he'd stop, spotting my inexperience and not wanting to bother with it.

"Are you a virgin, Nova?"

Swallowing, I nodded.

"But you've had boyfriends."

"Yeah," I whispered. "But never serious or anything."

"And they never got you off?"

I shook my head.

"A virgin who's never come," he muttered, but not like he was put off by it. More like he was intrigued. He pushed my hair back behind my ear, the rough callous of his fingers tracing the shell up and around and down my neck.

I shivered when his finger scraped along my collarbone until he reached the hollow of my throat and moved down between my breasts. His fingers rested there over the sheer material of my top, and he studied them like he wasn't sure how they got there or where to move them next.

I had some ideas, and I was on the edge of not caring if I looked like a fool and begged him to touch me again—to rip the flimsy material off and shred my lace bralette underneath and just fucking touch me. I needed to be closer.

Finally, his eyes lifted back to mine and sent a jolt down to my core. Parker Callahan had never looked at me that way— no one had. With so much heat and desire—a look I only saw in movies—filled with the promise of everything to come.

His fingers drifted to my left breast, and I whimpered when he circled the hard tip.

"Has anyone touched you here?"

Biting my lip to hold back more whimpers, I nodded.

"What about under your shirt?"

I shook my head.

His lips twitched, one side kicking up into a smirk that rivaled Ash's. He pinched the tip, making my effort to hold back crying out useless. My hips rocked without thought when he rolled the tight bud, shooting darts of pleasure to my core. Like a chain was connecting them, every brush and twist had me pulsing with need between my legs.

"Your body knows what to do, Nova, but I'm happy to help."

With that, he went back to kissing me, dropping his hands to my hips, and sliding me back and forth. Heat burned up my neck as I imagined what we looked like. I wished I had a mirror to watch us—to burn the memory in my mind and recreate it with every medium I could find.

He wedged his length against me and started thrusting to match my rhythm. His fingers left my nipple, and I almost screamed, demanding he put it back, but I didn't have time because the next thing I knew, he had his hand on the bare skin of my stomach, pushing up under my shirt and tugging the lace aside.

My moan was salacious and like something I'd only heard in the few videos I researched out of curiosity. I imagined them fake and overdone, but now, with his fingers on my bare skin, his palm covering my breast, I knew the moans were real and came from a place I never knew I had inside me.

"So fucking soft," he muttered. "Perfect. Do you like this?"

"God, yes. More."

"Fuck, Nova. You're going to kill me."

"I don't mean to," I panted. "I want to make you feel as good as you're making me feel."

"Has anyone touched your pussy before?"

I lost my rhythm, jerking harder in shock and another dart of pleasure over his crass words.

He chuckled, switching his attention to my other breast. "I'll take that as a no."

The heat grew down my chest, and I rocked my hips faster, not knowing if I should be ashamed of how his words hit me or how I wanted to reach the elusive edge that tickled just beyond my reach.

"But you've touched it, haven't you?"

"Parker, please."

"Tell me what it feels like."

"What?" I said on a panting breath.

"Tell me what your pussy feels like when you touch it."

I squeezed my eyes shut and focused on his hands, on his lips pressing wherever they could reach. I focused on the pleasure and told him because maybe he liked hearing it as much as I did.

"It's warm and wet. And so soft. Like silk."

His grip tightened on my hip, pulling me down harder to meet his chaotic thrusts.

"It's tight," I whimpered.

"Fuck, fuck," he grunted. "Just like I imagined."

I gasped.

"Oh yeah, Nova. I've imagined what your pussy would feel like. What it would taste like." I rocked harder and harder with each confession. "Have you ever touched a cock before?"

"No."

"It's hard but so fucking soft. The head is even softer and so fucking sensitive. I like to squeeze my dick tight and brush the tip on the upstroke. I like to swipe my thumb over the precum that leaks out. I like to imagine it's your tongue desperate to taste me as much as I am to taste you."

My nails dug into his shoulders, and his words drove me wild. It was too much, and I couldn't stop my body if I tried. I had no way of slowing it down. It came at me like a tsunami —you knew it was coming—impossible to miss, but unable to stop it and not knowing what you'd look like on the other side.

"Yeah, Nova. Fuck, yeah. Gonna come."

He used both hands on my hips, both of us bucking against each other. And when his mouth crashed down to my nipple, biting the hard tip through my shirt, I came. I exploded into another world and lost myself like a pebble in a raging ocean, at the mercy of the pleasure that consumed me. Everything blurred and only came back when Parker groaned, thrusting up. I forced my eyes open and watched his neck strain, his mouth part over each groan ripped from him only to sink into me. Each brush against me sent another aftershock of pleasure, and I never wanted to stop.

Finally, we slowed, both of us gasping for air and limp

from the onslaught. I collapsed my damp forehead to his and promised myself to remember this moment forever.

"Happy birthday, Nova."

"Thank you," I whispered just before leaning in for his kiss.

The kiss was just as languid as our muscles—lazy and slow. Before, we'd been releasing almost a year of tension, and now, we took our time to discover each other's mouths.

"I need to clean up," he said with one last soft peck.

I looked down to his pants, a wet spot blooming near the zipper. "Oh."

"Yeah, oh. These are my favorite jeans. I haven't come in my pants in a long time."

Something about it bubbled up, and I laughed.

"Sure. Laugh it up," he deadpanned.

And I did until he was laughing with me.

"Want to sleep in my bed tonight?" he asked, standing up.

"Yeah, that sounds like the perfect ending to my birthday."

"K. Let me go get cleaned up."

As soon as he disappeared into the bathroom, I ran to my room, giddy with the thought of laying in his bed *before* we fell asleep. Usually, he snuck into my room after the house was quiet, but what would it be like when we were both wide awake and already giving in to our pleasure? The possibilities had me floating around my room, looking for my sexiest tank top and shortest shorts.

At least until the front door slammed and our parents' voices reached down the hall, into my room, and ripped the night away. I heard muttering, and I just stood there frozen, unable to stop myself from playing the what-if game, imagining them having come home ten minutes earlier. What the hell were they doing home anyway?

My mom appeared in my doorway, pulling me out of my stupor.

"Happy birthday, Nova."

"Mom, what are you doing here?"

"The event was boring, and tomorrow's seminars were even less appealing than today's," she explained with an eye roll before going back to smiling. "Besides, I wanted to at least say goodnight to you on your birthday. I figured we could all go to a gallery or something and then dinner tomorrow. Maybe come back here for games. Just a family night."

"Family night," I repeated lamely.

"Yes," she said, clapping her hands. "It'll be great. But I'm beat tonight, so I'm off to get my beauty sleep and wake up refreshed for tomorrow."

I nodded slowly, still standing stupefied when she turned to walk away.

Coming to terms with my new night, I dropped the shorts and grabbed my sweatpants, heading to the bathroom to get ready for a night alone. I'd almost made it when I heard Parker's dad from his room.

"She wants to do a family day tomorrow," Brad said.

"A family day? With me?" Parker asked.

Brad chuckled. "Yeah. We had a talk this weekend, and it was good. Things have been a little tense, and she admitted she thought you and Nova could end up acting inappropriately. She thought she saw you two looking at each other a certain way."

Brad snorted like it was the most absurd thing, and I just wanted to run away and pretend I never heard anything. I wanted to delete this moment from my mind forever.

"I assured her that you look at Nova as a sister and that you'll take care of her like you would your own sister."

"Yeah," Parker said, sounding pained.

"Tomorrow will be good."

"Yeah. Good."

"Well, I'm off to bed. Those seminars were boring as hell and long. I need a glass of wine and some mindless TV."

"Night, Dad."

"Night, Park."

I darted into the bathroom before I could be spotted, leaning against the door, running over every word. I squeezed my eyes shut, hating all of it. Parker and I knew our attraction came with a wealth of issues. It was why we never bothered acknowledging them. It was pointless. But we had tonight, and although I started it with a promise of only wanting one night, somewhere between the wall and the orgasm, I realized I'd wanted so much more.

I forced myself to fall back into our routine, washing away any fantasy I'd foolishly concocted.

Parker's door was closed when I left the bathroom. It always was, and I shouldn't be bothered, but walking past it was harder this time. My covers clung to me like a twenty-pound blanket, and I struggled to relax when all I wanted to do was be in his room like we planned. All I wanted to do was be with my best friend and not worry about anyone else.

It took me a long time to fall asleep that night, going around and around with ways to make us work and always knowing we couldn't.

And just like every night, once everyone had fallen asleep, my door creaked open, and Parker's shadow crept toward my bed where he crawled in behind me, pulling my back to his chest. Unlike other nights, he pressed a soft apologetic kiss to my shoulder.

I held his hand tight and squeezed.

"I'm so sorry, Nova."

He didn't have to say what for. We both knew. So, I did what we always do.

I shoved it aside and didn't talk about it.

Why bother?

One night of giving in wouldn't change the fact that Parker Callahan was my stepbrother.

Not even the fact that I was starting to fall in love with him.

THIRTEEN

Parker

For four days, I did nothing but think about picking Nova up. I did my best to respect her wishes and wait to talk to her until I saw her today, but I had to force myself to put the phone down more than once. At one point, I'd even asked Oren to take my phone. He, of course, proceeded to send her selfies, which she at least reacted to but never wrote back.

The guys didn't bring up the situation but watched me like I was a bomb who could go off any minute. It wasn't far from the truth. From dawn until night, the thought of Nova being on tour with us after years of not talking and months of her refusing to see me twisted me tighter and tighter until I was sure I would snap. I vacillated between excitement and frustration, never really settling on one, the two mixed and mingled in some diabolical cocktail.

So, when I went to pick her up, standing outside her door, squeezing sweaty palms into fists, the last thing I expected was for a petite brunette with glaring brown eyes to be on the other side of the door.

"Hey, fuck boy," Rae greeted.

"Shit," I muttered.

"Oh, my god, Rae. Lay off," Nova called behind her.

Her flannel shirt fanned out behind her as she rounded the corner of the small entrance, baring her faded band T-shirt, stealing all the oxygen from my lungs.

You'll get at least a month to take her in. Don't stare like a drooling fool now.

She took the door from Rae's hands and pulled it open. Before I could squeeze past, Rae blocked me by pulling Nova in a hug. "If you need anything at all, call me."

"Thanks for helping me pack."

Rae smacked a kiss to Nova's cheek and faced me, walking right into my chest, forcing me back a few steps. Her glare held a fire so intense, I should have burned to ash right there.

"If you hurt her, I'll use every resource I have to make your life a living hell. And don't think I'll go the easy route and have you killed," she threatened with a laugh that kind of scared the shit out of me. "No, I'll make you endure every second of whatever I can come up with. And I can come up with a lot."

"Rae, I swear to all things holy," Nova scolded.

With a forced smile, Rae gently guided Nova back into the apartment and slowly closed the door, holding up a finger for just a moment. When Nova tried to open it back up, Rae held it closed and turned back to me like the she-devil she was.

"She likes you, and I don't know what the fuck you have going on with the succubus from New Year's Eve, but you better clear it up before even looking at her for more than ten seconds, or else I'll rip your eyeballs out with my bare hands and make you choke on them."

She held me right where she wanted me with the intensity of her narrowed glare, and I just stood there frozen like a statue—my jaw unhinged. I struggled to match the words she just said to the petite brunette in front of me.

"Jesus-fuck, you're violent."

"It's a gift." And with that, she let go of the handle and walked away like nothing had happened.

Nova stepped back, giving me room to pass inside. "Sorry about that."

"It's good. I guess I'm glad you have a friend to look out for you—albeit slightly terrifying."

She laughed and nodded, falling quiet. Her teeth worked her bottom lip, a sure sign of her nerves, and I didn't hate that I affected her, at least in some way.

"I wasn't expecting you to come."

"We signed a contract," I reminded her.

"I mean, I didn't expect you to be the one to pick me up. I figured they'd just send a car."

"Usually they do, but I offered to come with them to get you."

"Oh."

Another silence, and I shoved my hands in my pockets to keep from fidgeting. The lack of noise sat uncomfortably around us. Nova and I never did awkward or quiet. We had music playing or were singing or debating. I hated the way it squeezed in, making the small apartment even tighter.

"You ready to go?" I asked, needing to get out of the tiny hallway.

"Yeah. Let me just get my bags."

She turned and walked to the open area, leaving me to follow behind. The whole vibe of the apartment changed once I cleared the entryway. The walls were tall and white and open. She disappeared around a corner I assumed was her bedroom, and I took the time to look around for hints of Nova.

A sitting area in the corner with colorful throw pillows next to bookshelves and a TV, a small but modern kitchen, and what was probably the dining room, and the rest of the living room was covered in her art. The tall windows pouring light in from outside.

I studied her pictures on her shelves, taking in what I missed over the years.

A few more steps, and I noticed a nook behind her art and froze. "Holy shit."

"Yeah," she said, appearing just in time to take in my awe. "I like puzzles."

"I think that's an understatement." A low shelf covered the bottom of the wall, but the rest, all the way to the ceiling, was covered with finished puzzles. Like a gallery covering every inch of white space. It should have been hectic and chaotic, yet somehow, Nova made it work.

I kind of loved it.

"I mean, I like comic books, but I haven't plastered them over every inch of wall."

"Well, maybe you should."

I turned to find her studying me, studying the wall, two suitcases, and a backpack ready to go. "Want me to take one of those?"

"Sure. And can you grab that blanket?" She gestured to the one draped over the back of a chair. As soon as my hands grazed the material, I jerked back, tossing the blanket aside.

"Blech," I gagged, opening and closing my fists.

She watched me like I'd grown a second head until her pinched brows softened to a look of understanding and finally a laugh. "Still hate the feel of Sherpa?"

"Yes. That shit is the worst. It gets caught on my callouses, and just…" I shuddered, trying to put words to the texture. Almost like nails on a chalkboard. "It just feels wrong."

She snorted, and I mock glared when I walked past and snagged both suitcases. I walked out the door and turned just in time to get hit in the face with the blanket. On instinct, I reacted and started flailing to get it off me, only flailing harder when my hands rubbed the fabric.

Once I finally had it balled up and shoved aside on a suitcase, I found a hysterical Nova watching me. Both hands covered her mouth, and her eyes gleamed with unshed tears. Her shoulders shook, and I pursed my lips.

"Oh, sure. Laugh it up."

She wiped a stray tear and slapped her chest. "It was a blanket, not a box of spiders. If I would have known that would be your reaction—"

"You never would have done it?" I finished sarcastically.

"Oh, no. I would have done this so much sooner."

She started laughing again, and I forgot about the blanket. You could have thrown a thousand of those blankets on me, and as long as I got to see Nova laughing, I'd have endured it without complaint. I soaked her in and memorized every new line and freckle she earned from the sun.

When she realized I was staring, she collected herself, tucking a strand of hair behind her ear and looking to the floor. With a nod, she turned and locked the door behind her.

I led her to the car, and any playfulness we found in the hall vanished in the backseat. Instead, tension returned, increasing with each mile closer to the bus. Her silence worried me, and the way she kept chewing on the skin of her finger, her most anxious tell.

"You okay with this?" I asked.

She glanced at me before looking back out the window. "Yeah. It's just work."

It was so much more than work, and she knew that—we both knew it. I was just the only one willing to face it. Maybe without an escape, I could make her face it too. Just enough to clear the air and get us to stable ground.

"Listen, Nova." She stiffened, but I pressed on. "About Sonia—"

"It's not a big deal."

"It is."

"Nope," she declared, popping her p. "Besides, we're here."

"Dammit, Nova," I snapped, punching the locks before she could get out. I should have started this conversation before we even left the apartment.

Without looking up, she pressed the unlock just for me to hit it locked again. It was like two kids bickering in the backseat.

Finally, she slowly shifted to look at me, and if looks could burn, I'd be ash. This was going in the wrong direction. This was supposed to be an easier conversation playing off the laughter from earlier. Instead, we were diving headfirst into dangerous territory and sharp reactions.

"I will nut-punch you, Parker Callahan."

I met her glare with a challenging one of my own. We couldn't keep doing this. "Fine. Do what you need to do, but you'll at least listen before we get out."

Rolling her eyes, she fell back against the seat and crossed her arms, pouting.

"I didn't agree to Sonia being at New Year's Eve. Aspen dropped it on me."

"It doesn't matter, Parker."

"It does because you showed up there for a reason. You showed up to see me."

"And it was a mistake," she snapped. "I don't know what I was thinking because the reality is that a few phone conversations don't erase the past. It doesn't change who we are."

"I don't want it to be like this."

"How do you want it, Parker? For me to be your girlfriend?" She said it like it was the most absurd thing she'd ever heard.

"Nova…"

Her sigh carried more exhaustion than anyone should have to bear. "I'm just an old friend—your stepsister—here to work with you."

"That's not what I want," I growled through a clenched jaw.

"I think that's what it needs to be." She swallowed before facing me again, and instead of a hollow void from before, wariness shone through. "This life, Parker—being here—it's hard. You know I never considered being in the public eye, and when I tried...well, you know what happened."

It haunted me every damn day.

"I have my stipulations about public arrangements for a reason. I don't want to be out in the open without controlling the narrative, and that's all you are."

Her perfect freckles scrunched along her nose when she winced like the thought of remembering that flash of a moment hurt too much. Her eyes slid closed, and when they opened again, they were resolute, but nothing could hide the loss that echoed between us.

"I'm sorry, Parker," she whispered. "I can't do more."

And with that, she got out.

I was too stunned by the loss to stop her.

Why bother?

She was obviously gone long before I had a chance.

I had nothing left to do but enjoy the time we had and soak up every second.

I had to—it would be all I had left of her in the end.

FOURTEEN

Nova

THE BUS RUMBLED along the road, getting pummeled by the downpour outside.

I sat in the booth seat at the table, and Parker across from me. The rest of the guys lounged in the captain's chairs and couch, their instruments resting on their laps.

It was day three, and we had nothing.

In all fairness, the first day we stayed separate, as much as we could on a tour bus, Ash and Parker played a video game in the back, and I watched TV up front with Brogan and Oren. I allowed myself that first day to get settled—both physically and mentally. I still wasn't sure I was settled mentally. I'd pull the curtain of my bunk back and jolt a little at finding Parker coming out of the bathroom. So much like it'd been when we were teens.

However, with time, I accepted it.

I was on tour with Parker Callahan. I slept all of two feet from him with barely a curtain between us. Put that down on my list of last things I imagined ever happening.

"Oren, play that beat again," I asked.

I sat back on the seat, tapping my head on the wall behind me, sliding my eyes closed to listen. The sharp staccato of beats masked the rain. I hummed the possible guitar opening, and Parker picked it up almost instantly, strumming the sound I imagined. Brogan added rhythm, and Ash found the middle between guitars and drums.

It's good.

Peeking down at the notebook on the table, I found my moment and added the lyrics—at least the two lines we had.

Meeting Parker's gaze, I sang the first line. Then the second. When I reach the third, nothing came. I waited for Parker to pick up where I left off like we'd done so many times before. When I was stuck, he came in and vice versa. So far, I'd been the only one contributing.

Frustration bubbled up, and I glared with pursed lips. "Are you going to try, or are you just going to be a lump on a log?"

The music screeched to a halt, and Parker's lip curled into a scowl. "I *am* trying."

"Really? Because we've been at this for over an hour, and we have two lines that *I* came up with."

"Because it's your job."

"Well, we can't all be as good at doing our job as you are, Parker," I sneered.

His nostrils flared at my double meaning, and he looked on the verge of snapping. Instead of shouting like I half expected, he stared me down while he put his guitar aside and stood up. His chest heaved, and he looked down on me. I tipped my head back, meeting his intimidation with my own frustration.

The muscle in his jaw ticked, and I held my breath, waiting for him to say anything. Instead, he broke the stare first and stomped to the back of the bus, where he slammed the door behind him.

Oren's whistle brought me back to reality. I'd almost forgotten anyone else was there with us, it'd been so quiet.

"Well, while Parker pouts, I'm going to nap. I'm exhausted

from the show last night and slept like shit," Ash said, making a much less dramatic exit.

All the fight seeped out of me, and I rested my forehead in my hands and my elbows on the table. The two lines on the page mocked me. They weren't even that good, and I considered lighting them on fire just to release some tension.

Why was this so hard?

I almost laughed at the stupid question. Parker and I had a million issues between us, and it kept us from finding that sync we'd had as teens.

"Sorry, guys," I apologized. "I've never worked so closely with a band on writing lyrics. For the most part, I just sell them."

"Well, we do like to push people past their norm," Oren said.

"Remember when we made Aspen drink the worm tequila," Brogan recalled, laughing.

"Gross," I cringed.

"Add in everything else, and I think we all knew we'd hit some speed bumps." Oren shrugged before pushing his electric drum table aside. When he looked back up, something in his light blue eyes had me holding my breath.

"You know, I've wanted to apologize for a long time," he started.

"It's okay, Oren."

"It's not. You were part of us, and I don't know…I guess I never stopped to consider you wouldn't come with us. And when you turned it down, I got it, but I was too excited to think past myself."

"We all were."

A lump worked its way up my throat, and between my frustration with Parker, constantly being on edge, and Oren's rare sincerity, I almost choked on it.

Somehow, I managed to swallow it down. "Seriously. It's okay. It's over."

"We just never got a chance to apologize, and it kind of weighs on us," Brogan added.

I had so much bitterness that hid inside me, and it popped out when I least expected it. Before meeting Parker again, I would have said I'd dealt with my past and moved on. Now, I realized it lingered in the dark corners I refused to look into.

So, when Brogan's words held the slightest tinge of an edge to them, I easily recognized he had his own resentment. Because they hadn't just left me. I left them too.

"I'm sorry," I whispered.

And in typical guy fashion, he shrugged like it was nothing.

"Okay. Good. Got that out of the way," Oren said, clapping his hands together, back to his goofy self. "Now, you and Parker need to make up, and all will be fabulous. Let them lyrics flow."

"I think that's about half of Parker's issues," Brogan muttered.

"Oh, yeah," Oren said, wincing.

"What?" I asked. "What else does he have going on?"

Alarm bells rang, and my mind went rampant with the most improbable issues. Cancer? Dying? Wanted for a crime?

"His mom sent him an invite to his stepbrother's graduation. She gushed about how proud she was that he'd already been accepted into the top ivy league schools."

Brogan snorted. "Yeah, and when Parker reminded her he was on tour, she mentioned something about priorities and how his silly band could take a day off for family."

"Oh, shit," I drawled out. "When did he get that?"

"Last night, after the show."

"Fuck," I breathed, the anger from earlier draining out of me.

We'd struggled yesterday to get started but mostly worked our way through it. Today, it was like pulling teeth, but at least I understood why. Parker's mom was his Achilles heel. Shoving the paper aside, I pushed up from the booth and headed to the back of the bus.

I turned the knob, half expecting it to be locked. When it gave, I entered cautiously, not sure of my welcome. I popped my head in to find him stretched out on the u-shaped couch, his arm thrown over his eyes. I tapped on the door in case he didn't hear me, but he still didn't move. Deciding to take no answer as an okay to come in, I shut the door behind me and sat on the other side of the couch, facing him.

Well, shit. What now? I probably should have come in with a plan and contingencies, like if he laid on the couch and stayed silent, ignoring my presence. My heart dropped at yet another reminder of our reality. I could no longer come to him and get an open smile and easy conversation.

"I didn't realize your mom was still being a bitch," I started.

"Fucking Oren and his big mouth."

"I'm sorry. I know how stupid her words can be." I infused as much sincerity in my words, making sure any snarky comment waiting to pop out without notice stayed far away. I hated how that woman made him feel small and insignificant, and I'd hoped she'd had to eat her words as he rose to world-wide fame. It pissed me off that she hadn't.

"It's not a big deal."

"It is. It may be why you're struggling with writer's block."

"I'm sure it's part of it, but being able to understand that doesn't really change that I can't think of any words."

It might not, but I could approach him with a bit more empathy.

We both needed this to work. He needed a kickass album, and I needed the money, and adding our shit on top of his own shit wasn't helping.

"Listen, Parker," I started. When I stopped, he finally uncovered his face and pinned me under his ocean blue eyes that looked tired. It took actual effort to not fall to my knees beside him and run my fingers through his hair to soothe him—to comfort him like I always did.

But that wasn't my place anymore. My place was to do a job.

"If we're going to make this work, we need to be able to be around each other without bickering, and I know some of it comes from me," I admitted when he cocked a brow. "But it doesn't help when you keep bringing it up either. I just…don't want to talk about it."

The muscle in his jaw ticked, but he didn't fight me.

"So, let's just put it behind us and start fresh tomorrow. No more snarky comments and heavy history. A clean slate."

He raised a dubious brow, and I knew it was a tall order, but maybe if we both agreed to try, we'd at least have a fighting chance. I desperately needed an opportunity to bury these feelings, and if he kept cornering me to talk every day, I'd never get the chance to ignore them. They could sit in time out until I was done with my job, and then I'd face those demons. Just…not yet.

He looked ready to argue, and I pleaded with my best puppy dog eyes for him to agree.

Finally, with a heavy sigh, he muttered, "Fine."

"Thank you."

"So, what now? How do we make this work?"

"We're in Raleigh tomorrow, but you don't have a show until the next day, right?"

"Yeah, I think so. It all starts to blur together." He laughed, but exhaustion kept it from sounding anything but tired.

"Good. I have ideas."

FIFTEEN

Parker

When Nova said she had ideas, a museum was the very last place I expected.

She had me grab a hat and aviators when we left but passed me a pair of thick rim glasses and an oddly bushy stick-on mustache once we got there. Frankly, I didn't know how anyone would even notice me when she stood beside me. All eyes would be on her with her effortless style. Those billowy pants and denim jacket looked unsuspecting until she turned, and you got the full effect of her fitted cropped tank top. Maybe two inches of skin showed, but I couldn't focus on anything other than how much I wanted to figure out if she was as soft as I remembered.

"So, how is this supposed to help?" I asked, looking up at the white panels of the building.

"It's an art museum," she responded, like it answered all my questions. When I still gave her a blank look, she explained. "Art inspires art."

"I mean, I'll give it a try." My hope waned a little. When she said she'd had plans, I imagined something more than looking at paintings.

"So, part of our problem is that we can't quite find our

sync. So, we're going to play a game. We're going to observe the art, but while we're looking on, we're going to come up with our own story for it. One of us will start, and we'll have to alternate back and forth until we come up with something fabulous and absurd."

"Oooookay."

"Trust me." She turned to pay the lady, and I ducked my head low, but apparently, the mustache worked because the attendant didn't blink twice.

Thankfully, we came earlier in the day, ignoring Aspen's disapproval over the phone when Nova informed her of her plan. Add in it was a weekday, and other than maybe a few school field trips, it was pretty slow. Thank goodness.

"So, I take it you don't do many museums in your spare time?" she asked while we wove our way around the statues on pedestals.

I scoffed at the words, *spare time*. "Not that I have much, but a museum isn't the top of my list."

"You never did like art museums."

"The only paintings I truly enjoyed were yours."

"Ours," she corrected.

"Yeah, ours." I smiled at her profile, warmth spreading through my chest when she mentioned how it had been our art. Even though my contribution had been merely a dot. "But we do actually hit up a few museums when we can. I like the natural history ones because of all the dinosaur bones."

"Like a little kid."

"Hey, they're pretty cool."

"What else did you do?"

Her question was innocent enough, but it halted the growing heat with a cold bucket of reality. We didn't know each other anymore. We missed out on so much.

"We went on a lot of hikes. I think I've hiked almost all of Southern California."

"Is that where you live?"

"Sometimes. I have a house there I share with Ash."

"And the tiny mansion in New York."

"Yeah, that one, too. Also, the one—"

"Seriously," she cut me off with a shocked cry.

I laughed at her dropped jaw. "I'm kidding. I just wanted to see your reaction."

She shoved me but smiled. "What else did you do?"

"We went to a lot of concerts. That was us studying our art. From Lady Gaga and Katy Perry to Foo Fighters to Luke Bryan."

"Wow, you don't like country."

"I do not," I confirmed. "But he was entertaining. We learned a lot of stage presence at those concerts."

"That's awesome."

"It was. We have a lifetime of stories, which is cool. But things get busy, and concerts are harder to get to. Hobbies are harder to keep up with. It's great, but you have to adapt."

"Do you love it?"

I took a deep breath, thinking over it all. "Yeah, I do. Everything has downsides, and any job will have hard days. But I still love it."

"Good."

"What about you?"

"What about me?"

"Well, you're basically crushing the Instagram game, writing music for huge bands, and I'm assuming you do art, based on your pictures online. Or are you just painting and burning them?"

"You know, Picasso painted over some of his own paintings. Maybe I just do that?"

"Do you?" he asked, brows raised.

"Nah. But it'd be a cool find if I became famous later."

"So, what do you do with all that art?"

"I sell some of it. Just not consistently enough to count on it as income."

"Ahhh, the life of an artist."

"'Tis glamorous," she laughed. "I'm working on it, though. I kind of just started a bunch of hobbies. Hiking was a great way to escape and just have it be quiet, and I saw such amazing views that I wanted to capture forever. So, I picked up photography and started posting them. I didn't expect it to be what it is."

"Yeah, a million followers is a hell of a platform."

"And apparently, I lived under a rock, not quite realizing I could monetize it until Rae lost her shit on me."

"So, what's the plan?" I asked. Nova always made her way outside of the box in her own style. She always had a quiet power about her that emanated success. She just never shouted about it.

"I recently hired someone much smarter than me to help me make this into something long-term. Hence the tour. Apparently, brands want a face with the promotions. A few big sponsors recently pulled out on me."

"So, they want you to start showing your face?"

"Pretty much. And I guess I just haven't because …" I watched her struggle over the words like she wasn't quite sure herself. "I guess I never pictured it being that way, and I'm too stuck in my own idea of how it should be."

"What?" I mock gasped. "I'm shocked."

"Oh, fuck you," she said, bumping her shoulder into mine.

"So? Are you going to show your face?"

"I don't know yet. But I am trying to merge the three moneymakers into one. Sell my art on my platform. Keep traveling and posting. I'm focusing on that first."

"Sounds like a plan."

"Speaking of a plan, let's get started."

We browsed around from piece to piece. She started most of the stories, but I quickly caught on. At one point, she even picked a strong midwestern accent that had me choking back laughter. A very hip-looking couple gave us an alarmed side-eye which caused her to break character and laugh.

"I think they're on to us," I whispered.

"Nah, I bet they're just eavesdropping to get any secret details."

"I'm sure," I deadpanned.

When we ran into them again around one of the many freestanding walls, her voice grew louder. I fought not to laugh and focused on playing along, but the nasally voice with the absurd facts she made up had me on the edge of cracking up. Honestly, I could have done this all day. The easy comradery and play banter flowed without anything inhibiting it. Being goofy came natural together, and right then, we needed to find natural.

"My friend, Tina, made this one," she said loudly, pointing at the very clearly ancient Greek statue of a naked man holding a bat.

I almost jumped out of my skin at the sharp decibel, unsure of when this turned into shouting. I slowly turned my head to look at her with wide, concerned eyes. She gave an almost nod to the couple closing in and winked.

"You know. Tina," she continued. "She's the one with seven kids and two husbands. She uses one house to be a wife and another one to be an artist."

Fuck, it. I guessed we were doing this. It was then I remembered how willing I'd been to follow Nova where she led me—even if it was a little crazy.

"Ohhh, that Tina," I agreed just as loud as her.

The couple inched closer. "She said this was a representation of *Ope*. You know what all us Midwesterners say when they do something on accident."

"That makes sense. The way he's leaned back." I nodded before taking a turn at our act and faced another painting, using a matching accent. "You know Hank painted this one last week. Can't believe he did it while sleepwalking."

She snorted but held it together. "You know, Hank. He's famous for that. He even painted a room in the White House."

We moved from painting to painting, rounding walls, coming up with more outrageous stories than the last. We lost our hip couple but picked up a few more along the way. However, when we neared the front, a guard pinned us with a glare before making purposeful strides in our direction.

Switching back to a casual whisper, like we were the picture of innocence, we speed-walked our way through the various structures, trying to lose the guard. We rounded a corner, and I saw a private alcove to lay low in. Not thinking about it, I linked my hand with hers, electricity and want reverberating through me at the contact when my calloused fingers grazed her smooth skin. Apparently, I caught her off guard because when I tugged her with me, she stumbled, and I barely turned around to catch her.

Right. Against. My chest.

Her palms landed against me, flexing into the material. I looked down at her mass of red hair and forced myself to remain still while her eyes traveled up my chest, my neck, and finally landed on my lips. All I wanted to do was flip us around, pin her to this wall, and take her up on the offer coloring her eyes. I almost did when her tongue peeked out to slide across her lips. But then her gaze met mine, and with a blink, she masked the fire and backed away.

I reluctantly let go of the grip I had on her hips and cleared my throat. "Sorry, I found a hiding place."

"Good call."

Taking a deep breath, I looked around the wall just to keep from looking at her. "I think the coast is clear."

"We should probably get going. We don't want to push our luck."

"Yeah," I agreed. "Thanks for this. It was fun, but also it

was good to look at the art and analyze the emotions with our stories."

"Good. I had no idea if it would work. I'm totally winging it."

I tossed my head back and laughed. Nova always looked so unassuming but held more depth and ability than almost anyone I knew.

I loved it.

If I was honest, I loved a lot about her.

Even after all these years.

Always.

SIXTEEN

Parker

Two days later, and we were back on the road again. We'd managed to write a whole verse and chorus. It wasn't much, but mainly because time held us back over our inability to create together.

It wasn't great, but it was a move in the right direction.

Which was why, when Nova had me pick a movie I'd never seen and demanded time at the back of the bus, I didn't question it. I grabbed popcorn and shoved down all the crazy, hopeful ideas that said she was inviting me back there to spend time alone together—to rekindle what we lost.

In a way, she was. Just not the love and caring I wanted. Instead, she was trying to rekindle our writing mojo. But thirty minutes in and it kind of felt like the same thing, because if we were honest, our writing mojo came from a lot of our emotional connection, and it was that emotional connection that had us pushing the limits of right and wrong.

"Parker," she cried just before a popcorn kernel hit my head. "You have to take this seriously."

I wiped the tears from my eyes and tried to take deep, calming breaths to get myself under control.

"I'm trying, but your British accent is horrible."

"It's the best," she argued, throwing another popcorn kernel my way. This time I caught it with my mouth.

Her idea had us watching a movie neither of us had watched before on mute while we made up our own script for them. It took a while to get going, but once we did, I fed off her as much as she fed off me. Until she broke out the accent, and I died laughing.

She glared with pursed lips, and the movie was forgotten. I forced myself to keep my eyes on the screen and not her, but now that I'd taken her in, there was no looking away. Her red hair defied gravity in the way it balanced on her head in a mass of tangles. She lay stretched out on one side of the U-shaped couch, her long legs bare beneath gray sweat shorts. All that lean muscle on full display. Creamy skin with almost imperceptible freckles that you had to know where to look to see them. I'd made it a point to map each and every one when we were teens.

My phone buzzed beside me, and I begrudgingly pulled my gaze away from her to find a message from Sonia.

Sonia: I'm in Charlotte. Do you want to have dinner when you get here? It would be good promo for your show tonight.

And leave Nova? I didn't think so.

As if on cue, Aspen's voice cut through my thoughts from years of always drilling me. *You should do it for the job. Sales, sales, sales and promo, promo, promo.* But right now, the job didn't matter. Even sitting here trying to build a rapport to write music with Nova didn't matter. It was the relaxing and just… being that mattered. I eyed Nova and smiled because maybe having her around was what it took to remind me that I could still be me—just me—and that was okay.

Me: Not this time. Thanks for the offer.
Sonia: You sure? Does Aspen agree?

Me: She's not the one that matters. I do.

With that, I pushed my phone aside, irritated that these two women seemed like they were conspiring to corner me. It pissed me off.

"Who's that?" Nova asked.

"No one important." I decided to be vague over lying because I didn't want to say Sonia's name when we were having a good time.

"Not your mom?" she asked.

I flinched at the mention of my mom. "Why would you say that?"

"You just usually get that line between your brows when you hear from her. It's grown deeper over the years."

"I'll be sure to botox it," I joked.

She laughed but quickly sobered. "Does she still message you a lot?"

"Not really. Just when she wants to brag about her other family."

"Do they come to your shows at all?"

"God, no," I laughed. "Although, I did leave some tickets for my younger stepbrother, but they were never claimed. He said Mom wouldn't let him come."

"What a bitch," she hissed.

"That about sums it up."

"So, if it wasn't your mom, who else puts that line there?"

I quickly weighed the pros and cons of lying, and the cons outweighed the two-second reprieve it'd buy me. So, with a deep breath, I answered honestly. "Sonia."

"Oh," she said, looking deep into the bucket of popcorn like it held the answers to life. "What did she want?"

"Asked me to go to dinner."

"Are you going?"

"No. I'm doing this with you."

"Yeah, but I'm sure Aspen would want you to go. You know, for promotions."

She hadn't looked up from the popcorn, but she held her body tight like my answer mattered more than just an affirmation. Because how many times had I hurt her when I chose the job over her or when I thought it wasn't a big deal when I chose my job over her.

"I'm sure Aspen would want me to go, but I'm not going to." Finally, she looked up, her eyes softening when they met mine. "I'm exactly where I want to be—here with you."

I forced myself to stay quiet after that when all I wanted to do was tell her how much she meant to me and how important she was, but my words had been rendered useless by previous actions. So, I let my decision do the talking for me. I let it sink in.

She studied my face until finally, the smallest of smiles tipped her lips. "Good."

"Besides, I'd hate to miss another awesome accent."

"Oh, shut up," she scoffed, rolling her eyes.

"I miss having fun with you," I admitted.

She waved it off. "You have the guys to keep you entertained."

"True, but they're not quite you."

"Well, there's also all the women you've been with over the years. Didn't seem to miss much then," she muttered.

She winced as soon as the words left her mouth, and I let it slide. We were doing a lot better about starting fresh, but we weren't great. Too much lingered between us. Too much tension and resentment. And sometimes, if I looked close enough—too much love to be hidden. Instead, it got masked by the random snarky slipups we both made. Thankfully, we came to the unspoken agreement to let those slide. But they were still there as a reminder that what we were doing was nothing more than a veneer. Even so, I'd take it.

"What's the tattoo on your leg?" I asked, changing the subject.

She looked down to where her shorts rose up to expose close to her hip before tugging them back down.

"Oh, come on. You can't not tell me," I cajoled.

She bit her lip and studied me before finally releasing it with a sigh. I was grateful for the small space between us because I wasn't sure I'd be able to stop myself from soothing the rosy, plump flesh.

"Fine," she huffed, hiking her shorts back up. "It's a DNA breaking up into music notes."

I sat upright and hunched over, resting my elbows on my knees to get as close as possible while still keeping space. Fuck, her skin was tempting. The pale flesh completely unblemished beyond a few faint freckles and the elegant DNA strand with flowers woven throughout.

"Are those…" I squinted, laughing when I saw it. "Puzzle pieces?"

"I said I love puzzles, okay?" she defended.

"I love it. It's totally you. Now show me some more."

"Well, you have to show me some, too. Fair is fair."

"Done." With that, I whipped my sweatshirt over my head, leaving me in just a tank. I couldn't help but puff my chest up when her jaw dropped a little taking me in. I let her look her fill, knowing that as soon as I called her out, she'd stop, and I wanted to bask in her awe. Moving slowly to not startle her, I turned my arm to the back and pointed at the guitar pick with our band initials inside. "Your turn."

She showed me a minimalist mountain range behind her elbow, and I showed her my compass.

She showed me her Viking symbol on the other elbow, and I showed her the lotus blended into the compass.

She showed me the outline of the world map on her ankle, and I showed her mine adorning the top of my feet.

Through it all, we kept it innocent and light. Telling stories about how we got each one and the regrets of the others. While mine were an ever-growing collage on my arms, hers were sporadic, and like little hidden treasures I wanted to find.

"What was your first one?" I asked.

She narrowed her eyes and chewed her cheek, considering something. With a small shrug almost to herself, she turned her back to me and started pulling up her shirt.

Oh fuck.

I could keep my space from an ankle and an elbow, but the bare expanse of her back had me tipping over the edge, and I had to clench my fists to keep from smoothing both palms up her back and into her hair. Once the shirt reached her shoulders, she clutched it tight to her chest and looked over her shoulder. I didn't know where I wanted to look first. Her back? Her tattoo? Or her stunning profile?

"It's one of my favorite sayings," she explained, pulling my attention to the tattoo.

The fine script was impossible to read, so I fell to my knees and inched closer. A clean line drawing of a phoenix sat between her shoulder blades, one of the lines of its tail extended down her into sharp cursive.

I am the storm.

If Nova could be put into a tattoo, this was it. This was her. It was perfect.

And I couldn't not feel it on her.

Moving slowly, knowing I should pull back, but unable to stop, I reached for her. Her whole back tensed, but she didn't pull back when my fingertip just grazed the tip of the bird. I followed the gentle swirls and down the tail. With each pass—each second—I connected with her, her breathing picked up. My lungs worked overtime, too, struggling to match my racing heart.

I stroked down the letters, feeling each dainty ridge of her spine, wondering how long I could drag this out. Wondering how far I could take this. When I reached the base, I held my finger there just above the edge of her shorts and soothed back and forth. With each pass, I added pressure and stretched a little further.

"Parker," she whispered.

I added my other fingers, pushing up and in, centimeters from pressing my palm to her skin.

Then the door opened, and the guys piled in.

I jerked back to the couch, and Nova slammed her shirt back down. Oren blocked the door and looked over his shoulder at the other guys, missing the situation he just walked in on.

"We want to watch the movie, too. I love Jennifer Aniston," he proclaimed.

They stumbled in and made themselves comfortable on the couch, completely ruining the moment. I don't know what would have happened in that moment, but I felt the shift. I felt it in the way she kept watching me out of the corner of her eye, almost like she saw me differently and needed to study me.

Something shifted, and I planned to stick my foot in the door and burst it open.

SEVENTEEN

Nova

"What if we played this?"

Ash braced his feet under his captain's chair and rested his fingers along the neck of the bass, strumming the same chords we'd played so many times I'd lost track.

"*The wind erodes, exposing fissures in this rock.*"

I leaned forward, holding my breath, hoping that this time the words would come. He played the chord again with no words, and still, I waited. Parker looked just as on edge as me from his place in the other captain's chair next to Ash. We just needed a break. One small tip over the edge, and I knew we'd get it.

Statistically, after so many tries, we were bound to get something. Right?

"*And…*"

Come on. Come on.

Another chord, his brows furrowed in concentration like he could see the words but not make them out.

"And to be honest, right now, I'd rather be coming in my sock," Oren screeched, belting his own lyrics from his spot on the floor.

"Bro," Brogan grumbled, stretching his long legs out to kick Oren's thigh.

"Fuuuuck." Parker banged his head back against the seat.

"Like a frock or a dock or a cock," Oren kept going. "Or anything else that rhymes with rock."

"Fucking stop," Brogan demanded, kicking him harder.

When Oren balled up and latched on to his foot, Brogan sat his guitar to the side, and I had to uncurl from my position on the long couch to stop the expensive equipment from tumbling to the floor.

It'd been almost a month on the bus together—minus a few nights when I flew home to see the girls while the guys did publicity.

In that time, despite the odds, we fell into a routine. I continued to come up with ideas to help us feed off each other. It helped, but only so much. We built a foundation of friendship, but it only served as a cover, loosely built over the fragile tension and lust we tried to ignore. It simmered like magma under the earth's surface, waiting to erupt at any moment. Just like when he stroked my tattoo, we continued to find ourselves in situations that put pressure on my determination to hold off.

Anytime we got too close, I just managed to pull back and direct us toward the job.

Which was going pretty bad. In this time, we'd written all of two songs, and I didn't even love them. Maybe the tension lingered a bit too much to find the natural rhythm we used to have. Whatever it was, I didn't like it because the bottom line was that this was my job and my chance to build my businesses into one.

"How long have we been working on this song?" Ash groaned.

"Just today or including last week?" Parker asked.

"Three hours and thirty-seven minutes today," I answered. "At least four-hundred-and-ninety-nine last week."

"Sounds about right." Oren nodded, getting up off the floor. "You know what we need?" he asked, turning to the iPad on the wall.

We watched him expectantly, all muttering different variations of doubt when he turned the main lights off and left the accessory lights along the ceiling's edge on. Before the music even started, Oren's hips rocked side to side, only increasing our groans, tossing scraps of paper from our failed writing attempts at him.

It didn't faze him. When Billie Eilish came over the speakers, he danced to the kitchen, digging in the cabinet to come out with a bottle of tequila.

"Oh, no," I objected before he could get glasses.

"Oh, yes," he responded with a smile. "It's time to dance this funk out and drink tequila. We're bound to say something poetic with tequila."

"I don't think I've ever said anything poetic with tequila."

"Come on, Supernova," he coaxed, dancing toward the group.

I looked around, and the guys were already accepting their shots. I looked to Parker to gauge his reaction about stopping writing but was met with an amused smile and shrug before he downed the shot.

"At this point, I'm willing to try anything," he explained.

Three weeks and two mediocre songs sat next to me in my notebook. In less than a month, we needed to have at least five, and it wasn't looking good at this rate. Shaking my head, I agreed with Parker. I was willing to try anything, and while our adventures were helping, they weren't helping fast enough. "Fuck it," I muttered, taking the glass from Oren and shooting the liquor back. It burned down my throat, and I barely felt it settle in my stomach before I held my glass out for another.

"That's my girl," Oren crowed, filling my glass.

This time, when I looked over, Parker was the one assessing me, and I copied his shrug. "Why the fuck not."

The liquor hit my veins, and I rolled my neck to the beat, loosening my tense muscles. The chords sank into my muscles, easing them more. I closed my eyes and moved my shoulders first, working down to my hips, limited by my position on the couch.

Next thing I knew, hands wrapped around mine, jerking me up into Oren's arms. He narrowed his eyes in a sultry stare, pouting his lips, and held me as he swayed our hips to the music blasting through the speakers.

Laughing, I wrapped my arms around his neck and gave in to the rhythm. We all danced around each other, shouting lyrics, and letting loose. After those two shots, I decided to stick with water, but the rest of the guys finished off the bottle. More than once, Parker and I found each other and danced, but the guys around us helped keep me from staying too long. Not that it mattered because each time my eyes met his, each time his hands held mine to twirl me around, another crack formed in my resolve.

"Ooooo," Oren shouted between songs. "You know what we should play?"

"Oh, shit," Parker muttered. "The last time Oren said that sentence, I ended up streaking down a hotel corridor with just a hand towel."

"Hey, that was your fault for sucking at strip poker," Oren defended.

"No," I gasped.

"Yup."

I looked him up and down, imagining Parker's long, hard body running down the hallway, not at all covered by a towel. I kind of couldn't wait for Oren's idea, keeping my fingers crossed for strip poker.

"Spin the bottle," he cried.

"Uhhhh," Brogan interjected, looking dubious. "There's a lot of guys here, bro."

"Psshh, we're all friends. It's not like we have to make out.

We just have this empty bottle of tequila, and what else should we do with it?"

"Throw it away?" Ash suggested.

"Nah," I cut in. "I am one-hundred-percent down with this idea."

"I fucking bet," Parker muttered.

"Okay, you big babies. We'll do a truth or kiss version of spin the bottle," Oren amended.

"What the hell is that?" Brogan asked.

"I don't know. I just made it up. Let's figure it out together. Come, come," Oren said, clapping his hands. "Let's gather around."

I plopped down in my seat so fast, almost bouncing in excitement to get going. For some reason, I saw absolutely no downside to kissing every guy here. I'd just blame it on the tequila.

"I'll go first." Oren spun the bottle, and I looked up expectantly when it landed on me. "Okay, Nova. Truth or kiss?"

"Who do I kiss?" I asked.

Instead of answering, he waggled his brows.

I snorted. "Truth."

"Ugh. Fine. Okay. Soft or hard…tacos."

"Hard," I shouted like I won a prize or something. I took my turn and spun the bottle, landing on Brogan. "Truth or kiss, Brogan?"

"Definitely kiss."

The guys cheered with ooooohhs, and I pretended to primp my messy hair.

Oren quickly cut the cheers down with his drumsticks on the table. "Order! Order at the table! Brogan has chosen kiss, so Nova gets to choose who he kisses."

"Wait, what?" he screeched.

"Yes," I shouted.

"You have to answer the truth or kiss whoever Nova

chooses. If she didn't want to answer the truth, I would have made her kiss me."

"C'mon, Nova," Brogan pleaded dramatically with a pouty lip poking through his beard.

"Oh, no, no, no. You can answer truth or kiss Oren."

"Oh, fuck no."

And the guys began shouting again while I clapped my hands in joy.

"Truth," Brogan grumbled.

I narrowed my eyes, giving him my most threatening stare. "Did you fuck Amber on my bed that one night when we were all in the living room after the Barney's concert?"

He gave me his own stare back. "No."

"Oh, thank god, I still have those sheets," I sighed.

"She sucked my cock, and I ate her pussy, and man, was she wet and messy." Brogan smiled, cutting off my joy.

"Fucking gross," I shouted. The guys gave him high-fives, and I made a note to burn those sheets when I got home.

Brogan spun the bottle, and it landed on Oren again. He answered truth, turning down Brogan's offer to kiss his bare feet.

"I'm into a lot of weird things, but feet are a hard pass."

The next spin landed on Ash.

"Truth or kiss Parker," Oren declared, rubbing his hands together. I looked just in time to catch Parker's cringe.

"Truth," Ash answered.

"Who do you get all bent out of shape over every November?"

Only a slight moment of hesitation. There and then gone in the blink of an eye. The next thing I knew, Ash stood from the captain's chair, gesturing for Parker to stand too. "All right, bro. Let's not make a thing of it. Just pucker up and feel grateful you got a kiss from the great Ash."

"Wait, what?" Parker shouted. "Don't I get a say?"

"'Fraid not," Oren said, not sounding the least remorseful. "You joined the game."

"I didn't know the rules."

"Come on, Parker. Don't be a baby," I taunted.

He directed his glare at me, and I rested my elbows on my knees and my chin on my hands like a kid desperate to tear through her Halloween candy.

He narrowed his eyes more. "I'll get you back."

"Bring it on," I challenged. "But first, pucker up. And no pecking. We're not in middle school."

"Come the fuck on," Ash grumbled.

Brogan started to chant "kiss," and Oren and I joined in. When they stepped close, I stopped—I didn't have any air left in my lungs to say words. I waited on the edge of my seat as they inched closer.

As soon as their lips touched, they jerked apart. Oren and Brogan cheered, and I boo'd my disappointment. They may as well have been in middle school. As soon as they pulled away, both of them wiped their mouths with the backs of their hands.

"Pussies," Brogan called.

"That wasn't so bad," I said, nudging Parker's toe with mine.

He glared but couldn't hold it when I made exaggerated kissing noises. His lips twitched into a smile that stole my breath. More and more, everything he did stole my breath. It was an odd mix of laughing and joking with unexpected flashes of heat and so, so much more.

Ash spun next, getting Brogan. I should have known I was in trouble when he looked to Parker and then me, his lips twisting into this devil smile.

"What's your favorite ice cream?" he asked Brogan. "Or kiss Nova."

"I'll never fucking tell," Brogan laughed, standing from his spot to come to me.

Parker's eyes flicked from me to Brogan and back again. Before I could get a read on them, Brogan grabbed my hand and jerked me upright into his arms. He held me close, looking down at my mouth. I shivered when his hand slid up my back, pressing me closer. Not really because of Brogan's touch, but because the thought of Parker watching me be touched sparked a corner of my fantasies I only visited at night.

I tried to look to Parker to see his reaction. Brogan's intensity changed the playful mood. Not enough to stop because along with those serious undertones came a ripple of excitement. Brogan caught me trying to look away, and in the next instant, his large hand delved into my hair, making a tight enough fist to pull my attention to him and tip my head back.

"Look at me," he ordered in a deeper voice than I'd ever heard him use.

The gravel tone and sting in my scalp sent the first wave of reality through me. These weren't teenage boys anymore, despite how much they acted like kids. No, they were mature men who probably had women at the ready to let them explore whatever they wanted. I couldn't help but wonder what Brogan had explored and found he liked.

I knew I had explored and found a whole new world as I grew up. Just not with anyone else. I explored my sexuality through the internet and research.

It made me wonder what Parker had discovered about himself.

Brogan inhaled deeply, brushing his nose along mine, and I struggled to control my breathing, anticipating and waiting for his kiss.

But in the end—they may have been men with experience —but they were still the same guys I knew.

Brogan pressed his lips to mine, and I had less than two seconds to feel the rough scruff of his beard before his free hand pinched at my ribs, making me jerk back and squirm to get free, shouting for help.

When he finally let me go, I plopped back and crossed my arms. "Traitors," I called, glaring at each of the guys who were wiping tears from their eyes.

Brogan spun the bottle and set Oren up to be the one I kissed. He stood, bowing like a regal prince before standing me up and dipping me back with flair.

"My lady," he murmured.

"Kiss me, my prince," I demanded breathlessly, laughing, my hair brushing the floor.

"As you wish."

I puckered up and immediately screamed when his tongue slid along my cheek.

"Oren, that's disgusting."

He set me upright with a shrug and an unrepentant smile. "I've never had any complaints."

When he spun the bottle, it landed on Ash.

Oren rolled his eyes. "All right, I'll take pity on you and challenge you to kiss Nova. Besides, we know you'll never admit the truth if your penis is a micro-penis or an extra micro-penis."

Ash flipped him off, and for the first time all night, when I looked to Parker, he didn't meet my stare with a lighthearted wink and smile. There was trepidation and maybe something else—something heated.

Ash stood, uncurling his body from the captain's chair. He watched me, cocking his head to the side like a lion studying his prey before crooking his finger for me to stand.

Other than the music playing in the background, the bus hummed quietly down the highway, everyone else falling silent. With each kiss, the guys had cheered, but not now.

My eyes flicked to Parker, and my heart kicked harder in my chest. He lounged, legs spread, body leaned back without a care in the world—except for the way his fingers almost turned white with the way they dug into the leather of the chair.

Needing to lighten the mood to ease my nerves, I popped up and smiled. "All right, Ash. Lay one on me. And just an FYI, I kind of dug the way Oren dipped me, but maybe leave out the face lick." With a wink, I closed my eyes and puckered up like a kid in a movie.

"What can I say? I got a good dip," Oren joked, but it wasn't enough to loosen the tension of corkscrews twisting down my spine.

Especially when the next thing I knew, heat covered the front of my body and a large palm pressed against the small of my back under my shirt. My eyes shot open, and I was met with Ash's sharp jaw covered in a light smattering of black stubble so different from Parker's lighter coloring. His tongue slicked out along his bottom lip, and I wanted to look for Parker for…reassurance, maybe? That maybe the flash of heat I saw matched the embers burning brighter inside me.

I knew the guys watched me. I knew Parker watched me, and the thought of it had other emotions creeping out to mix with my nerves.

Excitement. Confidence. A hint of resentment and revenge.

Just over a month ago, I pictured I'd be like this in Parker's arms, waiting for this kiss. Instead, he'd locked lips with Sonia, and maybe, just maybe, I wanted to get back at him.

So, with a slight tremor, I rested my hands on Ash's hips. "You gonna kiss me or tell us about your penis."

His mouth quirked, and he huffed a laugh. "I'd happily show you my penis if you'd like."

I pretended to think on it before scrunching my nose. "I'm good."

He shook his head, his smile growing.

He leaned down, forcing my back to arch over his hand as his other hand came up to brush my hair off my neck, only so he could make a patch to breathe me in. "This is killing him," he whispered so only I could hear.

My eyes searched for Parker, only catching a glimpse of his tight jaw before Ash filled my view again.

"Let's make it fun, shall we."

"I thought we were already having fun," I responded breathlessly.

He gave me a stare that said I knew better and whipped me around until my back faced Parker. "Sit on his lap," Ash ordered.

My eyes widened. "What?"

"I said. Sit. On Parker's. Lap."

"Why?"

"So, I can kiss you."

"Oh, hell yes," Brogan mumbled from his spot.

"I-I don't—"

"Do you have a problem with that, Parker?"

I jerked around to watch his reaction over my shoulder. His heavy-lidded eyes met mine, and he slowly shook his head. His fingers eased from their death grip on the chair and slid around my hips, tugging me back until I had nowhere else to go.

My body sparked to life. If I thought the casual touches here and there over the last few weeks had sent me into a frenzy, it was nothing compared to the fire spreading its way through my veins. His long fingers rested in the hollow just under the ridge of my hips, and I gasped when I encountered the hard length under me.

"It's a normal thing around you," he murmured in my ear.

More heat swirled up from my core, and my nervous excitement grew. Each movement and breath against my sensitive skin hit me like gasoline until I was sure the fire would be a raging inferno, burning us all.

Ash moved between Parker's spread legs and leaned down,

looking to Parker first and apparently finding approval before focusing his attention on me.

His palm slid behind my neck, holding me in place before finally kissing me. It started slow—teasing—a sharp nip of his teeth and a soft flick to soothe the pinch. His hand landed on my waist, and I gasped, giving him the opportunity to dip his tongue inside my mouth.

Parker's hands gripped tighter, and I sucked in a breath, involuntarily grinding into his lap, loving the groan that vibrated against my back.

Despite Ash being the one whose mouth claimed mine, my focus centered on the way Parker's quick puffs of air heated my neck. On the way his chest rose and fell over his thudding heartbeat that matched my own. All my attention remained on every flinch and adjustment he made with my body pressed to his.

Ash finally pulled back with one last nip to my lips. My eyes struggled to slide open, not wanting to come out of the haze. I searched the depths of his dark eyes, trying to figure out what this was all about.

"Put the poor guy out of his misery and kiss him," he murmured before standing.

I struggled to make sense of his words until he reached back for the bottle and specifically turned it to face me. "Kiss Parker or tell us your filthiest fantasy you masturbate to."

"Oh, shit," Oren exclaimed. "I'm not seeing a downside."

Heat swelled like a living thing inside me, and Parker's hard cock pressed against my ass. Part of me wanted to fuck with them all and come up with something insane to get off to. Another part of me considered saying fuck it and going to bed. But the bigger part of me, the teen girl who wanted Parker—who wanted Parker without hiding it, the woman who'd done nothing but fantasize about him for years—that part didn't give a shit about anything else but feeling Parker's lips on mine.

At least, until I faced Parker, and for the first time all night, I didn't love the guys' eyes on me. I gravitated to his heavy-lidded gaze. I stood between his parted knees and even reached down to stroke the light scruff along his jaw. But when I tried to move my body into position to kiss him, I couldn't. After all this time, I couldn't imagine kissing him with everyone watching.

Kissing the other guys had been funny and joking. Kissing Parker was anything but light and playful.

I pulled my hand away, closing my eyes when his jaw flexed in frustration, wanting to block out the flash of hurt and disbelief.

"Seriously?" he asked.

The step back away from him physically hurt, but it was nothing compared to when he stood and towered over me until his will forced my eyes open. His glare flamed a hot blue, and I hated it.

"You'll make out with everyone here, but you're too fucking stubborn to just fucking kiss me. Even when you have the lame-ass excuse of it being a game," he snapped. "Jesus, Nova."

With that, he stormed past me, and after less than a second, my fight kicked in, and I turned to follow him. Just as he tried to slam the door to the back, I slapped my hand out to push it back open, only to slam it behind me.

"I am not stubborn," I shouted.

He laughed without humor. "You're one of the most stubborn people I know. The fact that you can't even accept it proves how stubborn you are."

"You have no idea who I am. It's been five years."

I toed the line, not wanting to talk about the past but also having a damn good reason to be cautious.

"I know. I fucking know, Nova. And if I didn't realize how deep your resentment went, I do after tonight."

"Tonight wasn't about resentment, Parker."

"Then what the fuck was it?" he asked, tossing his arms wide. "Please enlighten me. Tell me why you can kiss everyone but me. Huh?"

"Because you're you. Because with them, it's a game, and with you, it's not."

"That doesn't make sense."

"Tell me about it, because I would love nothing more than to just fucking kiss you."

"Then do it." He said it like a challenge and plea all mixed together.

I froze, my muscles contracting for fight or flight, and I had no idea which one my mind would choose until everything snapped into action—and he met me halfway.

My lips crashed to his and our arms wrapped around each other. His hands slid to my ass, and he lifted me up to wrap my legs around his waist as he walked us until my back hit the door.

With my arms around his shoulders, I held him close, holding on tight as tidal wave after tidal wave of emotion crashed over me, almost like I was caught in a riptide. I needed him to cling to, to survive. His fingers dug in, and I knew I'd have bruises on my pale skin, and I relished in them. I wanted them to remember every second.

His tongue pressed into my mouth, and my tongue played with his, remembering his taste like it was yesterday and not years ago.

We ravaged each other like desperate wild animals trying to cram the last five years into one minute—or ten minutes. However long it was. I lost myself in his flavor, in the feel of his flexing muscles that hadn't been there when we were kids, in the feel of his hard length pressing into me. I hadn't meant to, but I rocked my hips, unable to help myself, loving his groan of pleasure at the small movement.

His thumbs reached around the front of my ribs, barely brushing the underside of my breasts, and I gasped, thrusting forward hard to ease the shot of electricity to my clit. He took the moment to move his kisses across my jaw and down my neck.

"God, Nova. I missed you," he whispered for only me to hear. "I can't tell you how much I've missed you. How much I've dreamed of this—of you."

His confession added another tidal wave, and this one hit too hard. Fire burned up the back of my throat, and I tried to blink away the tears but failed. Before I could wipe it away, his lips moved back across my cheek, stalling when he tasted the wet salt.

Slowly, he pulled back, his own eyes cloudy with the same emotions raging through me. One of his hands abandoned my ribs and came up to wipe away my tears. When another slipped free, he kissed it away. He delivered soft, soothing kisses, bringing us both back to shore, where we could finally breathe.

Because I could.

In his arms, finally cracking through the band of tension that squeezed tighter and tighter each day, I could breathe again. Maybe for the first time since I last felt his lips on mine.

"I missed you too," I admitted.

A loud knock against the door jolted me so hard I almost jumped out of his arms.

"All right, party poopers. We're heading to bed," Oren called through the door.

Holding Parker's stare, the intense moment was broken, but a softness lingered around the edges. With a protesting growl of frustration, he set me down, and we opened the door.

"Sorry, guys. I guess I can't party like a rock star."

"We've got another month. We'll train you," Brogan promised, wrapping his beefy arm around my shoulders in a side hug.

"Can't wait," I deadpanned.

By the time we all got ready for bed, I could barely crawl into my bunk. Exhaustion clung to every muscle, making me feel both heavier and lighter from the emotional release. I closed my eyes and didn't even hear the guys shuffling around in their bunks or their usual jokes before bed. All I heard was the hum of the tires on the blacktop soothing me to sleep.

What felt like two seconds later, my curtain being pushed back woke me up, and I jerked at the shadowy figure hovering on the edge.

"It's just me," Parker whispered.

I stared, wide-eyed, watching his shadow climb into my tiny space. My heart hammered against my ribs so hard I was sure he'd hear it in the quiet, but if he did, he didn't mention it.

He moved slow enough that I'd be able to tell him to get out if I wanted—but I didn't. Instead, I scooted closer to the wall and made room for him just like I had when we were teens, and he snuck into my room at night.

And just like then, his hand found mine, and the worries from before slipped away.

For the first time in years, on a bus in the middle of nowhere, I knew.

With Parker Callahan, I was home.

EIGHTEEN

Nova

Vera: What is up?
Rae: OMG! It's been ages since we heard from you. Spill the tea!
Me: We talked three days ago.
Rae: Sooooo long ago.
Vera: Anyone got time for a FaceTime?
Rae: I wish, I have a gala to go to.
Vera: Someone is busy.
Rae: All. The. Time.
Me: I can't. The guys are taking me out somewhere. It's a surprise.
Rae: They know you hate surprises, right?
Me: I don't *hate* them.
Vera: Yes, you do. Remember the birthday surprise we tried to throw, and you hid in the bathroom for the first thirty minutes.
Me: It was very overwhelming.
Vera: Because you hate surprises.
Me: I'm sure it will be nice.
Rae: Is it a sex club?

Me: I hope not …
Rae: God, I hope so. I would be so jealous.
Vera: How's that boyfriend?
Rae: Side eye …
Me: LOL!!
Vera: Hahaha!
Rae: Keep us updated and make sure you memorize everything. I want to know it all. Every ridge, vein, and length.
Me: OMG! It's not a sex club!
Rae: But if it is …
Me: Then every ridge and length.
Rae: You're the best.
Me: Kisses. And we'll FaceTime soon. I have stories.
Rae: Ugh. How you gonna leave us hanging like that.
Me: Byeeee.
Vera: Bye bitch. I hate you for that cliffhanger … but have fun!

"Ready to go?" Parker asked.

I looked up from my spot at the table, transfixed by the way his white T-shirt pulled tight across his chest as he shrugged on his navy flannel button-up.

"Is that drool?" Oren swiped my chin, and I jerked back, slapping his hand and delivering a death glare.

"Yes, I'm ready whenever you are," I answered Parker like I hadn't been caught ogling him.

His smile was full of arrogance, and I rolled my eyes, stuffing my phone into my purse and shoving Oren out of the booth so we could stand.

"Damn, Nova. I may start drooling over you. And that ink? Nnng." Oren grunted.

I looked down at my relaxed, holey jeans rolled up for my Doc Martens, and my black Alkaline Trio concert tee. The shirt was cut off above my belly button, but the pants reached my waist, so it's not like I bared too much skin.

Except for the back, which had thin strips of the shirt tied to hold it together, baring the tattoo running the length of my spine.

Parker twirled his finger, directing me to turn. I held my breath when I heard his steps get closer, pulling my hair aside to bare my back. The rough pad of his finger started between my shoulder blades, where I knew the head of the phoenix rested. My muscles contracted, sending prickles of awareness down my spine as if chasing his touch as it trailed over the letters that went all the way to the small of my back. He'd seen it before, but every time he got the chance, he stroked his finger along the words.

"I am the storm," he whispered.

It had always been one of my favorite quotes about the devil telling the warrior she wasn't strong enough to handle the storm. I imagined being a bloodied and beaten down person struggling to stand, finding their footing only to take an aggressive step forward and baring their teeth, growling the quote back.

"Did you design it?" Oren asked.

"Of course."

I'd been camping in the desert with stretches of red rocks looking more and more like fire as the sun set. It'd been the anniversary of the day the court case closed on my trauma, and I'd stood on the cliff, looking out at the vast world—alone—but strong. I'd felt like a phoenix rising from the ashes, daring the devil to question me again.

I'd sketched it up and found a tattoo shop the next day.

"You'll have to design my first tattoo," Oren declared.

"You don't have any?"

"Have you seen any?" he asked like it was obvious.

Which I guessed it should have been, considering he strolled around the bus in the least amount of clothes. Sometimes even just a hand when he ran from the shower to his bunk.

"It's baby fresh skin, baby. Just waiting for your artwork."

"Maybe. My art is expensive," I taunted.

"I'm wounded," he pouted, holding a hand to his heart. "Would you like another kiss as payment?"

"I'll design one if you never lick my face again."

"Score."

"You ladies ready to go or what?" Ash asked from the bus door. "Car's waiting."

We piled into a black SUV with another one behind us for security. The guys assured they would be discreet and were going off the beaten path, but we got into Nashville this afternoon, and the fans could be crazy. I sat sandwiched between Oren and Parker with Brogan driving and Ash in the passenger seat.

"You look good," Parker said, leaning over close enough for his words to brush hot against my ear.

I turned enough to take him in from the corner of my eye, giving a sly smirk. "You don't look too bad yourself."

He huffed on his nails and buffed them on his shirt, puffing his chest out.

I couldn't help but laugh, and butterflies took off in my stomach. The other night caused a shift between us. We'd been on this knife's edge, balancing precariously between confronting all the issues that lay between us and all the desire threatening to bubble over. That kiss tipped us a little closer to the simmering fire.

It was like we went through a cycle of steps in our relationship. Friendship, desire we did our best to not admit to, desire we only showed in the darkness of night when he crawled into my bed, and then…and then we fell apart. We'd never actually made it past step three—or maybe we had, and that was step four—falling apart.

The realization that we'd moved to step three recently sunk the butterflies to the pit of my stomach. What if we were moments away from falling apart?

He bumped me with his shoulder. "You okay?"

I took a moment to really look at him. He was only twenty-four, but I could see the lines forming. A wrinkle between his brow when he scrunched them in concentration. The fine lines around his mouth and eyes that would only grow deeper with the way he inevitably enjoyed life. Would I be there to see it?

I didn't know, but I was there now, and if it was all I had, then so be it.

"Yeah," I said with a smile. "I'm good. Although, I'd be better if I knew where we were going."

His pinky stretched out from where his hand rested on his thigh beside mine and stroked my leg. The smallest touch and fire spread like ripples in a pond. "Almost there," he promised.

With a dramatic huff, I rested my hand on my thigh, meeting his pinky halfway, where we linked them for the rest of the drive. Our desire wasn't forbidden anymore, but it was like we didn't know how to actually show it.

"All right, Supernova," Ash called from the front. "Close your eyes."

"What? No."

When all he did was smile and nod at my objection, I pursed my lips but complied.

Parker's fingers linked with mine, and I held on tight. I could get used to closing my eyes and surprises if this was the payoff. The car rocked to a stop, and I squeezed my eyes tighter, fighting off the urge to peek.

"We have arrived," Brogan announced excitedly.

"Open your eyes," Ash ordered.

Four smiling faces scooting in close greeted me first, and I had to laugh at their hopeful looks. "You guys look like little boys showing off their rock collection."

"You mean cock collection," Oren snickered.

"Ew," I cringed. "Sooo, can we get out? Or is sitting in the car with you smiling at me the surprise?"

They all hustled, and I followed behind. As soon as they exited, they donned various hats to try and blend in. Parker tipped his black cowboy hat that clashed with his band T-shirt and flannel but still looked good.

Finally looking past them, I took in the glowing sign outside the purple building with green trim.

My smile slipped.

Karaoke All Night, Every Night.

Somehow, I managed to scavenge a slight tip to my lips, if not a little forced. I didn't sing anymore in front of people. I mostly only sang in the shower or in the car. Very few times, I sang with the guys in the last month while writing. They'd jokingly brought up how I should join them on stage at their next show, but I'd shut it down hard enough that they never pressed again.

The only other time we'd been to a karaoke bar had been for my birthday and marked the beginning of singing for me. It marked the beginning of the road to my worst nightmare. I didn't sing in front of anyone anymore because I couldn't do it without associating it with what happened.

"What are we doing?" I asked, laughing uncomfortably.

"Karaoke night, baby," Oren exclaimed.

"You guys really want to sing in a karaoke bar the night before a show in the middle of a tour? Also, I don't think we're that far off the beaten path to keep your identity hidden if you go on stage."

"Oh, yeah," Brogan agreed. "We're not singing. We wanted you to be able to sing."

My smile dropped completely, and my heart thundered, pumping blood so hard it rushed through my ears, making it hard to hear. The lights swirled around me, and I took a step back, the scrape of my boots against the gravel too loud.

"We remember how much you loved to sing," Ash explained, still smiling and completely oblivious to my turmoil.

"And yeah, asking you to come on stage was a bit much, so we figured a hole-in-the-wall bar would be cool," Parker finished.

My heart beat too hard—too fast. My lungs weren't getting enough oxygen despite how hard I was sucking in more and more air through my dry lips.

I didn't know what brought on the panic more—the thought of being on stage and singing in front of anyone or the realization that they didn't get it.

Moving from one face to the other, their smiles slowly dropped as the reality of the situation hit them.

They didn't get how haunted I was. I couldn't blame them completely because I'd never actually talked about it, but even an outsider would put two and two together. I more than made it clear I didn't want to sing. I didn't think I needed to go into the gory details of my recovery to make them understand.

Just because I didn't say it, doesn't mean it didn't play a role in every decision I made. Doesn't mean it wasn't a huge part of why I fought Aiken on remaining private. I shouldn't have to. I never thought I would have to.

But they didn't understand.

They didn't understand how I'd cut myself off from everyone after they left and stayed there until Vera and Raelynn pulled me out.

They had no idea how much I suffered, struggled, and mourned while they flourished in their dreams.

"Nova?" Parker called my name, but it sounded like we were on opposite sides of a tunnel. He stepped forward, and I stepped back.

"You don't get it," I whispered more to myself than them.

"What do you mean?"

His voice was so soft and hesitant, like he didn't want to startle the person on the verge of overreaction. Because he didn't. Fucking. Get. It.

"I said," snapping my head up to glare, enunciating each word. "You don't. Fucking. Get it. None of you do. Bringing me here? To sing on a stage? Like I'd ever fucking want to? Like you don't know better than anyone *why* I don't ever want to put myself out there again." I glared in disbelief, watching the confusion sink away to guilt. "You. Don't. Fucking. Get. It."

"Nova, we're sorry," Brogan said first.

"No." My voice cracked, and I stepped back, needing to get away from them before the lump in my throat broke free.

I turned and stomped to the other black SUV, throwing the back door open and climbing in. Parker was almost to my door when I hit the locks. I locked eyes with the wide-eyed guard in the back seat with me. "Take me back to the bus."

"Ms. Hearst, we can't leave them," he explained calmly.

"Then I'll get a fucking Uber," I growled, preparing to face the guys after I tried to run.

"No," the female guard driving stopped me. "Graham and Vince, you two ride with the guys, and I'll take Ms. Hearst back."

I met her understanding eyes in the mirror, and she nodded. The two guards hopped out, and thankfully, Parker didn't push in. We watched them talk in a circle with big hand gestures and scowling faces before piling back in the car.

"Thank you," I whispered.

"They're great guys, but sometimes, you just need some space," she said in understanding. Thankfully, she stayed quiet the rest of the drive and ignored any sniffles that slipped free from the back.

Taking deep breaths, I wiped at my damp cheeks and pulled myself together as we rounded the corner to the bus. I considered asking her to take me to a hotel for the night but knew we had to work on the music in the morning before they got ready for the show.

Fuck. I could only imagine how well that would go. Wincing at the thought of sitting with them to write some ballad, I fought to keep from banging my head on the window. What the hell was I thinking taking this job? I'd been naive, thinking we could just move on without anything from the past coming back to haunt us. I'd only been successful over the years at avoiding it because of therapy and my complete lack of surrounding myself with anyone who knew what had happened. But working with them was like jumping into the thick of it and keeping my eyes closed, trying not to bump into anything—and asking them to do the same.

Wanting to get on the bus before them, I considered my options. For now, I'd hide away in the back. It was the only place with something more than a curtain to separate me from them. Maybe tomorrow, I'd think more clearly. Maybe I could leave and just demand they work with me virtually, or I could send them songs to do with whatever they wanted. Anything sounded better than sitting around and trying to create magic.

I didn't bother washing my face—just grabbed my bag and a change of clothes and darted to the back. I'd been in there all of five minutes before the slam of car doors announced their arrival. Their deep voices murmured, and I clung to one of the square pillows to release some of the adrenaline pulling my muscles tighter and tighter.

"Did she leave?"

"Swear to God, if she ran."

Parker. I remembered his message from New Years and how he accused me of always running. And maybe I did, but I never ran from a good thing.

More doors slammed until the one to the bus opened and closed. Footsteps moved down the hall, and I held my breath, almost jumping out of my skin when the handle jiggled before a knock.

"Nova?" Parker called.

But I didn't answer. It was obvious I was here, but I didn't have anything to say.

"Nova, can you come out?" Pause. "I want to talk about what happened." Another pause. "Please."

"No." The last thing I wanted to do was talk about it. I never wanted to talk about it. I never wanted to think about it, and talking about it required thinking about it.

"Nova, come on. Open the door," he said with less patience than before.

"No."

A rumbling growl let me know he'd reached the end of his rope. "We're done avoiding this. It's been a tense month, and hiding doesn't help anyone. We have an album to write, and we're not flowing like we usually do. You do *not* get to run. Not this time."

I don't get to run? Not this time?

The words burrowed into my chest, twisting and burning, scraping past old wounds, opening them back up. It tugged off the sheets hiding the emotions I left hidden in the corner—the hurt, the anger, the resentment.

I didn't get to run?

How dare he.

Tossing the pillow aside, I shot from the couch and yanked the door open to an angry storm over an ocean, looking back at me. I fumed, meeting his glare.

I didn't get to run?

I stepped close, but Parker didn't back down. "You. Left. Me," I growled.

"You *all* left me. You convinced me it would be okay—that it would all be fine. And I believed you." My body vibrated with the words. Like the effort to hide them from even myself had been so great that now that it was set free, it couldn't handle the strain anymore. "You promised. And then you left."

I hated the way my voice cracked. I hated the small

hallway with Parker crowding me. I couldn't stand it, and I needed more air. I needed more space. It was too much, and I needed out. I stomped past and made it just past the kitchen when a strong hand gripped my arm. I whirled around and slipped into the self-defense training I'd had to take for years to feel stronger. I twisted my wrist, stepped in, and pulled my hand toward me, thrusting my elbow up and breaking his hold. But I didn't back away.

Parker stared with wide eyes, holding his wrist.

"Nova…"

"And then you left again. Except this time, you didn't come back."

"We did come back," he defended.

"Not when you promised," I almost shouted.

"You told us to go. I offered to wait, and you still told me to go," he shouted back.

"I didn't mean go forever."

His shoulders dropped, and he lowered his voice, almost pleading. "We tried, okay?"

"Yeah, well, trying wasn't enough—not the second time around. And I wasn't okay enough to wait for a third time," I admitted, hating when the first tear finally broke free, quickly followed by another. "I was hanging on by a thread."

He paced to the end of the bus before turning around and pushing both hands through his hair, tugging on the ends.

The confession rocked him, and I was too tired to care how vulnerable I was making myself by admitting it all. The last time I saw them before they left, I'd been a shell, unsure of everything, unsure of what I'd look like a week from then. So, I'd told them it was okay. I told them to go. I hadn't been prepared for them to not come back.

Admitting it all rocked me too, and my muscles ached with the effort it took to stand. Stumbling back, I fell back on the couch.

"We were selfish, okay?" Parker finally barked, like the

admission barely snapped free. "We were selfish dumb teenagers, all running from something. At least, they were running." He winced and ran his hand over his jaw. "And I just...I felt so much pressure to fucking make it. This was our chance, and I took advantage of how much you supported me. They looked to me to make the final decision—I was the only one that had someone to go back to—and I fucked up. I had my mom messaging me, and the managers pushing for more shows, and the guys happy, and I just...I...I didn't know what to do. I was selfish."

I hated that I understood. I hated that it hurt me to see the hurt in him. I hated that I never took the time to think about what it cost him to make those decisions.

Because I'd been a selfish teen too.

But my selfishness never hurt anyone else.

I squeezed my eyes shut, chewing my lip, trying to figure out the back and forth knot twisting inside me. The bus sat silent, and I didn't know what to say when he admitted he was wrong.

"And you never gave me a chance to fix it," he said, some of his frustration slipping back in. "I've lived with it every day and never got a chance to make it right. I always wondered what the hell happened or if you were okay. Not that I'm trying to compare my guilt to what you went through, but you were my family, and maybe..." His voice cracked, and he cleared his throat. "And maybe that was too much for me to understand as a selfish asshole. I let you down so much, and I didn't know how to fix it, and maybe I used it as an excuse to stay away, but once I *did* figure it out, you were gone."

"Yeah," I choked out, trying to wipe away the tears that wouldn't stop. "I didn't know how to handle it either. And no one around me knew. I was alone. I was alone with everything, and I didn't know what to do." I hated how I talked in circles, but it all fumbled out in a mess of words.

"I'm sorry," Parker whispered. He paced back in front of

me and held his hands out in supplication. "I'm sorry for it all. I'm sorry I left you. I'm sorry I was a selfish kid who didn't know a lie when I saw one. I should have called you on telling us to leave. I should have called bullshit and stayed by your side. I shouldn't have left." He dropped to his haunches and looked up at me with watery eyes. "Not a day goes by, I don't think of it. Not a moment I don't think about what happened to you when you were taken—"

"Don't," I cut in. It's one thing to talk around it, but I never talked about it because there was nothing I could do but satisfy someone's morbid curiosity. "It's done."

I sat there, slouched and exhausted from releasing the tension I held back in hopes that if I didn't acknowledge it, it wouldn't exist.

Parker slowly reached his hands for mine, and I let him. "I'd never been so scared. I'd never felt so incompetent. I couldn't help but think you were better off without me because I couldn't keep you safe like I promised. So, maybe I ran first."

"I never wanted to be without you," I whispered. "I loved you."

"I loved you too, which was why I thought I was doing the right thing."

I squeezed his hands tighter in mine because there wasn't anything left to say. We'd both made mistakes. We both fucked up. We'd both been a little selfish and doing the best we could with the nightmares that weighed on us.

I just didn't know what to do now. We sat in silence, the bus like a battlefield littered with our argument, unsure of how to clean up and make the next step forward.

But like finding a gem amongst the rubble, Oren called through the cracked door from outside, lighting the way.

"Well, just to clarify," he announced. "I loved you too."

I jerked toward the door to watch it open, and the guys

piled in with hesitance and somber faces. They must have waited outside.

Ash rested his hand on my shoulder. "We're sorry. We're all sorry."

"I'm sorry, too," I said. No matter how small a part I played in this, I needed to accept that I'd done damage too.

"How can we make it up to you?" Brogan asked.

I looked to each of them. "Just be here now."

"We can do that," Parker confirmed.

"And let me have the cushy bunk," I added, barely holding back a watery laugh.

"Aww, c'mon," Brogan groaned. "I'm the biggest one here, and it's the only one with the extra length."

Getting my smile under control, I fought for a blank stare and shrugged.

"Fine," he reluctantly agreed. "But only for you."

"Awww," Oren cooed, standing. He stepped over and pulled me into a hug. Each of the guys followed suit until we stood in the middle of the bus, holding on to each other. And I had to admit, it was the safest I'd felt in a long time.

I was home.

"Anyone want to play spin the bottle?" Oren asked.

"Yeah, but this time it's truth or touch my boobies," Ash said, wagging his brows.

I shoved my way free, laughing. "You guys are the worst."

"By worst, you actually mean best, right?" Ash asked.

"Maybe," I conceded.

"Yes," Oren shouted, throwing his hands up in victory.

"I don't know about you, but I'm tired as fuck," Parker said.

We all agreed and headed toward the back.

"Brogan, you can keep your bunk. I just wanted to see you sweat. It was reward enough."

"Cruel woman," he grumbled.

That night, Parker didn't bother waiting for everyone to

fall asleep before he crawled up into my bunk. And I didn't bother to hide how I tucked myself against him and curled up perfectly in his arms to fall asleep.

I told him I loved him then, but safe in his embrace, I wasn't sure I ever stopped.

NINETEEN

Nova

PAST

"Please, please, please, please." Oren bounced from foot to foot with his hands clasped together, his puppy dog eyes fully in place.

The other guys stood around waiting for my answer expectantly.

"I'm not even supposed to be in here. If they find out I'm seventeen—"

"Psh," Ash cut in. "Bear knows how old you are and doesn't give a shit."

Oren went back to the annoying begging. "Please, Nova. Please, please, please."

I looked to Parker for help. "We need the edge," he explained instead of helping. "The other bands are good, but if we had a girl singer with us, we'd leave no room to beat us."

"I never should have come to this battle of the bands," I muttered. Singing at a karaoke bar was one thing, but in front of their fans and judges with a real prize on the line added an expectation I didn't know if I could handle.

"Your voice is epic, and no one else has a girl singer," Ash said.

"And you know all the songs. You've sung them a million times at practice," Brogan added.

"Yeah, but these songs aren't duets. How the hell do you expect me to work around that?" I asked.

"Uhhh…I guess it's a good thing you and Parker screw around all the time making them into duets," Ash explained like I was dumb.

"That was only a couple of times," I grumbled.

"Enough for us. Besides, you guys have a freaky-deaky connection thing going on," Brogan said. "Probably that brother-sister bond."

Ash snorted, and I cringed.

"We are not brother and sister," Parker growled.

"I don't think I can do this," I said, mostly to myself.

Parker turned to me, sucking all the oxygen from our space when he slid his hands against my cheeks and tilted my face up to his. The world faded just like it always did with him. All I saw were his deep blue eyes. I held on to his wrists, finding comfort in our connection—in the soft skin on the inside of his wrists, where I found the soothing beat of his pulse.

"Nova," he whispered just for me. "You can do this. *We* can do this. I'm right there with you."

We may not have repeated that night—agreeing to not push the limits, but there was no denying the relationship between us. I didn't know much about intimacy, but the moments between Parker and me left me bare—stripped to nothing but me. I couldn't fathom anything more honest or close.

He made me better—brave. Hence, why when I would shy away, all he had to do was hold out his hand, and I trusted him enough to step into his light.

Just like I would now.

"Okay," I agreed with a nod.

His smile lit up my world, and it took all I had to remain

rooted to the ground and not press up, closing the gap to latch on to his beautiful mouth. Not a day went by that I didn't remember how perfect they'd tasted.

The guys whooped and high-fived.

I bounced around and shook out my limbs, waiting for them to call our name. I went out back and warmed up my voice. I'd never had professional training, but I knew my body well enough to know that first note was always hard to hit with cold vocal cords.

But all my nerves were for nothing. When I got on that stage, thirty seconds into the first song, the crowd faded. First, I lost myself to Parker, meeting his gaze during the first chorus as we locked into the perfect harmony.

Then, as we moved through the set, I lost myself to the music like I did with my art. I relaxed and danced to the beat Oren kept on the drums, played air guitar with my back pressed to Brogan. Jumped around with Ash and Parker during their most upbeat song. It was like any other practice of goofing around and having the best time.

I loved it. And I wouldn't have had it without Parker pushing me.

When the set ended, I bounced off the stage and was hoisted up into Oren's arms, and twirled around.

As soon as he put me down, another set of arms wrapped around me from behind. "Kickass, Supernova," Ash whispered in my ear.

Brogan mussed my hair with his giant palm like I was a dog who did a good job. I was sure my cheeks would crack from so much smiling, and when Brogan shifted out of the way, there stood Parker, watching with pride and awe—for me. Knowing I put that look of wonder on his face had me flying even higher. I patted Ash's arm, and he let me free so I could run into Parker's arms.

When I leaped, he caught me. I wrapped my legs around his waist and squeezed for all I was worth.

"Thank you, thank you, thank you," I whispered.

He smiled into my neck, and we held on for dear life like we were trying to meld our energy into one. "I didn't do anything."

"You know when to push me."

"It's okay to be in the spotlight, Nova. Don't let anyone tell you otherwise."

Almost desperate to place my lips on his, I somehow managed to divert and smack a giant kiss to his cheek.

"Hey, where's mine," Oren whined.

I blew him a kiss, and he caught it, rubbing his palm between his legs. "Gross," I said, pretending to gag.

As much as I didn't want to, I relaxed my grip to get down. What proceeded was the most erotic slide down his body, my mouth inches from his, my breasts scraping along every dip and curve of his chest, and I swore I could feel a slight bulge grazing my core and abdomen.

I whimpered when my feet finally touched the ground, not wanting to part.

"Haunted Obsession," someone called.

We parted and turned to find a tall, broad man strolling toward us. I almost had to do a double-take because while I'd never met Brogan's dad, this man looked like he could be Brogan's dad. But darker. An older, darker Viking built the same way as Brogan.

"Hey, I'm Grant Sommers from GS Productions. I was one of the judges and just wanted to come say how amazing I thought you guys were."

"Thanks, Grant. We appreciate it," Parker said, shaking his hand.

They all introduced themselves, and I lingered back, letting them have their moment. Except when he looked past the guys to me. "I didn't know you had a female singer, too."

"Hi, I'm Nova." I waved, taking a small step into the circle.

"Yeah, Supernova is our secret weapon. She basically keeps us all in line and sings when we can coax her to," Ash explained.

"Very cool." Grant looked me up and down but not in a sexual way. More like he was trying to piece together a puzzle. "Well, she may have been the weapon you needed to win. I'm only one judge, but you have my vote tonight. In fact, here's my card. Email me, and maybe we can set up some shows."

Parker accepted the card, and they all barely held in their excitement until Grant left. As soon as he rounded the corner, they jumped, shoved, punched, hugged, and even shrieked a little for joy.

The excitement kept pouring in when they were announced the winners of the night, winning a prize package, including money, equipment, and a spot to open for a band at a big concert venue.

By the time we made it back to the apartment, I was beat, but they talked me into joining them down on the basketball court in the basement for beers.

"That was fucking awesome. Best night ever," Brogan said. He leaned back against the cement wall, his eyes closed, a beer clutched in his hand, and a serene smile on his face.

"Dude," Oren said, abandoning the basketball he tossed around. He was the only one on his feet still. We all lined the wall, looking exactly like Brogan. Happy and tired. "Grant fucking Sommers. How cool."

"We're on the edge of making it. I can feel it," Parker declared.

"Thank god. I don't want to go to college," Ash said.

"If it takes a while, what will you do?" I asked, always looking at the practical side.

"Probably football," Brogan answered first, not sounding happy.

"My dad wants me to play basketball, but I don't fucking think so. He can fuck off with that," Ash grumbled. He didn't talk about his dad much, but when we did, it rarely sounded anything like love.

"What about you, Oren?" I asked. He was back to playing ball, this time with an imaginary ball. Just bouncing side to side, whirling around to fake out an opponent that wasn't there.

"Don't know," he answered, coming to a stop. "I kind of like Physics. Maybe I'll shoot for the moon. Literally. NASA sounds like a badass job."

Somehow, I forgot that Oren was the smartest one out of all of us. His mind was just like his body, working in overtime.

"I don't want to do anything but this," Parker said beside me.

"Solid," Oren agreed, holding his fist out to Parker.

Ash turned my question on me. "What about you?"

"Probably art school. I'd love to go to the Art Institute in Chicago."

"Not that you need art school," Parker muttered, bumping his shoulder to mine with a smile.

"I can always learn more."

Before we could say anything else, Oren shouted, making my heart jump up into my throat.

"Holy fucking fuck. Holy fuck. Yes. So much fucking yes."

"Dude, what the fuck is going on?" Brogan asked, looking just as alarmed as me.

"Someone uploaded a video to YouTube of us tonight—like less than an hour ago and look at all those fucking likes. Look at them!" Oren shoved the phone in our faces.

Ash snatched his wrist to hold him still. "Holy shit," he muttered.

Brogan shoved him out of the way. "Is that fifty? Fucking fifty?"

"Fifty shares?" I asked.

"Fifty thousand," Oren exclaimed. "We're fucking viral, motherfuckers." He abandoned his phone with the guys who still stared in awe and ran a victory lap, shouting for joy the entire way.

"They're talking about you too, Nova. About how amazing your voice is," Parker said with pride.

I pulled the phone over and scrolled through the comments. I saw the good ones, but I also saw quite a few others. "These are…kind of creepy. This guy commented seven times. Ew."

"'I'd like to see her open her mouth that wide for me,'" Brogan read one of the comments, cringing with me.

"The internet is a weird place," Ash explained, brushing off any concern. "You just got to block those sociopaths out and focus on the majority."

Thankfully, Oren came back to claim his phone, removing the temptation to give in to my morbid curiosity and read all the others.

"I can't believe this. Not that it means anything, but it's kind of huge," Parker rambled.

"I'm happy for you guys. You've been busting your ass this past year."

"For *us*," Ash clarified. "*We* have been busting our ass."

I held up my hands, taking a step back. "Uh, no. I'm not part of this."

"Hell yeah, you are," Brogan explained, hooking me back into the circle with a burly arm around my shoulders.

"I don't think so." I ducked out from under his arm, the thought a little overwhelming. Okay, a lot overwhelming. I just couldn't quite decide if the overwhelming was good or bad. I stood closer to Parker, hoping he'd back me.

"Don't go running to brother-dearest. We'll have him kidnap you and take you with us when we go on tour," Ash threatened.

"And I'll do it," Parker confirmed.

I turned to him with a dropped jaw. "Traitor."

"Come on, Supernova. You have to sing with us again. They love you," Brogan cajoled.

"Yeah, come on," Oren added, winded from his run. "We need you."

"You guys will be fine without me."

"Nah," Ash said. "You're like the glue that keeps us grounded."

"Truth," Parker agreed. "Brogan and Oren would be arrested ASAP if they didn't have you to be concerned about."

"They'll be arrested anyway."

"Maybe," Parker agreed.

"Probably," Ash confirmed.

"But," Parker said. "They will be less likely to be arrested as they will be on their best behavior because you expect nothing less."

"Come on, Nova," Oren whined, brushing his hair back and flexing. "I'm too pretty for prison."

"Me too," Brogan added.

"Say you'll be in the band," Ash pleaded.

"Nova. Nova. Nova," Oren started chanting, and the guys quickly joined in.

"Oh, my god," I groaned, laughing. These guys were crazy, and I couldn't imagine not doing this with them. "Okay. Okay. Fine. You win. I'll sing a few songs. Occasionally."

This time when Oren did a victory lap, he tossed me over his shoulder and took me with him.

I laughed, and the guys followed behind, my hair flowing all around me. All of it played out—surreal but amazing.

I'd had such an exhilarating time on stage. I loved it.

Parker reached out, and I latched on to his hand. He pulled me from Oren's shoulder and wrapped me in his arms.

Why not give in to the intensity a little bit longer?

Besides, I had Parker to keep me safe.

TWENTY

Parker

PAST

"Do you really think I should do this?" Nova asked me when we stood outside the apartment door.

I was just about to unlock it but stopped, giving her my full attention.

Even after hours of sweating under the spotlights and being exhausted, she still looked more stunning than ever before. I loved the way her hair curled along her hairline, the way her freckles showed more from where her makeup faded. Her bare lips, puffy from where she chewed the lipstick off all night.

I loved it all.

I framed her face in my palms, brushing my thumbs along the freckles I always loved to map, and stared into her emerald eyes, trying to remember why I couldn't lean down and kiss her.

"Nova, I can't imagine doing this without you."

Her cheeks pinkened up, and her teeth came out to chew on her lip again to hide the smile I couldn't get enough of.

"I've imagined this for a long time, even before I met you, before it had any form beyond an elusive shadow I knew I needed to have. But it was like each moment with you clarified that shadow. It shaped into something tangible. It shaped into something with you in it. This is my dream, and I need you there to help me reach it."

She nodded slowly, her smile growing. "Okay. I'll do it with you."

God, I wanted to kiss her then. I wanted to pull her in my arms and never let her go. It'd been a month since that night we gave in, and not a day goes by that I don't think about it—about her and the way she tasted, about the way she felt on my lap and under my hands.

Brushing my thumb along her lips, I considered it—could feel myself already leaning in when I heard laughter beyond the door. A reminder of exactly why acting on our attraction had to come to a screeching halt. It almost pained me to do so, but I dropped my hands and nodded my head inside.

"Sounds like the parents are still awake."

She dragged a hand through her hair and blew her cheeks out with a big exhale. "Yeah. We should head in. It's late."

Before sliding the key in the lock, I looked her over one last time. One side of her mouth tipped in a rueful smile matching exactly what I felt—hating being stuck in a position that kept us apart but aware there was nothing we could do.

"Look who's finally home," my dad called from where he leaned against the island. Gloriana sat perched on a barstool next to him, both of them holding a glass of wine.

"Look who's up," I shot back.

"Yeah, we had a bunch of Chatty Cathies at your dad's dinner tonight," Gloria explained with an eye roll.

"They weren't that bad," my dad defended playfully.

"Brad, we shut the restaurant down, and dinner was supposed to end at nine."

He winced, tipping his head side-to-side. "Okay, so they talked a lot." He conceded before they both focused their attention on us. "So, how was the show?"

"Good." I tried to play it cool, but nothing was holding back my smile.

And nothing was holding back the volcano of excitement next to me. Apparently, all she needed was to be asked and came to life like a firecracker. "Good?" Nova exclaimed. "They freaking won *and* had a top record executive come over to talk to them."

"That's my boy," Dad crowed, lifting his glass as if giving a toast.

My smile grew. I had to admit, I was lucky my dad always supported me. Sure, he would have preferred me to follow him into the world of business, but I'd never been into anything other than music. Even when my mom, who left us to start another family, got on me about having *real* dreams and aspirations with actual success that "didn't rely on a hope and a miracle," my dad always had my back. He never stepped out of my corner.

"He was amazing," Nova gushed. "They all were."

"Yeah, but we wouldn't have won without you," I rebutted.

"What do you mean?" Gloria asked, tipping her head.

Nova dropped her eyes to the floor, but not before I saw the blush stain her cheeks. I loved that she was so fair-skinned that I could see every emotion.

I bumped my shoulder with hers, wanting her to stop hiding. "We finally got Nova to sing with us, and she killed it."

"What?" Gloria asked again, her smile slipping.

"It's nothing, Mom. Not a big deal at all."

"No big deal?" I asked, shocked. "Even the record exec said Nova was our winning edge. She has such a unique tone that sets us apart."

"Nova," my dad gushed, completely missing the way Gloria finished her wine in one gulp. "How did I not know you sang? I guess you hanging out at practices makes more sense now," he laughed.

Nova perked up at the praise. "Yeah, it was pretty cool. Usually, I just help them out where I can with creating the songs at practice, but Parker pushed me."

"Well, I think you were willing to be pushed anywhere away from Oren bouncing around saying please five times in a second," I said, rolling my eyes.

"So, are you singing more?" Gloria asked, doing her best to mask whatever displeasure she found in Nova singing.

"I think so. I know it's new, but I really like it. It's a lot more fun than I ever expected it to be. And once I get over that initial hurdle of actually getting out there in front of people, I kind of lose myself."

Her mom nodded slowly, and a conversation passed between them I had no hope of understanding. I made a note to ask Nova later. Right then, I wanted to share the rest of the news.

"And someone recorded us at our show tonight and posted it to YouTube, and it's getting crazy likes. It's going viral." Now I felt like Oren, bouncing on my toes.

"And viral is good?" my dad asked.

I rolled my eyes and shook my head, leaning over to give him a shove. "Such an old man."

"Okay, okay. I know what viral means," he conceded. "What I don't know is what that means next."

"I don't know. Could be nothing. We could be going with our original plan of hustling over the summer at holes in the wall and not get far. We could get a call from Dave Grohl asking us to open for the Foo Fighters tomorrow and head out on tour with them."

"And you want Nova with you?" her mom asked.

"Yeah. She's a hit. The comments about her are crazy."

"What about school?" she asked.

For the first time all night, I slowed down. The perfect, hopeful future I imagined waking up to tomorrow had a mar on it I hadn't seen a moment ago.

I looked to Nova to find a rueful smile on her face like she hadn't even considered it either. I graduated in a couple of weeks, but she had a whole other year.

"She can finish it on tour. Kids do online learning all the time now."

"What about college, Nova?"

"I can just attend local shows and just sing there. It's not like I'm a vital member," Nova explained.

I scoffed. "Yeah, right. Look at these comments," I said, handing my phone over to Gloria before turning back to Nova. "You're more than vital to this band. Did we not already go over Oren and Brogan needing you to keep them from getting arrested?"

"That's a fair point," Dad threw in. "It will be a miracle if they make it to twenty-one without at least seeing a holding cell," he joked.

"There are a lot of men commenting on things other than your voice," Gloria grumbled. "My god. Some of these make me want to lock you away forever."

"It's the internet," Nova rebuked. "Those comments are nothing worse than the random guys who try to contact me asking if I'm looking for a sugar daddy."

"I just…" Gloria sighed, her shoulders drooping. "I just don't know what to think of all this."

The deeper Gloria's frown grew, the more it stole the light from our moment, and I wasn't ready for that just yet. "Either way, it's all nothing more than an off chance. A song going viral may mean nothing. No matter what happens, we've got a lot of work ahead of us. We're all just so excited about what may be."

"Besides," Dad tagged on, refilling Gloria's glass and luring her into placidity with the red liquid. "Parker will take care of her. He's like her bother, and he'll watch out for her."

It took all I had not to flinch at the punch to the gut. I just barely managed a smile. "Yeah. I'd take care of her."

Blame it on the Tequila

Gloria accepted the glass, shrugging. "You always did want a brother," she said to Nova.

"It all works out," my dad said, looking adoringly at Gloria.

I wanted to backtrack to before Gloria got upset. I wanted to go back to my dad patting me on the back and Oren running victory laps around the gym. I wanted to go back out in the hallway and kiss Nova before I was doused with the reminder of what I was expected to be.

"All right, Glor," my dad said. "How about we take our wine and head to bed. I'm fucking beat after that dinner." They walked past, stopping to pat me on the back with one last congratulations.

"I should head to bed, too," Nova said, some of the shine she came in with gone.

"Yeah, me too."

Because what else was left to say?

I managed to stay in bed for all of thirty minutes, listening to the murmur of our parents before everything went silent. I tried to focus on the dark, center my mind to a new tune that eluded me. Almost like an itch that went away as soon as you scratched it.

I turned this way and that, but nothing helped.

"Fuck it."

I threw off my covers and eased open the door, waiting for someone to make a noise, letting me know they were awake. When nothing came, I made my trip down the hall. I knew it would take only seven steps—five if I made them bigger. I knew one floorboard creaked when you hit it just at the right angle and how to avoid it on step three. I knew I had to lift up on the handle to avoid the door getting caught in the humid summers but didn't have to worry about it in the winter.

I knew to take a wide berth around the dresser along the wall to make it to her bed because she liked to change right in front and drop shit where she stood. I'd tripped over more than one pair of shoes and pants before.

I knew she slept on the right side of the bed, so I looked for the corner and used it to make my way to the left. I knew just the sound of her breathing and when she was awake because it grew a little quicker the closer I got.

We'd done this more than once a week, and it was like under the cover of night, we could pretend it didn't matter. We never kissed. We never talked about why I was there. We just let it be. Sometimes we'd hold hands and talk until we fell asleep, only to wake up curled into each other. Some nights we didn't bother waiting until we fell asleep and curled up right away.

Tonight was one of those nights. As soon as I eased in the bed, she rolled into my chest, the soft puffs of air heating my already too hot skin.

"I'm sorry my mom was such a Debbie downer."

"Don't worry about it. She's just concerned for you."

"Yeah," she answered a little too quickly.

"Is it something else?"

I swallowed down my groan when I felt the tickle of her fingers tracing my pecks. "I don't talk about my dad."

"No, you don't."

"He, uh ... he was a musician."

"Huh." The word didn't convey even an ounce of my shock. I started to worry my eyes would pop out of my head if they bugged out anymore.

"Yeah," she said with a laugh. "He wasn't anything big. But he wanted to be, and so he left us when I was young to chase it. Sometimes he would come back if he thought having a family would benefit him. He'd tried more than once to use the fact that he had a young daughter to get noticed or move ahead. My mom hated it—*I* hated it. Eventually, she had enough and kicked him out."

"Shit. I'm sorry."

Blame it on the Tequila

"It's not a big deal. My mom, just kind of, has a thing about it."

"It's understandable."

"I guess it's why I always avoided the spotlight. I didn't want to be like that."

A thought struck me then, hitting me harder than the brother comment. "Do you think *I'm* like that?"

Her head tipped back against my arm as she looked up through the shadows. "Like what?"

"Someone who chases the fame."

"No," she answered easily with a small huff of a laugh. "I've never looked at you like that. Even though you talk about how much you want it and never hide the fact that it's all you want, I've never thought you would leave important things behind for it. Also, my dad kind of just wanted it given to him. He didn't want to work for it. Probably why he never actually made it."

"Where is he now?"

"Don't know."

She shrugged, and I brushed her hair back, catching glimpses of her pale skin in the moonlight.

"I won't leave you, Nova."

"Don't make that promise because you might have to. As much as I want to, I may not be able to go with you."

I hated that truth. I wanted to say fuck it all and do as Ash threatened: kidnap her and make her stay by my side. "Okay, how about this? I'll always come back to you, Nova. Always."

"I can live with that," she whispered so close her words brushed my chin.

Her hands wrapped around my back and held me close, pressing her soft chest to mine. Tipping my chin, I cradled the back of her head and brushed my nose against hers, aching with the effort to hold back.

"Parker?"

I grunted, too scared to say anything.

"Just…"

Whatever it was, she let it go, and the next thing I knew, her lips were on mine. Even quicker than that, she was under me. As soon as our lips connected, the chains on my control snapped.

She spread her legs, cradling me between them, and it would have been so easy to shove our clothing aside and be where I'd dreamed of being since I met her, but this was Nova, and I knew that whatever happened tonight wouldn't change tomorrow. She deserved more than a fumbled rush in the dark.

Trying to slow us down felt about as hard as I imagined climbing Everest would be. I rolled to my side, delving my tongue into her mouth for a few more tastes to hold me over. With the intense pressure of my desire crushing in on me, I struggled to get a grip on my lungs as I finally slowed to a few pecks and eventually stopped completely.

"I hate this," she whimpered.

"Me too."

Before Nova, my focus had always been on music, and if a girl came along that intrigued me, I went for it. Then there was Nova. She intrigued me from the first smile and soft-spoken conversation. But once I got to know her, I saw the depth to her that matched my own. We just…clicked in an almost indescribable way.

I loved her. I wasn't really sure what that meant. I guess I always thought of it as if you loved someone, then you made them your partner, your lover.

Nova wasn't my lover, as much as I wanted her to be, but she was my partner—my best friend. My other half. She created this all-consuming tidal wave of this feeling—all the feelings—inside me, and I couldn't put a name to it, but I knew it made me happier than I had ever been before.

And when I tried to put a name to it, all that came out was love.

If this was love, then I'd take it. Because having her in my arms right now was all I ever needed, and I never wanted to let that go.

But if I had to leave like she said, I'd always come back because there was no living life without Nova. Of that, I was sure.

TWENTY-ONE

Parker

"Thank you, Columbus!" I shouted into the mic. "You've been amazing, and we can't wait to come back."

The crowd roared, and I closed my eyes under the flashing spotlights, basking in the sound I'd never tire of. My strap scraped my neck when I bent in half for a bow. Standing up, I flicked my sweat-soaked hair back and walked to the edge of the stage, tossing my pick out into the crowd like I had after every concert. Oren climbed out from behind his set and tossed out his broken drumsticks he used and abused throughout the concert.

He had more broken than usual after playing so hard.

The energy had been different this time around. More intense, and I think it had everything to do with the new energy we cultivated every day on our bus after clearing the air with Nova. It'd been about a week, and we'd already added four more songs to the playlist and cleaned up the others we'd barely scraped together before.

I think it had everything to do with the woman who stood off in the wings jumping and screaming along to each word of our songs. Every time I glanced her way, a jolt of electricity hit me, and I hit each note sharper than before. She'd come to two of the three shows this week, and it was like a puzzle piece that had been shifted just a little off-kilter clicked into place for us.

Like we'd said before. Nova was the glue that kept us grounded.

When we hadn't had her, we'd ignored the shift and focused on our dream, growing accustomed to the ill-fitting feeling. Like a rock in your shoe that you didn't have time to get out, so you just ignored it and eventually grew used to it. Until you were reminded of what it felt like to have that nagging pressure there all the time—then you realized how off you'd been walking this whole time.

Now, if only I could break through the thin veil holding us apart. I was so close, crawling into her bunk every night, not even bothering to wait and hide it anymore. We watched TV and talked about experiences. She told me about her favorite hikes, and I told her about our favorite shows. One night we'd laid on our sides, barely fitting in the damn thing with a pen and paper between us and jotted down lyrics like the tension constantly trying to bind us together bled into the paper.

With one more bow from all of us, we finally left the stage, getting high-fives and backslaps from the crew. Nova stood to the side, beaming with flushed cheeks, her lip firmly planted under her teeth. I moved to her like a magnet, and when she saw the intention in my smile, her hands came up as if to hold me back.

"Don't you dare, Parker."

"C'mon. It's not that bad," I said, plucking my damp shirt from where it clung to my chest.

"No."

"What about now?" I asked, stripping my shirt over my head.

She stopped walking backward and took me in. I loved catching her off guard without my shirt on. We all walked around the bus in various states of undress, but only with me did she freeze, her attention solely focused like I was a god.

"Is this better, Nova?" I asked quietly, now that I was only a foot away.

She swallowed and nodded jerkily. "Yeah. It's, uh—it's a start."

"What would make it better? How do I get you in my arms?"

The question snapped her attention from where it mapped every ridge of my chest up to my eyes. We weren't just talking about right then after a show. I meant all the time and not just at night either.

The flash of a camera stole her attention, and when she looked over my shoulder, her eyes blanked of any heat, and she stepped back.

"I'll catch you after you clean up and do the whole rock star thing," she explained, her eyes flicking to the journalist Aspen set up to write about our show.

She backed into a crowd of workers, doing her best to blend in and failing. Nova stood out to me among the masses, and I was sure I'd find her even with my eyes closed. But taking her in, I didn't understand how anyone could miss her with half her red hair down her back and a weird knot thing on top. She had on one of our band T-shirts she'd tied up over her loose, torn jeans that she rolled up over her snakeskin ankle boots. I snorted, loving her obsession with weird as hell shoes. And if that wasn't enough, she wore some sheer cardigan thing that hung to the floor. The deep teal made her look like a mermaid in the sea of black clothes everyone else wore.

Another flash directed at me, standing there with my shirt in my fist, pulled me out of my daze.

"You'd probably make the fans go wild if you took your shirt off during a show," the reporter commented.

"Nah," Ash cut in, his arm tossed over my shoulders. "If

he took his off, then I'd have to take mine off, and they'd forget who he even was. He'd cease to exist."

The other guys joined in, and we bantered, took pictures, and answered questions. It was actually a fun interview about our music and tour. Sometimes we got people who flirted or asked about our personal lives, barely touching on our music. I understood it and played the game, but it was always nice to have someone as passionate about music as we were.

"There you are," Oren shouted when we walked back into the room they'd set up for us.

Nova sat on the couch, swiping through her phone. "Yeah, I figured I'd wait here away from the chaos."

Also, avoid any attention directed her way. Any time we went out, she stepped back in the shadows, keeping a healthy distance in case any photos were taken. Or she didn't go out with us at all. Especially since her Instagram started blowing up even more than usual. She'd been posting intermittent photos of her working on lyrics with a stage in the background, hinting at more than just hiking adventures but never outright showing anyone's faces.

I kind of understood since any time I was pictured with a woman, people went crazy with ideas of secret dates and love affairs. But she was a songwriter, and it would be easy to explain away. Also, Nova herself was hard to peg down. She had a very small digital footprint.

"What are you guys doing tonight?" she asked, pulling me out of my contemplations.

"What we do best," Oren said with a wink. "Party it up."

"You have fun with that," she laughed.

"You're not coming?" Brogan asked.

"Nah. I'll probably head back to the bus. Enjoy some peace and quiet."

"Psssh, we're in hotels tomorrow night for Cincinnati. You'll have plenty of peace and quiet," Oren explained.

"I think I'll go back with her," I jumped in, saving her from Oren's pleas.

"Well, duh." Oren rolled his eyes and made thrusting motions, insinuating what he thought we would be doing.

"Hardly," Nova deadpanned.

"Besides," Ash said. "I'm gonna head to the bus, too."

"You?" Oren asked.

"Yeah. I need a fucking night of nothing. I'm hitting that six-week slump."

"Not the six-week slump," Brogan cried.

Ash shrugged. "Yeah, it'll pass."

It always did. We almost always hit it on long tours, the exhaustion creeping into our bones. Thankfully, we had a week off coming up soon that we tried to plan around this time, and it couldn't get here soon enough.

"All right, party-poopers. I guess it'll only be Brogan and me representing tonight."

"Please don't get arrested," Nova pleaded.

"I solemnly swear I will do my best not to."

"I guess that's all I can ask for."

Brogan held up three fingers next to Oren. "Girl Scout's honor, Mom."

With everyone's plans made, we parted ways. As soon as we got back, we took turns showering. Nova went first, and then Ash and finally me. Ash must *have* been really tired because, by the time I got out, his curtain was closed, and the soft rock he listened to at night played low.

Bypassing my bunk, I climbed into Nova's, smirking when her jaw dropped at my shirtless chest.

"I think I'm still hot from the show," I said, knowing the excuse to go sans top was weak at best.

She laid on her back, one side pressed to the wall and the other pressed against me. Wanting to look at her, I rolled to my side, propping my head on my hand, and just stared. I mapped the faint freckles across the bridge of her nose, the pink lips she drew her tongue across, her pert chin and slender neck. I traced the pale skin until it disappeared under the loose cotton tank top. My fist clenched to keep from reaching out to follow the same path my eyes took, especially when her nipples pebbled under the thin top.

I was damn near panting when her voice broke through my trance.

"What does this tattoo mean?" She fingered the oblong swirls and blurs decorating the side of my ribs, not at all hesitant to touch me.

Goosebumps spread from the light graze, and the shock shot straight to my length. I twisted off my side just enough to see the ink and remembered the night I got it. I'd been on a week-long bender, driving myself into the ground around a year after we left. I'd been home in New York and could have sworn I saw her hair blowing in the wind, and when I caught up to her, it hadn't even been close. I'd stumbled back to the apartment I shared with Ash and shattered every glass piece I could get my hands on in our kitchen, trying to do anything to ease the destroying tsunami of emotions I had over missing her—over being so damn mad that I didn't know where she was—over being so confused about the two taking up so much space and leaving no room for anything else.

Ash had come home and cleared a spot and sat with me, finally telling me it was okay to feel both, and apparently, all I needed was for someone to tell me it was okay.

We cleaned up, and the next morning, I went to a tattoo parlor and told them what I wanted.

"It's a design of a supernova," I finally answered.

Her finger froze. "Parker," she whispered.

Her eyes met mine in the dim lights of the bunk, but they sparkled like the star we named her after. A beat of need pulsed in the cramped area and matched the thrum of my heart, urging me to take, take, take. Before I could move, she shifted, tugging the side of her tank up to bare a familiar guitar line drawing in the same exact spot as my supernova.

I huffed a laugh of disbelief. What were the chances? "My drawing."

"It was good."

"It was shit," I laughed.

"Okay, I might have cleaned it up a bit."

I traced the rudimentary outline of the guitar I drew for her one night, up and down the squiggled frets on the neck, down to the initials P-C resting inside the body of the guitar. Taking it further—needing to—I leaned over and pressed my lips to the soft skin, soaking in her gasp. Barely lifting my mouth, I turned to her skin, loving the increasing rise and fall of her chest against my mouth. I edged her shirt up an inch further and nipped at the curve of her breast.

She cried out and slicked her tongue across her parted lips, and I couldn't take it a second longer. Moving slow enough to give her a chance to stop me, but with an urgency I knew we both felt, I adjusted myself up so I could reach her lips and latched on. She met me halfway, lifting her head off the pillow.

We'd kissed that night of spin the bottle, but this was different. This had been building and building and building, and there was no stopping it. This was years of waiting with the bare minimum between us, and I just wanted to live with her mouth on mine forever.

This kiss screamed desperation in the messy onslaught of our tongues fighting to taste each other, to memorize the give of her lips under my teeth, to never forget the angle she tipped her head to match mine perfectly. I sucked in every delicious sigh and savored every whimper. One hand delved in her hair to hold her up, and hers gripped my back to keep me close. I was so focused on finally kissing her that I couldn't think of anything else.

At least until she arched up, and her nipples scraped my

chest, a moaning whimper shooting straight to my cock. Then I couldn't help but let my body take control. I rolled over on top of her, gripped her thigh, and pulled it wide enough for me to situate myself between them. I rocked forward, determined to make that whimpering cry again.

"Parker," she gasped. "Ash is right there."

"Does that bother you?" I asked. When she didn't immediately say yes, I rocked again and leaned my forehead to hers. "Does it bother you that he can hear what you sound like in pleasure? That he's probably imagining exactly what you look like when you make that sound?"

"Oh god," she whimpered again.

I rocked softly, gliding my length up and down her slit, already feeling the warmth soak through the few layers between us. Trying to gauge her reaction, I watched her squeeze her eyes shut, and the faintest pink tinged her cheeks.

"It's okay if you like that," I said when she didn't answer. "It's okay to want to be seen, Nova."

Ever since I knew her, it was like she'd been too scared to be noticed by too many people, but when she was, she flourished. Unfortunately, life kept shutting it down, but a person could still be seen without being seen by everyone. An insane thought popped in my head that made me about a million times harder, and I could've been wrong, but the possibility of trying was too great to pass.

"Do you want to be seen, Nova?"

"No, I—"

"Not like a famous person," I clarified. "I mean, like when you kissed the guys the other night and sat on my lap…did you like them watching you?"

"I-I…" She swallowed. "I don't know."

"Did it make you wet? Because your nipples were so hard, it took everything I had not to give them all my attention."

She licked her lips, her brows pulled together tight, but she still writhed under me. "I—" Another swallow followed by a deep breath. "I know you have experiences, but I didn't experiment. Instead, I learned from watching porn."

"Oh, shit," I breathed, the shock and desire knocking the wind from me. "What kind?" I wasn't sure I could survive knowing, but I needed to.

"Umm…it was—was exhibitionism," she admitted, squeezing her eyes shut.

The blush grew so deep, it spread down her neck.

"Nova. Look at me." One eye peeked open and then the other. "There is nothing you could want that I wouldn't want to give you. There is nothing I wouldn't do to have you. And you admitting what turns you on has got to be the sexiest fucking thing ever."

"Yeah?"

"Yeah. And we already know I love the attention."

She laughed, but it died on a moan when I slid my hand to her ribs and pressed my length to her again.

"I bet Ash can hear you right now," I whispered in her ear.

Her breathing picked up harder, and she met me at the next thrust. Holding her stare, I pulled the curtain back halfway, holding my hand there, waiting for her to tell me to close it. The music from Ash's bunk had stopped—a clear sign he was dead to the world, but I wanted to give her the idea of being exposed—that he could be watching.

Her eyes flicked to Ash's bunk across from us but didn't protest. Instead, she gripped my sides and lifted herself so she could rub against me. It had to be the sexiest fucking thing I'd ever seen.

Needing more of her—to give her more—I slid my hand up her shirt, thumbing the soft underside of her breast. The skin pebbled, and I became almost desperate to see it. Cupping my hand around the curve, I kissed down her neck, losing myself in her wet heat, grinding closer and closer to the edge.

It was so much like the night on the couch when we finally

kissed, but with so much more knowledge and built-up desire. Pushing to see how far I could go, I drew my hand back to the edge of her top and started lifting it past the pale skin of her stomach. I fingered her ribs and looked to her for permission. Ash was most likely asleep, but with the curtain open, if he did wake up, he'd be able to see all of her.

She looked to his bunk again, a rosy blush warming her cheeks before looking back to me with a nod. Agonizingly slowly, I tugged the top up and over her breasts.

Holding her gaze, I leaned down and coiled my tongue around the tip, almost jerking back when I brushed against cold metal.

Holy fuck. Nova has pierced fucking nipples.

I think I just died and went to heaven.

Using my other hand, I lifted my fingers to the pebbled tip surrounded by two metal balls. She whimpered and groaned as my tongue flicked and teased with the gentlest of strokes across the buds.

"Parker, please," she whispered, arching up against my mouth.

Not being able to take it any longer, her whimpers growing louder, I sucked her nipple into my mouth. She cried out, and I thought I would come right there. God, I wanted to pull my shorts down, tug her flimsy pants from her body and push inside her once and for all, but as much as I loved exploring this with her, our first time together wouldn't be in a bunk bed of a bus.

It didn't mean I couldn't make her come other ways.

Abandoning her breast, I shifted my hand down. She rocked frantically, digging nails into any part of me she could get, crying out and moaning the sexiest sounds I'd never forget. She owned her pleasure, and the sight was stunning. When we were teens, she'd been hesitant and unknowing, and now she stretched and mewled and held me where she wanted me.

Again, giving her plenty of time to pull back, I fingered the edge of her pants, and when she didn't tell me to stop, I delved under, creeping my way between her thighs.

"Yes, Parker. Please."

"I bet Ash is stroking himself, ready to come with you."

Her eyes blazed but never left mine.

"He can't take his eyes off your pierced nipples. Such a good girl hiding filthy secrets."

Her mouth parted on a moan when I pressed between the soft folds of her pussy, encountering wet, slick heat.

"Such a dirty girl who wants everyone to watch her come."

"Yes."

I only grazed her opening to pull more of her wetness up to her soaked clit before she went off. She thrust, and I brushed back and forth, circling and tapping, resting my other fingers at her opening, on the edge of coming when I could feel her cunt spasming. She cried out, almost arching off the bed, and I pulled back to watch her explode.

She was stunning. All fiery red hair sprawled out, her beautiful breasts heaving and tight, her legs spread wide, rocking against my hand until she finally relaxed back against the pillows, dazed and sated, gasping for air. Her heavy-lidded eyes took me in, scanning down to my tented shorts.

"Come," she ordered.

Scooting back to my haunches, I held myself over her with one arm extended and used the other to tug my shorts below my balls.

"Oh, wow," she breathed, her eyes wide.

I slowly stroked my cock, length to tip, holding my breath when she reached out to finger the silver barbell across the underside of my shaft just below my head.

"Fuck, Nova," I grunted.

She skated her fingers across the head, collecting the drop

of precum before pulling away and stretching out like a fucking model designed just to get me off.

Having held off for too long, I jerked my dick harder, coming in less than a few minutes. I cupped my hand over the head and looked everywhere, from her perfect pale tits with barbells through them to her rosy pink lips, round and panting like the sight of me jerking off had her on edge all over again. I remembered how her pussy drenched my fingers from a simple swipe, and I came in my fist. My muscles tensed, and fiery pleasure shot from my head to my toes. Wave after wave poured out of me until I thought I'd collapse. I scanned the area for anything and found a box of tissues in the corner. Grabbing one, I cleaned up and crumpled to my elbows, my forehead pressed to hers.

"That may have been the hottest thing I've ever seen," she said, stroking her fingers through my hair. "Way better than any porn I've watched."

"How much porn do you watch?" I asked, laughing.

"Enough."

"Fuck, that's hot."

"Really?"

I collapsed to my side, curling her into me, and tugged the curtain closed behind me. "Nova, anything you do is hot. And these," I groaned, stroking her now covered pierced nipple. "That was a surprise."

"Your piercing was a surprise, too."

"I'm glad you like it."

I wanted to say so much more. Tell her about all the things I wanted to do to her. How I wanted her to stroke my piercing and how I couldn't wait to feel inside her. I wanted to have it all right there.

But she yawned, and I remembered where we were. Tonight wasn't planned, but it was beyond anything I could've asked for or expected, and I didn't want to push.

We crossed a line tonight we'd never crossed in our relationship.

I didn't want to push any further and tempt fate to send us back to the beginning like it always seemed to do.

So instead of telling her how much I couldn't wait to be inside her, I settled on wrapping her in my arms and falling asleep.

TWENTY-TWO

Nova

"All right, ladies," Aspen addressed the guys. "These two suites connect and have two rooms each. Nova, you're down the hall."

She passed me a key card with my room number on it, and a couple of weeks ago, I might have been grateful for the reprieve, but now I looked at the guys knowing I'd miss being crammed into a tiny space with them twenty-four-seven.

"We're here for three days, so please behave and show up for practices and events on time," she continued, looking around the room as if to inspect the crisp area for any wrinkles.

I couldn't imagine the penthouse suite to be anything other than top-notch, but I'd never stayed in a place as nice as this. At least not the top floor. But the guys lounged around and dropped their bags, propping their feet on the furniture, obviously used to the life of luxury.

"Will you be here too, Aspen?" Oren asked, batting his lashes.

She rolled her eyes, which she did almost every hour with Oren, but it was always with affection. Aspen stood with her back ramrod straight, intimidating in all black with a bold red lipstick. She screamed sophistication and power—the complete opposite of Oren's laidback personality. Which was why he prodded her so incessantly.

"I'll also be down the hall in another room," she answered.

"Well, if you get lonely, you can always join me."

"I'll keep that in mind," she deadpanned.

Oren pumped his fist, bringing out another small smirk from her.

"So, what events do we have? I know there's an interview in the morning," Ash asked.

"There's an event at the Contemporary Arts Museum showcasing musical art from local schools to raise money for arts programs."

"Very cool," Brogan said.

"Parker," she turned to him, her tone warning that what came next would probably piss him off. "Sonia is attending the event, so you can go as her date."

My gaze jerked to his, thankful to find a frown already forming. He gave me a small shake of his head before pulling his shoulders back as if preparing to go to battle with Aspen.

"No."

"Uh, yeah," she responded like he was stupid to even try and say no.

"I'm not going on any more dates with her. Our agreement needs to be absolved."

"Listen, Parker," she sighed, exasperated she had to even explain. "You have an album coming out soon and a concert to promote, and you have enough ballads on your playlist that fans go crazy over the idea of knowing who it's about."

"I don't care. I'm not going. Let one of the other guys go with her."

"No one will believe the other guys are in a relationship."

"True story," Oren called. "I think someone got a picture of me sandwiched between two girls the other night." Aspen glared, and he held up his hands. "Don't look at me. I was just dancing. Brogan was making out with like three different women before disappearing in the bathroom."

"Jesus," she muttered. "Like I said, you have an established relationship, and that belief equals oodles and oodles of money."

"I get that, but I'm ending this. As there was no set date, it shouldn't be an issue."

"The issue is the timing. Just get through the tour—maybe the album release, and then you can be done."

He let out a frustrated growl and paced away. Aspen let him have his moment before putting her phone aside and strolling to block his path, her black stilettos clicking each step of the way. "Beyond the contract, you gave your word to management that you would promote the band as necessary. I do believe you even scoffed and let us know if you had to bang a redheaded model every now and then to help the band, then you'd take it. That if this was the shit rock stars had to do, then it was better than you originally thought. So, I suggest you get over yourself and follow through."

Parker looked away, and I did my best to erase the last ten seconds from my memory.

"That was two years ago," he ground out.

"And look how well it's working. You don't get to stop now. So, show up and give every girl a face to imagine is them. So when you release the album, they buy it so they can imagine it's you singing to them."

"I just—" Parker paced away, dragging his fist through his hair.

"Everyone wants to believe the song is about them, Parker. They want to be the girl."

"What if we wrote a song about foot fungus and Daddy fetishes?" Oren asked.

"Even that one," she answered over her shoulder.

"But that one would be especially for you."

Aspen held up her middle finger over her shoulder before shifting to look at me. "Sorry, Nova. It's just business," she said, erasing any doubt of her knowing if Parker and I were together. She knew and apparently, didn't care.

I stood half a foot taller than her, and I assumed it would help me glare at her from a superior height, but when she walked past, I stumbled out of the way like her boss-bitch aura took up a hell of a lot more space than she did. Rae would be ashamed of how intimidated I was by this tiny powerhouse.

Before she opened the door, she turned back. "Sonia will be there at seven. Make sure to bring a flower or something sweet. Maybe a red one like you mentioned in your last album. Also," she narrowed her eyes. "Don't turn your cheek or shove her away this time when she goes for the kiss."

She didn't bother to wait to hear his rebuttal, and I really didn't want to hear it either.

"I should go get settled," I said, trying to slip away.

"Nova," Parker called. "You come with me."

"What?" I shrieked.

"Yeah. You be my date."

He might as well have suggested I go to the event just to bitch-slap Sonia. "That's a horrible idea. Could you imagine the headlines? *The other redhead. The Homewrecker.*"

He screwed up his face like I was being absurd. "They wouldn't say that."

I gave him a deadpan stare because we both knew that's exactly how it would go. Parker and Sonia hadn't even been spotted together since New Year's Eve, and articles speculated about marriage announcements every week.

He threw his arms wide. "Who cares if they do? If we're together, then we'll face it. I won't have to go on a date with her, and we get to be together."

"*I* care, Parker. It's so easy for you. They'd probably high-five you, but I'm doing this job so I can control the narrative for my business. Something like that would tarnish my reputation."

He shook his head but couldn't argue it.

"Listen," I said, softening my tone. "I want to go, okay? I *hate* the idea of you with her but showing up when another woman is expecting you. I may as well show up naked with a scarlet A painted on my chest."

"When will you be ready to put yourself out there? To be by my side?" he asked, his voice dangerously low.

"I-I don't know," I stammered, unprepared for him to turn this into me not doing it for him—for us. "I'm trying to find the right time to make it happen."

"There's plenty of times. Just take a selfie and post it. Done. We can take one together, right now," he offered sarcastically.

I stood my ground. "I'm not rushing this for you."

"So, we should just keep fooling around at night until holding hands in daylight fits your schedule?"

"That's not what this is," I snapped.

"Then what is it?"

Here we stood on the edge. Fall forward into new territory or fall back?

"Parker," I whispered, pleading with him to understand my position. Hating that we stood on opposite sides, unwilling to yield.

For once, I didn't want to yield for him. Maybe I wanted him to go the extra mile for me.

"I can't get out of this without burning bridges, Nova. It's my job."

It always was. I'd just hoped it wouldn't always be that way. Maybe I was wrong. "I understand. You do what you need to."

Baring his teeth, he crowded me against the wall out of sight of the guys. "Tell me it won't bother you that she's on my arm."

Swallowing, I looked away. "You know it will."

"What if I have to kiss her? For every single photo," he murmured against my cheek, my neck. "Again, and again."

To add insult to injury, he kissed the thudding pulse under the sensitive skin, and I pressed my head back to the wall, squeezing my eyes shut to hold back the fire trying to break free. But it didn't help because all I saw was her in his arms on New Year's Eve.

"I want you," he confessed.

"I want you too, but I can't," I said, adding finality to my words.

He backed up, shutters falling over his eyes. "Then I guess I have a job to get ready for."

Angry at his lack of understanding, angry at myself, angry at Sonia, angry at Aspen…angry at everyone who put us here, I pulled myself off the wall and stood to my full five-foot-eight height. Hardening my jaw like his, I leaned in and met him glare for glare.

"Fine," I snapped.

And with that, I tipped us back.

I stormed out to my own room, barely getting the door closed before sinking to the floor, letting the tears fall.

TWENTY-THREE

Parker

I CLIMBED out of the car, thankful for the mostly empty lobby and the security who kept a clear path to the elevator. The concierge pressed all the buttons, asking me about my night. I didn't really want to do small talk for all of the twelve floors we had to travel. I'd done nothing but small talk all night.

All I wanted to do was get upstairs and talk to Nova. I wanted to tell her about my night and crawl into bed behind her and hold her to me like we'd done the past couple of weeks. Like I'd dreamed of doing every night away from her for over five years.

I imagined her face when I let her know how the night played out. I imagined how she would react.

Then I imagined her not even opening the door to me—refusing to talk to me just like she had after New York.

An idea hit me, and I pulled out my phone to check on any online gossip sites that might have reported already on the event. Finding what I was looking for, I interrupted the concierge talking about his interaction with Brogan and Oren earlier and asked him a favor. He blinked a few times but happily agreed.

When I got off the elevator, I had an extra pep in my step,

and instead of turning left toward the suites, I went right for Nova.

I knocked on the door and stood off to the side so she couldn't see me through the peephole. I figured I'd have a better chance of her opening the door to a random knock than to me. At least, that's what I hoped for because if she turned me away now, I needed her to open it for the concierge later.

No answer.

Checking my watch, I saw that it was just about eleven and knocked again, knowing damn well she'd be awake.

Unless she left.

I hated the panic that squeezed my chest with that thought. I hated that the thought came at all. She'd run so many times before, and standing there waiting for her to open the door, I replayed through the argument we had before I left and tried to pick out if it would have led her into running or not.

I knocked a little harder.

The door jerked open.

"What?" Nova snapped when she flung the door open.

She looked side to side for who knocked so incessantly and looked so stunning in her black leggings and shirt that claimed *I hike because fuck people* that I couldn't do anything but smile, even though she rolled her eyes when she finally saw me and turned away.

"Go away, Parker," she grumbled, attempting to close the door.

I slapped my hand out before it could close and prowled inside. She met me chest to chest but was forced to back up with my every step forward. The door clicked shut, and she jutted her chin, but the green of her eyes swirled with indecision, hurt, and want. Even if she didn't want to want me, I saw it burning there. It reflected mine, a fire that ebbed and flowed but never died out.

"What the hell are you doing?"

Once we made it past the hallway and into the room, she shoved me back but only managed to put a few inches of distance between us.

"Coming to see you."

"No. I don't want you here."

"Nova," I said softly.

Only the lamp glowed from the end table. It perfectly illuminated the soft dusting of freckles on the bridge of her nose, the fiery highlights in her hair I couldn't help but imagine gripped tight in my fist. She stood before me, so stubborn, doing her best to make up for the six-inch difference between us. But while she glared, I took in every soft edge and elegant arch of her face, letting it etch itself on my soul and shine on the warmth that somehow grew each time I was with her. How did something so big keep growing inside me? She'd planted the seeds when we first met, and it twined with my veins, becoming a part of me, filling me to overflowing.

I saw it in her too, but she tried to hide it, and when she couldn't, she jerked away, pacing to the other side of the room, just to turn back with her arms crossed.

"What. Do you want. Parker?" she gritted out through clenched teeth.

For as tightly coiled as she was, I stood relaxed, my hands loose by my side, a smile at the ready. "You."

"Congratulations, but I'm not into open relationships." She barked a humorless laugh and threw her arms up. "Not that we're even in a relationship. I don't even know what the hell we're doing. In fact, I *never* knew what we were doing, so what's new?"

"If it makes you feel better, I never knew what we were doing either. I just knew how you made me feel and how much I wanted that—how much I *still* want that."

She licked her lips, swallowing, indecision marring her beautiful features. It was like watching a silent movie, a plethora of emotions displayed until finally settling back on irritated stubbornness. Back up went her chin.

"How was your date?" One brow rose like she had me cornered.

She had no idea.

I allowed my mouth to tip the slightest bit and dodged the question. We had maybe five more minutes before a knock came. "The event was great. The art was really good, and we raised a lot of money. You would have totally been in your element with all those artsy people. You know, you should have your art in a museum somewhere."

She blinked, struggling to follow my quick transitions. "Well, I'm not really into the red carpet," she sneered.

"You got to get past them quick—it's the worst part—well, that and the food. Not that the food was bad, just minimal. I had to swing my McD's on the way here, so I didn't wither away to nothing." Her brow furrowed, and her eyes widened when I shrugged my jacket off my shoulders. "But other than that, it was great. Other musicians of all kinds. Some fabulous art. Also, some weird art."

"What the hell are you doing?" she asked breathlessly.

I kept my face casual and rested my jacket on the back of the chair. "Getting comfortable."

"I-I don't want you here. Get comfortable in your own room."

"Liar," I whispered.

"No," she snapped. "No. You don't get to sleep in my bed every night and then ditch me to go on a date with some model."

"*I* didn't ditch *you* as I recall."

"No, you just asked me to lay myself on a platter for public consumption."

"No, I asked you to accompany me to an event."

"It's the same thing," she shouted.

"It's not. We could have come up with a solution, but you

Blame it on the Tequila

shut down; you didn't even give us a chance. But you know what, Nova," I closed the distance between us, bending my knees to meet her eyes. "I want you enough to push through the hard stuff."

"That's not fair," she whispered, her eyes glossing over. "You know there's more behind me not wanting to throw myself to the public. You know I want you."

I did know, and it was the first mention of her avoiding the spotlight because of the past. She hid behind so much frustration that I think she forgot it was there fueling her decisions. But, like I said, I would push through it all.

Standing tall, I took a step back and undid the top button of my shirt. "Then show me."

"That's not fair, Parker. Besides, even if I did try—what if I can't? Would you just leave me again and go see Sonia?" She sneered Sonia's name like it left an acidic taste on her tongue.

"I choose you," I answered simply, continuing to undo the buttons.

She watched me, her chest rising and falling, her eyes flashing between anger to push me away and needy desire. I got through three buttons when she managed to shove her anger to the forefront.

"No." She shook her head, tendrils of hair falling from the messy mass of hair piled on her head. "I can't do this. You need to leave." Another button undone, and she stomped her foot. "Get out."

With the most perfect timing, because I couldn't ignore her demands much longer, a knock rapped on the door.

"I'll get that."

I took the sheet from the concierge and gave him a hefty tip before turning back to find Nova still standing in the same spot. Stretching the paper out to her, I waited for her to stop staring at me and take it.

"I knew you'd be stubborn, but I hadn't expected this. But

if showing you is what it takes to make you believe me, then I'll happily show you."

I shook the paper, pushing it closer for her to take. She finally grabbed it, and I waited.

For the first time, I questioned myself.

What if this wasn't enough?

What if I showed her, and she still made me leave?

I guess I was about to find out.

NOVA

Parker and Sonia no more?

Parker Callahan from The Haunted Obsession and Sonia Caravin from the upcoming movie, The Harlots, looked anything but together tonight. Check out these exclusive pictures from the Music Programs Rock charity event tonight in Cincinnati. The couple has been on-again and off-again for almost two years, but tonight, Sonia's scowl looks anything but together again. When asked, Parker announced that he hadn't been with Sonia for a while but appreciated her friendship. Ouch! Talk about friend-zoned. When questioned about if he was already with another special someone, he clammed up tight. Me thinks drama lurks in the shadows with this juicy story. But don't worry, Caravin fans, our beloved didn't seem too torn up when she was spotted with male model, Aaron Jones, canoodling (quite heavily, I might add) in the corner by the end of the night.
Parker left alone before the event ended—not even giving this reporter a chance to soothe his broken heart.
Maybe next time.

Until then...

—Muah.

I LOOKED over the photos beneath the article. Sonia looked like a modern Jessica Rabbit with a sparkly red bustier and black leather leggings. She also looked pissed.

Parker looked…exhausted.

I looked from the Parker in the photo to the one standing in front of me. I almost couldn't handle the intensity of his blue eyes.

Hope, arrogance, nerves, fear, confidence, *heat*. So much heat.

He did this for me. He went against his management…for me. He put me first.

"What about Aspen? The contract?"

"I'll take my chances, and I'd do it again for you, too—a thousand times over. I'd only seen her once when we were in Seattle, and I told her then I was done. Aspen planned the whole New York thing. I almost blew a fucking gasket when I had to give up looking for you. She means nothing to me. *Nothing.* It's always been you, Nova."

"Parker." My heart thundered too fast like a pack of wild horses, and my lungs worked overtime to keep up. I closed my eyes, trying to read his face while also trying to decipher the whirlwind taking place inside me.

"I want you, Nova."

"It wasn't just her, Parker. There's more between us—"

"Then I'll tear it down with my bare hands," he gritted out like a wild animal. "I'm done, dammit. I'm done with *just* missing you. I'm not letting you slip through my fucking fingers again. I won't do it." As if to prove his point, he closed the gap and gripped my biceps, leaning his forehead to mine. "I *want* you, Nova."

The desperation and pleading bleeding from his words almost took my legs out from under me, and I held on for support. My resistance crumbled, and everything that seemed so important before faded away, leaving just me and him pressed together—no one or nothing else holding us back for the first time since we first laid eyes on each other.

"I know it's not perfect. I know we have things to work on, just please don't ask me to leave."

"I can't—"

"*Please,*" he whispered before I could finish.

Sliding my hand up his chest and around his neck, I held him to me as I tipped my head just enough to bring my lips a breath apart from his. "I can't let you slip away either."

A puff of air hit my lips like he'd been holding his breath, and my words punched his gut, setting it free.

It was the last gentle thing from him.

With a growl, he attacked my lips, and I met him with equal ferocity.

His hands abandoned my biceps and gripped my ass, hoisting me up, where I wrapped my legs around his waist. We spun, and things crashed to the floor when he swiped the dresser clear. We slammed against the hard top and the wall. I'd have bruises tomorrow, but I didn't care, I was too focused on picking up where he left off with his buttons. In the end, I clawed at his shirt until I gripped both sides, pulling with years of pent-up passion, sending buttons pinging everywhere.

His tongue plunged into my mouth, and I twirled mine with his, sucking like I wanted to do everywhere. I wanted to taste every inch of his skin, know every secret spot that turned him on. I wanted it all.

I fumbled with his belt, and he pulled back enough to pull my shirt over my head.

"I will never get over these fucking piercings. These tits I've dreamed about since I was a teenager." He palmed one and pinched the other, pulling a cry from my parted lips. "I'm going to worship them," he promised, starting to work on getting into my pants. "I'm going to worship all of you. But first, I just need to be inside you."

"Yes," I hissed.

Blame it on the Tequila

We slammed back into action.

The room became a symphony of groans, whimpers, heavy breathing, and the rustle of clothes. Something tore, and I didn't care what it was. I just needed him.

His pants dropped to his ankles, and his thick, hard length fell into my hands. I'd watched him last night—watched his rough grip around the soft skin and silver piercing, and I'd thought of nothing but feeling him since.

He released a savage moan, his hand fisting in my hair too tight when I slid my hand around him. I hadn't been with many men and none of them like Parker, but he filled my hand like he was made for me.

"Fuck," he groaned, kicking his pants free.

I stroked him softly a few more times, stopping to cradle his balls, while my other hand explored every inch of skin I could reach. I fingered the piercing in fascination, wanting to look at it but also wanting to get his mouth back on mine. I was in a sensory wonderland and didn't know where to go next.

He pulled away, and I almost fell off the dresser to chase his lips, but he quickly hunched down to dig in his wallet for a condom.

I trembled in anticipation, having imagined this moment for years. It was almost too much but not enough all at once. My head swam watching him slide the condom down his length, my hips rocked, already seeking more. When I expected him to come to me, he dropped down, kissing and biting his way down my chest, taking only a moment to suck my nipples into his mouth before descending between my legs.

I wanted to protest. I wanted to tell him to fuck foreplay, but he shoved my legs wide without care, making room for his broad shoulders. He used his thumbs to pull my folds apart and dove in. My whole body contracted at the first swipe from my opening to my clit. My fingers clawed at the hard wood, searching for something to hold me steady. He ate me like a man starved, sucking on my clit with purpose, pushing two fingers deep without warning, twisting and sliding until I thought my whole world would explode.

Just when I almost tipped, he stopped, standing to his full height, and kissed me—making me taste myself. His forearms tucked under my knees, and his palms gripped my hips, jerking me to the edge of the dresser. He pushed all the way in to the base, tearing a savage cry from my throat like it'd been waiting there for years.

For just a moment, he stilled, and we held each other. Foreheads pressed close, breathing each other's air, we made a moment, committing it to memory. The moment over seven years in the making. The moment we gave in.

He hooked one of my legs around his hip and used his free hand to cradle my face and tip my chin to meet his deep blue eyes. Everything fell away, and it was just me and him— Nova and Parker—like we'd longed for, for so long.

His thumb traced the arch in my cheek, the edge of my jaw, the curve of my lip, and I just watched him, felt him filling me. Finally, he pulled back one agonizing inch at a time, only to slam back in. It started slow and steady, a pounding rhythm full of intensity and need. But the desperation came roaring back, creeping through our veins, pulsing with more, more, more.

We lost our rhythm. Our soothing, searching hands became frantic again, grabbing on wherever we could. Our kisses no longer explored with intent but roved and tasted every inch we could reach. His nipple in my mouth. His ass under my clawing nails, his wavy, damp locks in my fist.

He rutted against me, thudding the frame behind me against the wall with each powerful thrust until I was sure it'd come crashing down.

And I didn't care if it did because, with each slide, my world came closer and closer to exploding into a million pieces, and all I needed was him to cling to, and I'd be okay.

His hand moved between us, his thumb slicking around my clit with quick sure movements, and I rocked harder, racing for the finish.

"Parker. Parker." I cried. I pleaded. I whimpered.

One more swipe, and I fell. I did my best to stem the ragged screams of pleasure by shoving my mouth against his shoulder, but it was useless because moments later, he joined me and clung to me as he tipped too. We fell in each other's arms into the abyss of pleasure. By the time the world came back into view, I was still in Parker's arms, and he was in mine.

Our sweat-slicked skin stuck together. Our chests heaved in sync, trying to catch our breaths. Our mouths still pressed to each other's flesh as if unwilling to part.

Prying my grip loose of his hair, I stroked my fingers down his back, just relishing the feel of him still stretching me, the feel of his naked skin under mine—a dream I wasn't sure would ever come true.

"That," he breathed, "was so much more than I ever expected."

He finally managed to support himself and pull back enough to hold on to the condom and slip free. As soon as he was gone, I already wanted him back.

Tossing the condom in the trash, he returned to hold me in his arms, brushing my damp, tangled hair out of my face so he could reach my lips.

Our kisses were lazy and slow and just as good as the frantic.

"Hold on," he muttered just before lifting me up and turning us to the bed. As gently as possible, he laid me back and rolled beside me.

"You, Nova Hearst, are wild."

I rolled to my side, fingered the supernova tattoo along his ribs. "Nonsense. I'm just trying to keep up with the rock star."

"Psh. You may kill me."

"Hopefully not. I'd like a repeat soon."

"Oh yeah?" He leaned forward and pecked my lips, nipping the bottom one. "I think I can stay alive for that."

"Good."

"How about you show me what you're working on over there," he nodded toward the notebook on my nightstand, "and then we can shower."

"Mmm," I hummed.

"Have you ever had shower sex?"

"Can't say that I have."

"Good. I've only been dreaming about it since that first time I walked in on you."

"Pervert," I joked, shoving his shoulder.

He rolled on top of me, flicking my piercing. "Yup. And I can't wait to show you every single perverted thing I ever wanted to do to you."

"Yes, sir," I breathed.

Fulfilling Parker's fantasies after denying us for so long sounded like the perfect night, and we set about doing just that.

TWENTY-FOUR

Parker

"So, this is what the great Nova, woman of the wild, does when she disappears into the woods?" I sank deeper into the warm water until it reached my neck, not taking my eyes off her. "Skinny dip?"

I'd seen her climb into the hot spring, confident in her nudity, but I didn't want to miss a single peek if she decided to stand up and give me a show. It'd been about a week since that night in the hotel and I refused to miss a second of it. So, when we had a few days break between shows without promo, I asked Nova to show me what she loved. It was the perfect way for us to connect away from everything.

"When the mood strikes," she answered flippantly, skimming her hands along the water. "Or whenever I need to get clean. Sometimes, I don't have access to showers."

I breathed a laugh, taking in the woman with the Sierra Nevada vista behind her, naked in a hot spring, her hair curling like flames licking at the mountain range. I remembered the girl who hesitated to show me her art and blushed at every compliment. I took the then and now and merged them into something more beautiful than what lay at the surface.

"When did you become so wild?"

She gave a coy smile from under her lashes and winked. "It's the quiet ones you have to watch out for. They're the rowdiest lying in wait for someone to share it with."

"Oh, yeah. I think it was all that porn you watched."

She tipped her head back, a laugh bursting from her lips. "I never should have told you."

"You should have sent them to me so we could watch together. You should have video chat me and let me watch *you*. In fact, let's make that a rule from now on."

"You couldn't handle it," she challenged.

"Puh-lease," I joked, putting on my best valley girl voice.

She bat her lashes. "I'm too wild."

"Oh, yeah?"

"Yeah."

I pushed away from the edge, venturing into the middle to close the gap. "Show me later."

"We'll see." Despite her doubtful answer, she leaned back, arching up to bring her pebbled tips to the chilled air.

At my growl, she giggled and submerged back in the water.

"In truth, I'm really not that wild. Usually when it's only just me."

"What about with the girls?"

"Sometimes. Rae can really pull it out of me. The third time we hung out, we went to a frat party, and I ended up dancing on a table."

"Damn. That would have been a sight to see."

"From the vague flashes of memory, I'm not sure it was."

"So, is that how you met Rae and Vera? At a college party?"

"Yup. It was love at first eye roll. We were people-watching in separate places in the room and very unimpressed. I caught her eye roll about the same time I did mine, and we clicked. In an odd way. When we saw Vera do the same, we roped her in."

"They're an interesting bunch."

She smiled and looked out at the sun slowly descending, causing the mountains' shadows to creep closer across the vast desert toward us.

"Did you miss not going to college?"

"No," I answered easily. "Not even a little bit."

She looked back at me, her nose scrunching up. "Yeah, I can't see any of you doing that. God, could you imagine Oren as an astronaut?"

Shaking my head, I remembered Oren barely making a front flip off of the stand his kit was set up on at the end of the concert last week. "Not at all. He's the very definition of someone dying after asking, *what does this button do?*"

"Yeah, space is definitely safer with him on drums."

Steam rose up, curling around her like I wanted to. The sun setting behind her cast her in a halo—she looked like an angel. My hands twitched to reach for her, and after so many years of denying myself, I didn't hesitate to close the distance. I gripped her hips, and her arms snaked around my shoulders as I sat back on the bench someone before us created. She straddled my lap, and instantly I hardened at the brush of her core against my cock.

She sucked in a shaky breath, and I considered pushing inside her right here, but we didn't have a condom.

So instead, I adjusted and enjoyed her warmth against me, raining gentle kisses along her neck and shoulders. She arched this way and that to give me access, dragging her fingers languidly through my hair. We moved like a dance with no end—no purpose other than to feel each other and be close.

"What about after all this?" she finally asked.

"I don't know." I pulled back to take her in, pushing the loose curls off her damp cheek. "I feel like we're just getting started in some ways. But I can also feel the exhaustion creep in quicker with each tour. Maybe I just need more breaks like this. Take some time to enjoy the quiet with you."

"I could definitely help with that."

"I've also been taking time to really understand and get to know all the behind-the-scenes action. The production and management. I could see myself producing later when my body has finally given up on touring." I shrugged, not really having thought about it. We all just lived in the moment and enjoyed every second. I'd only had to think about me, but with her in my arms, I realized I wanted to think about her too. "What about you? What do you want?"

Her shrug matched mine. "I got a degree in fine arts and minored in journalism—mainly for my mom's peace of mind—but I feel like I hit the ground after graduation and splattered in every direction. At the core of it all, art is my foundation. And I started a lot of these projects while I was in college, and now, I'm getting a chance to delve deeper. I write for various online journals about travel, I paint and do photography, I write music and go on tour with famous, sexy musicians."

"Hey, you better not be doing that with anyone else," I pretend scolded.

"You are definitely an exception," she promised.

"Good." I pecked her lips. "When you're a famous artist, will you still find time to paint me like one of your French girls?" I asked in a breathy, feminine voice.

She laughed, shaking in my arms, making it hard to sit still, but her smile made it all worth it. "Of course, I'll paint you."

"And we can't forget your Instagram fame," I added.

She groaned and rolled her eyes. "As I said, that was unintentional and solely based on my vanity of wanting to document my travels."

"Well, I'm glad you did. I may have spent more than a few nights scrolling through them all."

"Really?"

"Yeah, although, I'm concerned with the amount of times

you're topless out in the woods. I mean, who takes those pictures?" I'd never stared at a back as long as I had hers. She had a collection of her laying in lagoons, standing on the beach, sitting on the edge of a cliff—all topless from behind.

"What can I say? It's kind of freeing. And it's just me in those moments, and my camera stand."

"Thank god."

"I don't know, when I'm out here, I just…am. I'm not worried about the future or any of the pressures of making the right decisions. It's just me and the quiet."

"I can see that." I looked around, enjoying that it was just us. She explained that it wasn't usually this quiet, but the time of the year wasn't ideal for those who only dabbled in camping. So, the location was pretty isolated. "I think I like the quiet with you."

"Good." She dipped her fingers in the water, warming them before pulling them out again and stroking across the bridge of my nose and brows. "How's your dad?"

"He's good," I answered languidly. I closed my eyes, just feeling her weight on me, enjoying the soft strokes—soft and soothing. "Your mom?"

"She's good. We don't really talk much. Especially right now with my decision to stay on my path.

"Why would that make her not want to talk to you?"

"She spent all this time pushing to lock me away in an office, and instead, I am out on my own in the forest. Basically, her worst nightmare. But instead of listening to me and seeing that it's about what I want and not her, she's letting it tear us apart."

It was like we were checking boxes of basic questions to ask when catching up. We'd been talking for a while now, but we kept it mostly superficial or about just us and the now. Our parents had felt a little too close to the past, but since she brought my dad up first—no matter how simple—it was like she pulled the curtain back, allowing more to come through.

"You know, I never quite understood what happened between them."

"Your dad didn't tell you?"

"Nah, and since he didn't bring it up, neither did I. I tried to broach it once, but he changed the topic real quick, so I followed suit."

"Oh." Her fingers stalled for a moment but quickly resumed, this time pushing back into my hair. "They argued a lot toward the end. I think your dad wanted to keep it from you so you could focus on your dream."

"Why didn't you tell me?"

"The same reason. You were away, and there wasn't anything you could do."

"They argued before though and made it past it."

When she didn't say anything else, I cracked open an eye and took in her furrowed brow and pursed lips like she struggled over what to say next. I didn't push her, just stroked my thumbs along the hollows of her hips under the water and waited, sinking back into the sensual scrape of her nails now working the nape of my neck.

"After…everything that happened, I guess tensions got higher, and they started arguing again. I know my mom was stressed over what happened. Your dad was worried about me and didn't really know what to do. I…didn't make it easy."

"It wasn't your job to make it easy on anyone."

"Either way. I didn't help by hiding away, moving through the motions with a pair of headphones locked in place. I could've said something."

I gently pressed my lips to hers. "You didn't owe an explanation to them."

"I know, and my mom didn't make it easy to talk. After I got home from the hospital, she went a little crazy. It was like all the years she hadn't spent being over-protective were crammed into those first few months, becoming a helicopter mom. It was like the only thing she could blame was giving me too much freedom."

"Yeah. I know she blamed me for what happened, and I wasn't there for her to take it out on. So, I'm sure that didn't help with everything else going on."

She pulled back, the lines between her brows deepening. "What? How did you know she blamed you?"

My confusion mirrored hers, and I took a moment to consider that her mom never told her about my visit. But why would she when all she wanted to do was keep me as far from her as possible?

"I looked for you."

Her hands stopped completely and slid to my shoulders, helping her scoot back to the edge of my knees. "What?" she asked again, barely a whisper. This time there was no confusion, but instead, disbelief.

"Of course, I looked for you, Nova." How could she assume I'd just given up? I'd been busy, but I never wanted to abandon her. Even if she abandoned me without giving me a chance to fight. "When you stopped taking my calls, and then my dad called to tell me they'd gotten divorced, I came back. But you were gone. It was like you vanished—no social media, you weren't at school. I couldn't find an address. Nothing. Your mom switched jobs and changed back to her maiden name, which took me a while to figure out, but it was something—somewhere to start. I went to go see her because why not?"

She searched my eyes, her chest heaving with each revelation I shared, her eyes brimming with tears.

"She fucking laid into me when I walked in. She told me she'd hide you from me if it was the last thing she did because of what I let happen to you. I, uh, I didn't take it great." I winced, remembering the way I'd got raging drunk and trashed the mostly empty practice space we'd held onto. "The guys cornered me the next day, pretty pissed since I canceled two shows to stay in New York to find you."

"Jesus, Parker."

"They made me choose, and in that moment, I made an emotional choice—I made the easier choice to go with the path of least resistance. I chose the safer one, and I'm so sorry I didn't fight harder."

A tear slipped free, and I wiped it away before it could even reach her chin. She studied me, swallowing again and again, and I sat there, letting her process everything. Barely a moment passed when she took a deep, shuddering breath and lifted her chin, pulling her shoulders back.

My Nova, I thought, taking in her strength and will, the sun fully setting like a fire behind her. *My supernova.*

"It's in the past," she declared. "I didn't know, but there isn't anything we can do but be here—now."

"I think I like that plan."

"Good."

With a decisive nod, she reached past me, pressing her front to mine, stealing my breath, and electrifying me right back into the moment. I was halfway to gripping her to hold her in place when she pulled back with her camera.

"Take a picture of me," she ordered, climbing off my lap.

She turned around and stood until the water rippled against the small of her back. With her red hair shining brighter in the dying sun, her pale skin bared, perfectly decorated with the beautiful art she'd created, she stretched her arms wide. I ogled the firm lines of her back and the delicate curve of her neck. She was strength and beauty and everything I could ever want in a woman.

I took a few shots, being extra careful to not shift and catch any of her breasts. But once those were done, I said screw it to caution and kept clicking as I shifted around her. When she saw me rounding her side, camera lifted and still clicking, she gasped and jerked her hands to cover her breasts.

"Oh, c'mon, Supernova," I coaxed. She pried her middle fingers free and stuck her tongue out. "Real mature."

"Well, let me take some pictures of you naked, then."

"You want a dick pic? Because I will happily pose for one."

"Of course, you would.," she laughed, rolling her eyes.

"I have a better idea," I said, closing the distance and pulling her into my arms. Flipping the screen, I positioned it as best I could and snapped a pic just as I pressed my lips to hers.

She abandoned her breasts and wrapped her arms around me. Losing myself in the moment, I randomly snapped, giving most of my attention to the woman in my arms. I walked her back, arching her over the rocks where she stretched her arms out and back. Pulling the camera back to my eye, I pressed my hand over her pale breasts, fingering the hard ball through the petal-soft nipple, growing harder at her gasp, and shifted my fingers enough to cover the bare minimum. My tan skin stood stark against her pale flesh, and I snapped. Her chin a shadowy blur beyond the exquisite line of her body arched back.

I took picture after picture as we shifted. My mouth on hers, on her chin, neck—her nipple. She stole the camera when I lifted her up and buried my head between her thighs. She dug her hand into my hair, and the whir and click of the camera had me diving in, even more turned on by her memorializing me eating her pussy.

When both of us were on the edge of desperation, I picked her up and practically ran to the camper van for a condom. The camera was tossed aside, and nothing else mattered for the rest of the night but her and me.

The way it should've always been.

The way I was going to make damn sure it always did.

TWENTY-FIVE

Nova

Warmth. More warmth than I expected on a morning in mid-February.

But then the warmth shifted, and the creak of the van doors preambled the bright sun pouring into the small space.

Then the warmth was back, and this time, I wasn't just warm, I was wet.

Wet kisses started at my knee and worked higher. If this was a dream, I didn't want to wake up.

A large hand pushed my thigh up and back, broad shoulders making themselves at home between my legs. A rough thumb swiped through my folds up to my clit. I gasped, arching up to follow when he pulled away. Before I could protest, a tongue took the same path as his thumb, and I moaned as it slowly swirled around where I needed him.

I fisted the sheets and dug my heel against the mattress, trying to gain more pressure, to move right under his tongue instead of the torturous circles around.

"Parker," I whimpered. "Please."

His laugh vibrated against my skin, sending tremors all the way down to my toes. Another long slow lick from my opening back up, sucking on my folds before finally returning back to my clit. This time two fingers worked their way inside me, curling and twisting, and I couldn't take not seeing him. I squinted against the brilliant morning sun and edged even closer to coming when I took in his tan back sprawled between my legs.

I burrowed my hands into his hair and rocked my hips faster and faster, racing toward my orgasm. A third finger joined and pushed deeper—harder. His tongue finally flicked across the sensitive bundle at the same time he sucked, and within seconds I was coming. Every muscle in my body pulled tight, the waves of pleasure surging through my nerves until I was crying out and riding his face to get every last ounce of euphoria.

I fell trembling back onto the mattress, gasping for air, dipping my chin just far enough to look down my body and watch him smile up at me as he swirled his tongue through my folds, bringing me down from my high. I committed the image of *the* Parker Callahan between my legs, the tip of his tongue gathering my cum from every inch he could reach. I was so entranced by the sight, the stunning rocky desert behind him couldn't even pull my attention away.

His hard cock stood tall when he leaned back onto his haunches, finally releasing my thigh, and I could think of nothing else but wanting to return the favor.

"Good morning," he finally greeted me.

Instead of saying it back, I moved quickly, pushing him back against the wall of the van.

"Here I was thinking you'd be more relaxed after an orgasm."

"I want more."

His hand snaked into my hair, holding me in place so he could kiss me and let me taste myself on his lips. "By all means, take what you want," he murmured.

Despite my orgasm, I wasn't any less eager to have him. Need pulsed like a beast inside me, and I sucked, kissed, and bit my way down his body. I sucked the soft head of his cock between my lips when I finally reached where it laid against his abs, moving to leave sucking kisses down his shaft until I reached his balls.

Gripping his thick length in my hands, I stroked my thumb along his piercing, sucking one ball into my mouth and then the other. I held his heavy-lidded gaze and dragged my tongue from base to tip, returning the favor of teasing. His abs flexed as I stroked the tip of my tongue around the metal and flicked between the slit on his head. He growled when I wrapped just my lips along the tip and gave a sucking kiss, but not going further.

I moved back down to tease but didn't get far. He grunted and drove a fist into my hair, pulling me back up. I met his wild eyes with a challenge in mine. His fingers tightened, and the sting only turned me on more. His other hand wrapped around mine, where I gripped his dick, directing it to my lips to paint them with the precum leaking free.

"Put my cock in your mouth, Nova," he ordered softly—almost dangerously. I knew he'd never force me or hurt me, but I liked how on edge he was.

I lashed the tip with my tongue before sliding across my lips to collect his flavor. "Make me," I whispered.

"Fuck."

With that, he jerked me forward and pushed my head down at the same time as he thrust up, both of us groaning. He didn't push far because of his piercing but did push against my throat. He had control for only a few thrusts before I took over, done with teasing and just wanting to feel him stretching my mouth, pushing against my tongue, tasting him. I twisted and stroked my hand to meet my lips and closed my eyes, losing myself to his groans and grumbled swear words.

His breathing picked up, and when I was sure he'd spill in my mouth, he pushed me back, moving so quick I could barely keep up. He flipped me over to my stomach and got behind me. When I heard the crinkle of the condom wrapper, I reached my hand back and stopped him.

"I've got us covered," I explained when his brows pinched together.

His jaw dropped. "I've-I've never—" he stuttered.

"I want to feel you, Parker. I want to feel all of you inside me."

"Fuck, yes," he breathed, snapping back into action.

He gripped my hips, pulling me up to my knees, but leaving my chest to the mattress, and lined himself up.

"Are you sure?"

"Please," I begged.

Swiping his head through my folds, coating himself in me, teasing my clit before finally pushing in. Just the head and back out, again and again until I wanted to beat my fist against the bed and scream.

"Parker," I growled through gritted teeth. I tried to push back, but his hands held me in place.

With a laugh, he kept one hand on my hip, and the other slid up my spine, pushing me into the mattress more as he eased inside—fucking finally.

I whimpered at the intrusion, desperate to move but unable to. He curled around me and inched out and back in, slowly at first. But when I started pulsing around him, he gave in. I shifted to all fours, trying to gain purchase against his rough thrusts, crying out with each one. Looking over my shoulder, I watched him stare down at where he fucked me, his abs contracting into a perfect rippled six-pack. His tongue slicked over his lips, and I needed more. I needed to be closer.

Pushing up, I reached back, rising to my knees and twisting to get his lips under mine. He groaned into my mouth, and I fed off his pleasure, feeding him my own whimpers when he palmed my breasts and tweaked my nipples.

"You are so warm—so wet," he breathed against my skin. "I'm gonna fill you up with my cum."

"Yes. Please."

"Look at you, getting fucked raw, begging for my cum. All with the doors open for anyone to see."

I flicked my eyes outside, knowing no one was there, but liking the extra shot of adrenaline at the thought of someone out there.

"They're probably watching these perfect little tits bounce from how hard your pussy is taking my cock."

"Oh, god," I whimpered. He knew how much it turned me on—he knew my fantasies.

"They'd be so hard from watching you they'd have to get their dick out and stroke it, imagining what it feels like to be inside you—imagining what it would feel like to tongue fuck your sweet cunt."

"Yes, yes."

"Would you let them, sweet Nova?" he asked, his hand skimming down to between my folds. "Would you let them eat your pussy while I fucked you?"

I should have been embarrassed—ashamed, but with Parker, I could always be me—honest and free. So, when he tapped my clit, I didn't hold back. "Yes," I whimpered.

He groaned, pushing in harder—deeper. "I have a confession."

"Tell me," I pleaded.

"I'd like it too," he whispered. "I like the idea of you in my arms as someone else touches you. Because they can touch, because I allow them to. Because even if they can touch and taste, I know you're mine."

Pressing my forehead to his cheek, I gave over to him. "I'm all yours."

He gave another slap to my pussy, and I came again, this time harder and more intense. Everything faded, and I almost fell forward, but Parker held me tight, fucking up into my spasming pussy, chasing his own orgasm. I started floating back to earth just as he started coming. He slowed to powerful, hard thrusts, spilling his cum inside me, holding onto me with a bruising grip, groaning his pleasure into my skin.

We both collapsed forward into a heap. He slipped free and looked for a shirt to clean up with while I relished in the feel of his orgasm slipping from between my legs. Needing to see it, I got up to my elbows and had a whole other tremor rack my body at seeing the sticky fluid coating my thighs. I reached down, dragging my fingers through the mess—our mess.

"Jesus fucking Christ. There's never been anything sexier," Parker muttered.

He watched me, a white shirt in his fist. Falling back, I arched my back and dragged my wet fingers up my body and around my nipple.

"Fuuuuck." He rolled to face me, leaning down to suck the wetness from my nipple while he cleaned between my legs.

He kissed his way up my neck to my mouth, where I got the slightest taste of the both of us—tangy and salty and so much Parker. It was perfect. A few more soft kisses, and he brushed his nose against mine before just looking at me.

"You, Nova Hearst, are everything."

That look. His words spoken with awe. His arms holding me safe. His body over mine. All of it seeped like warm chocolate through my veins.

"Parker." I barely breathed his name, scared of what I would say next if I put too much force behind his name.

I love you.

He smiled and delivered one last peck. "I'm going to go make breakfast. We need to fuel up because I'm going to need to fuck you again. A few times."

I watched him get up and pull on sweatpants that hung precariously on his hips. Rolling to my side, I smiled, wanting to watch him all day.

"Why don't you go paint?" he suggested.

I looked over my shoulder, finally taking in the beauty of

the morning. It matched the beautiful feeling shaping inside me. It'd been there all along but in disarray until I could finally gather the pieces enough to put it together. Maybe painting would help me sort out the last bit and clarify what to do next.

I grabbed the first thing I could find, which ended up being a pair of baggy denim overalls, and tossed them on, grabbing my items and heading out.

With the first stroke of my brush to the canvas, something already began to ease inside me.

I didn't poke or prod at it, instead losing myself to the colors and blend and sounds around me.

Music reached through the open doors of the van, and Parker's voice followed, slipping in place.

This my mind whispered. *This is what we've searched for.*

I'd run for so long from one thing to the next, always pulling back and holding a part of myself by the door in case I needed to run, but I didn't want to anymore.

I didn't want to live scared.

Fear hadn't been the driving force behind my decision to remain private, but I always knew it played a role. I never wanted it to rule me, so I ignored it. But ignoring it didn't make it any less real, and I needed to face it if I wanted to step forward with my business—with Parker.

I loved him.

I loved him enough to at least give everything I had to try. And to do that, I needed to bring both feet through the door.

"Scrambled eggs and bacon, my lady." Parker set the plate down with a bow before checking out my painting. "It's just missing one thing," he declared. And just like he had all those years ago in my room, he grabbed a brush, dipped it in a color, and placed an inconspicuous dot somewhere in the painting. Making it our art. "Perfect."

He plopped down, and I couldn't help but stare at every little move he made as if seeing him for the first time—this time with both eyes open, fully facing him rather than half turned away.

"You okay?" he asked around a bite of bacon.

"Yeah." I blinked, snapping out of my daze. "Just still baffled how you can eat that." I pointed at his plate, and the same disgusting grape jelly smeared all over it.

"It's delicious. I think it's the cheese that really makes it," he said around a big bite.

"So fucking gross." But still, I smiled because it was one of the first memories I'd created with him, and every time I saw him on tour eating it, I couldn't help but smile.

We sat in our folding chairs, enjoying our eggs and bacon in the unusually warm weather, in the middle of a desert. No one was around but us, and all I could think about was when we got back. With a deep breath, I closed another door on any chance of backing out. "Will you take me on a date when we get home?"

He faced me slowly, my words so much more than asking him on a date, and he knew it. "Are you sure?"

The hope in his eyes lit a fire in my heart, and I couldn't help but smile and nod. "Yeah. I want you, and it may take some work, but you're worth it, and I'm done losing you. I want to be wined and dined by *the* Parker Callahan."

His answering smile was everything. "I can do that."

"But let's take it slow, okay?" He tipped his head, not understanding. "Can we maybe try low-key places—maybe keep things quiet for now? Give a little time for the Sonia debacle to settle."

"Of course," he answered easily. "This life isn't for everyone, but I think if we both work at it, we can make it for us. We can meet halfway."

"I can do halfway."

He smiled through the rest of breakfast, and I couldn't help but smile right along with him. Before he got up to throw everything away, he took a deep breath like he wanted to say something big, too.

I froze, bracing for the impact of whatever had him looking so cautious.

"Listen, I know this is like giving an inch and taking a mile, but I was wondering if…" Another deep breath and his hand shot through his hair. "I was wondering if you could go to the Grammys with me?"

"Uhhh…" I didn't want to turn down his first offer, but that was also one of the biggest, most public events to go to.

"No red carpet. You could meet me inside at the table," he rushed to explain.

I considered my options. The Grammys were in a month. A lot could change. And the idea of skipping the cameras and questions was very appealing. It also gave me time to move forward with Aiken's plan and slowly start revealing Nova Hearst to the world—or at least those interested in me.

"I think I can do that," I finally answered.

"If you can't, I understand. I know it's a lot. I would just… love to have you by my side. I've never gone with anyone I really cared about."

I remembered how jealous I was when I saw the pictures of him and Sonia walking the red carpet last year, and a petty part of me jumped for joy that he hadn't really cared if she was there.

"We'll take it slow, and I'll make a plan, but I can do that."

He beamed brighter than the sun, making any nerves one-hundred-percent worth it. "Like I said, everything."

TWENTY-SIX

Nova

I DATED MORE in the past three weeks than I had in my entire life. I imagined this is what the women on *The Bachelor* felt like. Exclusive dates in a different city every few days. Figuring out creative ways to remain isolated, which sometimes led to extravagant dates like a hot air balloon picnic or bungee jumping. Although the guys came with us on that one. All squeezed in between traveling and shows.

It'd kind of been the most amazing three weeks of my life. When we'd come back from our trip, boarding the bus hand in hand, everyone had been sitting around, including some of the crew. They'd taken one look at us, and a mix of cheers and groans followed. I'd been thoroughly confused until everyone started pulling out their wallets and exchanging money. Apparently, a bet had been going on for a while.

It'd been…nice. Almost too good to be true. The intrusive thought reared its head at random, and I shoved it away each time, living for the moment.

Like tonight. We got into Chicago this morning, and the guys had practice, but the night was ours before the show tomorrow. Parker was wining and dining me like a true date. I'd bought a special dress approved by the girls.

He's gonna fuck you so hard in that. I can't wait to hear all about it. Rae practically squealed when I told her about our trip and that I finally gave in to him. Vera smiled like the caring friend but tagged on that she also wanted to hear all about it. A pang struck my chest, and I made a note to FaceTime them tomorrow.

Another pang hit me, but this one was full of nerves. Chicago was the biggest city we'd been to, and Parker had a restaurant he was dying to take me to. He apparently knew the chef and had gotten us a private reservation. I'd been sharing more on my Instagram, receiving lots of exclamation points in the emails from Aiken, but I had yet to show my full face.

The latest one, in particular, might as well have painted a target on my back. I'd stood, decked out in my hiking gear, in front of the tour bus with my hat pulled low. Oren and Ash flipping the camera off in the background had been a dead giveaway as to who I was writing music with. I posted it yesterday morning, and already countless articles commented.

After three weeks of things going great with Parker and me, I felt confident in starting the process of tying myself to him. He'd stood his ground with Sonia when Aspen tried to make him take it all back. He stood by me. I trusted he wouldn't leave me to deal with the fallout. I trusted he wouldn't hurt me.

But with the added pressure of my last post, my caution with being in a big city with lots of photographers waiting for the band skyrocketed.

"You just have to make it in and out, and no one knows we're coming. Once we're there, we have a private table away from prying eyes," he said to me in the back of the car.

I could have laughed at how he was basically giving me a pep talk like it was game day. All we were missing was a dry erase board with Xs and Os and lines laying out our plan.

Turned out we hadn't needed one because we made it in

without issue. Sure, there were murmurs as we passed patrons already seated, but photographers didn't pop out like Jack-in-the-boxes. And the dinner had been fabulous, the company even better. We'd shared a tiramisu I could have married, but with each bite, my nerves spiked again, knowing we still had to make it back out.

When Parker noticed my growing anxiety, he ordered a couple shots of tequila. We talked until my limbs relaxed, and nothing mattered but getting back to our hotel to follow up on the filthy promises he whispered across the table.

"You look ridiculously stunning." His eyes scraped across my cleavage where the deep vee of my beaded dress barely clung to my curves.

More heat surged through my veins, and I finished off my last drink. "I think I'm ready to go now."

"Thank god."

We kept our heads down, and I realized the one downside of a sparkling dress and chunky ankle boots that added enough height to bring me closer to Parker's—everyone saw me. But I cared less with the tequila and desire bubbling to the surface. It was the only excuse I had for why I turned and smiled when a flash went off just before we reached the SUV.

Parker followed me into the car and blinked with eyes just as wide as mine. We sat frozen, staring at each other while I replayed what I'd just done.

"I blame it on the tequila," I whispered.

It broke the tension, and we both burst out laughing—mine just held an edge of panic to it.

"I can see your head spinning," Parker murmured. He shifted to face me, sliding his hand over my knee and up my thigh. "Let me distract you."

By the time we reached the hotel, Parker had my panties in his pocket and my lipstick smeared on his mouth. My carefully crafted messy bun *actually* looked like a messy bun, and despite the orgasm he just gave me, I was more eager than ever to get upstairs.

Another photographer waited for us at the hotel, but this time I ducked my head. I couldn't hide the blush staining my cheeks at our disheveled appearance.

Despite the attendant in the elevator with us, Parker stood behind me, making love to my neck with open-mouthed kisses, grinding himself against my ass. Not that the attendant would have stopped us—they were paid for discretion, and Parker and I liked to dabble in our fantasy of exhibitionism. We never said it loud or pushed too far—merely toed the line.

I was ready to pounce as soon as we opened the door to our room. The hotel had an apartment-like suite, and all the guys stayed together, but they'd made plans to be out tonight. The idea of fucking on as many surfaces as possible before they came back had me almost ripping the handle off in my eagerness to get inside.

Except, not all the guys were gone. Ash sat leaned back on the couch, one foot propped on the coffee table with his bass in his lap.

"Hey, lovebirds. Nice dress, Nova," he greeted, looking me up and down.

"Hey. I thought you were going to that party?" Parker asked, struggling to not sound disappointed.

"I did. And it was lame. Oren and Brogan left to chase some pussy, and I wasn't feeling it. So here I am."

"If only everyone knew, the party animal, Ash Finch, would rather lounge back with his bass over some pussy." I sighed dramatically, and his brows shot up over me saying pussy.

"Let's keep it our little secret."

"Deal."

"So, how goes dating life?" he asked, turning his attention back to his bass. "Based on the sounds coming from your bunk every night, you guys obviously enjoy each other."

My eyes shot wide, and my face flamed. "Oh, my god. I'm so sorry," I muttered through my hands covering my face. Of course, they had to know and hear, but no one ever said anything to make me confront the moans and whimpers Parker pulled out of me.

"Don't be. I basically jerk off to you coming every night."

My hands dropped along with my jaw. He took me in from the corner of his eyes, the dark smirk in place.

Parker apparently didn't have any of the shock rendering me speechless. "Oh, man, Nova will eat that up," he muttered.

"What?" Ash asked, his hands stalling over the strings.

"Yeah, Supernova here likes porn—specifically exhibitionism," he announced, stepping up behind me.

"Parker," I gasped.

Ash shifted his full attention to me, the dark pools of his eyes swirling with who knew what. Sin. Dark promises. "Oh, yeah?"

"It's just Ash," Parker explained. He slid his hands to my hips to soothe me, and I realized he was right. It *was* just Ash, and honestly, in the small bus, my fantasy might have been the tamest among the guys.

"Yeah. Just me." Ash set his bass aside and rose from the couch, prowling closer like a panther to close the distance between him and his prey. "And if you ever want to fulfill this fantasy—I'd happily be the man to play the role."

Parker's hands squeezed tight at Ash's suggestion. I was sure he was taunting, teasing—being typical Ash, but there was also truth behind it. And feeling Parker's reaction to the suggestion spurred my own, and rather than laughing it off, we let it linger and grow.

The idea swelled, taking me over.

I met Ash's gaze, stepping to the edge of his darkness, the promise lapping at my toes like waves on a shore, begging me to come in. My nipples hardened at the thought.

Parker pressed his front to my back, his hard length

against my ass. A shiver raced down my body when he pressed the gentlest kisses up my neck to nip at my ear.

"What do you think?" he whispered, his breath teasing the hollow of my ear. "You want to let Ash be our voyeur? Want to turn our little game into a reality?"

Ash's eyes finally freed mine to watch Parker's hand trail up my stomach to swirl his fingers around my nipple. I clenched my jaw to fight back the whimper, failing when Ash made a show of adjusting his length in his pants.

My head fell back to Parker's shoulder and rolled to meet his eyes—the pupils almost completely blocking out the brilliant blue. "Do you?" I asked.

He pushed his dick into me harder. "You know I do. But only if you're okay with it—only if it turns you on."

Closing my eyes, I took stock of my body. My nipples pulled tight and aching. Every time Parker gently brushed them, a string of electricity shot to my core, pulsing with need. Wetness coated my thighs, and I ached to feel anything between them to ease the building need. Did I want this?

Yes.

Did I want it with Ash?

I met his eyes again for only a moment—but a moment was all I needed. With Parker's arms around me, the answer was easy.

Yes.

I rolled my hips, biting Parker's chin. "You know it does." He groaned, his muscles tightening behind me like an animal ready to pounce. "No sex," I clarified before we got too far into the moment.

"No sex," he agreed. His hand shifted from my hip to between my legs, cupping me, looking directly to Ash. "This is mine."

"Fair enough," Ash agreed. "Maybe just a taste?"

"She does taste awfully sweet," Parker murmured against

my neck, his hand gently massaging between my legs, inching my dress higher.

Air brushed the wet heat between my legs just before his fingers slid through my folds. I gasped at the swipe and burned with the knowledge that Ash caught his first glimpse of my pussy—that he'd get more than a glance by the end of the night.

Parker stroked his damp fingers along my bottom lip, and my tongue followed, tasting myself.

"I'm gonna need a bed ASAP," Ash growled.

We moved to Parker's room just off the living room, and the French doors clicked closed like a director's clapboard starting the action. Parker gently brushed his fingers up one arm, across my back, and down the other. "How would you like her?"

"On the bed. Legs spread wide. I want to eat her pussy."

I'd always called Ash's eyes the pools leading to sin, but those were empty words compared to the depth of desire in them now. I'd had no idea how deep they went, but I knew I'd get a glimpse tonight.

Parker directed us to the bed, scooting back until he was pressed to the pillows. He shed his shirt before pulling me up between his legs—my back to his front. Ash's shirt went next, and I marveled at the lean ripple of muscle covering every inch. He'd always been ripped, even in high school, but over the years, he bulked up and had a few tattoos across his hard flesh. He crawled up the bed and never looked away from my gaze once. Not even when Parker's calloused tips started at my knee and scraped up my thigh, hitting the hem of my dress and tugging that to my hips.

The cool air brushed starkly against the wet heat saturating my core. Just the slightest sensation felt like too much, like a feather in the wind waiting to be tipped over the edge, but it was nothing compared to when Parker gripped the inside of my knees and pulled them apart.

Ash's eyes dropped then and landed on my core like a physical touch, dragging a needy whimper from my parted lips. My chest heaved for air, trying to keep up with my racing heart, pumping adrenaline and fire through my veins. Needing an anchor, I linked my fingers with Parker's and held on.

Ash scooted closer and, without looking away, asked, "What about her tits. Can I play with them?"

"If she'll allow it."

I nodded before he finished answering.

Ash's hand moved at a snail's pace closing the distance between us, and when he finally reached me, it was a butterfly-soft touch, stroking the smooth wet folds. Up one side and down the other, each time with a little more pressure, the circle closing in until he parted my pussy and finally circled down around my opening and up past my clit. I rocked my hips, searching for friction, only earning me a dark chuckle.

"Eager."

"Horny," I growled in response.

Another deep laugh, but as if his finger was attached to his body, when he leaned forward, his finger slid inside. Another finger joined the first, and he stopped a breath away from my mouth as if he wanted to taste me there but knew he couldn't. He locked me in his gaze, inches apart, and slid his fingers in and out, the sound of my core trying to suck him back in obscene and blending with my whimpering cries.

"She's tight," Ash uttered.

"So fucking tight. If I was a less jealous man, I'd let you feel it yourself, but unfortunately for you, I'm not."

"I'll take this."

"How many times did you fantasize about Nova in high school?" Parker asked.

I almost scoffed and said never for him when he shocked me. "So many times. I jerked off to the thought of bending sweet little Nova over the couch in our practice space and fucking right through that little virgin hymen." At my wide-eyed stare, he smirked and shoved in hard, pulling a cry from me. "But not nearly as many times as you did."

"I think I have everyone beat. Her pussy was all I thought about. Totally worth the wait."

"We'll see." Ash leaned in and diverted to my chin, sucking down my neck into my cleavage.

As he progressed lower, Parker worked the other side, tugging both straps of my dress off my shoulders. As if Ash was waiting, as soon as the material cleared my nipples, he pounced, sucking the tip into his mouth, flicking it with his tongue.

"Pierced fucking nipples. Fuck yeah," he said in awe, almost to himself. He tortured and teased, moving from one breast to the other, working in tandem with Parker—while he sucked, Parker played. All the while, his fingers twisting and pulling and swirling until I was sure there was a mess on the bed under me.

Finally, Ash skipped over my bunched-up dress and wedged his shoulders between my thighs, his hot breath gentle puffs to my overly sensitized skin. I tried to thrust up to reach his mouth only to have him pull back and tsk.

"Please," I whimpered.

"Supernova is a desperate little beggar. I fucking approve," Ash taunted.

Parker's laugh rumbled against my back, and frankly, I wasn't sure this was what I imagined being tortured by two men at once was like.

No, it was better. Yes, I wanted Ash to make me come, but the torture added to the tension, pulling the string tighter and tighter like a twisting screw, and I knew that once it snapped, it'd be heaven.

I trembled against Parker, holding on to wherever I could reach of him, my forehead growing damp from balancing on the edge for so long. Ash took his sweet time, sucking my folds, lapping along my thighs, barely brushing his tongue inside me, and ending with a light flick of his tongue to my clit. I wanted to wait patiently and scream all at once. I hadn't even begun coming, and I already felt torn in half.

Parker added to the painful pleasure by cupping my breasts, teasing the tips with swirls and pinches until I wanted to sob in need.

When I started to lose myself to the moment, Ash latched on tight, sucking my clit hard at the same time he shoved three fingers deep, and like I'd touched jumper cables, I jolted over the edge. Screaming moans ripped from deep inside me as I came fully apart, watching this man devour my pussy.

"Fucking. Again," he ordered like a savage animal, diving back in for more.

"I-I-can't—"

"You will," Parker demanded in my ear. He pinched my nipples, and right as I started coming down from my last orgasm, another took hold, and I flew even further.

Ringing crescendoed, and black closed in around the edges, my body just one long pulsing orgasm.

"Need you," Parker groaned against my neck. "Need inside you."

Ash pulled me toward him, still fingering my pussy as Parker rustled out of his clothes behind me.

"I'm gonna watch you ride him, imagining it's me. I'm gonna sit right there," he nodded to the chair in the corner, "and watch him stretch that tight little cunt around his fat cock. I'm going to see everything."

His words kept me more on edge than his fingers.

"I'm going to watch your tits bounce from him fucking up into you so hard. I'm going to watch your ass grind on him, imagine crawling up behind you and fucking that tight asshole—both of us at the same time."

"Parker," I whimpered. I needed him.

"Show me," Ash ordered, releasing me.

He did as promised and moved to the chair. Like a woman possessed, I turned to find Parker waiting for me, already stroking his thick length, and I couldn't wait another second to have him inside me.

I crawled over him, holding him tall at my entrance, and sank down. We both groaned, and I didn't stop until he filled me with every inch.

"Fuck, you're so swollen and wet."

Resting my hands on his chest, I lifted up and fell down, rocking my hips back at the same time. My legs shook from the exertion of holding myself so tensely when Ash ate me out, but nothing would stop me from having Parker.

"God damn," Ash groaned. I glanced over to find him with his dick, just as long and thick as Parker, in his hand, using a rough, fast grip.

Parker pushed up, hitting deep inside, and I focused my attention back on him. I rocked harder, racing toward another orgasm, unsure how I could survive another one. Parker gripped my hips and pulled himself up to suck on my nipples, and helped me move. I held onto his head, sinking my fingers into his damp hair, and ground myself down to get friction on my clit.

"You are fucking perfect," Parker muttered against my chest. "I'm gonna come, baby."

"Yes. Please."

He fell back again and held me in place as he fucked up inside me, taking his thumb to brush my clit. All the while, Ash watched. I saw what he told me he would see, and the picture was too much. I came. My nails dug into Parker's chest, and I held on, squeezing his cock tight until moments later, he spilled inside me.

When we both came down, my skin prickled with goosebumps from the sweat drying on my skin. Behind me, rustling clothes let me know Ash was dressing, and it was probably time to cover back up, but I couldn't bring myself to care.

Instead, I sat atop Parker and enjoyed every lingering pulse around him. The bed dipped before warm lips pressed to my shoulder. "Thank you," Ash said.

With that, the door opened and closed, and it was just Parker and me.

He laid me back, slipping free to roll on top, and kissed me until I was sure I'd pass out.

Again, like in the van, and almost every time after, he pulled back, looking deep into my eyes like he was truly seeing me, and what he found made him happy. "You're everything."

And just like every time before, I struggled to choke back the words I love you.

I didn't know why I didn't just say it. Maybe some girlish thought that I needed him to say it first? Maybe just lingering fear. Whatever the reason was for me not saying it, it didn't affect how much I loved him because it swelled more and more each day until I had no more room to give. He filled me, and I couldn't remember it being any other way. I didn't want to.

He got up to get a towel and wiped between my legs before tossing it aside and pulling me into his arms.

All at once, the shock from the photographer, the excitement of Ash joining us, and just the comfort of Parker's arms, hit me, pulling my lids down like weights.

Happiness engulfed us both because we finally made it. We finally broke out of our loop, and we were making this work. We'd finally got what we'd wanted all along. I fell asleep feeling invincible—confident in our future.

Nothing could shake us.

I was wrong.

TWENTY-SEVEN

Parker

PAST

THE CROWD CHANTED OUR NAME, and we each looked to each other with massive, goofy-ass grins, all thinking the same thing: *This is it.*

This was happening for us.

It was by far our biggest show yet with the rowdiest crowd. When Nova joined us on stage halfway through, we really hit our stride—*I* hit my stride. I'd locked eyes with her, and everything faded away—even the hundreds of fans singing our song —*our song.*

And it couldn't have happened on a better night. We'd walked in, and the bartender let us know some music execs were stopping by to check out the performers tonight.

I tossed my pick to the crowd like I was some actual rock star, and Oren joined me by lobbing his broken sticks up, and girls reached for them like they were the bride's bouquet at a wedding.

Fucking surreal.

We practically floated off the stage, and I only had one thing on my mind—Nova. After our night talking to our parents, things had been…harder.

We'd worked harder once school was out, constantly fighting for our next spot on a stage.

Nova worked harder on hiding her growing anxiety over the comments directed at her and the letters that still came. At the end of each show, a letter waited. Every video to YouTube included twenty comments from the same person. But nothing ever happened, so we pushed it aside, focusing on the next performance.

And Nova and I had to work ten times harder than ever before to keep our bodies in check. Every day my muscles clenched with the need to pull her into my arms and have her, but somehow, we held back.

But there was no holding back tonight when the surge of adrenaline hit.

The guys all chest bumped and manly hugged our excitement while Nova stood back laughing, but as soon as they parted, there she stood, and I couldn't stop my body from gravitating toward her if I tried.

I walked over, my eyes locked on hers, getting the same look in return. Without any warning, I bent down and picked her up, her legs wrapping around my waist, and kissed her. Every kiss hit just as intensely as the first time, and I wasn't sure we could pull back from it anymore. I didn't want to.

"You're amazing—everything," I whispered against her smiling lips.

"I don't want to stop kissing you," she admitted.

"Then don't. Ever. Fuck everything. We'll figure it out."

She nodded, and I went back in for more. In that moment, I could have said we'd make it to the moon, and I'd believe it. We were on a high.

Sliding her down, I groaned when she made a point to press her hips to mine. "Tease."

She winked and backed away, going to help the guys pack up their equipment. They'd been so engrossed in their own post-show high that they hadn't even noticed Nova in my arms. Not that I cared.

By the time we got packed up, we were ready to join the crowd and enjoy the concert.

"I'm going to run to the restroom first," Nova let me know, her eyes taking on that wary edge again.

"Meet us out there," Ash said.

"Wait," she shouted, her hand reaching out to stop them. "Can you wait for me?"

"Uhhh…why?" he asked.

I hit his shoulder and gave him a hard stare, silently reminding him of the letters she got that put her more on edge each time. Each show, she looked around more and more like the guy writing the notes would pop out and announce it was him to make it easy on us. Each note grew a little more detailed, never failing to be handed to us before the end of the night.

"Nova," he began with a confident smile. "You need to stop letting this admirer get in your head. We told you, he's probably harmless."

Her jaw ticked when he said admirer when she firmly planted this person in the category of stalker. "It's just that, a letter came to the house last week."

Alarm jolted through my veins. "You didn't tell me that."

"I didn't have time. You were at practice, or Mom was around, and I wanted to ignore it…later."

Later, as in at night when we went to each other to relax.

"It's not like it's hard to get an address. I mean, hello internet," Oren added with a laugh. "Seriously, Nova. It's probably a prank. Don't worry about it."

"Instead," Brogan cut in, "focus on how epic we're going to be. Think about our bad-ass rock star future when we make it big."

She forced a laugh. "Yeah."

"So, we'll see you out there after you take care of girly stuff?" Ash asked.

She looked to me, and I smiled reassuringly. "I'll be right here, waiting for you," I promised. The bathrooms were a few feet away, close to backstage.

"Thank you."

The guys bolted as soon as I offered to stay back, but before she could turn away, I snagged her wrist and tugged her back for one more kiss. God, I loved kissing her. She backed away with a seductive smile, worries gone, and part of me wanted to skip the concert and find a place for just the two of us.

She'd been gone less than five minutes when the guys came hurtling back with the bar manager, Joe.

"Dude, we got to go," Ash declared, bouncing on his toes.

"Uhh, why?" I asked.

Oren slapped his hands on Ash's shoulders, joining in on the excited bounce. "The music exec from Hinge Records wants to talk to us before he leaves."

My eyes bulged, that statement sinking in. "Are you fucking kidding me?"

"Nope," Ash answered.

"But we got to go now. He has some red-eye flight to L.A," Brogan explained.

"He asked to meet you in the back office," Joe explained. "I let him know I'd make it happen."

"Holy shit. Holy shit." I joined in their bouncing, unable to stand still. I thought I'd explode. Nova was going to be so fucking pumped. "Let me just wait for Nova."

"She's still not back?" Oren asked.

"Dude, did you see that line? We don't have time to wait that long," Ash explained.

"He said he didn't have much time and needed it now," the manager explained.

"I told her I would wait." The adrenaline flooded my

brain, and I struggled to piece together a well-thought-out plan. I tried to look to the bathroom to see if I could find her in line. "We can't have the meeting without her."

"She might have already made it in, but the line inside is always long, too," Joe piped in.

"Fuck," I muttered. I looked to the bathrooms again, searching for her red mass of hair, and turned back to face three eager sets of eyes about to club me over the head and drag me off.

"Come on, man. We can't miss this." Ash rested his hand on my shoulder and pulled me close. "This is our fucking chance, Parker. *Our chance.*"

"Listen," Joe said. "I'll hang out here and keep an eye out for her and bring her back to the office when she's done."

"Yeah?" I asked. It seemed like the perfect solution.

I couldn't wait to see Nova's face when she walked in to us meeting with an executive from freaking Hinge Records. She'd fucking die.

"Okay," I said when he nodded. "Thanks, man. I really appreciate it."

"No problem, kid. This doesn't happen often, so I'm glad it happened here. Just remember where you got signed."

"Signed?" Oren crowed. "How fucking cool would that be?"

We walked in with barely any composure, our anticipation bursting at the seams. The executive, Beck, greeted us, and we hit it off like we were old friends. Everything in that office moved in a blur of jokes, a couple of beers, and finally an offer.

While I was making my dreams come true, I had no idea Nova's were being stolen from her.

Not until it was all said and done, and I walked out to find Joe behind the bar. I looked at the time and realized over thirty minutes had gone by, and I knew the line in the bathroom wasn't that long.

Maybe she decided to watch the concert instead of coming back to the office. She did always claim the band was more our thing than hers, but I still wanted her there.

"Hey, man, where's Nova?" I asked Joe.

"Not sure," he answered, not even looking up from pouring drinks. "I got called to the bar, so I asked Niall to keep an eye out for her."

"Niall?" The busty blonde next to Joe raised a dubious brow. "The one currently making out with some guy in the corner? That Niall?"

Niall was a drummer from another band that played before us, and I looked over, seeing the guy who was supposed to watch Nova otherwise occupied. The first drop of dread hit me, and like a rock to water, the ripples quickly spread.

"Did you happen to see a redhead come out of the bathroom?"

"Nova?" the blonde asked. "Nah. I haven't seen her since she came off stage. Good show, by the way."

"Thanks," I responded offhand, my mind already scrambling for an answer to where Nova was.

Maybe she left? Maybe she was pissed I didn't wait and went home?

God, please let her be at home.

I hit her number and called only for it to ring.

God, why hadn't I sent a message to her letting her know we were in the back? Why hadn't I called first? Why hadn't I taken the time to let her know? They guys could have started the meeting without me.

All these thoughts hit me now with a clarity I hadn't had before. I'd been on a single track, and everything faded away. When the guys looked at me like I had all the answers—like they couldn't go back without me, I ignored everything else.

"Fuck," I hissed when it reached her voicemail. I sent off a quick text and then another.

"What's up, bro?" Brogan asked.

"I can't find Nova."

He looked side-to-side like she'd pop out. "I'm sure she's around."

"I told her I would wait for her, and I didn't. Fuck."

"Dude, chill," Ash said.

"What if something happened? What if—"

"Stop overthinking. You're letting those notes get to you."

"Of course, I am," I shouted.

"Parker," Ash put both hands on my shoulders. "It will be fine."

Famous last words.

"Are you guys looking for the redhead from your band?" a girl beside us asked.

"Yeah, did you see her?"

"Think so. She was being carried out by some guy—didn't get a look at his face, but he had your build," she gestured toward Oren's lean body. "She looked trashed. I wasn't even sure it was her, but then I saw those sweet blue suede boots she had on."

My whole world crashed in on me like a black hole, everything—all at once, like an anvil from a mile above. I wasn't even sure how I was still standing, as my legs shook like jello.

"Dude, are you okay?" Her voice sounded like it came from the end of a tunnel.

Someone shook me.

My stomach roiled.

She was carried out.

She looked drunk.

Nova hadn't had anything but water all night.

I promised her I'd wait.

I promised her I'd protect her.

I promised her I'd keep her safe.

I promised her she'd be fine.

"Parker!" Ash shouted an inch from my face. "Parker! Look at me."

"I promised…" I breathed.

"It's okay. We'll figure it out," he said, but his eyes held anything but surety. His eyes brimmed with the same panic consuming me. "Let's start looking for her. Brogan and Oren are already outside."

"Call 911," I ordered someone—anyone.

I snapped into action, but we all knew.

We were too late.

Any hope that maybe I was wrong was dashed to nothing but dust when the cops questioned us later that night.

"Do you have the notes?"

"No. She tossed them."

"But there are comments on YouTube," Oren offered.

"We already looked at those. It's being sent to our department, but it's not much to go on."

"Why didn't you come to the police?" a female officer asked.

"I guess we didn't think it was that big a deal. That he was just an admirer," Ash explained, looking the least confident I'd ever seen him.

"An admirer?" she repeated, her face scrunched in disgust. "More like a stalker."

"More like a serial killer," another officer said, walking up and passing a file to the two questioning us.

"A what?" I asked, speaking for the first time.

The female officer scanned the pages before meeting each of our eyes. She looked like someone who shows up at your door to let you know a loved one has passed, and everything in my body started breaking down before she even started. One word reverberated through me like an earthquake.

No.

No, no, no, no, no.

TWENTY-EIGHT

Nova

PAST

INTENSE THROBBING POUNDED against my temples. I squinted against the bright sunlight pouring in, only adding to the pain. My tongue scraped across my dry lips, and I struggled to swallow—my mouth like the Sahara.

Trying to massage my temples to ease any of the pressure came to a halt when metal scraped metal, and I couldn't move more than a couple inches. Like an electric shock to my heart, I jolted, opening my eyes to find my left wrist cuffed to a metal headboard. My stomach churned, and bile burned up my throat. I barely held back the vomit, probably because panic squeezed my throat too tight to even breathe.

Oh god. Oh god, oh godohgodohgod.

Flashes of how I got here bombarded my already frantic mind.

I was at the show. I was in Parker's arms. I was kissing Parker.

I had to go to the bathroom, and he promised to wait. *He promised.* But once I finally made it through the line, no one was there. I asked one of the members from the other bands, and they turned to me with glassy eyes, slurring something about how he went to go talk to some music executive.

When I asked him where, he shrugged and walked away. I'd been a ball of excitement, already riding a high from the show, but then to know that the guys had a music company interested in the band had me practically floating. I'd just needed to find them.

I'd been so gone in my excitement, I'd forgotten to keep looking over my shoulder at every turn. I'd forgotten why I'd asked Parker to wait for me in the first place. At least, until I'd turned a corner down a barren hall, looking for the offices, and felt a prick in my arm. I thought maybe I'd scraped myself and looked over my shoulder to find a large, dark shadow looming. The same dark shadow that haunted my nightmares. The one I dreamed about each time we played a show, and I got another letter waiting for me at the end.

The one I asked Parker to protect me from.

The one he promised he'd keep me safe from.

The one the guys laughed at and said it was probably some teenybopper.

This nightmare was anything but a teenybopper.

And I was anything but safe.

I'd opened my mouth to scream, only to have a beefy hand slap over my lips and catch me as I fell, the drugs he injected me with working too quickly to fight.

I jerked my wrist, cringing from the screech of metal on metal. With a quick glance around the room, I saw I was alone, and the last thing I wanted to do was alert whoever had taken me to the fact I was awake.

Taking stock of my surroundings, I stalled over the picturesque room. Simple grays and whites, clean lines. Hell, even a flower arrangement sat on the nightstand. I wasn't sure if the normality of the room caused more panic or less. Maybe because I expected a mattress on a floor or some dingy trailer that reeked of desperation and evil. Instead, my mind had to wrap around the nightmare I was in with the warm scent of vanilla floating around me. It felt like some kind of mind game to lure me into comfort before the worst—the calm before the storm.

Creaking reached through the closed door opposite the bed, sounds like footsteps coming up wooden stairs. The sun shining through the mostly-shut blinds let me know I wasn't in a basement, so that meant I had to be on the second floor. As the steps got closer, my mind swirled with options. I could pretend I was asleep, but that would leave me lying vulnerable. But I was already vulnerable cuffed to the bed. And who knew if he'd even care if I was conscious or not.

I looked side to side and made a quick decision to roll off the side of the bed, wedging myself in the space against the wall. It was a false sense of protection, but I'd take what I could get.

The door creaked open, and I held my breath.

Footsteps faltered as if frozen before a soft chuckle squeezed my lungs even tighter than I thought possible.

"There's no need to hide," his deep voice said, almost amused. "But I'm glad you're awake. I hated drugging you." He rounded the corner, giving me the first real look at his face. Like the room, he was normal—almost handsome. If this was a movie, I'd expect him to be the good guy coming to rescue me with his warm brown eyes and tousled brown hair. He looked attractive in a non-discrepant way. Muscular, but not bulky. Dressed nice, but casual, in jeans and a plain black T-shirt. Not at all the balding man with a beer belly and stained tank top.

Just like the normality of the room, it only served to add to my panic.

He leaned against the wall, arms flexing as they crossed over his broad chest, taking me in crouched in the corner.

"You're just as beautiful as I imagined. I've watched you online, I don't know how many times, and come to all your shows, but I never allowed myself to get too close. I wasn't sure I trusted myself until I had a plan in place."

He stepped sideways to edge between the bed and wall, coming into my space, but thankfully, stopped to sit on the bed. I lifted my chin and forced the most stubborn don't-fuck-with-me look I could muster. His legs almost reached where mine balled up to my chest, and I considered lashing out and kicking him with all I had but decided to save my energy and wait him out. If he wanted to keep space for now, then I would take it.

"The first time I saw you, you were singing in the YouTube video. Then to find out you were in New York, I just knew. I had to have you."

Don't poke the bear. Don't provoke him. Bide your time.

I repeated it over and over, clamping my jaw tight against the acidic retorts I wanted to give about people not being owned. The more I watched him, the more his simple look appeared as a veneer, and I was in no rush to find out what it covered.

"Nova, Nova. You were impossible to miss, and I didn't want to take you randomly. I wanted to prepare you. You got my notes, right?"

I refused to give even the slightest head nod.

"I never thought those *boys* would leave your side," he sneered.

His words sent a sharp reminder through my already fragile heart, planting the first seed of blame.

If they hadn't left me, I wouldn't be here.
If they hadn't pushed me to join the band, I wouldn't be here.
If they hadn't joked about my fan mail, *then I wouldn't be here.*
If Parker had kept his promise to keep me safe, I wouldn't be here.
If I had been more important than talking to a producer, then I wouldn't be here.

Not having enough room for the weight of those doubts and resentment, I shoved them aside.

Blame it on the Tequila

"But then, there you were, walking all by yourself, like you were looking for me. Were you looking for me?

Realizing I wouldn't answer, he shook his head and laughed. He took his time to look me over, not missing an inch. He looked at me like I was sprawled out for his perusal rather than huddled into a ball. His eyes finished raking me over and flashed back to meet my hard gaze. The first crack in my strong act fissured under the glimpse of the real monster beneath the mask.

His lip curled up slowly, and he shifted, reaching toward me. With my fight or flight in full effect and flight not an option, I snapped my teeth, forcing him to back up.

He jerked back, just barely escaping my bite. He looked to his hand and back to me. I braced myself for the force of his wrath—my muscles coiling, ready to fight. Instead, he laughed.

"So, feisty," he hissed, his eyes sparking with something I didn't want to dwell on. "I knew you would be with all that red hair. Don't worry. We'll become real close soon enough."

His eyes drooped with a look I knew all too well. I saw it from Parker all the time—desire, heat, want, need. Except with this man, bile churned up my throat, and I almost hoped I had a chance to spew it all over him.

The thought of Parker only added to the nausea.

My heart cracked deep and wide. Why hadn't he waited for me? Why had he left?

The man sighed and slapped his thighs, making me jump. "Later," he promised. "Right now, I need to get my pet some food. I had everything else planned, but in my excitement, I forgot to get nutrients to help us keep our energy up for all the work we'll be doing later."

The way he said work hammered another blow against my strength, and all I wanted to do was crumble and beg to be set free—beg for this not to be real. With all my effort to not fall apart, I forgot to stay silent.

"I'd rather die," I gritted out.

He frowned. "Don't say that, pet. I promise I'll make you like it."

"Fuck. You."

"When I get back. I promise." He winked like he was being funny, and I imagined clawing my nails down his face.

He edged his way back out to the foot of the bed, and I could almost breathe again with him on his way out, but he stopped and turned back, studying me. "Show me your tits."

My eyes bulged, and I coughed, choking on my own breath. "No," I growled.

One hand moved to the wall, and the other rested on the mattress, leaning in closer. He was still too far away, but the intention of intimidation was not lost on me. "Show. Me. Your. Tits," he ordered, his calm veneer slipping even more. Simple brown eyes vanished, and a wild darkness took their place as he stared at the part of my chest my knees couldn't cover. "I just want a little teaser. You don't always wear a bra, and I've done nothing but stroke my cock all day, imagining what they look like. They're so small, and I just…I need to see what color your little nipples are."

His voice edged on a hysterical desperation that scared me more than anything up to that moment. When he started closing the gap, taking small steps to come back to me, I broke my silence and screamed. I lashed out with my feet, hoping to scare him from getting too close, and screamed as loud and wild as I could.

"All right. Fine. Shut the fuck up. Jesus," he shouted, backing out again. "Just stop fucking screaming."

I did once he passed the bed and was two steps closer to the door. I could only imagine how I looked—a feral animal with my hair wild and teeth bared.

"I'll make sure to get some duct tape while I'm out," he grumbled just before he slammed the door.

It wasn't until the creaking of the steps stopped and the

Blame it on the Tequila

front door slammed that I even considered relaxing a single muscle—too scared that if I did, I'd fall apart while he could still come back and find me weak. A car door slammed, and the engine faded. Only then did I allow myself to fully sink back against the wall, and it was as if I'd been holding a tsunami back. As soon as I stopped giving it everything I had, it crushed my weak defenses, and I crumbled.

Sobs wracked my body, and as mad as I was that Parker left me, all I wanted was to be with him—to have him come storming through the door to my rescue. Anything. I just…I needed him.

I needed him even when he hadn't been there.

I needed him.

I needed him.

It was all I could think of, crammed in the corner, losing faith I'd make it out of this. Wondering if I did survive, who I'd be on the other side.

"I'm going to die here," I mumbled through cracked lips.

My stomach cramped in on itself, and I curled around it, wishing the hunger pains would stop. They had to stop eventually, I reasoned. Eventually, my mind would give me the blessing of blocking out the physical pain because the mental one was enough.

My captor left and hadn't come back. I wasn't sure how long it had been since I'd had water. The first night, I'd cringed while giving in to drink the water from the flower vase. I'd almost thrown it right back up, but I'd been desperate and didn't know how much longer I could wait until he returned.

If I'd known he wouldn't have come back at all, I would have saved the water, making it last.

I had no idea I'd be left chained to this bed for who knew

how long. I'd lost track. I knew it hadn't been that long, but I was so tired, and my body ached. Sometimes I passed out, not knowing for how long. Did I miss a night? Did I miss two? How long could a person go without water? Five days? Or a week? Or was that food? I tried to remember the obscure facts I'd seen on a TV show somewhere, but I could never focus long enough to figure it out.

Not that it mattered anyway.

Because I was going to die here.

I'd been grateful at first when the man hadn't come back. More time between me and misery. More time for me to think of a way to escape. I'd thought about dragging the bed to the closet in hopes I could find something to get free—only to find it bolted to the floor.

I'd stretched to reach the window, hoping to discover neighbors close enough that I could get help from—only to find nothing but land. I wondered if I was even in the state of New York anymore. It hadn't stopped me from getting it open and screaming. I'd screamed until it hurt to breathe, the air too rough for my raw throat.

I'd wriggled my hand, forcing it into the smallest shape possible to slide free of the cuff, only to result in a raw wrist. I'd considered breaking my thumb like I saw on a show one time, only to figure out there was nothing I could actually use and that I was too scared to pull it off.

Now, laying here in my own waste, I didn't care about fear, but now I was too weak to break a cracker, let alone my hand.

Now, I just wanted the earth to have mercy and let me pass out for good.

Now, I just wanted to quiet my mind, frustrated with the pendulum of hope, too scared, too desperate, too angry.

After the first night, I almost hoped to wake up to the sound of his steps coming up the stairs again. I hoped maybe he got caught by the police, and they were questioning him, and I just needed to hold on a little longer.

When I woke up the day after that, and he still wasn't there, a hesitant form of acceptance crept into my mind, spreading as the hours passed. I took the time to wonder why? Was it all a joke? Did he kidnap me just to scare me and leave me here? Did he have multiple personalities and his other side came out and forgot about me? Did he die? Did he just change his mind? Or was this his plan all along? Or was he waiting until I was desperate enough to be grateful for his return?

Not a single idea filled me with anything but angry fear.

And through the hours and waiting and thinking, one person stayed on my mind more than anyone else: Parker.

That was a whole other kind of pendulum. Missing him and needing him. Doing nothing but imagining him bursting through the door, apologizing as he crumbled at my feet and saving me. Hating him for lying. Hating him for leaving. Screaming my anger as if he had been standing in front of me instead of this horrifying shade of gray and white.

All of that, only to crumble all over again and beg for him to find me because I loved him, and I needed him.

I closed my eyes, imagining him on his knees, begging me to forgive him for being so selfish and leaving me to talk to some producer. I imagined telling him it was okay and falling into his arms, but even my daydream stuttered over that, tripping over the resentment. I hated that I thought it but hated it even more because it was true. Sometimes I almost laughed at the irony of being left behind by a musician who forgot about me to follow his dreams. Maybe this was my destiny.

Another sharp jab like a knife cut through my abdomen, and I rolled to my side, my other arm aching from being held in the cuff.

A thud sounded, and I couldn't tell if it was my blood sluggishly attempting to pump through my veins or my imagination. Whatever it was, I ignored it. Why bother when I was going to die here.

But then a louder crash came, impossible to put down to not being real. Especially when it was quickly followed by shouts.

"FBI," a deep voice bellowed.

It reached up the stairs and pumped one last push of adrenaline through my body, and I struggled to sit up. I pushed to my elbows and shouted, barely managing a squeak. Trying to swallow was fruitless, my mouth like sandpaper, but I tried again.

This time I made a sound, and I did it again and again and again until I heard the same noise that started all this—thuds of steps coming up the stairs one creak at a time.

It wasn't until a man in a jacket marking him as FBI came in with his gun drawn that the wall came down, uncovering the hope I'd blocked off. My body shook with sobs even though tears didn't come.

Everything moved in a blur. They got my wrist free while barraging me with question after question. Other footsteps moved around the house, but I kept my eyes on the stairs just beyond the door. Freedom. I needed to get out of this house.

They had to carry me, but I would have crawled to see the sky. I'd never been so grateful to be outside—to feel the cool night breeze on my skin. I was loaded in the back of an ambulance and faded in and out, catching snippets of them telling me I was okay, that I would be okay.

But I was pretty sure that even now that I was free of the house, I was never going to be okay again.

And despite being free of my cage, the pendulums continued to swing.

I couldn't wait to rage at Parker for not putting me first.

I couldn't wait to see him, to find safety in his arms.

I couldn't wait to slap him for not waiting like he promised.

I couldn't wait for him to hold me.

I couldn't wait to scream at him for leaving me.

I couldn't wait to tell him I loved him.
Back and forth. Back and forth.
I wasn't sure which side I'd settle on. All I knew was that no matter if I had anger or hope, I needed him there.
I needed him to not leave me again.

TWENTY-NINE

Nova
———

It's amazing what the mind can convince itself we're capable of.

Sure, I could bungee jump off that bridge. I put myself up at the top, imagine myself looking down, and taking a deep breath past my fear. All I'd have to do was take one tiny step forward, and I'd be in it, exhilarated and brave.

But then you're up there, and we didn't prepare for how strong our body could react. We didn't prepare for our nervous system to throw us into fight or flight mode so fast our legs almost give out. We didn't prepare for our body's reaction to reach out at the very last second and latch on to the safety we know, no matter how much we told ourselves we'd be fine, that the platform was boring, and we'd regret not taking the jump.

None of it mattered when your heart pumped so hard you were sure you'd pass out. Right then, nothing else mattered but feeling safe, solid, known ground under our feet.

When I strolled out of the bedroom the next morning after my night with Parker, a smile on my face, ready to refuel after all the work we put in, I was still on the platform. I was still hopeful, already strapped into my harness, still brave and ready to jump into the future with Parker.

But then I saw Aspen pacing behind the table, looking less put together than I'd ever seen, in yoga pants and band shirt, her hair in a messy bun. It was like staring at the edge of the platform that led to the abyss—the first tingle of something not quite going as planned.

I tried to backtrack, not wanting her to catch me strolling out of Parker's room in just a robe. But before I could get far, she tossed her phone on the table, and her eyes snapped to mine.

Her expression was hard to place. Disappointment, frustration, pity? Not a single one had me wanting to figure out what was going on. The guys sat around the table, all pushing food around their plates, looking like someone kicked their puppy. Ash's eyes popped up to mine, and despite the dread creeping its fingers around my neck, heat from last night clashed with it, bleeding into my cheeks.

He smiled, but it wasn't his usual smirk—no, this one almost held an apology.

Sensing the abyss waiting for me, the first drop of adrenaline kicked in, and I stepped back, only to collide with Parker.

"Hey, Aspen." His rough morning voice that had woken me moments ago, filling me with warmth and so much love I'd burst, now stood like a wall blocking my escape. I wanted to turn to him and beg him to run and hide with me—nothing good waited for us out here. "What are you doing here so early? We still have a couple hours until practice."

"Why didn't you tell me? We could have prepared," she jumped right in.

"Told you what?" he asked.

"That you two are fucking. I knew you had a thing between you, but I didn't realize this much."

"We're not just fucking," he argued.

She didn't even acknowledge what he said because the fact that we were fucking was the least of her concerns. "Why the hell didn't you tell me the full story about what happened to her before I pulled her on board like a PR nightmare," she snapped, pointing at me.

"What the hell are you talking about?"

"They know," Ash cut in, his voice weighted and tired. His muscular arms crossed over his chest as he leaned back in the seat, staring at his full plate of food. Slowly, his gaze lifted to mine, and he explained the apology I noticed earlier that had nothing to do with last night. "A photographer got a photo of Nova last night coming out from you guys' date. It was a head-on photo, so they were able to dig deeper into the *hippie-redhead that Parker switched model-Sonia for.*"

"Fuck," Parker muttered.

"No," I breathed.

I stood on the edge of the platform, eyes squeezed tight. My flight response told me to bolt, run, hide. My fight told me to open my eyes and look. Knowing it would only make things worse, I stormed over to the table and snatched the computer Aspen had open, clicking through the tabs. One after the other, the depth of the fall loomed in front of me, growing with each picture of me smiling at the photographer before climbing in the back of the SUV last night right next to one of me leaving the hospital almost six years ago with broken posture and hollow eyes.

Parker Callahan, from The Haunted Obsession, Caught with His New Love Interest: The Last Victim of the Serial Killer, The Backstage Slicer.

Leaving the five-star restaurant, Kovoks, Parker was spotted climbing into the back of an SUV. Before this mysterious redhead climbed in with him, she posed for a photo, appearing to be none other than Nova Hearst. Sound famil-

iar? It should. Her case made headlines as she was the last victim, and only one to survive, in the clutches of the notorious serial killer, Hank Dalton, also known as the Backstage Slicer. He was known to capture his victims at concert venues and keep them for prolonged periods, only to leave them out in the open months later with their throats cut and hundreds of incisions at varying stages of healing, leading investigators to believe he sliced into his victims each day.

A horrid fate Ms. Hearst was lucky to escape from when Mr. Dalton died in a car accident the very next day after taking her.

It looks like Hearst's luck didn't run out just yet as she's nabbed the attention of the lead singer and guitarist of Grammy-nominated band, The Haunted Obsession. After his recent split with long-time girlfriend, Sonia Caravin, it's hard not to compare the two, especially with so many similarities. I guess it's obvious Parker has a thing for redheads.

The article went on, but I'd read enough.

I should have kept my eyes closed. I should have turned back.

All of a sudden, every light I'd avoided for years shined brighter than ever, leaving me nowhere to hide. Everyone who wanted to would be able to stare and gawk and wonder and constantly ask questions, poking and prodding at my past—a past I desperately fought to move past—to not talk about. But the population had a sick fantasy with gore—fear mongers wanting to be a part of your terror to validate their fears. Because the knowledge that things happened wasn't enough—they wanted it to be theirs too.

I knew the victim of the Backstage Slicer. We were so close it was like it was my experience too.

I *hated* it. I *hated* talking about it.

I knew I couldn't hide forever. I never wanted to. I never wanted it to dictate my future. Each step I worked towards being better and the steps over the last month to show my face

—to show the real—had all been calculated so I could control how it came out.

Now, it slipped from my fingers in a chaos I had no hope of controlling.

This was it.

I stared down at the abyss, fully strapped into my gear, my muscles coiled tight. All I needed to do was let go of the bar and fall, having faith that the panic-filled vision of me crashing into the ground wasn't real and the bungee cord would hold me.

This was it.

I looked over my shoulder, taking Parker in. His hair rumpled from where I ran my fingers through it this morning when we still lazed naked in bed. His defined shoulders and biceps decorated with bits of ink that I'd traced with my tongue. The blue eyes I loved to watch darken with pleasure. But there was no pleasure now. His lips pulled down. His brows scrunched with frustration.

This was it.

I told him I could do this—that I wanted this.

I asked him to take me bungee jumping.

I still wanted this. I just couldn't do it alone. So, I reached my hand out and took my first breath when he slid his fingers through mine.

Parker wouldn't leave me to handle this alone.

"I've been on the phone with PR all morning, and we have a plan," Aspen explained, back to pacing.

I jerked my attention to her. "A plan?"

"Yes. We need to spin this."

"I don't-I don't understand."

She looked to Parker, and he stepped close to my side, running his free hand up and down my back. "She's good at this," he explained to me.

Trepidation crept in—a hint of something not quite

Blame it on the Tequila

coming together right, but I pushed on. "Okay. What's the plan?"

"We don't want this to negatively impact the band, not after all the work we put in this year. The guys filled me in on some of the details, and if anyone comes forward to accuse them of neglecting the letters, then it could put them in a bad light. So, Linda is calling the main news shows: *The Today Show, Good Morning America, Ellen. Oprah,* if we can get it. We're going to use this."

Use this.

The words crawled around my throat, squeezing. "Use what?" I whispered.

I glanced at Parker to read his reaction, but he seemed to be hanging on to Aspen's every word like it was gospel.

"Your story. We can make it work. We say you came on tour with Parker to write about your experience. We can do talk shows and push that the new album has songs focused on you and Parker and how you reunited to write about your tragic past."

"What?"

"The fans will eat it up," she kept going, growing more excited. "Boys, you are going to explode. With this kind of natural publicity, you'll skyrocket."

Nausea churned like lead, and I looked to Parker. I searched my lifeline—my safety. "Parker?"

He met my gaze, brows raised as if looking to me for confirmation of the good idea. As if he didn't know it was everything I didn't want.

That look—the one that said he didn't hate the idea of using this to make his jump to another level a little easier, blew me apart. It found every weakness and crushed me. My limbs went numb, and my hand slipped from his.

I stepped back from the ledge of the platform. His brow softened from hope to confusion to hurt. Another step back, and realization hit. He shook his head, pleading with his eyes to stop.

But it was too late.

Another step back.

"I trusted you," I whispered before darting past him to the bedroom.

He followed right behind me, slamming the door. I wanted to run to the bathroom, but I needed to get out. I needed to get off that ledge.

"Don't do this, Nova," he pleaded.

I shoved clothes haphazardly into the bag. "Don't to what?"

"Don't leave."

"What? Would you rather I stay and play your little puppet? Would you rather I sit by with a smile to be used?"

"No. That's not what I want."

"Bullshit," I accused. "I saw it. She said the words, and you ate them up."

"Dammit, Nova," he growled, shoving both hands into his hair. He tugged at his strands before throwing his arms wide. "I'm not good at this. I don't know how to fix this for you. Aspen is good at this, so I just…"

"She didn't fix it for me, Parker. She fixed it for *you*."

"No, she fixed it for *us*. There's not a good way for anyone to come out completely unscathed, and this covers all the bases."

"That's the thing, Parker. I don't want to even play the game, but here I am, basically being used as the damn ball."

"Well, Nova, the game is my job. I'm doing my job, and it's exhausting and hard and not always what I want to do, but I have responsibilities."

I closed my eyes, trying to see through the storm raging inside me—past and present swirling too close to separate. Is this what it would be like? Always coming second? Would it be just like my father? The question knocked the wind out of me, and I needed out of that damn room—I needed air.

"I just…I need time to think."

"No, you need time to run."

He stood in my way of escape, and my panic flashed to anger. I stood tall, gritting my jaw. "No, Parker. I need space because I expected you to not choose your job over me every single time, and apparently, you aren't capable of it. How many more times am I going to have to step aside for your job? Will you leave me behind again because your *job* is more important? Will I be left to the wolves again while you achieve your dreams?"

He stumbled back like my words were a physical blow.

The direct hit didn't ease any of the pain wracking my body. Instead, it only made it worse. Tears broke free, and my chest shuddered over the sobs I fought to hold back. He closed the gap between us, gripping my biceps. "I know it's hard, but, Nova, I want you. I don't want to lose you again. I *need* you with me."

"No…not really." I pulled back, shrugging my bag on my shoulder. "You never did."

"Don't you dare walk away," he ordered when I shouldered past him. "Don't you dare run. For once, don't be a coward and fight."

Just like that, my muscles tensed all over again, and I whirled around. "I am *not* a coward."

"Then stop acting like it," he snarled, taking a challenging step forward.

"You have no idea what it's like—what it *was* like. I'm already exhausted, Parker, and all I want is to *not* talk about it anymore. All I want is for you to go out there and tell them to fuck off."

"You think I want to face this? I don't. It was one of the biggest mistakes I ever made, and it haunts me every motherfucking day. Not a moment goes by that the guilt doesn't weigh me down like a ten-ton truck. But, goddammit, Nova, I busted my ass to get here. I faced doubt at every fucking turn my whole life, and I can't just say fuck it when I want to. I fucked up before, but I can't let my past define me. I can't let it keep me from a future I dreamed of—a future with the woman I love by my side not always trying to run."

His words slammed into me, knocking the wind from my lungs. "Don't say that," I breathed.

"What? That I love you?" For every step I fumbled back, he followed. "I've loved you for so long that I don't even know what it's like to not have this feeling taking up every spare spot in my body. It's part of me. *You* are part of me. You always will be."

Too much. Too much. Too much.

I couldn't breathe. It came at me from all angles, and all I wanted to do was ball up and be alone and ignore everything crumbling down on me.

"No. Parker, I can't." I shook my head, backing up more, lashing out blindly—pointlessly. "Go do your job, Parker. It's what you always wanted."

"Don't, Nova. Please," he pleaded through clenched teeth.

He stretched his hand out for me to take, and I stared, remembering the way they traced every dip and curve of my body. For a moment, I considered taking them, holding onto him, and taking the leap into the abyss.

But familiar, solid land stretched behind me.

"I'm sorry," I whispered.

And then I turned and did what he accused me of.

I ran.

THIRTY

Nova

REGRET HIT me almost as soon as I left, but my feet refused to turn back. I went to the airport and booked a ticket to the closest I could get to New York. On my flight to Pittsburg, I clung to the merry-go-round of emotions, not sure how to let go when everything swirled around me like a blur.

As soon as I dried my eyes from crying, indignant anger burned. As soon as the embers cooled, defeat pulled me down into despair, where I started crying again. I hated it. I hated the way they blurred together and left me a mess I didn't know where to begin to untangle. I didn't know which thread to pull first without falling apart.

The only thing I did know was that I needed to get to solid ground. I needed to make the spinning stop.

When my flight landed, I didn't take my phone off airplane mode, too scared of what waited for me. I booked a mini-cabin for the night before renting a car the next day after I peeled myself out from where I hid under the covers. I blasted music on my drive through the mountains. I tried to focus on the trees and the rocks and nature all around me. I tried to blot out the thoughts by belting out lyrics, but it was useless.

Nothing could distract me from my argument with Parker. We both lashed out. We both dug our heels in and landed blows that were wrongly delivered. We both acted without thinking. We were both wrong.

But one thing he was right about: I was a coward because I was the one running.

In the moment, it had filled me with an all too familiar feeling. The one where we only made it so far before falling apart. It's like I'd been waiting for the other shoe to drop, and once it had, I gave in to the inevitability without trying to change anything.

So, I ran, never giving us a chance to figure it out together. I let the past dictate my future, and I hated it. It was like shining a light into the dark recesses of my mind, calling me out for not *actually* handling my trauma like I thought I had.

Seeing it there pissed me off. I wanted to rip it out and never let it back in again. I wanted to be strong, not a façade of strong waiting to crumble as soon as the past crept from the shadows.

I said I wanted to bungee jump, so dammit, I would bungee jump.

Which was why halfway through my drive, when I saw a sign, I veered off the road. Fate heard me, and even if it was only metaphorical, I needed to prove to myself that I could.

Because Parker Callahan said he loved me and, without a doubt, I knew I loved him too.

I loved him more than anything, including my fears.

I followed the signs and refused to back out.

I pushed past the racing heart as they strapped me into the harness. I focused on slowing my breath when they walked me to the edge. I closed my eyes and pulsed my sweaty fists open and closed, standing at the end of the platform. And when push came to shove, I opened my eyes and stared into the abyss.

Blame it on the Tequila

My legs shook, but when I looked at the valley of trees and rocks, all I saw was Parker's face asking me not to leave.

One more deep breath.

"I can do this."

I jumped.

By the time I reached New York, I still hadn't turned on my phone, leaving me unsure of how I'd be greeted. Not that it mattered. We stood by each other no matter what. So, with a deep breath, I knocked.

The door opened and—

"It's about fucking time." Rae propped one hand on the door and the other on her cocked hip, looking like a disapproving mama who wasn't going to let me back inside until I explained.

But I couldn't explain because, in the next second, I broke down in tears.

"Dammit," she sighed. "You're ruining my anger at you disappearing without an explanation."

With that, she let go of the door and yanked me in her arms, squeezing me more tightly like she could strong-arm my soul back together. I clung to her and let her guide me inside to the couch, where she stroked my hair.

"You and Vera get one pass and one pass only. If you come crying to me again, I'll be killing people. I'm not equipped with the emotions to handle my best friends hurting."

I sniffed, wiping my tears, trying to get myself under control. "I know. I'm sorry."

"Oh, no. Don't you dare apologize. I'm glad you finally came to me. I've been freaking waiting. Vera took two seconds before her ass was at my door, and here you are, making me wait two days."

"Yeah," I responded lamely. Another moment I was faced with my cowardice.

"Hey." She dipped her head, trying to get me to meet her eyes. When I still hung my head, she gripped my cheeks and forced me to look. "It's okay, Nova. If you need time, then you take it. As long as you know, we're here, and let us know you're safe."

"I should have told you everything. I should have called. I didn't mean to shut you out," I admitted through a fresh wave of tears.

I didn't mean to shut anyone out, but I couldn't deny that maybe I'd been hiding more than I wanted to admit. Maybe I'd been controlling more than just what I shared with my art. All this time, I'd been fighting Aiken on showing my face because I wanted to stick with the brand I created, but really, I was just hiding—even from my friends.

"Ha. Girl, you cannot shut me out. I may be biding my time in the corner, but I'm in here," she tapped my head. "And if you tried to make me leave, I'd laugh in your face, and Spartan kick the door down to get back in. You and Vera are my bitches, and you've accepted me. There's no going back."

Laughing both hurt and felt good at the same time, but at least I could still laugh.

"You just need to process it differently."

I laid my hands over hers, where they held my cheeks and smiled through my tears. "Thank you."

"Any time. Now, speaking of ways to handle our shit, let me grab some alcohol and get to the bottom of this."

I didn't even argue when she came back a few minutes later with a bottle of wine for each of us—sans glasses—and a bottle of tequila.

"I feel like this is turning into some tradition," she said, scowling at the alcohol on the table and back to the crying woman on her couch. "I'd like to skip it, please. No crying

Blame it on the Tequila

over guys for me, thank you very much. But I am always up for a night of drinking straight from the bottle."

"I'll keep the vodka on hand," I promised, deciding against the tequila and sticking to wine. "Speaking of, how's your boyfriend?"

She stiffened for half a second before shaking her head. "Oh, no, Miss Nova. This is about you."

"It was worth a shot." I shrugged, lifting the bottle.

I took a long swig, the dry berry flavor washing away the salt from my tears. If only it could wash away the exhausted hurt wrapping around every muscle and bone in my body. I was exhausted, finally ready to lay it all out there and ask someone to help me carry this load weighing me down.

A soft knock had Rae back off the couch. I knew who it would be before she even opened the door. We were a tripod —we worked better with all of us together.

Vera entered, coming over to the living room all sleek, composed, and calm.

My mind flashed to when I came barging in almost six months ago to find her in the same situation I was in now— crying on Rae's couch, clutching a bottle of wine. I'd been anything but composed.

"What? No trying to break down the door like She-Ra?" I asked with a soggy laugh.

She scrunched her nose and shook her head. "Nah. I know how dramatic Rae can be with her messages. Besides," her eyes locked on me, and I saw the focused businesswoman who matched her husband's force. I leaned back, bracing myself. "I'm saving my energy for you."

"Oh, damn," Rae muttered. "Mom is mad at you."

I glared at Rae, but she just smirked, passing a bottle of wine to Vera before plopping down on the chair beside the couch. She pulled both legs up in criss-cross apple sauce and leaned in like she couldn't wait for story-time.

Vera took her time setting her purse and coat aside before

sitting down beside me. "Now, explain why the hell you couldn't respond to a message after we discovered your past from the media of all places. If you're going to fall off the face of the earth, at least send us a message to let us know you're alive."

Damn. She did reprimand me like a mom. But then she drank straight from her bottle, bringing the image of the woman in pearls scolding me together with my best friend.

"I know," I sighed. "I'm sorry."

"Why didn't you tell us? About before?" she asked gently.

"I-I—" I stuttered and winced, swallowing to try again. "I never talk about it. It's the reason I don't talk about knowing Parker, because usually with that story comes the other, and I just avoid it."

"Fair enough," Rae chimed in. "Sounds like it was a fucking shitshow."

"And we know Rae avoids talking shitshows at all cost."

Rae mimed zipping her lips and throwing away the key before turning more serious. "You don't ever have to talk about it. We all have things we hold close to our chest that we don't want to talk about." She shrugged before looking away for another drink.

Rae appeared as the perfect, fun, socialite, but a lot brewed beneath the surface. She hid it well, but this was an instance we got to see more than she probably wanted.

"The point is," Vera added, "that we want you to know that you *can* come to us if you just want to talk about anything."

"I know that," I said, adding more sincerely. "*I know that.* I really do. You guys are my best friends, and I love you. It was just nice to go to college and be far, far away from the girl who was taken. And as time went on, I just never talked about it, and I convinced myself that I didn't need to."

"It's not like we had a lot of conversations where you

Blame it on the Tequila

could bring up that one time you were kidnapped," Rae muttered.

I snorted, and wine spewed from my lips which only served to make me laugh more. Then all three of us were laughing until I cried again just because it felt good to feel my chest shake and rumble with happiness. But when you opened the gate to one emotion, others followed.

"Nova," Vera cooed, pulling me into her arms.

Rae reached across to hold my hand.

"I fucked up, you guys. I fucked up with Parker."

"No," Vera tried to say, but I shook my head.

"I did. I love him so much, and I ran from him like I always do. And I said mean things on my way out the door."

I broke down the argument and how I ran when push came to shove. I hated admitting out loud what a coward I'd been. By the time I finished, I was almost out of tears, leaving sniffles and wet cheeks. Rae moved over to my other side, being a good friend and keeping me hydrated with wine through the story.

"Has he called?" Vera asked.

"I-I don't know," I winced.

"Nova. Hearst," Rae reprimanded. "Stop being a little bitch and turn on your damn phone."

I hesitantly pulled the phone from my purse and just stared at the settings. What if I swiped and there was nothing from him? What if there was only a message from Aspen letting me know she was firing me and that I could pick up my belongings at the local Goodwill? Before I could sink further into my what-ifs, Rae snatched my phone and turned airplane mode off.

My phone notifications went insane, and I immediately wanted to make it stop.

When I reached for the device, Rae strong-armed me and started tapping buttons. "Let me just turn off some of these pointless things." More swipes, a few eye rolls, and a lot of scowling with muttered death threats to whatever was being said. "Now, I think I deserve an award for not snooping. I would like my reward to be you telling me every letter of those messages and maybe sending me a dick pic of the Viking, please."

"What?" I snorted a mixture of nerves and laughter. Only fucking Rae.

"I'll give you a second to read through them," she explained, passing the phone back to me.

Rock Star: I'm so sorry. I was shocked, and I reacted.

Rock Star: Not just shocked. I was terrified. Here I was trying to keep your privacy safe, and I couldn't even do that. So, when Aspen started taking control, I let it happen because I don't know what the fuck I'm doing, and the last time I failed you, I really fucking failed.

Rock Star: Then I got angry. You looked at me like I should know what to do, and I didn't. I felt useless, and it pissed me off.

Rock Star: Nova, I still don't really know what to do, but I do know whatever it is, we need to figure it out together. I've spent the past five years having someone tell me what to do, and it's frustrating as hell sometimes, but it's easy.

Rock Star: I get so focused on my job and proving myself to everyone that I forget to think about me and what I want. And Nova, I want you. I meant what I said.

Rock Star: I wish you would pick up. I wish I could say all of this to you in person. I wish I wouldn't have to say it at all. I wish I could promise I won't screw up again. I wish for a lot. But mostly, I just wish for you to be here.

Rock Star: At least let me know you're safe. At least give me that this time before you disappear.

THE MESSAGES CAME over time yesterday. But nothing today. Had he changed his mind?

My fingers hovered over the buttons to respond, but I couldn't form any words.

"Well?" Vera asked.

"He apologized."

"That's great."

"But that was yesterday, and he hasn't sent anything today, and his last message sounds irritated, and what if I fucked this up too much?"

"Well, it's a good thing we're not in middle school, and we can just ask him," Rae said sarcastically.

"What if he won't give me a chance?"

"Psshh. Of course, he will," Rae said. "You're Naughty Nova. Who turns that down?"

I laughed but shook my head. "I'm serious."

"So am I. You're a bomb-ass bitch that can handle everything," she said fiercely.

"I don't feel like it. He was right to call me a coward. I always run."

"You're not a coward. You just need a few seconds to process things," Vera chimed in. "You may appear calm, but that fiery redhead is in there, and when you get hit with something big, you just need time to chill for an hour—or a couple of days."

"Yeeessss," Rae agreed, drawing out the word. "Remember that one time her mom tried to buy her a condo in Connecticut?"

"Oh, my god," Vera groaned, clapping her hands. "She left for a week to…to…

"Colorado," Rae filled in.

They talked across me like I wasn't even there, and I watched in awe as they listed off a character trait I hadn't realized was quite so obvious.

"But you always come back when you've had time to think it over. Like with your mom. You called her up and very politely told her fuck no," Rae reminded me.

"But I can't always run."

"No, you can't," Vera agreed. "So, you work on it. The fact that you recognize it is half the battle. But there's also nothing wrong with asking for space to think, just maybe let the people you love know you're not falling off the face of the earth beforehand."

"What if he doesn't want someone like that?"

"He'll have to learn if he wants to keep you," Rae said.

"And he'd be a complete dumbass to not want you."

"Especially when you show up at the Grammys looking like fucking fire," Rae exclaimed, almost bouncing in her seat.

"I don't know. I—"

Rae's finger pressed to my lips, halting me mid-excuse. "Mama Rae's gonna take care of you. Now hush and say thank you."

I managed a smile under her finger and muttered, "I love you."

"Close enough," she conceded.

Vera wrapped around my back, and Rae hugged my front. I'd needed the mountains to process—just like they said, but if

I had to choose one over the other—I would always choose this.

All I had to do was win Parker back and prove to him that I may need a second to process, but I would always choose him, too.

THIRTY-ONE

Parker

"Parker, were you in love with your stepsister? Will we be singing any songs about incestual love on the new album?"

"Fuck off, Oren," I grumbled.

"Hey, man, I'm just prepping you for the red carpet tonight."

"He's not wrong," Aspen confirmed, walking closer with that damn makeup pad thing again. "Now that they've uncovered everything about your past with her, it's a free for all."

"If you try and put makeup on me one more time, I'm going to break it."

She gasped and glared, holding the rectangle to her chest like it was her baby. "I'm just trying to help you look more human."

Shaking my head, I turned back to the full-length mirror in our suite. I adjusted the sleeves of my suit jacket and cringed at the man staring back. Between the tour, fielding questions at every turn, and missing Nova, I looked as tired as I felt. I knew I looked like shit, but I refused to cover any of it no matter how much Aspen tried.

I hoped Nova saw me on TV tonight and realized what a fucking mess I was without her. I wanted her to see the dark

Blame it on the Tequila

circles and dull eyes. It was hard to sleep when all I saw on the inside of my lids were her tears and mouthing *I'm sorry* right before she ran.

I was tired of watching her run from me.

I wasn't even mad this time.

Not like when we were kids, and I raged for months on end.

Not like on New Year's Eve when irritation hit harder than anger.

No, this time? I ached. Without any other emotion to take up space, all that throbbed and weighed me down was the intense need for her. It both flooded me to bursting and left me with a hollow pit only she could fill.

When she left, I called and called with no answer—not that I expected one. But when it started going straight to voicemail, I knew exactly where she had run to. We'd gotten to know each other better than ever before, and I didn't need to wonder where she was this time because she'd gone where no one could reach her—the mountains.

I considered calling Raelynn for all of a second, but honestly, I was slightly terrified.

I considered just showing up to find her, but with the Grammys on top of everything else, I had nothing to show but open arms and me begging on my knees for her to come back. Not that I even knew how long she'd stay before running again, even if she did come back. I'd thought she'd stay this time.

She said she could do this with me, but at the first bump—a very big bump—she bailed. Not that I blamed her. Hell, each time I walked outside, someone cornered me, asking about her kidnapping. It wasn't even my story, and I was exhausted by it. No wonder she never wanted to talk about it. Add in the tidbits and revelations about our pasts and how we met, and the reporters fell on it like a bunch of savages who hadn't eaten in a week.

The thought of doing it choreographed by Aspen filled me with dread.

It left me, for the first time ever, questioning if this career was really worth it.

"You're messing up my suit, bro," Oren shouted.

"It's a fucking T-shirt," Brogan shot back.

"That has a suit on it," Oren explained slowly.

"Can you at least wear the jacket?" Aspen almost begged.

"Say please, baby," Oren cooed.

"Fuck you and wear the jacket," she deadpanned.

"Ooo," Oren shuddered. "I love when you swear at me. Makes me hard."

"Gross."

"And I'll wear it, but only because I look damn good in this red," he claimed, tugging on the dark red jacket.

Ash smacked him in the back of the head, and Brogan smacked him from the front.

I shook my head, watching them act like fools, and was reminded that this band wasn't all about me. We were brothers, and we didn't abandon each other. If I tried to run, I had no doubt they would drag me back, and I'd be grateful for it—except for the part of not having Nova with me.

My fists clenched, and my shoulders hung heavy under the weight of frustration and defeat. No matter how many ways I spun the issue, I couldn't find an answer. How could I want something so much and not know the first thing about making it happen?

"Sonia will be there," Aspen said.

"No." I leveled the most serious stare I could muster. "We talked about this. I said no more tricks, not more jumping through hoops. I'm a musician, and if that's not enough for people to pay attention, then so be it. I'm done trying so damn hard when our music should be enough."

"I know. I called management and let them know your

ultimatum of walking away if they pushed it. I was just saying. It's my job."

"I know," I answered exhaustedly. "I'm glad they let it go."

"Me, too."

She studied me a moment with a sad smile, and I hated it but braced myself for it. If I was going to wear my hurt all over my face and walk down the red carpet, then I'd open myself up to the same scrutiny she gave me.

Maybe I should have accepted the makeup.

"Let's go, bitches," Ash announced. "Car is waiting."

Too late now.

We piled into the back of the limo and opened the bottle of bourbon waiting for us.

Aspen poured us all a glass before holding hers up. "To winning a Grammy tonight."

"To winning all fucking six Grammys," Brogan corrected.

Managing a semblance of a smile, I clinked my glass with the guys' and tossed it back. I should have been on cloud nine, just as pumped as the rest of my bandmates. For the first time ever, we were nominated for six Grammys. We'd only been nominated for our first one last year, and it had only been one. And with all the cheers and laughter around me, all I could think about was the empty spot beside me.

She was supposed to be here, holding my hand. She was always supposed to be here from the very beginning.

A ripple of quiet worked its way through the car until no one said a word, and I looked up, finding four sets of eyes look away as soon as I met them.

"What?" I asked.

"Nothing," Oren answered, snapping back to life, shoving his phone in his pocket.

Everyone rustled, now avoiding looking at me. Brogan put his empty glass to his lips, and Aspen buried her face in her phone.

I looked to Ash, knowing if I pushed, he'd tell me what the

fuck was going on. He gave the most forced smile I'd ever seen—more of a grimace than his usual smirk. Now, I really knew something was off.

"What?" I asked more forcefully.

Ash sighed.

"Don't," Oren pleaded.

"Fucking, what?" I almost roared.

"Nova posted to Instagram," Ash explained, passing me his phone.

Just hearing her name hit me, knocking the wind from my chest. I looked at the outstretched phone like a bomb, knowing I would take it but hoping maybe I wouldn't. Giving up, I snatched it and looked down. It was a Reel, so I hit play. It started with her from behind, her red hair loose and blowing in the soft breeze. Like I already knew, the mountains and valleys stretched beyond her. She looked like she was standing on the edge of the world.

A violin beat played as the camera backed up, and she took off running. It was then I noticed the harness and framing on either side of her. As soon as she reached the end of the bungee jumping platform, a video voice said *run*, and she turned in slow motion, striking a finger gun pose, smiling wide at the camera as a rock version of the violins played.

She shined with the sun behind her, her hair a fiery halo. Her face lit up with happiness, and I had the biggest clash of emotions—like two tidal waves slamming together. She was happy, and I was happy for her. I'd been worried she'd been harassed like me, despite not appearing in any reports, and here she was enjoying her life—without me. That realization pulled any joy plummeting to the pit of my stomach.

Nova was happy without me.

Fuck. I wanted to stop the car and get out right now. Fuck the Grammys, fuck all of this. Now, *I* wanted to run away and not look back. I'd imagined her hurting like me, and now this—this slap in the face.

"I'm glad she's happy," I managed, passing the phone back to Ash.

"She showed her face," Brogan pointed out.

"I noticed."

"She never shows her face," Oren added.

"Well, good for fucking her," I snapped.

They blinked at my outburst. For the first time in weeks, a flicker of anger emerged, but I knew it would be dashed by hurt all over again.

"Aspen," Ash called. "When do we get another break?"

She flipped through her phone. "Not for a while. And the ones you do have are small and filled with promo."

"Maybe we can find one of those promos for Parker to miss."

"Why?" I asked.

"So you can go get her."

"It won't change anything," I muttered.

He watched me—studied me until I wanted to squirm and demand he leave me the fuck alone.

"Then at least go for closure," he said softly. "All the times she left, you never got to say goodbye."

Just when I thought I'd experienced the lowest, something proved me wrong. *Goodbye*. The finality of it kicked the chair out from under me and left me flat on my back.

Fuck. Fuck.

I clutched my chest. I didn't know how I would make it through the night.

"Holy. Fucking. Shit," Oren said slowly. His eyes were as wide as his dropped jaw, glued to something outside as we pulled up to the event.

"What?" Brogan asked, shoving Oren out of the way.

Oren pushed him back and rolled down the window, which had Aspen slapping his arm and telling him to roll it back up. But it was too late, Oren leaned halfway out, his dropped jaw shifting to a wide-ass smile.

"Supernova," he shouted. My heart jumped up into my throat, and I froze. "You beautiful, crazy-ass, bitch. Look at you, standing there like fire."

"Ow, ow," Brogan shouted, leaning behind him.

I sat frozen to my seat, wondering if each revelation was really a mirage of insanity and none of this was real.

"Dude," Ash said, looking out the tinted windows from his seat. He slapped my shoulder and shook me, a real smile on his face.

The guys didn't feel Nova's loss like I did, but they did feel it. We were friends—a family, and she didn't leave just me.

They all jumped at the chance to believe, and I didn't know how it could be real.

"Parker!" Ash smacked my head. "Are you going to fucking sit there all night?"

Oren and Brogan scrambled out with Aspen gracefully behind them. Ash scooted down the bench seat toward the door and looked at me like I'd lost my damn mind. I kind of thought I did. If I got out, and she wasn't there, I'd crumble. Then I'd pick myself up, just to climb back in the car and copy her.

I'd run. Everyone else be damned.

With a deep breath, I scooted to the door and closed my eyes, trying to prepare for whatever waited for me.

The sun shined and blinded me a second from the dark interior. I blinked, and like a dream, the guys parted, and there she was—like a miracle, more done up than I'd ever seen. She was stunning.

My heart pounded like a freight train, and my muscles ached to run to her. She wrung her hands and chewed on her pink, glossy lips.

"Wow," I breathed.

I looked her up and down, from the full, black, silky skirt to the pale strip of skin bared between the skirt waist and the white tuxedo-like top that looked like it got cut right under her chest. And her eyes—I never wanted to look away. They shined like emeralds hidden in the smoky shadow of her makeup.

"Hi," she greeted, taking a hesitant step forward.

Her eyes glossed over, and she looked away when I didn't move. Ungluing my feet from the pavement, I closed the gap but stuffed my hands into my pockets to keep from gripping her to me.

"What are y—" I tried to ask but choked off.

"I said I'd be here."

"Nova, you don't have to—"

Her eyes shot up with determination. "I don't want to miss another moment of you achieving your dream. I don't want to miss another moment of you."

"Nova..." I blinked, trying to process what it all meant—trying to adjust from the other side of the pendulum I'd been on in the limo.

"Dammit," she hissed. "I didn't plan how much I'd want to run into your arms. I just wanted to be here."

She blinked back her tears and gave a hesitant smile, and it hit me. I'd let go of the pendulum and landed on my feet with her in front of me. The words sank in, and I smiled back.

"Fuck it," she muttered.

It was the only warning I got before she closed the last foot and threw her arms around my neck. I caught her and buried my face into her soft hair, inhaling as deep as I could to make up for every second I hadn't been able to have her. I held her to me like I wanted to make us one, and she could never leave again.

"I'm so sorry, Parker. So, so, so sorry."

"Me too."

"Guys," Aspen said. "Why don't you step over here for some privacy."

She guided us to a small alcove behind banners and equipment. People still moved about, but it was mostly workers and not anyone chomping at the bit to invade a private moment.

"You've got about five minutes before we have to go."

"Thanks, Aspen," Nova said.

With a nod, she left us.

We stood still for less than a second, and then my mouth was on hers. My hands re-exploring every inch of skin I could find—desperate for her. Her tongue collided with mine just as needy. Small whimpers escaped, and I seriously calculated our chances of making it to the limo and taking an extra fifteen minutes. We could be late, right?

"I can't believe you're here," I said between kisses.

"I had to be."

"I called."

"I know." She pulled back just enough to meet my eyes but not enough to separate. "I needed to show you. I want to be with you—if you'll have me."

I barked a laugh. "Of course, I'll have you. Fuck, Nova. I've wanted you from the second you walked into that apartment, charcoal staining your hands clinging to more art supplies."

She gave a watery laugh and sniffed before turning serious. "I'm sorry I ran—again. I'm working on it. Rae and Vera so kindly pointed out that I need space to process. I somehow missed it, but seeing it now, I know I can work around it. I can be honest and ask for pockets of time before I just plain vanish. I can promise to always come back and work it out together."

"Good, because as much as I don't want to, I can promise I'm going to fuck up. I'm going to need you to stay and remind me I messed up and help me fix it. In return, I can give those moments of space—as long as you always come back to me. And promise to take me with you, even if it's only in your heart."

"Parker, there isn't a moment I haven't carried you with

me," she admitted. "I got a new tattoo."

"Yeah?" I asked, confused by the change.

"Yeah."

She shifted, tugging the edge of her dress shirt up a couple more inches to show thin, elegant script along her ribcage under the soft swell of her breast.

"I carry your heart with me. I carry it in my heart," I read the words.

"I've always thought of that quote when I thought of you," she admitted.

I stroked my finger along the letters, shuddering right along with her when I grazed her soft skin.

I stood tall and pulled her back in my arms, but before I could lean in for a kiss, she framed my face in her hands. "Parker, I love you. I can't remember a time I didn't. And I know I've run a lot, but I want to show you that I'm here—I'm all in. I posted my face on Instagram," she confessed with an edge of panic to her laughter.

"I saw. You looked so happy."

"Because I was coming to you. I love you," she said again.

I gripped her hips tight, pulling as much of her against me as I could. "I love you too. I always have. I always will."

A single tear slid down, and she dabbed it away. "Stupid makeup."

"You look beautiful no matter what."

"I love you."

"I love you, too."

Just as we were going back for another kiss, Aspen poked her head around. "Time to go."

I groaned but pulled back. "Do you want me to get someone to take you to your seat? I should be in soon."

She shook her head. "I'm walking the red carpet with you."

"You don't have to do that."

She pulled her shoulders back, her chin held high. "I

want to."

Smiling bigger than I thought possible, I reached my hand for hers, finally filling the gaping hole when she slid hers in mine.

We made it around the corner before she let go. Only because the guys bombarded her and jerked her into their arms.

"Missed me, didn't you?" Ash muttered so only we could hear.

She rolled her eyes. "Yeah, right."

"Fine, your pussy missed me."

"Fuck off, asshole," I grumbled but smiled.

He backed up, his hands held up in surrender. "Hey, I'm just saying I'm here whenever you need me."

She shook her head and laughed, coming right back to my side, where she stayed the whole length of the carpet.

She fielded all the questions with grace and sarcasm that had me laughing more than any red carpet before. My favorite was when one reporter asked her if she thought it would have hurt if Hank had made it back and started cutting her.

I almost stepped in for such a crass question when Nova put on an over-the-top British accent and answered. "'Tis but a flesh wound. I would have bit his kneecaps off."

The reporter blinked and blinked some more. Meanwhile, I choked on a laugh and pulled her away before the reporter could place the quote from Monty Python and the Holy Grail.

Before we knew it, we made it to our seats, and with Nova by my side, we won four of the six nominations. When we won best album, I made it a point to thank my girlfriend, Nova Hearst, for always being the inspiration behind my songs.

Now that she put herself out there how she wanted to, I could finally let everyone know that Nova Hearst was mine, and I was hers.

Epilogue

NOVA

"Thank you, Vegas. We couldn't end our tour in a better place."

I watched Parker walk to the edge of the stage and toss out his pick, quickly followed by Ash and Brogan doing the same. Oren tossed out his broken sticks and they all bowed to the raucous applause.

My eyes burned, taking them in, huge smiles on their face.

Parker looked over his shoulder and met my eyes in the wings and I bounced on the balls of my feet, barely holding back from running out there to drag him off stage.

Over a year and the tour was finally ending.

One more bow and then he made his way over, passing his guitar off to the crew.

Before he could make it, I launched myself at him, wrapping my legs around his waist and kissing him as he walked us off.

"I love you," I whispered.

His lips stretched into a smile under mine. "I love you, too."

"Get a room," Brogan shouted playfully.

I rest my forehead on his and breathed him in, so unbelievable grateful to be in his arms without any worries holding us back. The fact that I hadn't seen him in two weeks also added to my exuberance.

Once we finished the album, he continued his tour and I continued to grow my brand, attending concerts, traveling to secluded hikes in my new van, taking pictures of it all.

"You ready?" he asked.

"Born ready."

With a soft chuckle, he let my feet hit the ground. "Let's go, Supernova."

We made our way to the exit, hand in hand, receiving well wishes and back slaps from the crew all the way out the door.

"It's about fucking time," Rae called from where she leaned against the black SUV.

Vera slapped her arm and shook her head. "Ready to go?"

"Yup." I answered.

"Why are we riding separately again?" Parker asked, not letting go of my hand.

"Because you can't see me before the big day," I explained.

"Ugh."

"Stop being a drama queen and let's go," Ash said as he walked past toward the second black SUV.

"Just one more," Parker whispered, leaning down to press his lips to mine. When he finally pulled away, I couldn't stop smiling. "See you soon."

I backed away, piling into the backseat. Vera sat in the driver's seat and Aspen climbed into the passenger side, while Rae climbed in back with me.

"Strip," she ordered.

"We're sure these windows are tinted?" I asked, already kicking off my shoes.

"Promise," Aspen assured. "I've had to do more than my fair share of quick changes."

Aspen and I had clashed in the beginning, but I stood my ground against her with what I would and wouldn't allow for publicity and in the end, I think I won her respect, which led to a friendship of sorts.

I quickly changed and sat as still as I could while Rae pinned my hair back and applied my makeup. The Vegas lights flashed by and I barely saw them, too focused on getting to Parker.

By the time we pulled up, I barely let Vera stop before I tried to open the door.

"Not so fast," Rae said, pulling me back by the elbow.

The guys all waited outside in black jeans and black shirts. Parker stole my breath with his black button-up shirt, undone at the neck. I wanted to bury my face into that sexy crook and breathe him in.

"I'll go get them inside," Aspen offered.

She stepped out and I bounced my leg.

"I'd ask if you want to run, but I'm pretty sure the only place you want to run is down the aisle," Vera laughed.

"Is it that obvious?"

"It might be more obvious than the cheesiness of this chapel."

I looked at the small building with fake flowers decorating the arch and recalled the gold and cream interior we saw in the pictures online. It screamed corny-Vegas-wedding and I wouldn't have it any other way.

Nico walked out to let us know they were ready and with my arm latched through Vera's and Rae's, the doors opened, and I walked toward the man I'd been dreaming of being my husband for longer than I could remember.

Time stood still. The music started and Parker finally saw me. His eyes raked over my white-lace crop top and white flowy pants. He smiled his approval when he got to my white high-heeled ankle-boots.

With a kiss on my cheek from each girl, I closed the small gap between me and Parker. With tears in both our eyes, I slid my hand in his and married my best friend.

"You may kiss the bride," Elvis finally declared.

Parker and I crashed together. What our kiss lacked in finesse, it more than made up for in happiness and passion. We clung to each other like we'd spent a lifetime apart rather than only an hour.

"I love you so much."

"I love you, too."

Cheers erupted and Elvis announced us as Mr. and Mrs. Parker Callahan.

It was perfectly short and sweet. We'd been years in the making and I hadn't wanted to wait another second.

He'd asked me to marry him on the red carpet of our second Grammys together—forever memorialized by the paparazzi—and I'd almost demanded we skip the awards and get married right then.

We compromised with Vegas.

"Where to now?" Oren asked when we all stood outside after pictures.

"I don't' know about you, but I have a car waiting to take us back to our suite."

"What?" Ash asked. "No reception?"

"Oh, we're partying," I said, waggling my brows at Parker.

"Yeah, but it's a no pants party just for me and my wife," he said, pulling me close.

Wife.

I'd never tire of it.

"Evan just texted me about a party at the Bellagio," Brogan said.

"I'm down with that," Rae interjected.

Brogan turned to her with a smirk, but before he could say anything, Austin cut in. "Don't you have a boyfriend you should call?"

"You're not her boyfriend?" Brogan asked confused.

"Nope, he's just my forever wedding date," Rae explained.

Blame it on the Tequila

Austin's scowl showed how much he appreciated being called *just* anything.

"Well, then by all means, come along. I know I'd love to have you there," Brogan assured, scanning her from head to toe.

"I am not going to some random hotel party," Austin grumbled.

"Vera will go with me."

"Girl," Vera stepped back. "I love you, but Nico and I have plans. It's our first trip after the baby and we are making the most of it."

Rae stuck out her tongue. "Party poopers. I'll just go alone."

I looked to Austin with wide eyes. "Please. I don't want to have to skip out on my wedding night to make sure my best friend is safe."

"What?" Parker almost shrieked.

I reassured him with a wink.

"Fucking fine. I'll go. But we're not staying long," Austin demanded.

Rae smiled proudly and I turned to face my husband. "Now that that's settled, let's get the hell out of here. I've got plans for you Mr. Callahan."

"I like the sound of that *Mrs. Callahan.*" He opened the door of a hired car, but wrapped his arms around me from behind before I could get in. Dipping his hand low, fingering the top of the apex of my thighs, he leaned in and nipped at my ear. "But I have plans, too, and they start as soon as we get in this car. However, there's no privacy glass, so you better be quiet."

A shiver worked its way up my spine. Even more eager than before, I pulled away and nibbled on his full bottom lip before whispering, "If it gets leaked to the press about what we do in the backseat of cars, we can blame it on the tequila."

RAE

My head pounded with beating drums. No, not just my head—my whole body ached.

The last thing I remembered was finally talking Austin into enjoying the night and taking a shot of vodka with me. Followed by many more. Everything after was blur.

Not even sure if I made it back to my own room, I managed to squint open an eye at the blinding sun. Cream curtains didn't give a clue as to where I was, but then I saw my teal suitcase opened in the corner with my dress from last night tossed haphazardly over it.

Good. I made it back to my own room.

"Fuck," I muttered.

A deep groan came from behind me. Apparently, I hadn't made it back to my room alone.

My boyfriend would *not* be happy about that. I guess it was a good thing I broke it off before leaving.

With a deep breath, I prepared to roll enough to face whoever laid in bed with me.

Please be hot. Please be hot.

"What the fuck," the deep voice said.

Not any deep voice. Austin's deep voice.

I'd know that sexy rumble anywhere.

Oh, thank god. He must have just stayed in my room when we made it back. Also, I kind of liked the idea of him not finding some girl to bang while he was in Vegas. Not that I'd delve too deeply into that emotion. Ew.

"How much vodka did we have?" he asked.

"Too much? No enough? I don't know," I answered, rolling to my back.

His thick arm came into view when he rubbed at his face. "I got to piss," he grumbled.

"So sexy," I deadpanned.

"I turn on the extra charm just for you."

"Lucky me." I looked over and bat my eyelashes just in time to watch Austin stand fully naked from the bed.

As if in slow motion, we both looked down at the same time.

I'd known Austin for over five years, lusted after him from day one. But I had never, ever seen him naked.

"Holy. Shit," I said with awe. I knew he had to be big everywhere, I just hadn't been prepared for how big.

"Holy shit," he shouted, snatching a blanket to cover himself.

It was then, I saw the flash of gold on his finger.

I jutted my hand out and pointed. "Austin, what the fuck is that?"

It was then I saw the flash of gold on *my* finger.

We both held up our hands and eyed the matching gold bands, trying to piece the night together.

Unable to come up with anything, we both looked up with wide eyes.

"We did *not* just get married in Vegas," I said.

"I think— I think we did."

Acknowledgments

My family: Thank you for always understanding and supportive. Thank you for the cuddles after a hard day and laughs when all I want to do is rip my hair out. I couldn't do this without you being the foundation holding me up. I love you.

Lucia. We formed a friendship over sarcasm, grass, and early mornings. Thank you for always getting up with me and pumping me up with your energy. Thank you for always cheering me on and shit-talking me into getting my work done. Thanks for always be honest and never judging. Thank you for all the laughs. You're the best, Mama Lucia!

Karla. Thanks for always being there every step of the way. Dream Team!

Serena. You're the lady behind the scenes making this all work. Thank you for everything you do and keeping me sane and always talking me down and calling me out on my shit. Best. PA. Ever!

Najla Qamber. Whew! This cover! You always do the most amazing work and I'm so lucky I found out all those years ago!

Valentine PR. This group of ladies is amazing and take

so much pressure off my shoulders so I can write with confidence knowing everything else is being taken care of. Megan, you've been an amazing person to work with and your ability to make me laugh and feel better knows no bounds! Thank you!

Kelly. Thank you for being an amazing editor. Thank you for being an even better friend! You give me the confidence to publish a book I know is the best it could be because of you.

Julia. Thank you for always being able to beta read and squeezing me in even when you're swamped.

Review team. You ladies are wonderful, fun, kind, and beyond supportive. Thank you for every share, every review, and everything in between. You guys are the real MVP and I loved every second of you impatiently waiting for Nico and Vera!

Lovers. You guys are my safe place. You guys give me the best book recommendations and make me laugh. You're more than I could ever ask for. I can't tell you how many times I've scrolled through your comments and have been brought to tears. Thank you for being such an awesome group.

Bloggers. To every single one from personal pages to the bookstagrammers. You all work so hard and take beautiful pictures and write such amazingly kind words in reviews. I don't have enough words to let you know how much you all mean to me. I couldn't do this without you.

Readers. You guys rock my socks off. Thank you for taking a chance on my words. Thank you for taking the time to read something I've created. You're the best.

About Fiona

Fiona Cole is a military wife and a stay at home mom with degrees in biology and chemistry. As much as she loved science, she decided to postpone her career to stay at home with her two little girls, and immersed herself in the world of books until finally deciding to write her own.

Fiona loves hearing from her readers, so be sure to follow her on social media.

Email: authorfionacole@gmail.com
Newsletter
Reader Group: Fiona Cole's Lovers

www.authorfionacole.com

Also by Fiona Cole

ALL BOOKS ARE FREE IN KINDLE UNLIMITED

Where You Can Find Me

Deny Me

Imagine Me

Shame Me Not Series

Shame

Make It to the Altar (Shame Me Not 1.5)

The Voyeur Series

Voyeur

Lovers (Cards of Love)

Surrender (A Lovers Novella)

Savior

Another

Watch With Me (A Free Liar Prequel)

Liar

Teacher

Blame it on the Alcohol

Blame it on the Champagne

Blame it on the Tequila

Blame it on the Alcohol - Book 3 (Coming late 2021)

Standalones

Just for a Little While

Printed in Poland
by Amazon Fulfillment
Poland Sp. z o.o., Wrocław

92691681R00211